WITHDRAWN LIBRARY

D1094858

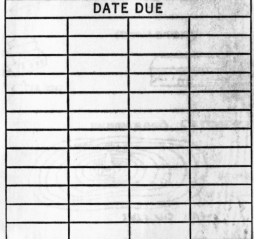

ISLAND
OF SAINT
CYPRIAN

WESTER

GRAVEYARD

BRIDGE

THE
GENEVIEVE

VILLAGE

The
Godforgotten

The
Godforgotten
by
Gladys Schmitt

HARCOURT BRACE JOVANOVICH, INC.
NEW YORK

First edition
ISBN 0-15-136065-0
Library of Congress Catalog Card Number: 77-182333
Printed in the United States of America

B C D E F

" . . . to the children . . ."

The
Godforgotten

Chapter I

The wise thing, the seemly thing would have been for him to get up off his knees with the rest. But he remained where he was while their cassocks and wooden crosses went by him, flapping or knocking against his side. The contact was intrusive and cold.

Not that he was more pious than the others. He had said the whole service of Complines by chill rote. The Latin words had fallen meticulously from his lips, but there had been no passage between his numb mouth and his scarcely living heart. Now that the late prayers were over, he added his own prayer, the only one that fetched anything up these savorless days:

> O Lord, show me Thy mercy,
> according to Thy will and Thy knowledge. Amen.

None of those who were walking up the aisle and out of the chapel knew of the existence of that prayer. He had come upon it in an ancient manuscript, had hoarded it as some of his ghostly brothers hoarded tangible things—a pair of fur slippers, a sliver of amber, a carved ring. It could offend neither the divine nor the human with its next-to-nothingness, its total and unfeeling submission.

3

O Lord, show me Thy mercy . . .

He said it again in the emptying chapel, in the light of the single torch held near the portal. Only three hundred years after the Lord had torn Himself out of His carnality with a cry, the hermit fathers had uttered it in the Egyptian desert. They had used it as a medicine against heat, thirst, sores of the skin, and the devil of dull emptiness that haunted the glare of their noons.

. . . according to Thy will . . .

And he was saying it eight hundred years after them, in a city called Cologne, in a Christendom they had purified to small purpose at great cost. Somebody coughed. The torch wavered. The lay brother who held it had probably grown tired of waiting. Let him wait—he had doubtless waited for worse reasons before.

. . . according to Thy will
and Thy knowledge. Amen.

He got up, stubbornly unhurried, watching his own shadow thrown forward on the damp flagstones: tonsured head, spare body, a thin hand raised to pull up the cowl, to put the cowl between himself and the lay brother, himself and the world.

On his way up the aisle, he knew that he had gotten nothing out of the prayer. For weeks now its power had been draining away from it like blood. And tonight it had fallen out of theology and into history. The fathers of the Egyptian desert—he might as well admit it—had lost the bright auras that sealed them off from time. They had descended to the level of his usual preoccupations; they were the same now as Caesars and Emperors. Well, let them take their places among ordinary mortals. In his cell he had an unopened volume of Livy, for which his eyes hungered. That, with the butt of a candle he had filched from the scriptorium, would take care of him until he slept.

"Father Albrecht—"

He looked past the edge of his cowl and saw that the one who held the torch was the lay brother Thaddeus. Christian charity

4

would not serve his need: Brother Thaddeus simply wearied him. A big body—twenty-five years had not stripped it of its baby fat. Blond hair too carefully squared across a round forehead. Small uneasy eyes. A mild mouth—and in its very mildness it was somehow provocative.

"Yes, Brother?"

"Our father the Abbot will receive you now."

"But I never asked him to receive me."

"No, Father, I know. It was *he* who asked—"

He stifled the "Why?" His work in the scriptorium neglected. . . . His manner cold and remote of late, without a trace of Christian love. . . . Candlelight showing night after night under the door of his cell while he read, read, read. . . . Never Scripture, never the holy commentary, always and only heathen history. . . . "Dye your wool once in that purple, and it will never again be white"— so the Sainted Jerome had said. It was true—the brain in his skull and the shriveled heart in his chest were purpled; and he could not regret it, let the abbot invoke against it all the faceless angels of Heaven and all the slimy devils of Hell.

"So the abbot sent you to find me?"

"Yes. I am here at the express bidding of our reverend Father." The title was uttered with the sort of respect that only a young man could give it. He himself, being forty-nine, could never bring it out without a shade of mockery.

"Where should I go?"

"To his chamber, Father. It is late and he is waiting."

"Consider me on my way, Brother. God forbid I should delay his hard-earned sleep."

It was not in the nature or rank of the lay brother to acknowledge the irony. "Shall I light you to him?" he said.

"No, no. There's light enough."

"God be with you then, Father Albrecht." The formula of farewell was scrubbed clean of any hint that God's attention might be called for at the coming encounter.

"And with you, Brother." He could not say the name: it had

5

become unleavened dough, like its possessor. He stepped into the night, heard the chapel door closing behind him, and looked up at the moon, faceless like the angels, small and distant in the mist.

✠   ✠   ✠

In Cologne, in high summer, a man would do better if God had not doomed him to breathe. The air of the city flowed in upon the walled square, bounded though it was by Cathedral, chapel, Chapter House, and abbey house. And that air, invading his nostrils, carried with it the essence of human indecency: smoke of today's burnt suppers, taint of yesterday's decaying fish, stale urine, old excrement.

As he walked along the roofed portico past the windows, he saw candles being snuffed out: now to the cold prayers, and after that to the cold sheets. Well, other lives were lived in other places. . . . He wondered whether at this distance he could catch the scent of his ancestral orchards on the other side of the river, of the quinces and apples that he used to see at night, the globes turned white by the light of the moon. He remembered a certain tree, a quince, with a twisted trunk so old and grey that it might have been carved out of stone. But he had no part in it. It was gone with all the rest. Fortress and field and fold, marsh and meadow and woody stretch —everything had gone to his elder brother, who had followed Peter the Hermit on the Crusade and died in sanctity in a dry land. Come autumn, and grown nephews whom *he* would not know at sight would be carrying the first fruits of that orchard to church— as if God could eat.

As for himself, he would remain imprisoned to the end, in a brown cassock, in a damp grey Chapter House, in a black city whose towers affronted the sky, whose narrow and crotchety streets gave off a brainless jabbering by day and this mean stench by night. Well, he had his Livy and his candle—yes, and the end of that candle was sticking out of his belt for the abbot's delectation. To catch a dilatory monk with a stolen candle butt—that would be almost as gratifying as catching out a boy in a barn with his member in his hand.

6

And he would see himself damned before he gave his superior any such equivocal delight. He took the candle out of his belt and laid it carefully on a sill under a trail of ivy. He raised the big bronze ring of the knocker and let it come down hard against the door.

"Come in." It was an old voice, cracked by seventy winters, and he wondered whether his own voice would sound so, given another twenty years.

The narrow room was a place of stateliness and order. In the center, on the long table in front of the Abbot's chair, burned two candles, each as thick as a man's arm and set in a wrought-iron candlestick—metal curiously twisted into blossoming vines. Fresh rushes had been laid on the floor, and the new arras covered every inch of the wall.

"Peace, Father," he said, covertly inspecting the new arras. He had not yet seen it, and for weeks it had been the talk of the whole brotherhood. It was the gift of the wives of the Great Ones of Cologne, a gift they had embroidered with their own hands. At the Abbot's back were the Cardinal Virtues, springing out of a half-circle of orange flame. On the opposite wall were the Seven Deadly Sins in their animal fleshings. Our reverend Father had asked that these be hung directly before him, within the habitual range of his eyes, no doubt as an edifying example of holy self-admonition.

The lion for Pride. This the abbot could glance up at without misgivings, sure that his mild satisfaction in the peace of the riotous city—a peace which he had established for God and the Church of God—could never be mistaken for Pride.

The serpent for Envy. And what was there for him to envy? Sardonyx and lapis lazuli weighted his withered fingers, gold chains and crosses shone solid through the brushed silvery web of his beard, a bearskin lay under his feet, and ermine was folded over his shoulders against the draught.

A unicorn for Wrath. But then, all wrongs done against him were righted before he had time to resent them. A punished offense breeds no cankers, and whoever offended the dignity of his office

7

was punished by sundown under the Rood and by the Rule. It was easy enough for him to say "Peace, my son" in an even voice, when God was always going beforehand, arranging for his peace.

"Are you in health, my son?"

"Well enough, Father."

The scorpion for Lust. But it was to be taken for granted—and only God knew how much he himself wished to believe it—that a man's loins are delivered from that scorpion before he has counted his threescore and ten.

"I am very glad to hear it." There was emphasis on that. That moved from the shadow of courtesy into the substance of intention. Father Albrecht put his face forward out of his cowl, as a snail will put horns and head out of the shelter of his shell. For the first time he saw the frail old man on the other side of the table not as the embodiment of authority, but as a presence with whom the occasion required him to make some exchange.

"—very glad to hear it, for you have not seemed well."

He shrugged. They raked his nerves, those fingers stirring in his direction. "I am neither sick nor in health, Father," he said. "If the dysenteries and fevers of summer are over, the rheums and coughs of autumn will soon be setting in." And furthermore, he thought, it is time to get on with it. Probe away, probe away—a babbling prelude is no kindness to me. Accuse me, accept my *mea culpa*, measure out my penance, and let me go to my book.

"Sit down, my son."

Erect, ungiving, moving only at hip and knee, he let himself down—no more present than a statue—onto the chair.

"You hold yourself as if you expect me to chide you. I do not intend to chide you."

"No?" He made certain that his voice carried neither relief nor gratitude.

"No, my son. If you have scanted your duties and seemed cold at prayer and oversolitary and too much taken up with books, these things may have their roots in a justifiable restlessness. It has occurred to me that you have never left this city. Weeks and months go by, and you never set foot outside this square."

"I have no itch to wander, Father." He did not try to hide his scorn for the commonality of the brotherhood, who made a world's wonder of the monasteries to be visited along the routes to the great shrines. Oh, the wines, the goose-feather pillows, the tilts of wit, the rumors, the scandals, the rabbit stews! But, for him, voices shrill after enforced silence were an assault on the ears, and anything more than the usual fish and bread and salad brought on pressure in the head.

"Yet, if there were God's good reason for you to journey, and journey far, my son—"

Why, then he would find another God's good reason to get out of it. It was enough that this puny idol of the faithful of Cologne should tell him what volumes to buy for the scriptorium. It would be easy to marshal arguments against sending him westward to the rough court of the Angles where not one in fifty could read, or northward to the saving of souls in countries where night and day were a confusion of shifting slants of light. Perhaps there had been a time when his heart would have leaped to it, but that time was long gone; and his face stiffened with contempt for the old self and the foolish heart. "If my Father will excuse me, it amazes me that our Lord should make such an unsuitable choice," he said.

Rage—more of it than he had anticipated. He waited while the abbot swallowed twice, and was the more discomfited because he could not tell whether the quaking cheeks and the trembling hands were the work of his jab at authority or his flippant irreverence. When the voice came, he was not surprised that it was low with a struggle for self-mastery.

"According to your vow of obedience, you will go wherever I send you."

"Yes, Father."

"And I do not send you upon my own whim, but to labor for Almighty God."

"Yes, Father." To take the tonsure—he had always known it—was to forge fetters for your own feet.

9

There was a discreet shuffling behind the arras. Faith, Hope, and Charity billowed out in turn until Brother Thaddeus found the opening and came through it, carrying hot bread on a silver platter in one hand and steaming wine in a silver goblet in the other. He sensed contention in the air at once: round head down, eyelids unlifted, he went away more adeptly than he had come.

The abbot raised his look from the spread before him to the stubborn subordinate who was hindering his enjoyment of it. "It seems to me you are in no state to give proper attention to the grave business I have to broach to you," he said. "I will say only this much for the moment: you will be going far away, to a place where no monk has set foot for more years than I would wish to tell you now. Go to the chapel and pray for the gravity of mind to hear and to accept. When you have so ordered your spirit, come back. I would suggest half an hour or more of meditation and prayer."

He allowed himself a long stare at the delicacies on the table. The smile was his private indulgence, lost as it was in the darkness of the cowl. He made the slightest of bows, turned his back, and moved toward the door. "Peace," he said, going out, and knew that the muffled "Peace" which followed him came from a mouth too avid to delay any longer its first bite of bread.

When he stood again under the small fogged moon, it struck him that it would not matter where the abbot sent him. In youth a man attaches himself to creatures and places by what he takes for sinews grown out of his own being, carriers of sense and blood that cannot be severed without almost mortal hurt. But afterward, in his autumn, he comes to see that the bonds have withered into —or have always been—things no more integral than cobwebs. One gust, and they are snapped and borne away as though they had never been.

Then, passing the sill, he saw the white of the candle butt through the living black of the ivy. There was a chair, there was a small circle of light, there was a volume of Livy—these he was to lose, and these and their numb peace were dear. It was this meager loss that assailed him, stronger in him than curiosity or foreboding or anger; and he had to tell himself not to strike his hand against the sill in his bitterness.

✠   ✠   ✠

He could be dismissed to the solitude of the chapel, but nobody was there to see whether or not he got down on his knees. He paced the familiar aisles in dark that carried the shimmer of precious things: crucifix, reliquary, gold-threaded altar cloth. Try as he would to keep his mind open as a night meadow, bats of fear swooped down upon it. The places the old man could send him! Southeast to a tribe of Bulgars fallen off to the Byzantine rite; northeast to a raw city with onion spires. With orders to stamp out one of a score of heresies: Image-smashers. Arians who refused to concede that Christ was made of God's very substance. Horse-brained serfs who had taken it into their heads that the Millennium was here, and ran ranting in the fields of bliss, burning their masters' barns, pinning stolen splendors over their rags and filth, and coupling where and as they pleased.

Yet none of it could really devastate his desiccated spirit. He was not what he had been—vital and therefore vulnerable—almost thirty years ago in the days of Father Carolus. Stepping over damp flagstones, he remembered that business in the words in which it had been set down in the Chronicle of the Chapter House: sparse words surviving in his brain and nowhere else. For the latter doings of Father Carolus were anathema. A sharp knife had long since cut away the pages where they had been recorded; and whoever happened on that part of the book bethought himself of the works of the Devil and made the sign of the cross.

In the year of our Lord 1076, the plague having been in the city and half the townspeople being in mourning, pitiful God sent to us a great light in our darkness. Came unto us Father Carolus, bringing with him in a box of cedarwood the Blessed Ursula's left hand.

And I was eighteen then, goaded by the scorpion to clutchings and spillings. If I was continent, dreams provoked me. If I con-

11

fessed, the need was upon me again before my penance was done. And there was no monk in the Chapter House who took it as I did for a mortal spiritual sickness. A small sin, they said, common to men. Better than with other men or with women. Better than with beasts to get monsters. Were we not, all of us, of the flesh and weak? What was there to do but have patience and pray for it to pass?

Came unto us Father Carolus . . .

Out of Italy, of Lombard stock. Big as an elk in frame, with a ponderous tread, but meager in flesh through prodigious fastings. Sallow blunt face, battle scar on the shaven crown, iron-grey curls on the forehead. Eyes that did not shift like other men's from side to side, but up and down, drawn by Christ's eyebeams and the howls from the pit.

And he preached to the brotherhood and to the afflicted people. And his eloquence was plainly from God, for his tongue was honey and fire. He preached chiefly of the fallings-off of the brothers, especially in matters of lechery and self-tainting and concubinage, saying that no hand which besoiled itself in an evil place was fit to touch the high things of the Lord.

Fire and honey for cleansing and healing. No, now, I said to myself, wait a few hours, and you will see him at Tierce. At noon you will hand him a napkin at table, and that will sustain you until Vespers. Between Vespers and Complines you will hear his voice reverberating over the heads of the townsfolk in the Cathedral. And after that you will be worn with adoring this strong servant of God, and you will sleep. Three days, four days, and the starved scorpion bit no more. And I confessed to him and told him how my deliverance had come at his hands. And those eyes, the color of amber, making their great sweep from the highest to the lowest, stopped for an instant on me.

On the Feast of the Epiphany, at dawn, in the abbot's chamber, he opened the cedarwood casket and showed the hand of the Sainted

Ursula to our reverend Father and to the six of the brothers most advanced in years. The hand was as white as the stone called alabaster, and was utterly untouched by decay. And, though there could have been no blossoms about, for the city and the fields around it were covered with three handsbreadths of snow, all who were present bore witness that the room and the whole square were filled with the fragrance of roses.

I did not see it. But even if I had been there, I would not have seen it. By that time my eyes were so strongly drawn to him that they could not have been held by a splinter of the True Cross.

A sennight more we were blessed with the presence of Father Carolus. Before he went from us, our lives were as they had never been within the reach of memory. We were at peace with ourselves, with each other, and with God. We walked a little on the way with him beyond the city gates, and there he stopped to hallow the new graveyard where those who had died of the plague had been laid in haste.

Peace and snow and the still knowledge that the place from which he had departed was not truly empty. On that wall his huge shadow had fallen. On that end of the table he had propped his elbows. On that flagstone in the chapel floor I had gone down on my knees, and standing just there he had said: "But God is merciful, beloved little Brother in Christ. Go and wish that you will not wish to sin, and you will sin no more." With the sin gone, purity became the prime property of daily things: taste of melted snow water from a metal goblet, innocent savor of flaked whitefish, smell of a new-baked loaf, as if it had a soul, an odor of sanctity of its own.

Leaving us, Father Carolus journeyed northward. He promised that he would send messages to us from the next Chapter House, but we have not heard—

There the chronicle broke off, and the prudent knife cut away the pages, and the prudent Bishop of Cologne consigned them, with Father Carolus and all his works, to everlasting fire.

The traveler had never gotten to the next Chapter House. Serfs looking for kindling had found him in a frozen pond, only the head and one arm above the ice, and these gnawed by wolves. The cedarwood box was not dragged out of the water until spring, and the hand inside it was duly attested to be made of marble, doubtless filched from the arm of some pagan she-devil of Italy. The Bishop of Trier knew of him and had set summoners on his heels, but they had moved slowly because of the bitter season, stopping to exhibit the scroll of his sins at every well-stocked monastery along the way.

He was a fraud. He had never taken the tonsure. Weary of the slow gains of a petty merchant, he had thought to make a fortune in false relics. A chest he had left behind in Ravenna contained a collection of bones, some of them human but most from deer and dogs. The gross wit of the monastery found congenial stuff in his story:

"What preacher of the Purification believes that, in the case of John the Baptist, two heads are better than one?" "I know not." "Father Carolus."

"How is it that Saint Radigunde can play the viol, the psalter, the trumpet, the bells, the drums, the sticks, and the cymbals all at the same time?" "How is it?" "Father Carolus has given her four hands and three feet."

But oh, the thaws of February tainted, and the earth itself unacceptable, showing forth out of the pocked snow. Food inedible, prayers an empty muttering, sleep made unbearable by evil dreams.

Corruption at the core of holiness—from that time on he had lived with such knowledge. It crawled out at him in the pink worm which turned iris root to carrion. His skin crept with it now because the rats had come out of their hiding, sure he was gone since he had stopped to rest with his elbow propped on a window sill. He could hear them scurrying over the reliquary, chasing each other in their lechery round the foot of the crucifix. Poor Brother Theodatus, somewhat touched in his brain—they drove him wild. After every celebration of the Eucharist he came with a broom and swept and swept, horrified that a crumb of Christ's body

14

should find its way into a rat's guts. . . . He put his hand to the nape of his neck—it ached, the chill of the chapel was seeping in. But there hung the moon, barely higher in the milky sky, and it was plain he had not stayed out half his time. He began to pace again, up and down the right-hand aisle, whistling through his teeth, walking past slits of windows, past grey fog divided into even sectors by black stone. To whistle secular music in God's sanctuary—there was canon law against that: "He who in a holy place offends through blasphemous or libidinous music . . ."

Heigh-ho, in spring the squire will go . . .

He conjured up a girl's body, lean as a January she-wolf's. Her hair came almost to her waist, coarse, lank, and unbrushed. The eyes in her starved face had the dull luster of a stick of charcoal.

> Heigh-ho, in spring the squire will go
> To the dancing-field where the kingcups grow
> And twenty fair daughters of margraves and earls
>   Dance, dance, dance,
> Dance in a circle and dance in a row.

As for the sick-hearted clerk, he will take himself to the nearest tavern. It had been a bad week. He had looked secretly into the reliquary to make sure that it did not hold a bone from a dog. He had been seized three times during the *Kyrie* by hideous silent laughter. What was there to do with such a brain? Stupefy it with drink.

That year April was sordid. The sky never entirely cleared; a weak sun drew water through a perpetual haze; and every evening there was rain or sleet or wet snow. There was a casing of sleet on him when he came into the tavern and found a place in the chimney corner, apart from the others. How was it that he could remember the whole company? Two young men in silk edged in fur. A priest from a bishop's train. A fleshy house-dame who squealed like a pig, laughing at nothing. Three serfs and a weaver's apprentice, all far gone and very companionable. Yes, and she, Elspeth. Her father was a welder of bronze but had been abed

15

these many months, spitting blood. When she could leave him, she lent a hand at the tavern, and in return for her fetchings and servings the tavern-keeper let her carry the day's slops home.

> Heigh-ho, in spring the squire is trim.
> Not one eye in forty but stares at him
> Through golden webs of shining hair.
> > Dance, dance, dance.
> The squire is ruddy, the squire is slim.

And the clerk on an evening's stolen leave from the Chapter House? Slim, but scarcely ruddy. A bony boy in a soaked cassock. Brown baby-fine hair curling from the tonsure around the nape and ears. Pale, bitter eyes of no particular color. A face too narrow, a spare mouth too grim, a nose too thin and turned a little to the right at the tip. Nothing but her duties could have drawn her to him. "Chopped radish and salt with your mead, Brother? Take, take. There is no charge for the savories."

> Heigh-ho, the squire will take his place
> Hand to hand and face to face
> With one fair daughter of Saxony.
> > Dance, dance, dance
> On rosemary, marjoram, dill, and mace.

It could be called a kind of dance, as he remembered it. She came and went, advanced and withdrew. More chopped radishes and salt? Was it true there would be a convocation of bishops here come midsummer? Another goblet of mead?—and she was not scant in the serving. Christ, how wet he was—and her arm, long and thin, brushed against him. What a night! Spring indeed! He must be chilled to the bone! And his hand, as if by a will of its own, went out and found its way through the side placket of her skirt, and there was no shift, there was only skin, feverishly warm and damp. At that, she stood stock still and said solemnly, as if she took it to be her duty to warn him: "Brother, your hand is not on a pilgrimage to Jerusalem."

16

The tavern-keeper sent her to the kitchen to look to the meat on the spit, and he fell to shivering. His teeth knocked together, he had to prop his chin to steady his jaws. Seized by a mortal heat, he deceived himself into believing he was perishing of mortal cold.

She came back and reported the meat roasted and carved. She tweaked the ear of one of the gallants, whispered to the drunken house-dame, sprinkled water on the neck of a sleeping serf, and came to him again. "Shivering, Brother? In that soaked wool you could take your death. Come into the kitchen. Nobody's there, and I have a towel, and there's a fire."

The kitchen was hot, empty, and eerily alive with the mutter and snap on the hearth. She handed him the towel and turned toward the doorway in consideration of his modesty, but then turned round again and came slowly, drawn by the lodestone of his nakedness. "Jesus, Son of God, how white you are!" she said. Her hands went out and stroked him, starting at the hollows of his cheeks and moving downward. Her mouth was open, her eyes were transfixed.

Dance, dance, dance—

On the floor, among vegetable peelings, with laughter and curses sounding over their pantings and strivings—they had not thought to shut the door. Quickly, yes, and so expertly he knew with the performing that all men have that road by rote: among the sons of Adam, there is no such thing as a virgin heart.

Dance, dance, dance—

At the end of it, in an aching bitterness, she said, "Well, I have gotten you warm, Brother, whether or not I have gotten you dry."

Heigh-ho, in spring, in the dancing-fever,
They walk apart to the cool of the river,
And the breast is bared, and the ring is given.
   Kiss, kiss, kiss.
And the troth that they plight, it will last forever.

17

Five months, six at the most. The carts of harvested apples were coming past her father's house that morning when he saw that she wanted more of it than he did and reproached her with her avidity. "But I must take what I can every time," she said in a whisper, for the dying father had coughed and turned in his sleep. "I cannot take it or leave it, like any wife. I never know whether you will be coming back."

Two or three times after that, and each time he was more put off by her insatiable seeking. Women were what the Church held them: the sulphurous pit into which men were dragged by the Devil, the darkness that obliterated serenity and reason. Her hands smelled of onions. She could not find time to keep herself clean. An old mildewed rag in a cupboard at the monastery had a strangely familiar smell, and he knew it smelled like her hair. To prayers, to penance—it was a venial sin in one who had not yet taken his final vows and might without mortal sin choose to leave the brotherhood and marry. Through a bout of autumn fever that could be taken for punishment, into a convalescence that seemed like absolution.

For months after his slow recovery he had veered between high purpose and triviality. He began to write a life of Saint Ursula, the virgin gospel-bearer martyred here at Cologne. Perhaps it was the futility of his efforts to give her a body and a face that took him out of the mainstream of his studies, sent him up a tempting rivulet, and landed him in a quagmire of facts about the Roman legions—the waggon trains that provisioned them, the weapons assigned to the auxiliaries. How many times in a day did he get up from his copyist's stool to wash himself, to brush his hair, to press down the folds of his cassock? Scholarship and elegance— he strove to make them both his own; and with his labors and his vanities he managed to keep the welder's daughter out of his thoughts, if not out of the dreams that assaulted his sleep.

He saw her again on Saint Stephen's Day, in the Cathedral. While he chanted in the choir, she stared up at him, stripping off his cassock with her charcoal look. Oh, she was shameless, well on her way to a whore's life, and—according to her father confessor—more than a little mad. As for his own father confessor, with more forbearance than could be expected he asked why, if a monk must think of a woman, it must be one of the foul daughters of Lilith instead of some faint earthly likeness of Mary, Mother of God.

Well, they were dead and gone, Father Carolus and the dark whore Elspeth. If the old man sent him through ice floes to the Norse, separation from them could not be more complete: he did not know where they were buried, had never prayed for the mercy that passes understanding beside their unhallowed graves. And the child of Mary on whom he had set his mind at the bidding of his father confessor? She was still among the living, but as remote from him as the dead.

He studied the moon again, higher now, risen close to the black arch of the window. Half an hour, no doubt, yet the abbot had said "half an hour or more" and would be at a disadvantage if drowsiness were added to the heaviness brought on by bread and wine. Oh, they were equivocators, all of them, including the father confessor who lay somewhere under these flagstones. What had he meant by that hint of his? Certainly not that a young monk should deal with a daughter of the Great Ones of Cologne as he had dealt with a welder's child. Girls cherished in the high houses were the ewe lambs of the flock—the tithes and alms of their parents bought a bond for their purity. Two possibilities then—and he had not seen them clearly in the days when he wrote about Saint Ursula and brushed the sheen into his hair: Choose a young woman simply to brood upon, build a crystallized fire in a frozen life of celibacy. Or acknowledge that some men are not made for unworldliness and cannot hope to be rewarded with the highest churchly offices. Choose to marry and to remain in minor orders, a worldly priest over whom abbots and bishops sigh and shake their heads, saying they hope for the day when the Church is purified and every priest is a cloistered celibate.

All equivocators, and he as much so as any of the others, now

19

that it was no longer a matter of simple lust. To knead desire and loving-kindness into one piece, to wrap a woman's body in the scent of a spring morning—thinking back over the arcs of twenty-eight years, he saw that it had called for a certain deliberateness, a certain set expectation.

A solemn day of festival, half churchly and half civic, in Cologne in the May of his twenty-second year. For decades, a mast of the ship that brought Saint Ursula here to her death had stood in the Cathedral; and every ten years the damsels of the city wove a new sail for it, sometimes white for her purity, sometimes red for her blood. That year the sail happened to be white. He could still see it, carried at its corners by those four considered most beautiful; and they were beautiful enough with their hair undone and their red robes showing bright under the pale sky, in the dull street. But the one he chose was not among these four. The goaded pride that had brought him now to think of himself as superior to every other monk in the Chapter House did not carry over to matters of love. It was a girl who came toward the end of the procession that caught his eye, a slight girl without jewels or any added coloring on her cheeks and lips. Perhaps she drew his notice because she halted a little on her left leg. Ah, lame, he thought. Lame and not overweeningly happy with herself. . . . As she came closer he saw that she was very like him, might even have been taken for his sister. Her eyes, like her dress, were a vague blue, the color of a jay; and her hair was the brown of a dead leaf, brushed to a sheen and spread carefully over her small breasts.

He waited on the Cathedral steps until she came up, long after the billowing sail, when most of the monks and priests had already gone in. She halted near him, uncertain of her balance, and they looked at each other, and her whole thin-skinned face was molded and lit up by a diffident smile. His hand went out to help her up. "Thanks, Brother," she said in a breathy voice. The reality of her touch strengthened the as yet unnamed intention: all through the service he felt as if she had left something —a petal, a dried leaf—in his hand.

20

Afterward in the refectory, there had been celebratory wine; and that, too, had helped him to get on with it, to ask the right questions and elicit the necessary answers from those who knew more about her than he. Her name was Ermintrude, a name used often in the northern ballads. She was seventeen and not yet spoken for, doubtless because of the lameness. But her dower would bring her a suitor in time: she was sole heir to her father, a knight who owned a solid house in the town and a fortress with fields and forests southward along the Rhine. Had he thought, while he drank and listened, Not bad for a second son who had inherited nothing but what was saved to be handed over with him to Holy Church?

Yet perhaps time and a hungry life had taught him to be too harsh with that spring day and with himself. There were other things, too, and he remembered them, stopping near a niche to lay his cold hand on a carved saint's cold feet. The smile, the light unasking touch. What they had said at table of her learning, how her script was better than any monk's, except, perhaps, his own. Her chastity, her shyness, her scrupulousness. The unanswerable questions she was forever asking her confessor: If a woman put up her mouth to a man in a dream, was she in a state to take the Lord's bread? Could one be called a good almsgiver if anything was held back—anything not truly needed, like a piece of moleskin or a yard of silk? What was the penance for striking a pet dog?

And his own father confessor had leaned across the board to connive in whatever questionable matter was afoot. "Her father and mother are great almsgivers," he said. "Our abbot is much indebted to them and sends them little gifts now and again. Next time, I will see to it that you are the carrier. A pot of our basil would not be amiss."

Our basil, our verbena . . . "Come again next Thursday after Vespers, if you can, Brother." A piece of honeycomb, a page copied in his own hand from a life of Saint Cuthbert . . . It was a quiet household, smelling of fennel and fresh rushes. They made it easy for him to take his time. "As like as brother and sister," said the mother. The father made him feel he was doing them a charity by dropping by after supper. In the embrasure of the window there was an everlasting game of chess in progress, and, until he had come, two had played and one had been companionless.

She too was careful—so careful that he had no occasion to ask himself "What am I doing?" She spoke to him of the saints and her soul's seeking as if he had been a second confessor. She sat three paces distant from him and begged his leave before she used his arm to help herself from her chair. If silence came upon them where they sat apart, she would turn aside and take up a book. "You are not here to listen to my chatter," she would say, giving him the quick shy smile. "Go take my mother's place at chess, and I will read a little."

It was when he sat at a distance from her, hunched over the game with her father, that he felt most what he had intended to feel. Not that what hung in the room was glitter out of old tales and ballads. It was more with him as if he were looking at a semiprecious stone set in silver and given such beauty as it had by its very isolation. She—she set apart for him, and by that made worthy. Her slight neck bent over the book, her hand wandering up to the corner of the page she was about to turn, her voice breathy with God knows what—shyness, gratitude, unlooked-for happiness.

"Will you have another slice of the pudding, Brother?"

"Not now, Ermintrude. Lay it by."

"For later this evening?"

"Oh, no, your good mother has stuffed me. For next Thursday, if it will keep."

"Oh, are you coming next Thursday? How good!"

"But I always come on Thursdays."

"So you do. And yet"—as he heard it, another voice raised a dark echo in his heart—"I am never sure you will be coming again."

Other women tied their men like falcons to their wrists. He

22

saw enough of it in the houses of the Great Ones of Cologne, in the Abbot's chambers, where he went often, missing Complines with permission. His life of Saint Ursula, finished and much copied, had gone west as far as Ghent and south to Chapter Houses in seven cities in France. When the name day of the martyr came round, it was he who was chosen to preach in the Cathedral, and for the first time he knew the force and timbre of his own voice sounding over a mass of adoring heads. Furthermore, what he had seen as faults in his person turned out to be assets in the eyes of others: it seemed he was "ascetic" rather than "bony"; his bearing was "dignified" instead of "stiff"; the right-hand slant at the tip of his nose was "distinguished" now, no longer "queer." And if she did not presume on his time after the fashion of riper beauties who always kept the leashes taut, she showed no more than common sense. With so much promise opening up for him in case he decided after all to take the final vows, she was wise to welcome him whenever he could come—even if it were only one Thursday in three or four—with the same quiet smile.

Two birds in the hand—he saw it now and could not tell how clearly he had seen it then. It was her father confessor who had taken it upon himself to point out that one of the birds was languishing. "Have you taken the trouble to notice," he had said, "that our spiritual sister Ermintrude is falling off in health?"

"No, truly?" It sickened him to think of it: his shoulders slanted forward in Christian concern. "What is her complaint?"

"Her mother tells me that she never sleeps. She is afraid to lie down in her bed."

"But why?"

"She is afraid of evil dreams."

Time, high time for him to make his decision. He did not show his face in the refectory that evening: he stayed, pleading sickness, solitary in his cell. There, thinking of her strained eyes and thin cheeks in the gathering August darkness, he had been assailed by so strong a tide of tenderness that he had fallen to bitter weeping. Go to her—explain, temporize, renounce in a loving and self-

23

accusing speech—but go to her at least. Yet it was hard to find an empty evening. So many knights and squires and elegant ladies claimed him as their confessor now. Besides, he was doing what he could about bad blood between his abbot and the bishop: they were quarreling over a piece of land, and only he, the darling of them both, could serve as a go-between. So it was weeks before he could find time to visit that house again.

The same room, the same smell of fennel and fresh rushes. The chessboard still set up near the window, the carved pieces reddened now in coppery October sun. She tried to smile when he came in, but the smile was grotesque. She had marred her face in trying to mend it: there was a spot of berry juice on each cheek, and lines of charcoal covered her light brown brows. The strain was intolerable, the talk false and halting, the food offered in courtesy a kind of torment. He had stayed half an hour and taken his leave, invoking God's blessing on them like any other monk.

He had never entered that house again. For months he had walked out of his way to avoid it, and when his meandering route ceased to seem monstrous and began to seem ridiculous, he resorted for the first time to the snail's way: he crept by the wall with his cowl pulled far forward to hide his face. Not there, but in other unexpected things the sweetness of what was lost was palpable like an incurable wound; the ache came back with the smell of certain herbs, the taste of a pudding, the sight of a chessboard set out for the game.

And the glory for which he had traded her and her inheritance? It had flared up brilliantly, and then it was gone. Where? Under the flagstones he paced tonight, into the grave with the abbot who had seen promise in him. To Regensburg with the transferred bishop whose favor had left him at a height he could not sustain. The Great Reform had been sending its emissaries to Cologne, and into the eye sockets of every one of them he had put the rolling eyes of Father Carolus. There was much sanctimonious talk about celibacy, and he sneered at it, remembering the welder's daughter and her bony body and sour-smelling hair. The scorpion bit, and he committed the small sin and openly defended it, possibly because abstention was high fashion these days. Old Latin and earth-stained scrolls concerned him more than Christ crucified; and the new abbot did not discourage his obsession. If Brother Albrecht virtually lived in the scriptorium, it was doubtless for the best. A disaffected monk with a formidable brain could prove a dangerous enemy. It was wise to keep him satisfied in an out-of-the-way and honorable place.

And she, their spiritual sister Ermintrude, had not taken herself off to a nunnery to pray for her rejector. Not a year later she had married a knight of substance and dignity. Not negligible as a man, either—still in his thirties, dark and well-made, with a falcon's face. That limp which he had thought would make her always the second choice of secondary men had not stood in the way of a high alliance. She came often to the Cathedral, leaning on the knight's arm; and later she came surrounded by tall sons and fair daughters, he did not know how many. Years ago he had lost count, telling himself he did not care.

There were times when he saw her more closely in the chapel, and light seemed to shine through the tight skin of her face, light of thankfulness for an undreamed-of gift. Then, if his eyes encountered hers, a shadow and a wonder would pass across the brightness, letting him know that she had loved him first and that in some inexplicable way she loved him still.

He had not seen her for five months, and their last meeting was not one he cared to remember. She had come to the Chapter House on a March morning to put gold into the alms box, fat hens into the kitchen, and polished maplewood bowls into the refectory. He had talked to her briefly in the abbot's chamber; they had stood near a window, and in the full sunlight he had seen with senseless anger that her skin was netted over with fine wrinkles and marked with pale-brown spots. It was as if she had affronted him, had deceived or betrayed him by growing old. She had asked the abbot for a sprig of the monastery's famous

25

basil, and *he* had been sent out for it and had deliberately delayed in bringing it in. Coming back with it, he had found her gone and the abbot aggrieved. He himself had felt the more ashamed because there was no way of making amends: he could not go tagging after her with the basil, and she would be wounded when another monk appeared with it at her door, and she would be leaving for the country soon. He would simply have to put the matter out of his thoughts until she came back on Saint Michael's Day next year.

Saint Michael's Day next year? He was roused out of his long brooding. When that day came, where would he be? But he could entertain the question with his mind only. The present into which he walked like a ghost was without substance, bloodless after his journey into the past. Snapped tendrils, and the ichor of the spirit drained away long since, and the mind, too, benumbed and dazed. The body went on of itself making the habitual gestures, straightening the aching shoulders, pressing down the damp folds of the cassock, smoothing the greyed hair. Where am I? Anywhere? Yes, going under the roof of the portico toward the abbot's chamber. And this is my hand—old, old—that lifts the knocker on the door.

✠　　✠　　✠

The room seemed different. The candlelight was less yellow—whiter and more intense after his long stay in the dark. The old man was not so drowsy: like a little fire that flares up if one dry stick is thrown on it, his frailty had taken life from the wine and bread. On the table in front of him two documents were laid out. One of them, covered with writing, curled at the edges—plainly it had come rolled up over a long distance and still bore fragments of the scarlet seal that had held it fast. The other, a map, was divided by creases and had been hastily drawn: the strokes of black ink in one corner had been blurred by the sweep of a monkish sleeve. He stood apart, unwilling to show himself curious or anxious. "Come, sit down and look," said the abbot. "These are for you, my son."

26

For him? But he saw as he seated himself that the bits of red wax were pieces of the seal of the Father of Fathers in Rome. The rolled parchment must have been brought by a papal legate out of the Everlasting City, up the mountains, across the Alpine pass. He could not make out the small script without craning his neck; and that he would not do under his superior's eyes.

"Here, look at this map," said the abbot, pushing it toward him over the table top.

On the right side of it, a river was drawn in a series of wavering parallel lines. The Yser, perhaps—he remembered seeing the Yser drawn in some such shape before. Coming down from the river and covering the lower right-hand half of the map was a forest of pines and deciduous trees sketched in as peaks and branches. To the left of the forest ran a jagged coastline; and a wide waste of waters on the other side of it was indicated by crested waves, a coiled sea serpent, boats, some fish—the sea, the westward sea.

Somewhere along the western coast then, probably to establish a new Chapter House. Workaday business—he had no heart for it, but he supposed it could be done. He as well as another could set out with a few companions, meet the master mason waiting for him at the chosen site, keep order among church serfs while the stones went up row on row and the land was cleared for outbuildings and fertilized for vegetables and grain.

"Do you know this river?"

"I take it to be the Yser."

"So *he* thinks—our Holy Father in Rome."

And how had *he* gotten into the matter? The founding of new Chapter Houses was the concern of bishops and abbots. Rome intervened only when two orders clashed.

"He thinks it is the Yser, and our bishop here agrees."

"But there is already one Chapter House along the Yser—"

"Chapter House? This has nothing to do with a Chapter House and very little to do with the Yser. The business on which you are being sent is out there." The ringed old hand came down among the crests and fish, on what could be taken only for the sea. "Out

27

here there is a promontory—an island—a promontory—" He
paused because a spray of spittle had come out of his mouth and
stained the map, laying him open to the charge of senility. "It is
not as witless as you would seem to think," he said, though his
listener meant to seem to think nothing. "It *was* a promontory,
and afterward it became an island, and now it is a promontory
again. Peculiar as it may seem, that is exactly what took place. I
have it stated somewhere here in the Holy Father's document."

A promontory—an island—a promontory out there in the waste
of waters. . . . While the abbot sought with a stiffened finger for
the right spot on the curled parchment, he himself glanced at the
map. Something was tentatively suggested there: an irregular circle
sketched in faint dots, as though the monkish map-maker had
hesitated to give more definite form to a thing so open to doubt.

"Yes, here is what he says," said the abbot, wiping his lips. " 'A
large promontory, supporting a flourishing community of brothers.
. . . On the rolls of Holy Church in the year of our Lord 998, and
not heard from since. . . . Called at that time Saint Cyprian's. . . .
A rich property, with its own fields, herds, flocks, vineyards, villages, and a town. . . . Connected to the coast of the mainland by
a narrow isthmus which seems to have been totally submerged in
a disastrous flood. . . . A Cathedral, a Chapter House, a nunnery.
. . . In the town, many houses, some of wood and some of stone.
. . .' "

He was on the point of saying "Unbelievable" but altered it to
"Very strange."

"Yes, strange, but there are witnesses. Three times in recent
months life has been sighted there, once by a fisherman washed far
out in a gale, and twice by travelers from a high place on the
opposite shore. Our brothers and sisters in Christ—only God
knows how many of them—have been living there, out of the eye
of Holy Church, cut off from everybody for almost a hundred
years."

Somehow he could not take it in. He was not even trying: he
was remembering a dream. Although it was emerging for the first

time into his waking thought, he knew he had dreamed it more than once before, changed in detail, perhaps, but in the main and in the dazed mood it brought with it always the same. It began in ordinary life, in the Chapter House, on any morning. He was walking up the circular stairs to the tower, he was opening the door that led out onto the roof to do some usual thing: see whether a cracked tile should be replaced, clean out a clogged gutter, take in some fruit left out there to dry in the sun. But instead of opening onto tiles and old leaves and magpies' nests, the doorway issued directly onto another level, a meadow stretching straight out from the threshold, sunlit, with a few stripped birches; and the unexpected vista was so known, so charged with a sense of release that it begot a swollen warmth, a fullness of amazement and recognition around his heart. . . .

"Almost a hundred years," his superior was saying. "Nobody knows what has happened to that brotherhood in the interim, nobody can tell whether they have fallen into loose practices or even heathenish beliefs. Our Father in Rome is deeply concerned for the state of their souls. That is why he has sent to me in their behalf, and I have chosen you to bring them back into the fold."

The last sentence—sanctimonious, sententious—almost dissolved the remembered dream. "Why should I be chosen for it?" he said.

The old man fetched up a sigh and let his back rest against the ermine. "Since the day I was made abbot here," he said, "you have asked me a great many questions, and with you they are always a means of voicing a complaint. 'Why should I be chosen?' you say, and what you mean is 'I have been singled out to be ill-used and put upon.' "

"My reverend Father himself pointed out that I was no wanderer. To find the way through such a forest—"

"Do you take me for a fool? It never came into my mind that you could find the way by yourself. How you will get there is no concern of yours—you will have a proper guide and pack beasts and provisions. Everything that is needed will be provided."

29

"Yet, if I may ask, seeing to it that my voice is duly humble—"

"The voice is not what I objected to. It is the spirit—the anger and the arrogance. Ask whatever you will."

"Why should so difficult a task be assigned to a monk who has scarcely proved himself worthy? Why, out of all his devoted sons, should our reverend Father settle on me?"

"You see? You resort to titles, and in saying them you mock them. Whatever comes out of my mouth"—he blushed, doubtless recalling the spittle—"you will mock, not to others—you are no babbler, no betrayer of confidences—but you will mock it nevertheless in the secret places of your heart. I have chosen you for three reasons: that God should be well served, that His lost children should be well served, and that you yourself should be freed from whatever shroud you have been winding around yourself these many years. For it seems to me—and, whatever you profess, I know it seems so to you also—that you walk among the living as if you were one of the dead."

"And the dead—" he could not repress it— "are they the ones best fitted to serve God?"

"In certain instances, yes. Or so, after long consideration, it seems to me. If your heartstrings are not tied to our heavenly Father, there is this at least: they are not tied to anything else. When I send you away from this Chapter House, I tear you away from nothing. Nothing but your books and scrolls and your fixed intention to read until you drop into your grave."

He had no answer. All of that was unquestionably so.

"As for God's lost children," said the abbot, "with them, too, you may prove more serviceable than you think. Pride sometimes gives way before the small claims of the pitiable, and an empty heart is a heart open to receive. There is this also: you hate this monastery and these times. And whoever goes to that island—that promontory—will step out of his times as well as his rooted place."

He could still conjure it up, though now it was more remote: the meadow with the stripped and shimmering birches, April made manifest to a child's eyes.

"Those brothers of Saint Cyprian's," said the abbot, tapping the relevant spot on the parchment, "cut off as they were from Christendom for a hundred years, would not even have heard of the Rule of Saint Benedict. It is possible that you will find them keeping wives or concubines—it is still so with some of us now, and very likely it was so with all of them then."

His impulse was to turn and stare at the scorpion, exorciser of whatever half-corporeal image was taking shape among the skin-pale branches of his dream. But there was no need for him to turn. His will itself expunged whatever was being shadowed forth— daughter of Lilith, daughter of Mary, daughter of Aphrodite the Cyprian. Strange that her epithet should have been woven into the name of a martyred saint and then passed on, dyed in his blood, to the lost land. . . .

"I believe you consider yourself bound by the Rule of Saint Benedict."

His face came forward out of the cowl. Partly in arrogance and partly out of an inexplicable necessity to deal in all honesty with the old man on the other side of the table, he said, "If I may ask —and there is no complaint behind it—why do you take that for granted?"

"You accepted the Rule when you took your final vows, and, as I understand, you took those vows at some cost. You have obeyed it—"

"Not in all things. Not to the letter."

"Who obeys any sacred rule to the letter? How have you trespassed?"

"I do not sleep in the common chamber with my brothers. On grounds of sickness and sleeplessness, I requested my own cell. But in that cell I have slept less than I did when I lay down with the others. I take candles from the scriptorium and sit up reading half the night."

"One paternoster for every month you have read there. You can say them on your way to Saint Cyprian's. And, lest you take me to be in my second childhood: I knew you were not sick, I knew you did not sleep, I knew you read. But perhaps the very breaking of that requirement has brought you to see it was not so unwise. Your freedom has not, so far as I can see, given you much peace."

"I have not labored in the fields, either."

"No—that, too, I am aware of. Expediency as well as charity has taught the brotherhood to temper that particular obligation. The glory of God is not increased when a hand that writes a fine script is ruined planting turnips. It is no pleasure to Him to see the weak burst their hearts to lift what is light to the strong. As for the rest, the major obligations . . . ?" He looked up, and there was a kind of merry malice in his red-rimmed eyes.

He considered the major obligations. Obedience? Grudgingly given, but given. No personal belongings? The borrowed volumes had been returned with regret, but he had always returned them. Chastity? He had touched nobody except by necessity, he had never laid his dry hands even on the heads of children since he had taken his final vows. "In the rest, I am guiltless in the act, though imperfect in the spirit," he said.

"Who is perfect in the spirit?" The thin old shoulders went up in a shrug and sagged into the folds of ermine. The eyes that had encountered his were withdrawn, looked vaguely at the new arras, and, suddenly tired, blinked against sleep.

"When am I to set out?"

"The day after tomorrow. All things are arranged for, as I said. Haste is in your interest. While summer lasts, you will not be in much danger from the wolves and boars, but summer is on the wane, and we cannot tell how long it will take you to cross the forest and find the isthmus. Even with the best of guides, you could lose your way, so you must be given plenty of time." He suppressed a yawn and rolled up the parchment to make it plain that the interview was at an end.

But who could stare at the map and think of the day after tomorrow without being assailed by questions—specific, earthly, urgent questions having nothing to do with the dazed quiet of the vista from the top of the roof? What was known of the lost folk

32

on the promontory? Where was the isthmus? Up there, close to the mouth of the Yser, or southward where the sleeve had smeared the lines? Was it anywhere? Had anybody truly seen it? And, if it had really emerged from the water, why had the people of Saint Cyprian's never walked over it to seek out their brothers on the opposite shore? The dotted lines among the fish and boats— were they projections of an existing body of land, or were they the dubious recording of some mad vision that had happened to visit a fisherman and two travelers in the same year?

The map was plucked from under his eyes, folded on its creases by the stiff old fingers, and laid flat under the rolled-up parchment. "Let not your mind be troubled. It is in God's hand, and God will look to it," the abbot said.

"I *hope* so—"

"Good. Continue in hope. Hope alone, even without faith and charity, has been known to work wonders."

The old man was at it again: the pious saws were rolling off his tongue by rote. His brief vitality was all burned out—his eyes were veiled by his seamed eyelids, and his head shook with his effort not to nod toward sleep. There was nothing to be gained by staying, that was plain. All he could do was get up, utter the required "Peace," and take himself out.

Passing the abbot's window, he saw a spot of whiteness through the black of the ivy. His candle butt—he recognized it with something close to wonder: it was as if a month had passed since he had left it there. He stopped, meaning to take it, but then went on erect and empty-handed. He could not see himself reading, not even the new Livy, not tonight.

☩   ☩   ☩

Not since the heyday of Father Carolus had he felt such yearning to let out the workings of his mind and heart. In the time of waiting he often thought what a fool he might make of himself, how he might babble if there were anybody in the brotherhood before whom he could unleash his tongue.

33

He could not sleep the first night, and during the next day's waking hours, images presaging sleep and endowed with all sleep's license took shape in his brain. At breakfast he saw himself standing on the prow of a fishing boat and knew suddenly that he needed no place on which to plant his feet, that with the slightest shove he could go on ahead of the hull, his soles scarcely skimming the waves. He walked in meditation round and round the square, and sometimes the black walls were porous and crumbled away, and sometimes the irregular building blocks all turned into hexagons and made up such a great dripping honeycomb as had been promised to the Jews. Or he would look up at the sky and know—dizzy with the knowledge and with tilting his head—that it stretched out forever over everything that lived. His body seemed scarcely corporeal, buoyed up by a sense of lightness and release.

Then again there were hours when he did not want to move: the beating of his heart was so loud and fast that it dominated his existence and drove him up to his cell. There he sat crouched over, listening to the pulse of his mortality, feeling it in his head and throat, knowing that he was terribly afraid. Then he felt a forked branch of the uncharted forest catch him by the neck and hold him dangling like Absalom. Or, riding on a donkey down a deserted road, he felt a knife going into his back and knew he had been attacked by thieves and had no hope of a Samaritan. Or he lost his footing on the slippery isthmus and went down, and water heavy as molten metal closed over his head.

But a little bread and fish were enough to revive him. A warmth, seductive and equivocal, spread tingling to his fingertips. His hands —he had to keep a watch on them in the actual world—reached out in his imagination to touch, to stroke, to know. Sometimes the cheeks and temples of a girl-child's earnest face. Sometimes a smooth hand extended to him out of a sleeve. Sometimes a naked foot, bare and high at the instep and the arch, stopping near him in a race or flight, close to his face where he lay in snow.

Dreams, a fool's dreams, and they were knocked out of him soon enough. The journey was taken out of whatever airy overworld he had been wandering in and set flat down on the earth

34

when the abbot told him the name of his traveling companion. He would be guided and attended—and there was to be no arguing about it—by the lay brother Thaddeus, the fat dolt, the unleavened loaf of bread. Why Brother Thaddeus? He let the question be what it was—an outright complaint; and he got his answer in an impatient voice, emphasized by sighs of aggravation. Because Brother Thaddeus was a woodsman's son. Because he knew such insignificant things as how to kill a wolf, tell edible berries from poisonous ones, handle a pack donkey, cut a path through a thicket, chart the direction by winds and stars. Perhaps his Latin left something to be desired, perhaps he was unacquainted with pagan history, but even as exalted and cultivated a mind as that of Father Albrecht might see that God could have His reasons for creating such common clay for service in a holy cause.

After that exchange, he carried his anger where he had carried his fear: to his cell. Mean and small—cell and journey were both of them mean and small. He kicked the soggy rushes about on the floor. He bruised his hand by striking it against his reading stand. He tramped on a plump spider and was the more enraged to find nothing left to exult over, not so much as a spot. Days, weeks perhaps, with Brother Thaddeus. God in Heaven—how was he to deal with such a man, eat with him, sleep beside him? What could they talk about? And the worst of it was that what the abbot had said about wolves and poisonous berries was as inescapable as the stones of these four walls. He himself would be utterly helpless without the brainless lump of dough—could not wield an ax, mix a batter, load a mule, use a kindling box, tell north from south. He had given his life to God in exchange for a roof and a fire and poor fare, and now he was mocked for the lack of what he had been promised in return for everything else.

On that last evening in the Chapter House he had a foretaste of what lay ahead of him, saw how much officiousness could be brought to the bland surface of Brother Thaddeus. The lay brother bustled in and out, informing him unnecessarily about arrangements and supplies. A cold nod, a turning away after a brief answer did not discourage him. His small eyes under the too carefully

35

trimmed yellow hair begged for, even insisted upon a look. His consultations were loaded with "we" and "you and I." He called the journey "our mission"; his references to "our isthmus" and "our promontory" were so offensive that it was hard to reply with civility. Complines was a blessed retreat from his intrusions. And when the service was over, even bed seemed insecure. Every step in the hall made him think it would be still another report, something to be added to "Our reverend Father has graciously told me to load the Livy for you" and "We are to have dried fruit and smoked fish as well as the flour and the cured meat."

He wanted a confrontation, an occasion for an outburst. It could not come over the loading of the donkeys: that, the abbot had said, was strictly the lay brother's business. But the new officiousness was certain to be pushed too far—snatches of sleep were possible for him only with that assurance. And it *was* pushed too far at the setting out when the two of them walked under a lead-grey sky over to the three beasts standing ready near the black tower.

Brother Thaddeus, his self-importance fattened on a farewell breakfast, walked a little ahead of his superior. Beyond his bulk, it was possible to recognize two of the donkeys, the ones that were draped with saddle cloths. There was a small inoffensive animal called Patches and another slightly taller one that the abbot—to show his freedom from superstitious prejudice against pagan literature—had named Cicero. It was toward Patches that the lay brother advanced. Good, Father Albrecht thought. At least he has the grace to assign the bigger one to me. But Brother Thaddeus only let his hand come down on the withers of the insignificant animal. "Here, Father," he said, "you can ride this beast."

His heart began to race and he had to make an effort to keep his voice low. "Why, if I may ask, have you assigned this one to me?"

Brother Thaddeus plainly heard no anger, took it for a legitimate question. "Because Patches here is such a tractable beast, the quietest one we have. He has been to Trier and back three times, and once when we took him to Regensburg—"

He was not listening. The third donkey, the laden one, had caught his eye. It was larger and bonier than the other two, and he

36

saw at once that he and it shared a bond. It was galled and it twitched under the leather sacks as he was galled and twitched under the world's stupidities. Furthermore, there was a dignity about it: among donkeys, it was obviously highborn and delicately bred. The proud eloquence of its wet eyes was somehow intensified by the veined vulnerability of its inner ears.

". . . So, if my Father will mount—" Brother Thaddeus was saying.

"This one." He pointed to the laden donkey. "This is the one I will ride."

"Asmodeus?"

"Asmodeus, since that is his name."

"That *is* his name, and a very good name for him, too. Asmodeus was a demon, and so is he."

"Indeed?" He stepped away from the mild Patches and laid his palm tentatively on the demon's lusterless hide. The muscles twitched under the touch as if they were remembering some dark and primal wrong. Then they quieted, and the long head turned slowly, and he was fixed again by the large moist eyes.

"Really, if I may presume to advise my Father—"

"I am advised, and I—"

"But Asmodeus is already loaded—"

"You will have to unload him then. If you had asked me beforehand—"

"But our reverend Father told me that I—"

"Shall we go back and lay the matter before him?"

It was scarcely a risk: he knew that Brother Thaddeus would never have the heart. The covered portico was deserted—the last of those who had come out to wish them well had gone back in. The brotherhood had already sloughed them off and was about its usual business: at a second-floor window a boy's high voice was practicing an *Alleluia*; a saw was tearing at wood somewhere in the back garden; through the open door of the kitchen came the clink of dishes and pans. To materialize on a doorsill after a formal departure . . . Brother Thaddeus shrugged and went about the work stolidly, without haste, in spite of the large drops of rain that had begun to spatter onto the flagstones. Bag after bag he un-strapped, laid on the back of Patches, and strapped again. His only show of annoyance was to thrust the Livy somewhat vigorously into his superior's hands.

But now that the confrontation had taken place and his author-ity had been established, he felt little satisfaction. To lend a hand in the consequent labor would have been an unthinkable degrada-tion of his own rank; sweat trickled down the lay brother's face—it was no light task for him in the thick, dank weather; and it was impossible to put out of mind how cheerfully and with how much bustle he had done last night what he was undoing now. A melan-choly, a vague regret spread over everything within the range of sight. The dull towers—would he ever lay eyes on them again? Would he come back to eat and drink from those clinking tin dishes and cups? Would he lie at the end as his dwindled ambi-tion had taught him to believe he would: in a modest coffin under the flagstones, his hands folded over his chest, his feet stiff and vertical, the toes lifting the cassock at the hem? . . .

"Well, now, Father," said Brother Thaddeus, attempting ease and goodwill, "there you have Asmodeus."

"Thanks, Brother." He mounted and drew his cowl around his face, wanting no traffic with the small quenched eyes. As he set-tled his weight, another quiver ran under the rough hide.

"You're very welcome. I only hope you will still be thanking me come noon."

There was no arrogance—it was only another attempt to make light of the hurt and embarrassment. He groped after words that would add up to an appropriate answer, could not find them, let it pass. Rain—heavy, squeezed-out drops of it, as if the grey sky were old and had forgotten how to weep—fell on them and around them as they rode out of the square into the foetid street.

✠　　✠　　✠

The change in him began almost imperceptibly, in his dealings with the demon on four legs. For the first ten days of the journey,

38

he rode Asmodeus two-thirds of the time and walked beside him the rest. Brother Thaddeus doubtless thought he was afraid of the beast; he turned away considerately whenever there was a struggle, never allowing himself the satisfaction of the look that says "You see?" Fear there was to be sure when the tense neck creaked and the stiff position of the long ears showed that the veins in their linings were purpled with a surge of angry blood. But fear was only half of it. Something else prompted him to dismount and walk whenever they came to paved or level places—a feeling he had not experienced for so long that he did not know whether to call it pity or awe.

Whatever it was, it was not at all like the lay brother's contemptuous fellowship with Cicero. Brother Thaddeus got down only when they stopped for provender or rest, and then he stood by and sneered at the things the animal would eat. "Look, there he is again," he would say, "back at the burdock. He eats anything—garbage, too—he's worse than a pig." And he would push his fleshy palm against the animal's nose. Neither of them paid any attention to Patches. That creature, laboring along under sacks and leather bags, was no more a subject for conversation than certain monks who get through their duties on a level that calls for neither praise nor rebuke.

Sometimes when they paused in a lane to let a flock or herd go by, Brother Thaddeus would do something his superior found incomprehensible and shocking: he would fling himself forward until he almost lay along the beast's back, hugging him, sinking his hands into the belly where nipples and sex were buried in the coarse pelt. "Must you lie on him, too?" Father Albrecht said, wondering that he could sound so casual and jocular.

"But I am not lying on him. I am doing him a kindness by holding up his guts."

"His guts would need less holding up if you walked him now and then."

He could not imagine himself performing the same service: it would be an unwarranted familiarity. He instinctively turned aside

39

when Asmodeus pissed or relieved himself in soft blobs. He never touched him without good reason and was particularly careful to avoid any contact with the trembling ears. Since the first day, he had always addressed him by name: "Well, now we will rest awhile, Asmodeus." "See here, Asmodeus, somebody has left you a mouthful of hay." He had been talking to the donkey constantly, spontaneously; and he knew suddenly, with amazement, that speech with a beast had led him imperceptibly into speech with another man. The two of them, talking to Asmodeus and Cicero, found themselves talking to each other. And Father Albrecht, listening to himself when he addressed the lay brother, knew that his voice lacked the formality and restraint of the tone he took with the demon, was more like his companion's easy, half-jeering way with Cicero.

The wonder was—so he told himself—that there was any talk at all. Whatever kind of talk it was, it served for the occasion. The country through which they were passing was an ordinary stretch: fields, manor houses, villages, forest lands mastered and held in check. Nothing as yet to resemble even faintly the points and twigs on the bad drawing, no glint of water between the trunks of beech and oak. The uncharted forest was known of but seldom mentioned by those from whom they got fresh vegetables and bread and milk. The sea was a rumor: if he spoke of it, the listener shrugged and gestured vaguely toward the west. Moving through such a commonplace stretch of the world, he and the lay brother needed no more than commonplace communication.

"So, Father, you did not like the house-dame's boiled eggs?"

"I prefer eggs when they have not been boiled in the same basin with shifts."

"Oh, but you missed the worst of it. There was a soiled baby-napkin, too—I saw her drop it in."

"*You* ate them, that much I saw, and you are always at Cicero over what he puts in his guts."

"But look, Father, there is a difference. *I* eat out of humility whatever charity hands out to me. Cicero eats trash out of stupidity."

40

Or at dusk, in an inn or a hayloft or some manor kitchen where they had settled for the night and he sat dreaming over the open Livy:

"Why hold the book, Father? So far as I can make out, you have not read a single word."

"How can I read? You catch me up at every sentence with your yawning."

"Can you hear me yawn?"

"Hear you? You may not know it, but you have a yawn as loud as a lion's roar. You make me wonder what manner of mind Saint Jerome had that he could write all those treatises, cooped up with a lion."

"Do you believe it, Father?"

"Believe what?"

"That the holy Jerome called a lion out of the desert and tamed him and taught him to eat no meat."

"Ask me tomorrow. Your yawning has put me half asleep."

Not much in the way of human discourse, but better than what he had expected: chilly silence on his part and churlish silence on the other's. He made do with such exchanges by day and counted heavily upon an hour with Livy before he slept. But though he never gave up, never failed to open the book, he never attained what he looked forward to. He took gratification from the weight of the volume on his knees, took pleasure in the precision of black ink on cloudy parchment; he even sensed the forcefulness of the Latin style. But he knew the book no more intimately than he would have known, by stroking it with the back of his hand, a face closed up in sleep or death. Livy eluded him. He could not really read. He thought he had been reading and knew of a sudden that he had fallen asleep and dreamed—of what? Something that had quickened his breath, something that had brought gooseflesh and a peculiarly delicious chill out on his arms; but he could not conjure it up as an image, nor give it a name, nor know whether he had been held motionless in a frozen present or washed out into an incalculable future or dropped back into a past beyond the reaches of memory.

On the tenth day of the journey they came upon a village where the people knew more and talked more of the great forest. It was at once a new and a very old village: fresh huts and houses, smelling of sap and saw, had been raised on the sites of other dwellings put to the torch by the Norse a hundred years ago. Beams and lintels for the construction had been dragged by oxen from the woods into which they were to travel, and while they ate a decent breakfast at the table of a bishop's steward, they heard reports from some who had seen the vast waters from certain high places three days' journey from the town.

It was to be a bishop's town, a western outpost, and it would seem that God's eye was upon the enterprise: last winter had been mild; the clearing had been begun early in a clement spring, and now the first harvest was coming in and was nothing short of magnificent. The steward's son, a piping tow-headed lad of nine or ten, engaged himself to take them to the square. There was a church going up there, and they must have a word with a certain Brother Matthias who was supervising the work, and a look at a certain Saint Pelagia who had been sent from Italy and was just out of her packing case.

Something in the place or the season moved him profoundly as he went on foot with Brother Thaddeus behind the lad. He felt weakly exalted, wanly blessed, as though he were taking his first stroll after a long sickness. It was as if he and the town were sharing a mild resurrection. The pale gold of the late August sun, the smell of dug earth and cut wood, the shaken shadow of leaves all begot in him a sweetness utterly beyond communicating in the sort of talk established between him and his companion. In silence they walked into an open space heaped with partly dressed stones. In silence they went from one to another of the booths put up for metalworkers and masons. And when the supervising monk finally appeared, they found that he was the only one there: it was a saint's day, and the booths were all empty, and the hammers were still.

If he had encountered him in the Chapter House back in

Cologne, this Brother Matthias would not have aroused any particular interest. He was a thin, red-headed, grave monk with a jaw overlong and slanted to one side; and this malformation made his glance seem always to be running ahead of his lips. They did not speak of any weighty matters; in fact, Father Albrecht was reluctant to spoil their enthusiastic converse with the complicated explanation of his mission; it was enough to spend half an hour with an equal, chatting of masons and marble saints and the history of Siena, from which the newly risen Pelagia had come. He forgot the mission, forgot the time, forgot Brother Thaddeus.

And when they had taken their leave of the long-chinned brother and were on their way back to the steward's house to see to their donkeys, he was made sharply aware of the extent of his forgetfulness.

"A fine talker, this Brother Matthias," he said, uncomfortable with the protracted silence.

"I could not judge of that. I caught very little of what he said."

"His jaw is malformed."

"Yes, badly."

"I took a liking to him. I thought we might go back to him later in the day and make our confessions."

"To *him?*" The lay brother had stopped short and turned round to face him. Red was spreading up over his heavy jowls. His small eyes were hard with anger and pain. "Now, truly, Father Albrecht, you cannot expect me to confess to *him.*"

"Why—why not?" He stammered because he had seen the answer before he finished the question.

"According to the Rule, *you* are my confessor—before we left, our reverend Father told me so."

It was true, the cure of Brother Thaddeus's soul was plainly his obligation. He had forgotten it, put it out of mind because he wanted no dealings with that soul. It was as distasteful to him as an uncooked slab of bacon. Like the thick body in which it lived, he could not touch it without disgust. I am no confessor, my duties these many years have been with books, he told himself, making a

43

blank of his face. Yet here they were, that body and that soul, beside him in a place drained of all its former beauty and intimations. "You are quite right. I should have offered to confess you earlier. I will see to it after supper this very day," he said.

But after supper there was, fortunately, no occasion. They had come upon the outskirts of the fabled forest and had met with the church serfs who were there to fell the great oaks for the lintels and beams. With these serfs—kin in the spirit, since his father had been a woodsman—Brother Thaddeus blatantly enjoyed himself. He used their strange woodcraft terms in a boastful voice, joined them in their coarse songs, drank too much of their mead, forgot to chart the road by the position of the stars, unloaded Patches with bad grace, and fell early into a snoring sleep.

For his superior, it was a haunted night. He could not tell whether it was body lice or wood lice he kept feeling on his skin. A sullen and erratic wind sprang up, and in his doze he more than once mistook the noise of the boughs for a sound he had never heard: the voice of the sea. A red full moon, half blotted out by a tree trunk, hung in the doorway of the hut where he slept; and, sighting it after an elusive dream, he took it to be a moon cut in two and imagined that some calamity would fall with the severed half of it onto the sleeping world. Asmodeus was restless, plagued by insects and unfamiliar sounds, and answered rush of wind and cry of crickets with stamping and whinnying.

He sat up on an alien pallet and tried to take imperious control of his fantasies. To impose disorder upon the universe was a trick for overleaping his gross neglect of Brother Thaddeus's soul. But when he tried to imagine himself listening to the lay brother's confession, determination left him. Doomsday's somber majesty, embodied in the halved moon, was more acceptable than the thought of his fellow traveler coming close, fat and sweat and all, to lay a round head and an account of crass fallings-off in his lap or on his knees.

And in the morning, the whole aspect of the journey was changed. There was nothing left of the lightness that had almost

44

opened into quiet exaltation among the sawdust and building stones of the new town. It was partly because the sky itself was hidden from them now by the multiplying branches of the woods. The forest had its own splendors: twitter and screech of wild birds, dart of blue and speckled wings, mushrooms cropping up around ancient boles in unbelievable stains of scarlet and purple, white-veined skeletons of leaves on blue-green carpets of needles from the pines. But the talk and the jests were no longer possible, and Asmodeus hated those sinking carpets, and Patches took to balking and shuddering under the load, and Cicero reared and neighed at the sight of the first doe. Also, there was a new pride in the lay brother's bearing. *He* knew the way; *he* could laugh at the fright of the beasts; *his* silence was the silence of concentrated thought, not the silence of embarrassment.

Late in the afternoon they came to an abandoned hut. The sun shone through cracks between the boards, pouring heat in upon accumulated heat. There was a smell of urine and rotted flesh; three pans, coated with an unidentifiable loathsomeness, stood on the floor; and spider webs sagged everywhere, heavy with dust.

"A hunter's hut," said Brother Thaddeus, breaking the day's wordlessness. "Look—" he pointed to a livid mess in a shadowed corner, "that's a skinned creature, a little one, caught for fur. Well, he'll not be wanting the place until winter. He'll be back then for moles and squirrels."

"Shall I confess you here?" He did not know why he had said it. To punish and subdue his flesh with the stench? To absolve himself by making the hard thing doubly hard?

The lay brother looked at him in bewilderment, dragging his hand over the back of his neck. "Here in this hole, Father? With all this stink? Confess me in the open—wherever we decide to stay for the night. There must be water close to here. The hunter would never have built a hut unless there was a decent spring."

"But why would he leave a carcass here to rot?"

"Slovenliness."

"Why would he want to come back to such a smell?"

45

A knowledgeable woodsman's smile, an inferior's gratification over the mysteries of his own low world, enlivened the doughy face. "There won't be any smell next winter. Come December, you'll find this mess all dried up."

Knowledgeable he proved to be on every count: the water he expected gurgled out of a cleft in a mossy rock; stakes and cross-bars had been set up for drying the hides of larger animals; a slab of granite was encircled by stones to shelter a fire. They watered and tethered the donkeys and washed themselves in the cold, earth-smelling yield of the spring. Quickly, aptly, Brother Thaddeus gathered dry twigs and used the flint box, mixed water with ground grain, sliced salted meat in strips; and within less than half an hour he was serving up pork wrapped in edible pancakes and pouring out spring-cooled wine.

The clearing where they ate was on a height. It would have been an excellent place for the lay brother to do what he had failed to do after last night's mead: determine their position and settle on the route they should follow by the guidance of the stars. But an evident uneasiness made his self-assurance dwindle while they sat eating together; he looked one way and another and sniffed the air like a restless beast; and by the time the blaze had burned down to embers, Father Albrecht knew the cause. The stillness around them was total—the wind had fallen, and a dank mist was beginning to rise. "There's one star. It will be some time before we can see the others," Brother Thaddeus said. And then appeasingly, as if his own fault might be lessened if he forgave and helped to expunge another's, "Confess me here. There's a fine stone seat for you, and I can kneel on the pine needles. I will make it a short business. I have been examining my sins all day, and I have them by heart."

Why he should have felt confined and oppressed, he did not know. The patch of open sky, so pale that the leaves looked black against it, the evidently renewed goodwill of the penitent, the small-ness and triviality of all human things, shrunken as they were here in the vast spread and evening stillness of the earth—these should have been antidotes against his disgust. But disgust surged up in him the moment the lay brother, taking the ritual position, laid his forehead, heavy as a hound's, on his ghostly father's knees. It was exactly as he had known it would be: his flesh crept, his nostrils and lungs rejected the smell of the man. And it was the harder for him because he seldom listened to confessions any more and habitually made his own after the new fashion, at five paces' distance with his face covered by his hands.

"Father, I have grievously sinned and am heartily sorry."

"God is merciful. What is your sin, my son?"

"The sins of gluttony and drunkenness. At the sight of any food, even the vilest, my belly yearns. I ate what would have fed three at the serfs' table last night. As for the mead, I drank so much of it that I fell into a stupor and forgot to examine the stars."

He suppressed the spontaneous, frightened "Are we lost?" He scratched his cheek—an insect had lighted on it—and said in the required voice, drained and distant, "Gluttony and drunkenness are insidious sins, my son. They heat the body"—he moved away from that quickly, sorry he had mentioned it—"and they addle the brain. Say twelve paternosters and eat no—" He was about to say "no meat," but that was plainly ridiculous. Was this great lump of a man to maintain himself on pancakes through a journey? "Eat no more than you must to put down the craving. Never eat for pleasure. Eat only for sustenance."

"And the drunkenness, Father?"

"You are too scrupulous," he said, thinking how the drunkenness had sprung out of his own obvious preference for the long-chinned brother. "I have never seen you drunken before last night. Say three more paternosters, and put the matter out of your head." His tone—he knew it—had grown impatient and querulous. He waited a little and reassumed the ritual voice, a voice that seemed to be censured, even mocked, by the rolling reaches of the forest and the pale arc of the firmament. "If these are your only sins, my son, you do not stand in urgent need of confession. As I said, God is merciful, and—"

47

"Oh, but I have more grievous sins than those, Father." The neck twitched, the forehead rolled against his knees, and he thought irrelevantly of Asmodeus.

"Well, then, name them, my son."

"I am lecherous as a horsefly. My soul crawls with lechery."

He was amazed and appalled to hear it. This great oaf, hidden under mounds of baby fat? This porcine, phlegmatic hulk? It was not reasonable, of course, but he had always taken for granted that only thin, inwardly driven men were tormented by lechery. "Surely you have not been with a woman, not since you last confessed in Cologne," he said, trying to circumvent the actuality by a preposterous conjecture.

"Been with a woman? God forbid, Father. I have never been with a woman. I would not do such a thing while I ate God's bread. Besides—"

"Besides?" He said it coldly. Had the stone on which he sat had arms like a chair, he would have tapped upon them in impatience.

"Besides, I do not even know whether I could be with a woman. Let me only think of a woman, and—"

"And?"

"I spill my seed."

"Oh, now, truly—" It was a protest against the vulgarity, the naked familiarity. The forgotten obligations of the confessional reproved him, made him twist the protest into something else. "Truly, if it is as easy as that, consider it of no more weight than a manner of relieving yourself. We are all men, and—" He stopped, aware that darkness had closed him in, darkness of his own making. His cowl—it had hung back over his shoulders these last ten days— he had pulled his cowl over his head and close around his face.

"That serving maid in the steward's kitchen—her skirt had somehow gotten into the crack in her nether parts, and—"

He cut it off with a brisk churchly lift of his hand. "Pray to Saint Anthony, and I will pray in your behalf. God is merciful and will grant you—"

But the plump fists which had hung at the thick thighs until

48

this moment clenched now and in violent and intimate protest beat, actually beat, on his knees. "I am not finished, Father. You push me, you hurry me, and I must finish." He could not see the face, but he knew that, where it rested on his lap, it was ludicrously and pitiably distorted—a baby's squalling face begrimed by tears.

"God forgive me, Brother. Go on then."

"I am guilty of the sin of anger."

"Toward whom, my son?"

"I am afraid to say it."

"A thing said in confession is a burden lifted from the heart."

"Well, then." It came out as a sigh, a blast of hot invading breath. "I am angry against you."

"Me? Why?"

"That you hold me so cheap."

"How—how did you come to that conclusion, my son?"

"No, now, stupid as I am, I am not so stupid that I cannot see it."

"If my talking with Brother Matthias so unsettled you—" He was doing the unthinkable. He was engaging in wily deception against a soul in the confessional. He fell silent, and the utter stillness around him moved in upon him. Within and without there was a vacancy, a void that could not tolerate God.

"Not cheaper than Brother Matthias, Father. Cheaper than him I know I am. But can a man—any man—be cheaper than a beast?"

"A beast?"

"I have seen it these ten days. I am a poor thing in your sight beside Asmodeus."

It was true; he had no answer; it was simply so. And his mind seized on the reason, disregarding the man whose head weighed upon his knees. All things on the ladder of being strove to fill with the elixir of their spirit the confines of their kind. The spirit of the beast Asmodeus filled up the donkey as wine generously poured will distend a wineskin to its full limits. The spirit of Brother Thaddeus left the species man limp and insufficient, impossible to love. He breathed deep and outstared the admonishment of the single star.

49

He lied, in the arrogance of his reason and the aristocracy of his own fullness. "Ask the saints to take away your foolish imaginings. You are my soul's son, dearer to me than a dumb beast that does not know God," he said.

"Truly, Father?"

"Truly."

"What penance, then, for my foolishness?"

"For foolishness there is no penance. Go and sin no more. Peace."

But peace, even with the most flaccid of creatures, could not be bought so cheap. The glance that passed between them when the pentinent got up was brief and veiled. All their dealings with each other that evening—except the short exchange at the end of it—were halting and spuriously considerate. He felt forced to sit and stare at the Livy because Brother Thaddeus had brought it to him and made a blaze for him to read by; and the fire was too hot, and the book was a burden, and his eyes smarted from the smoke. His resolution to pay no visits to Asmodeus was useless as well as false: he could not refrain from looking up at every sound the donkey made, and he knew that the lay brother could tell how grudgingly he was denying himself. And, when the mist thickened and the night cries of the forest increased his uneasiness, he did not feel called upon to give Brother Thaddeus any further assurance that he had been forgiven for his neglect in the matter of the stars.

"The sun set over there—am I right, Father?"

"Yes, but I cannot be sure you are pointing due west."

"More to the right?"

"More to the left, since you ask me."

"Would you say, then, that due south would be there, over that big pine?"

"No, more in the direction of that bald cleft hill. But you are the one who knows."

"But there are no stars, Father. It might be better to stay where we are until the stars come out tomorrow night."

The prospect was maddening. "By no means," he said. "We will go on in the morning as we planned. If our way is south"—anger put an unwarranted authority into his tone—"we should move in the direction of the bald hill."

"If that is what you wish, Father."

"That is what I wish."

It was not until Brother Thaddeus was rebuilding the fire against total blackness and possible wolves that he thought: Merciful Jesus, we could very well be lost.

✠   ✠   ✠

Lost . . . It was a word he could ponder while they were on the outskirts of the great forest. But once they were in it, once he knew what it was, he could not face the thought, not for several days.

The branches that intertwined above their heads were as thick as he had imagined the trunks would be. The real trunks outdid in mass and moss and stony age any trunks he had ever dreamed could exist. It was dark under innumerable needles and crowding leaves: he rode hunched over, confined between the ground and the lowest boughs, through a perpetual eventide. The path that Brother Thaddeus had expected to find and he himself had taken for granted kept failing to materialize. The air was thick and humid—the sides of the donkeys labored taking it in. And certain sights undid him, whether or not they were horrible in themselves: a white owl with a rodent trailing from its beak, enormous black and scarlet mushrooms clustered in the decayed bole of a tree, a flower with a mouth that gaped after some obscene devouring, with a greenish throat marked with spots the color of blood.

There was also the silence into which all their noises dropped to be swallowed up—a vast indifferent silence netted over with its own chattering and scurrying but annihilating everything else. The lay brother, looking for the path and often hacking a way through underbrush and thornbush and thicket, made noises that would have wakened sleepers in the city; but here they were paltry sounds, muffled and echoless.

51

It was against this silence that he spoke, voicing questions. And once the first question was out he saw that his connection with Brother Thaddeus had undergone still another subtle change. It was the woodsman's knowledgeable son, the wielder of the ax, the man who would find the elusive path, to whom he addressed himself. "When will we stop to wash ourselves?" he said.

"We can *stop* whenever you like, Father. But as for washing ourselves—considering how little water we can carry with us, we had better not do that until we come to another spring."

He had asked only to pit his voice against the stillness. But now what he had asked at random became a matter of life and death. There was an oiliness, a scum upon him. Every part of his body not covered by his cassock was bitten by insects; he felt sticky with sweat, tainted with the resinous exudations of the pines. He could not bear it that his nails were cracked and blackened, that he was adding his portion to the steamy stench which moved around them wherever they went, that the backs of his thighs were galled by creases in the damp saddle cloth. It was infuriating too that his companion, whacking away at what looked like an interminable growth of thorn, should say lightly over his shoulder what *he* did not want to hear. Yet it must be heard and even accepted with a show of good grace. Better to stink than to thirst—and now that he thought of it he was thirsty. "Is there much likelihood of finding a spring hereabouts?"

"Oh, there's bound to be a spring. That one"—he pointed to a squirrel hanging head-down on a trunk and flicking his tail and watching them silently as they passed—"could never live if there were no water. But where it is or whether we'll find it or miss it, I do not know."

Since the answers were sure to be humiliating and appalling, he saw to it that the times he asked questions were few and far between. Hours would go by when the chattering, scurrying hush would remain unbroken. Sometimes a whole morning or afternoon —it was hard to say which because of the indistinct and characterless light—would pass without a word. He even schooled himself to hold his peace when darkness, quick and total, came down upon them, scarcely leaving them enough of the dying light for gathering wood for a fire. "Night again?" he said, but he said it to himself in a whisper. And, as "night again" and "day again" were repeated, were multiplied beyond accurate conjecture, he saw the puckers of worry appear under the sweaty fringe of blond hair. No wonder. The meal sacks were half empty; the chunk of meat was a third of its original size; the dried fruit and smoked fish were gone. And he was loath to ask and ask, to make himself seem like a child who plagues a preoccupied elder with foolishness.

Yet there were times when the oppression lifted because the aspect of the forest had changed. The trees stood separate from each other, light sifted in, clusters of spiked flowers broke the overpowering and hostile green—delicate pink, innocent blue. Relieved of the necessity to plod and whack, Brother Thaddeus would get back up on Cicero, would blow on his ruined palms, would break the stillness with a "Thanks be to God!"

"Could it be that the forest is thinning out, Brother?"

"Oh, it *is* thinned out—"

"Thinning out for good?"

"For good?"

"In a way, I mean, that would show we are coming close to the sea?"

His companion, having gotten down off his mount again, was walking over stones and moss through shaken coins of light that showed how much flesh he had lost, how slack his skin hung on his bones. "No, Father, I would never say that," he said, leaning over, feeling the moss with his swollen and blood-clotted hand. "You only find such glades toward the middle, not on the edge of it. I would never say . . ."

His preoccupation with the business of feeling and the fact that his wide buttocks were presented to his superior were as maddening as what he said. He looked gross and stupid bending down, crouching over. "What are you doing?" It was loud, but it begot no echo.

"Looking for the path, Father."

And all of a sudden it struck him: there was no path. Brother Thaddeus might know all the lore of pathfinding, but God had not given him the imagination to see what would happen to a path in a hundred years. Encroached upon by grey lichen, covered over with dropped needles and the skeletons of powdered leaves, crossed and recrossed and scratched away by the feet of the scurriers—who could find it? It would have been buried before he was born.

His heart stammered and stopped. The hateful silence moved in on him before the loud pulse began to beat again. "Let it alone. Stop scratching for it. You will never find it that way," he said.

"Then how am I to find it?"

"God knows."

At no time during the next three days did he tell his companion what he knew. He suspected himself of offering up pity as a bribe in the court of God: if he pitied this wretch and did not exult over him, they might reach a height, might see the veil of murk torn away from the guiding stars, might hear the voice of the sea. But the lay brother's behavior altered enough after the exchange to show that he had guessed what had been left unspoken. The pancakes served up at the evening meals were smaller and smaller. He cooled the shrunken supply of meat whenever he could, laying it on a slab of rock to keep it from rotting; and he was constantly waving his hands over it to keep away flies. Once, after he had cut his shin in his wild whacking away, he said without malice that, path or no path, they might have done better if they had started toward *his* big pine instead of toward Father Albrecht's bald hill.

A daze settled upon all of them, including the donkeys. The nature of the beasts had revolted at last against forest fare: their bellies swelled, they kept ambling off to one side, their eyes had a yellowish cast. Patches—a nonentity through the early part of their wandering—took on a new distinction: he was obviously the one who would be first to die. During the days when he manifested that fact by stretching out his neck, foaming and having fits of shudders, something else became undeniable, something

54

Father Albrecht had pushed out of mind though he had guessed it long ago. They were not going anywhere, in any direction. They were going around in a maze. Certain sights—a tangle of roots thrust out in such-and-such a way, two lines of trunks converging at such-and-such an angle, an area of bark peeled off to leave an unforgettable shape—he had a horrible conviction that he had seen them before.

This, too, he kept secret from Brother Thaddeus. He might never have revealed it if it had not been for the death of Patches. The poor beast fell when there was least reason, in an easy open stretch, after watering at one of the rare springs. Fell with a sound that was echoless like all their noises. Fell with the legs stuck up and the bloated belly white as a maggot. Fell with an empty meal sack under the withers and the volume of Livy under the head.

"Done for, poor creature," said Brother Thaddeus, getting down from Cicero's back, and going over, and tugging at the book.

"Let it alone."

"I thought you would want it."

"Why would I want it?"

"Well, then, I might as well get back up on Cicero and—"

"No!" A rage scalding enough to annihilate pity for the dead beast and himself and the dolt he could call fat no longer boiled up in him and made him shake as Patches had shaken in the final agonies. "Take a knife, and walk, and cut crosses on the trees, you fool!"

"Why?"

"Because time and again we come back to the same places."

"Truly? Why did my Father never tell me?"

Useless, nothing to lean on, worse than nothing. He lashed him with words: "You are the woodsman's son—you are the one that is supposed to know. Do we have to come back to that—that—" He pointed at the sprawled carcass, and pressed Asmodeus's sides and rode ahead.

Thereafter there should have been stark enmity and total silence between them. But the boiling out of his rage had left them both inexplicably softened. He himself felt like a child contrite and undone after a long spell of sobbing; and whenever he saw the lay brother turn aside, he guessed that he had turned aside to weep. The blur of tears washed over the hard lines of everything: the realization that he would die and rot unburied in this forest; the certainty that there had never been an isthmus, a promontory, an island; the bitter knowledge that his life was to be torn from him because travelers and fishermen had dreamed a dream. . . .

"It is a strange thing, Father—" They were moving on, uselessly, back in the old formation, the lay brother leading Cicero and going a little ahead of his superior with the blunted ax in his hand.

"What?"

"That I should keep wondering which service they will be saying next at the Chapter House—"

"That is natural enough."

He did not know why he should have said it was natural. Through the whole journey, the Chapter House was the thing that had come least often into his head. Yet, given the softening of his state of mind and the blur of tears drawn between him and the actualities, he could see why his companion would brood on it, would yearn after the chants with their lingering resonances, the herb garden where vegetable horror was tamed and aromatic and blameless, the stone blocks shaped by men's hands and put together for men's use. It was not what he himself wanted, but a person must long for something. And, seeking something to desire, knowing himself to be in that respect poorer even than Brother Thaddeus, he fastened—with a deliberateness which reminded him of his first encounter with Ermintrude—on the new town. For hours he would ride with his head down, remembering what he could of that outpost on the edge of the world unknown: smell of new wood, lines of half-dressed limestone blocks, rafters as yet uncovered by thatch or tiles. If only the abbot had sent him *there.* . . . If at this moment he could be stepping out in a clean cassock to greet a mason or a family of settlers just arrived. . . .

If he could have stepped over the threshold of the tower into the sun-drenched, expectant emptiness of the square—

He was sleeping, fainting, perhaps dying. He had actually fallen forward, and Asmodeus, startled, had gone down on his knees, and he saw in his unwilling waking that he was in the forest, and swift night was coming down, and Brother Thaddeus was as weary as he, so weary they could agree amicably that it was better to take risks with wolves and boars than to trouble to make a fire.

But the next day he began to question both his obsession with the new town and the childishness that had begotten it. Perhaps "childishness" was too innocent a name. Perhaps, when a man was about to die, he lived out in his last days a kind of fore-shortened senility. He exorcised the image that had been a comfort to him yesterday; he kept his mind where his body was: lost in this vegetable hell. Looking on at himself—it occurred to him that his soul might already have moved a little distance from his person—he saw what he hated but could not put down: the shaking awkwardness, the whine in the voice, an old man's fretfulness.

There was, for instance, the difficulty about the meat. It happened at noon—they could tell it was noon because the trees were set less thickly here and the source of light shone white and blinding behind clouds directly overhead. For breakfast they had taken only water and some roots carefully chosen and washed and chopped up by Brother Thaddeus, and the taste had been refreshing to the dry and coated tongue. "Shall we eat the same thing as we had for breakfast, Brother?" he said.

His companion had cut off a piece of the remaining meat and was holding it in his hands. He looked down at it and fetched up an exasperated sigh. "Truly, now," he said in the voice of one who resents uttering what ought to be obvious, "a man must eat some solid thing once a day, and the proper time to eat it is noon."

"Did you come upon that in the sayings of Asclepius?"

"If my Father means to tell me that I am ignorant, I admit it:

57

I never heard of this Asclepius. But so much I do know: if a man takes nothing but roots for the first two meals, he will fall on his face before he sits down to the third." Stolidly, without encountering his superior's look, he laid the cut of meat and two knives on what was to serve as their table. This time it was a big bough cleft in two by lightning, grey with age and covered with moss.

For days the places where they had eaten had all been in shadow. Now what he was about to put in his mouth was all too clear in the harsh white glare. There was a ring of bone in it, and inside the bone was a greasy lump of marrow as yellow as cheese. The meat was slick, looked as if it would be slippery under the touch. And there was a tainted iridescence upon it; the colors of corruption came and went, now purple, now green.

"I will not eat it."

"My Father must eat it."

"Do you presume to say 'must' to me?"

"No, no. Whatever I say, you catch me up. I only meant that you must eat so that you do not starve—"

He got up and stepped back, gagging. The meat was suddenly crawling. The putrescent odor of it had called up out of the grey rot of the log a whole tribe of reddish ants. "Let me alone!" He turned and walked away. "Starve to death I will"—he shouted it back over his shoulder—"but I will not die with my belly bloated by putrid meat." He went his way on foot, leaving the dolt to eat if he could, wanting to come upon the next stretch of dense forest, another thicket of thorns at which he could tear away bare-handed, another tangle of trees where he could terrify the lay brother by getting himself temporarily lost.

But what lay before him was not to his purpose. There was no growth of thornbush and little underbrush. The firs were fewer, far outnumbered by the deciduous trees; the tall planes, shedding their bark, stood half-naked in the white stare of the sun. It struck him that an unusual number of torn and splintered trunks were lying about and that the ground beneath them was brown with leaf mash and scattered only here and there with blue-grey

58

needles from the pines. The forest, that obscene outcropping on the body of the earth, had unaccountably thinned out. The glade through which he walked was plainly sparse enough to be penetrated by lightning and invaded by strong gusts.

It seemed irrelevant now that he had walked off to punish and worry his companion. The comparative openness of the mesh of leaves above him, the rare solitude, the light-headedness which came of having eaten next to nothing, all unaccountably cheered him. His sight had been baffled so long by lack of distance that he simply took pleasure in the unobstructed view. And, looking ahead, he saw a gleaming irregular oval some fifty paces beyond him. He took it at first to be water—a marshy spot, a pond. No, water it could not be—even his cloudy brain could tell him that: water could borrow such a yellowish luster only from a sunset, and the sun was standing straight over his head. He stepped across fallen trunks toward the pale expanse, a sight so strange that he wondered if some demon had put it there, if it could be like the clumps of palms that had appeared and disappeared, on the dry trek to the Holy Sepulchre, before the famished knights of God.

It was not water, of course. It was—the inexplicable presence of it held his attention less than its beauty—a small patch of some kind of grain. Rye, wheat, barley—he did not know one cereal from another, had not laid eyes on a rooted stalk since he had been a child. There it stood, a miracle of lightness in the brown and grey and green of leaf mash and rock and moss, of a delicate dry tint that eased and blessed his sight. He rejoiced in the straightness of the stems; he thought he had never seen anything more pleasing than the heads; each grain lying against its fellow, leaving its fellow room to breathe and grow in order and civility. "Who would believe it—a patch of wild grain," he said aloud, bending over and running his palm across the spikes, for every head wore a spiked crown of pale gold.

Whereupon, foolishly, he went down on his knees at the brink of it—pondlike, it had a brink—and tried to increase his pleasure, to feel its spikes press against his face, to see whether it exuded

59

any smell. He even broke off a stalk and chewed on it, as boys will chew on timothy grass when they walk in rural lanes. It did not, of course, yield him what he longed for, the taste of new bread, but it had a taste of its own. Something questionable, something that reminded him of a marketplace of a Friday morning, stayed on his tongue.

It seemed that he had somehow been provided for here. A big slab of stone, unshadowed, stood close to the little crop. Letting himself down upon it, he felt its warmth go gratifyingly into his aching buttocks: yes, for several days, without knowing it, he had been affected with chills. The ground on either side of him—his head and arms hung down and he was too tired to lift his chin—the ground on either side of him was sparsely scattered with leaves spotted with yellow and streaked with red; and the air that flowed down on him no longer carried a damp heat, actually carried a dank cold.

Autumn had come, and after autumn would be wolves and winter. I had better bestir myself, he thought. Even now the lay brother could be passing him by, screened off from him by some configuration of trees. But that realization only gave an edge of malice to his enjoyment of the solitude. He reached for another stalk and snapped it off and chewed the grain and saw again the Friday market stalls: scales, grey and gold and salmon red, and round dead eyes. Fish—it tasted like fish and should have roused his disgust; but what was fishiness compared to putrid meat? He swallowed and felt the grain passing down his cramped gullet and into the slack bag of his inner emptiness. I should not sleep, he thought, and slept. . . .

When he woke up, there was no telling what time of day it was. The clouds had evened out into one mass of greyish whiteness, thick enough to blot out the sun. What was around him had undergone a remarkable change: the colors had been intensified, seemed almost to burn and glow. The parts of the trunks that had shed bark were like ivory pilasters lighted from within, the leaves burned sardonyx and ruby, the grain burned gold. Only in jewels had he ever seen such colors; that he was parted from Asmodeus and Brother Thaddeus and Cicero was of small consequence beside this splendor; nothing distracted him from contemplating it but some cobwebs that had somehow gotten themselves fastened to his face. They were maddeningly persistent, those cobwebs. He tried without success to brush them away with the back of his hand, and when he plucked at them he had no better luck: the tips of his fingers tingled and were awkward and numb.

He fell to gazing at one small stripped plane tree. The longer he stared, the more he became convinced that the delicate trunk was expanding and contracting, slowly, evenly, taking in and letting out tender and deep-drawn breaths. No trunk, he thought, no trunk at all. The pale body of Saint Pelagia shown to him by Brother Matthias in the empty square of the new town. But there she had been clothed and here she was naked—how exquisite the rising and falling of her small breasts. And there was Brother Matthias just behind her: his red hair glowing, his white chin pulled out and out in a veritable excess and beauty of ugliness, blue eyebeams shooting from his gentian-colored eyes. The sight was so intense that he had to let down his own eyelids; and when he raised them he did not dare to take it in again at once—he thought to ease into it more slowly by looking down and sidewise at the lesser brilliance on the ground. But what—what? It was not his look, it was his whole person that moved, shifted without any effort to the very edge of the slab of stone. Shifted? Was propelled, or magically propelled itself. I'll wait a bit and try it again, he thought. But why go sidewise, if I can go up as well? He closed his eyes for an instant, took a deep breath, and went up easily, at will. In air as pure as snow water, himself transparent and glittering like a sun-pierced icicle, he hung above the square of the new town.

And quiet it was on a saint's day down there, with the heaps of stones turned turquoise and the shadows of the booths empurpled: every shadow of a slightly different hue, each a unique and separate violet. Doves, pearl-breasted and necklaced with emerald and amber, came up at him out of the rosy dust—it was their wings that begot the crazy tickling itching on his face. Fortunate, too, that the stalls had not yet been set up in the expectant emptiness. Stalls would mean fish, and he had, God knows, enough of that in his mouth, in his stomach, oiling and loosening his guts. And with that he lost the trick of it and came down, was down on the stone slab again, was a spirit caught in a loathsome sack of flesh that was vomiting and oozing from behind. Bad, worse than spilling one's seed, to make such a mess of oneself. . . .

Sleep awhile then, and let the badness pass. He did, and it subsided, and, from the looks of the sky, the process of renewal had not taken very long. The important thing—he understood it now—was to pay no attention to certain things like itchings and numbness and vomit and excrement. Stare at the trunk, get it to stir and breathe; and there was Brother Matthias on the other side of it, nodding encouragement, holding out his cordial hands. He lifted those hands palms upward, as God might gesture a soul toward Heaven, as a loving father might gesture a child to take its first step on a flight of stairs. Hang back? Refuse such consideration, such loving-kindness? Not he. One breath and he was out of the mess and flesh of it—out and up; and, in humane and courteous brotherhood, the long-chinned monk had joined him in the glassy upper air. Side by side, a little apart, they stood on nothing above everything. They reached their hands toward each other, but there was no need for them to touch. Flames burst from the tips of his fingers and enveloped his companion's alabaster wrist without doing it the slightest harm. And yet the flames were real enough—the numbness had passed over into something else: his hands, his feet, his itching cheeks were all on fire.

But it would be gross and stolid to consider these bodily afflictions now. Saint John the beloved, he who had leaned upon his Master's breast—had the seething oil in which the heathen dipped him boiled away the memory of that embrace? With gestures that spoke—for something had stopped his burning ears to outer sound and all he heard was the roar of pain in his head—with exquisite pointings and openings and fallings of finger and palm and wrist —the long-chinned brother was showing him, if not all, then at least a goodly part of the world.

This time from a much greater height. The roofs of the town, the rosy square, the building blocks were all so small he could have held them in the palm of one flaming hand. All around the town, in an irregular circle, stood the emerald peaks of the forest. He could make out the heights where the fire had been built and the confession had been made: thin as a needle stood the big pine; no bigger than a lentil was the bald hill. And from the bald hill, westward and downward, led a declivity in the expanse of needles and boughs, a deeper green than the rest, not emerald but a velvety bluish green. A path—he had been right, he had known from the start that the path was just there; God had given him—he saw it from where he hovered—a holy second sight whose power had been debased and ill-used by Brother Thaddeus in his stupidity and drunkenness. An exaltation seized him. He flamed and trembled. In his transport, he caught hold of the long-chinned monk who floated there beside him. He embraced him— had not such an embrace been permitted to Saint John of Patmos? —he kissed the eyelids closed over the gentian-colored eyes, the elongated chin, the garnet lips. Upon that his companion, graciously, if loudly and definitely, said, moving apart, "Not so, dear brother of my spirit briefly met on earth." And, as if to ease any wound inflicted by the withdrawal, he bent down and conjured something up, something pale and naked, drawn through the crystal air by the magic of his hands. Then she was there between them—Saint Pelagia, half breathing plane tree, half woman, her ivory-colored side pressed against his body, cheek to cheek, thigh to thigh, emanating a balm that took the sting from the enveloping fire.

There were three then to see what was to be shown: the small but unbelievably clear new town, the great forest, the bluish path

63

that led down from the heights, the thinning outskirts blazing with the reds and golds of autumn, a beach so white and minute that it looked like a trail of spilled salt, and beyond that—as God had told him in the aristocracy of his spirit—the westward sea.

That sea was a melted opal, vast, stretching out forever. In it were blended the purest and palest blues and greens. The edges of the waves were tipped with flickering lines of orange and red and gold—water blessed with the beauty of fire. He drew the Sainted Pelagia into the circle of his delight. He held her round the waist, laid his head on her cool bare shoulder, claimed her lips. His mouth stung lightly, deliciously as it encountered hers. He saw the reason when she turned her head aside: her breath was issuing out of her in the form of luminous five-petaled flowers. As they passed into the air and fell toward the earth, these flowers became stars. They settled in loose constellations, garlands lightly bound and falling apart, on the square among the heaped building stones, on the heights, on the crowded pines, on the glittering beach, on the perpetually moving opalescent waves.

Ah . . . Pressing against her side, he spilled his seed, and that, going from him, was like the trail of a falling star mingling with her flowers and not at all out of place. Brother Matthias did not see or was courteously pretending that he had not seen. He pointed at something: the isthmus, the isthmus stretching from the beach and covered with crocuses. Had autumn gone and winter after it? Had the crocuses already sprung up, nourished on the purity of melted snow? And beyond the isthmus there was the promontory. It was as if here liquid opal had congealed: a blue cathedral with fiery towers, a cool green village, the earth itself a powder of turquoise and lapis lazuli. "More beautiful," the monk indicated by pointing first to his left and then to his right, "far more to be desired than the new town."

Which was certainly true and would have been a cause for unmitigated bliss if the monstrous fish had not heaved itself up, parting the waters. Its head was iron grey; its round eyes were dull with the coming-on of death; it spewed in spasms; it tainted the sea with the taste of fish-oil and the color of blood. God, God, God—he clutched at the Sainted Pelagia in his agony. His guts were wrung to bursting. It was not the great fish but he himself who had been fed poison by a demon. It was he who was voiding and vomiting, lying on his face in the glade, dying—for who could so suffer without being at the point of death?—biting on lichen with his tainted teeth, tearing at a log with his flaming hands.

Yet the spasm did not kill him. Looking up after it passed, he glimpsed the hem of Brother Matthias's cassock receding, disappearing behind a thicket. "Brother, Brother, in Jesus's name!" he screamed. And then more quietly—for it was not seemly to shriek after a withdrawing spirit—"Seeing what has been between us, will you leave me here to die alone?"

But the departure and the sickness were not the worst of it. What was unbearable was that he should be here after where he had been. All the colors were bled away; all the breathings, all the possibilities of transmutation were gone. Rocks were smudged rocks, boughs were drab boughs, leaves almost merged with the mash they lay upon. He himself, stretched on the ground, was not marked off from it. He and his existence were so spiritless and mean that he thought he might well already be dead, compounding with insensate clods.

Some fifty paces from him there was a stirring. Three figures came forward between the thick trunks: two wretched beasts and a human being whose face was made of mud. Memory, sunken under fish-oil and a leaden weight of waters, tried to struggle up to claim them. Those ribs in a loose hide—was that Asmodeus? That blob of slipping clay—was that the lay brother's face? As the three drew closer—slowly, ploddingly, after the swiftness he had known in his ecstasy—the face took on some semblance of humanity. It was made of slack flesh, pitted and discolored. As it bent above him he stared at the lines that ran from the corners of the nose to the ends of the lips. They looked as if a plough had dug them out of a soaked March field: furrows, furrows in wet earth. . . .

"Father—"

65

He could not answer, seized as he was with a fit of dry retching. He could only think how ravaged the poor wretch was, what horrors starvation and long wandering had wrought upon him. Could anything be as pitiable as that hanging face?

"How is it with you, Father, in the name of God?"

"I thought just now that I was dead." He stretched out his fingers toward the grain, dull yellow like sodden hay.

Brother Thaddeus, seeing what he pointed at, let out a madman's cry. "Rye! Holy Jesus, Father, that is rye!"

"Is it? I would not know one grain from another."

"It is rye, and some human being has been tending it. Otherwise—"

Asmodeus and Cicero came up from behind him, avid for the crop. The lay brother pushed them back easily by their noses: they were even weaker than he. "Wait, let me see," he said, and inspected the grain. "I do not like the looks of it, the beasts had better not touch it. There are purple spots all over the heads, and it smells like rotten fish besides."

"I ate of it—"

"Ate of it?" The big hand—it also was made of mud—came down on his forehead, flat and wet and cold. "Dear Father, you are very sick—"

"Yes. Sick to death, very likely. But tether the beasts and try not to distress yourself." He wished to say some kindlier word, but could not manage. His tongue thickened, and he fell back into a sleep he took for death.

When he stirred again, he saw that the donkeys had been tied to a tree. Miserable creatures—he pitied them both—they were straining their scrawny necks after the grain. The stench about him was less; and after long pondering he concluded that the lay brother had stripped away most of his filth along with his cassock and had covered his nakedness with two empty meal sacks that smelled of dust. Nobody was about. A tinge of washed-out red was spreading over the dun sky. He gazed up at it and grew dizzy and heard a rushing sound. A storm wind coming in upon the open glade? A roaring in his head? He would have liked to stop up his ears to determine whether the rushing was without or within; but the lifting of his hand was enough to set his whole right arm on fire. He closed his eyes and sank again into the grey vortex of nothingness. But something followed him down the funnel of the whorl: another cry. . . .

Sleep, and yet another waking, and the swishing sound still with him.

"Father—" The voice was urgent, almost wild.

"Leave me in peace, my skin is burning, let me alone."

"But you must rouse yourself." Brother Thaddeus stood at his feet, his flabby fists clenched, the furrows of his face running with tears. "You must rouse yourself, because I have seen it."

"Seen what?"

"The shore—the isthmus—I have just come back from there. I went to look for help, to find whoever it was who tended the rye."

"Are you out of your senses?"

"No, as God is my witness. Not half a mile from here—listen! You must rouse yourself, you must let me put you upon Asmodeus. Listen!"

It was so, he heard it himself: the sound was the roar of the westward sea.

Chapter II

$\mathcal{F}$or a long time he knew little, and even of that he was uncertain. Stone walls, hung here and there with faded tapestry, surrounded him. A raftered ceiling was above him, crossed sometimes by thin autumn sunlight and sometimes by candlelight. He lay on softness and was given over to the ministrations of hands.

So, he thought—when thought was possible—an infant lies, willing nothing and expecting everything. The hands came into the surrounding vagueness: washed him, fed him, folded the covering back or pulled it up to his chin. When he fell to retching, they held a basin for him. When the flames burst from his body, they eased him with damp aromatic cloths. They even cleansed him of the excretions by which he was made to understand that his spirit was still tied up in the loose bag of his body. They had been waiting on him for what seemed to him many days when it struck him with amazement and shame and guilt that they were *women's* hands.

Two pairs of them, so far as he could make out. One old and rough and blunt—the hands of a peasant. The other so well-formed and carefully tended that he confused them now and again with the ones he had dreamed of back in the Chapter

68

House: almond-shaped nails, long fingers, veins showing through delicate skin. This second pair touched him tentatively, the eloquence of their compassion held in by a wincing fear of hurting him or putting him to shame. Hands of women, and he should have been nursed in his sickness by his ghostly brothers—a fact which he kept repeating to no purpose. The old voice said "Yes, we know." The other voice said "Rest, rest," and trailed off on a sigh.

His sight was affected, and there was guilt for that also. He could see what lay at the far boundaries of his perception and what came very close to his eyes, but everything between lay in impenetrable mist. Retribution for the more than human clarity with which he had seen exhaled flowers and the trail of a falling comet and Brother Matthias's gentian eyes. He who has seen with the sight of angels pays thereafter by seeing little. Never to read again, never to take in the parchment page and the circle of light upon it and all the quiet blessings within the close confines of a little cell. . . . He whimpered, and the blunt hands—it was they that happened to be serving him at the moment—drew rough knuckles across his cheek.

For, questionable as it was, he had commerce with those palms and fingers. Caught himself grasping the old ones when the retching seemed to be shattering his ribs. Kissed the smooth ones when they lessened the burning of his skin with a cool aromatic cloth. She of these long, hesitant fingers—what sort of woman was she? Not since his infancy—he believed he could remember the touch of his mother—had he had dealings with such giving hands.

One night he woke in candlelight and saw at the opposite end of the room a dumb show so strange that at first he took it for a dream. Two monks—and monks they certainly were, since they were dressed in cassocks, though the cassocks were fantastical beyond belief—two monks were sitting at a long table, busy with some sort of game with counters. Small blocks of stone, polished and varicolored, were being passed between them, laid down on the wood, picked up again. Concerning the placement of these stones, they were having earnest differences: they frowned, made gestures of dissent, shook their heads. They spoke, too, but soundlessly. No, he had not lost his hearing. One of them—the taller and elder of the two—laid a finger across his thin lips and cast a warning look in the direction of the bed: they were whispering in order not to disturb what they took to be his sleep. Then I will seem to sleep and learn what I can, he thought; and he watched through the slits of half-closed eyes.

He fixed his sight first on the elder of the two. He was not really old—at a guess somewhat past forty. Nor was his cassock very strange on second look. It was of undyed greyish-white woolen, loosely woven and fringed at the neck and the bottoms of the sleeves. He was narrow-boned, with a long fair-skinned face —remote, abstracted. He was neither shorn nor tonsured. The length and the strangeness of his face were emphasized by a straight fall of hair of so pale a yellow as to be almost like flax. This hair seemed to annoy him—he moved his head impatiently to get it away from his cheeks, out of his eyes. Once, when he was peering at an arrangement of bluish blocks, he took an exasperating lock of it and held it between his colorless lips.

His companion was dark and leathery, as if he had spent his life in sun and wind. His hair, his eyes, the crescents of his nails were black. He had a beaked nose and a mouth too ripe for the rest of him—head and figure suggested not the austerity of prayer and fast but the hardness of constant exercise. He treated the stone blocks with a decisiveness that seemed to disturb, even to shock his fellow player. At one point he pushed them all aside with a gesture of contempt. Contempt—*his* cassock had plainly been made in contempt, in mockery of all cassocks. It was russet—a color unthinkable on the mortified body of a brother. The wide sleeves were lined with a vivid sky-blue. And on the chest—no, it was impossible, surely he was imagining things— there was a cross in yellow, and the cross had been stitched on upside down.

70

Then I am in some mad kind of monastery, Father Albrecht thought. They must have moved me, taken me out of the hands of the women while I was in one of my deep sleeps. . . . But no, that was not so. The same bed, the same walls, the same strips of faded arras, the same rafters. Still, where had the women gone? Worn out with long watching? Sick—God forbid!—tainted by his disease? Not real?—an even more distressing thought. He could not take the tending hands out of actuality and reduce them, like the Sainted Pelagia, to irreclaimable dreams. As he lay unmoving and silent, telling himself that he must not sigh or whimper, he heard a sound that had become familiar: the opening of a door. And there, under his eyes, spreading a coverlet over him, tucking it around his shoulders, were the compassionate hands. They were in no haste: they put his hair back from his forehead and smoothed the bolster before they disappeared into the milky mist.

He closed his eyes and waited. When he looked again, there were three instead of two: the woman was at the table where the queer game of blocks was going on. She was made after the manner of the ancient wooden likenesses of God's mother that were carried in ritual processions—smooth and round of brow, with breasts delicate yet swollen as with holy milk; narrow of waist and slight of hip—it had been established by the learned scholars of the earliest days that Mary never lost her youth, but received her crucified Son in the same body that had born Him, marked with sorrow, yes, but still in the April of her days. She moved lightly around the table, looking down at the blocks laid out by the two monks. The candlelight that shone down on the board shone up on her face. There were hollows in her cheeks and temples, and the light brown of her hair was muted, probably greyed. No, she was older than the Virgin, though the careful timidity of her bearing gave her the air of a child. As she passed the fantastical monk in her circuit of the table, he swung round on his haunches and blew her a kiss. Which she acknowledged, plainly with irony: she spread

71

her grass-green skirt in an exaggerated sweep and bowed from the knee. Behind the other monk, the fair-skinned one, she came to a stop and bent so close that her breath must have stirred the hair on his crown. But he was absorbed in the game and did not look up, and after a little she stepped aside and was gone.

All that night reality kept moving in upon his sleep. Between drowse and drowse he saw the two monks stand up, drop the varicolored counters into a leather bag, and depart, leaving the candle behind. In the midst of an effort to recall a curious dream, he found himself emptying his bladder into a pot near the foot of the bed, and knew with surprise that this was the first time he had sat up to do it without help. The wax-smothered flame went out, and he heard footsteps and wondered if she were coming toward him. It would be strange to feel her hands upon him, now that he could conjure up in the blackness the woman to whose person they belonged. But the footfalls were not hers —they were heavy, and they went off into soundlessness. Somebody —a man—said far off: "In the ten years that I have served in this castle, I have never known . . ." So it was a castle, it was no monastery. And what was he doing, lying on his back and waiting for her to wipe his face with a dampened cloth and breathe upon him through the dark? Against all reason, to say nothing of the Rule of Saint Benedict—yet how was *he* to blame? It was not his doing: he had been carried into this chamber, laid on this bed, and a blessed bed it was, clean and warm. . . . Bird-cry on the edge of another dream—such a screech as he had never heard: gulls, cormorants, great birds of the sea. . . . In a castle, on an island, on the island of Saint Cyprian, divided for a hundred years by a tidal wave from Holy Church and the world.

More sleep, the light sleep of one who has really had his fill of sleeping. Dawn, a windy morning—red light spreading under his eyelids, cold gusts crossing his naked arms—but he neither got himself back under the coverlet nor opened his eyes. For she was in the chamber—he knew it and he waited. Her hand

72

reached with fearful carefulness under the nape of his neck and raised his head.

"A little water—take a little water."

It was said with a strange accent, in a whisper. The metal rim touched his mouth. He swallowed and let her lay his head back on the bolster, put his hair away from his cheek, dry his wetted chin.

But I am awake and aware, he thought. I could sit up, I could open my eyes.

Something trailed across his face, perhaps her sleeve, perhaps her hair. "Ah . . ." she said aloud. Out of dread of waking him? Out of weariness? Out of pity? Certainly out of something so profound and private that to open his eyes upon her now would be a kind of invasion. She covered him, and he turned on his side and went on feigning sleep until he knew that she was gone by the creak of the closing door.

This room in which he had been deposited by a will not his own was very large. It suggested a castle whose spaciousness had declined into bleakness, whose splendor had fallen into ruin. Scarcely a figure could be made out on the faded arras that masked part of the grey stone wall. Table, chairs, iron brazier, lightless torches fastened to the rough blocks by rusted iron bands—everything was ancient without honor. Something—perhaps the wind, perhaps the whitish blankness of the window behind the table where they had played the inexplicable game—convinced him that he was high up, very high. If he were to step out of *this* window . . . No, he would not sleep and dream. Yet snatches of former dreams encroached upon his waking: expanse of sun-drenched meadow, birch tree moving its arms to peel away its own dry bark, honeycomb oozing with richness behind the drab fall of the tapestry. . . . He had read a curious treatise once on the ambrosial sweetness, the blissful coolness and plenitude of the Virgin's milk. . . .

Footsteps again. Why should be fling up his arm to cover his face? To shield himself against imminent danger? To hide what

73

years had made unlovely and sickness had further ravaged? To enable himself to see without being seen? What he saw under the crook of his elbow—and it was unwelcome—was the tall monk, he of the long face and the troublesome pale hair. He stood at the foot of the bed, too close to the pot of urine. His eyes, steady and of a strange cool grey, gave nothing out and took all things in. "No," he said, turning his face toward the open doorway, "there is no need to come, he is still sleeping."

"Is he covered?" It was she who said it from somewhere out in the hall.

"Covered and resting at his ease. For the time being, it would be better to let him alone."

Footfalls retreating, and the door pulled to, but not altogether shut, and she and the monk first whispering, then speaking, then raising their voices in what was evidently a difference.

A difference over something that should—or should not—be let into the castle. At first he took it to be some wild thing: a hound or a falcon that had not yet been tamed. She, flirtatiously pleading, was for letting it in. He—stern, making his intentions known in a flat baritone that did not give them much authority—was for keeping it outside. "No, really, we have tried it before. Enough is enough," he said.

"But these days she is very mild and tractable. She has done no harm whatever in the garden."

A cat, perhaps?

"Then keep her in the garden."

"But if I promised to sit in the kitchen while she is there? If I never take my eyes off her?"

"It seems to me you could find a more pleasant and profitable way to occupy yourself."

"Only for a little while, Alain? Only long enough so that she could warm herself by the fire?"

"Look now, Julianne, I have said no, and no is what I mean."

"A little kindness—she is such a miserable thing—"

"A little kindness, a little kindness—you use this matter to make a monster of me. And I am no monster—" He raised his

74

voice and she answered with a "Hush!" "It does not make me a monster"—the flat baritone was louder still—"that I mean to live in my own house in peace."

"Must you shout?"

"A little kindness, and she sets the arras on fire. A little kindness, and she poisons my mastiffs. A little more kindness still, and the poison will be in our broth and the fire will be set under our beds."

A woman, then. What kind of woman?

And the monk went on to make an end of the matter, "She has a devil in her one day out of seven. Today she is sane, tomorrow she is mad."

But Jesus, Jesus! Anguish assailed him—anguish at the immensity of his task, anguish at the dullness of his brain that could grasp nothing until it was thrust into his face, anguish at God knows what else. Things here were as the Holy Father in Rome thought they might be at their worst: these were not monks, not even celibates. She and this "monk" were Adam and Eve, lord and lady, man and wife. They shared this castle, ate together, slept together. Night after night, coming here to perform her ministrations, she had gotten up out of another man's bed. It was unbearable: the place where he had lain helpless and she had tended him—he yearned to be out of it, he thrust the hateful coverlet aside. And saw himself—skin and bones in a threadbare shift. Old body, sick body, not to be trusted on its feet. But able nevertheless to make a prop of the bolster, to sit upright. There. When you have finished your breakfast, eating cheek by jowl, come and find me so.

They came into the chamber together, as he had expected. Or had he fully expected it? He experienced another pang when the two stood side by side between the high grey blankness of the window and the foot of his bed. And he felt the more exposed and compromised because he could not see their faces though the white light behind them was shining straight into his own face.

"A good morning to you, and nothing but good mornings from

75

this day on, Father." It was she who said it, with her strange accent, in her careful voice, yet with the muted fervor of a full throat. "Over these three weeks that I have nursed you here, there was many a time when I was afraid—"

The cool-eyed monk broke in. "I am Alain, lord of this castle and a Brother of Saint Cyprian." If he knew that no man could be invested with both titles in the sight of Holy Church, he did not show his knowledge. "And this is Julianne, my lady and the chatelaine."

The bow with which he answered was as formal as conscience required. "I am grateful for your many kindnesses," he said. "Nevertheless, I—"

"Ah . . ." It came out of her in pity and tenderness and such apprehension as cries out to a child about to hurt himself. "You are tired, Father, you are still very weak. There will be time enough to speak of the many things that must plague and puzzle you. Only, for the time being, try not to distress yourself, try to rest."

"Yes," said her lord. "There is no need for you to trouble yourself. The lay brother Thaddeus is well, and properly lodged. Both of your beasts have been tended and healed and are well fed. As for the rest, as she says, there will be plenty of time."

He stiffened his aching spine into authoritative straightness. "No, there are certain matters that have already waited too long," he said. "I ask you, as my son and daughter in God, why I am here, where—in consideration of my office and my mission—I could not possibly belong."

Their heads—featureless because of the glare behind them—turned toward each other. It was she who turned back to him first, pained and wondering. "But you were very sick, Father, sick almost to death. Where would we have kept you—where else?"

"In the monastery, to be tended by my brothers."

"In the monastery? Ah, now, Father, a hundred times we have told you, Berthe and I—though perhaps you did not hear in your fever—"

76

"The monastery of Saint Cyprian," said the monk, slowly, as if he were speaking to a mind still clouded, "is in no condition to receive the sick. It is a ruin."

"A ruin?"

"A ruin, Father—roofless, muddy, rat-infested."

"Then where are the Brothers?"

"In their own households. Some in the village, some in the town."

He steadied himself against the bolster. What lay beneath the vacant sky beyond their heads? Into what chaotic desolation must he drag his worn and unwilling body now? Monks coupling and breeding—mud, rats, ruins. "Your abbot—am I to take it that you have an abbot?" he said.

"Oh, yes, Father." It was she who spoke, eager to offer him something. "Surely, we have an abbot. The Abbot Ottric—a very good and devoted man."

"Then I will get up and go to him."

"There will be no need," said the monk. "He will come to you."

"It would be better if I—"

"Ah, now, Father"—her voice again, so desperately beseeching that he thought she must be wringing her hands—"you must not think of getting out of bed. You must lie down at once under the coverlet. We will bring the Abbot Ottric to you. He will be very glad to come."

"When? Today?"

"Let us bring him tomorrow. Surely, Father, you can wait one more day. This is the first day you have been without the fever."

She was right: he had outreached his strength. Bits of shimmering silver, small as midges, trailed across the barren square of sky. "Very well, tomorrow. But no later than tomorrow," he said.

"Certainly. Tomorrow, in the early evening." She stepped forward, ready for such services as were no longer to be thought of. He looked beyond her and shook his head. "For what you have done, my daughter, I am grateful. But I am a monk, and only another monk—"

"Here, then," said her lord, "let me help you."

77

But these other hands were scarcely more acceptable, though they dealt with him gently enough. He stared with fixed eyes at the rafters, he suppressed his breathing and counted the beats of his own heart until the two of them—her lord first and she after him, bowing her head and holding her skirt close to her sides—went out and left him alone.

✠   ✠   ✠

Since the arrival of the strangers, the Abbot Ottric had been calling himself to account, body and brain. What he saw in the faces of others gave him no pleasure. He knew by their solicitous questions and their show of consideration that in a few weeks he had aged three or four years.

Long ago he had forgotten that he was a peasant by birth set to rule over many descended from lords and knights, and now that knowledge was bitterly present to him again. He saw himself constantly in his mind's eye: swart, squat, as muscular as if he had spent his whole life sowing and reaping. He deplored his stocky arms and legs, the way his broad nose was flattened against his face, the coarse and intractable curls, all gone to an ugly grey, that grew on his thick cheeks, squared-off chin, and ball-shaped head. The lay brother Thaddeus, whom he had not yet seen—his very uncertainty made him insist he would see nobody but his clerical peer—had in his imagination a more acceptable person, more dignity and elegance. As for the other one, lying abed in the castle—by the old woman's account he was like the sandstone statue of a saint chiseled out by a master craftsman who knew and loved his art.

The old woman, coming home from her nursing in the castle, had made the stricken traveler seem an appropriate bearer of the heart-shaking tidings. Her descriptions of his person and what he had said in his fever dreams had done more to destroy her man's trust in his own mind and spirit than the tidings themselves. Who was he, Ottric the peasant abbot, to give an account of his charge to such a one? Of late he had found himself stopping in the middle of sentences, stumbling over words, forgetting names, confusing the near past with the far past. There is no use trying to mend it now, he told himself. I am what I am, and I know what I know. There is nothing to be gained from writing down lists—who knows what he will ask? There is no profit in reading the Book again—when the stupid sleepiness is not upon me, I can say whole pages of the Book by heart.

Yet the stupid sleepiness *was* upon him. And when the news that he would be expected to make his appearance came from the castle, what small determination he had summoned up seemed a fool's arrogance. The news came late and filled his little house with the crackling air of panic. The old woman Berthe, warming her stiff joints on the hearth, was doubtless sensible in arguing that he should do nothing, that whatever the day after tomorrow might bring he could deal with better if he ate and slept. Yet she could not talk him out of it. In the dark, alone, in a devil's wind that came at him out of all four corners of the tattered sky, he set out with his lantern to have a final look at the Book.

The night conspired with the heaviness in his head to wreak confusion on the order of the years. It might have been the very night before the onset of the all-obliterating flood. He was walking that part of the bowl-shaped island where the rim kept narrowing. Fifty paces or so, and he would come upon the rickety wooden bridge that marked the spot where the rocky edge had been chipped away and the sea—oily and black to the left of him—had dashed in upon the land. Nor had it ever flowed out again, not all of it. From the perilous ridge along which he made his way by lantern light, he could see water on his right as well as on his left. The great main square, from which the steep terraces of the city once had risen, had been filled up forever by the invading flood. Down there to his right, at the bottom of the bowl, was the Cathedral of Saint Cyprian wrapped forever in its watery shroud, as invisible, as irreclaimable as if it had been sealed up in a gigantic leaden cylinder two miles wide and half a mile deep.

79

There was the bridge—dullard that he was, he had forgotten about it. As though he were blind or a child not yet steady on his feet, he walked over the slippery planks, feeling his way along the splintered and sodden railing. There were days when he crossed repeatedly and never gave it a thought. But tonight it was as if Leviathan were about to heave himself up out of his century of sleep. That, too, was a foolish thought: if the beast *should* heave up, it would make no difference where he stood. That danger was an absolute and would do no less to a man drowsing by his own fire than to one who stood on the dizzying edge of things.

Once he was beyond the bridge, he had no reason to be wary about his footing. Here the land that made up the rim of the bowl widened out, was broad enough to accommodate an ample path and to nourish brush and trees. Twigs and low boughs struck at him and stung him. What leaves were left rattled like parchment in the crazy gusts. There was room for dwellings, but there were no dwellings. For some reason he could never account for, this holiest of all the places left to the people of the island after the calamity had become abhorrent to them. There was nothing here but scrubby wilderness giving way after half a mile to scattered crosses, stone sarcophagi set among stunted trees, memorial statues leaning to one side and blunted by the perpetual blasts. Only the dead had a home now in the precincts of the Chapter House of Saint Cyprian.

As for the Chapter House itself, all that was left intact was the chapel and one outbuilding divided into cells. The rest, in the black hour when the earth had quaked before the onslaught of the tidal wave, had been gutted by fire. It was toward the chapel that he went, up the ascending path, led by a wan beacon now, a light in one of the upper windows. Some brother had come here before him, driven by restlessness or a quarrel with his woman to read or meditate in the scriptorium; and, though he was thankful for the directing light, he had no appetite for company.

The cell reserved for him was the largest, just to the left of the entrance to the chapel. He passed through the square hall, pondering the incongruous splendor revealed by the lantern light: Four pillars of green granite, crowned with gold capitals and polished like mirrors. A bronze statue of Saint Cyprian sent from Saxony, the gift of some lordly bishop whose name was forgotten together with the sins he had meant to expiate by his generosity. A floor made up of blocks of alternating green and yellow marble, no longer neatly separated and aligned, trodden one into the other by wet and weary feet. The wavering floor extended into the abbot's cell. Weeks ago, Berthe had given him two bear-skins to cover it; at his age, she had said, he should not walk on a damp cold floor. But he had never troubled to lay the bearskins down. The lantern light showed him the disconsolate heap of worn fur in the corner, along with the stone walls, the high three-legged stool, the high reading lectern, and, on the lectern, the Book.

Footfalls sounded above him, hollowly repeating themselves. "Who is there?" he shouted, and his own voice came back at him before the reply.

"Eustace, Father. Is there any way I can serve you?"

A bitter answer broke in his head, and he bit his lip, knowing himself muddle-minded enough to utter it. What he wished to say was: Yes, either take my daughter or leave her once and for all. What he said was: "No, my son. I have a lantern and there are candles here. I need nothing. I came only to have another look at the Book."

Once he had lighted the candles and set them on the lectern, once he had got his weight centered on the creaking stool, he did what he always did. Like a peasant scenting oncoming rain or the first furrow, he closed his eyes and smelled the Book. In its smell was its wonder and its terror. It smelled of smoke—or at least he believed it smelled of the smoke in which it had been born. His nostrils inhaled the faint choking odor of the old conflagration. Then he exhaled and, still with his eyelids squeezed down, he felt the cover. Rough, untooled, and damp—definitely

81

damp even to his numb fingertips. Properly prepared, he turned back the cover and opened his eyes on a fine but wavering script and read:

I, the Abbot Benno, write these things in this new book. For the four elements have leagued themselves against the old book, and it is no more. The cover and the pages have been consumed in fire. The chronicler who set down the words welters in water with the Cathedral of Saint Cyprian. And all this has come upon us, together with the Last Day, out of the great turmoil stirred up by the hand of God. As for me, anguish unstrings me when I ask myself for whom I write, seeing that all the race of man, save only we few unfortunates, are gone from the face of the earth.

I do not know what year I should have written at the top of this page. If I remember aright, and two of the remaining Brothers assure me that I do, the last date put down by the dead chronicler was the month of October in the year of our Lord 997. The month should stand, but who can vouch for the year? According to those most learned in matters of the Last Day, that day was to come when the millennium filled up its measure: that is to say, in the thousandth year after the birth of the Babe. Now, there is a difference of three years between 997 and 1000, and what am I to think in the dullness of my despair and the knowledge of all men's ignorance? Surely, they that have kept chronicles over ten centuries could have fallen into the little error of three years. Shall I write, then, "October, in the year of our Lord 997" or "October, in the year of our Lord 1000"? Indeed, since time is finished, and the children of Adam—all but us, rejected wretches that we are—have been taken as was foretold out of the world, can I write any year? Or, if I write either 997 or 1000, can I write that a year which comes after the end of all things is a year of our Lord?

The following items must be set down this night, though why and for whom I do not know:

I: All the ships and boats that lay about the island went under when Leviathan raised himself up, nor is there any mast or net or sail left upon the surface of the sea.

II: The isthmus is submerged. It is no more.

III: The line of the opposite shore is changed. One said he

saw it rise and fall away. Now we see neither cliffs nor trees. IV: A count has been taken, and thus it stands: of eight hundred souls, not more than three hundred have outlived the event. We make the following surmised disposition of our dead: Three hundred lie, together with the Cathedral and the Square and the houses on the lower terraces, in the water that rushed in through the cleft in the rocks.

Fifty and more—all Brothers of the Order of Saint Cyprian—died in the monastery by smoke and fire.

One hundred and more were buried in mud or crushed under falling stones.

The rest we cannot account for, except in the case of three who died without injury or mark of injury where they sat mending nets on a cliff that faced out to sea. These, it is said, are the ones who saw the eyes of Leviathan when he reared up out of the waters, and his glare was such that their horror at it burst their hearts.

Why is my own heart unburst within me? He who is charged with the keeping of the flock after the Last Day—it would be better for him if he were dead.

He stopped and brought one hand down on the page and struck his forehead with the other. He was doing exactly what the old woman had said he would: trying to read it all over again page by page—impossible even if he had had a week on his hands and could have read day and night. He took a solid quarter-inch of page-ends between thumb and forefinger and turned at random, pausing at the first date.

December, Saint Stephen's Day or thereabouts, 997 or 1000 or 1, if we count as 1 the year of the end of the world.

Now that the dead are buried, and those who were mortally sick through the calamity have also died and been laid away; now that the water in the basin at the center of the island is frozen at the edges and we are as much at peace as we will ever be, I, the Abbot Benno, have called the flock together among the ruins of the Chapter House; and, having counseled one with the other, we have agreed upon these things:

I: The nuns can no longer live in the nunnery because it is infested with water-rats, and many of the sisters have died of fever there, and some have gone mad. Henceforth they will dwell, two and two parceled out together, in houses in the town.

II: Since there is not room enough for the Brothers in the desolation of the Chapter House, it will be with them as with the nuns.

III: The people of Saint Cyprian's will provide all the surviving clerics, male and female, with daily bread and with garments to cover their nakedness.

IV: The begetting and bringing forth of children in a world which is ended, in which there is no time and no hope and no law to guide the ways of men, is not to be thought upon. Therefore, no man will lie with any woman, and no womb will be quickened, and every soul will pray earnestly for its own last day. For who would call up feeble life into the void? And who could have any desire except the desire for death?

V: Since all has been taken away from everyone by the inscrutable hand of God, it cannot be said of anything, "It belongs to such-and-such a one," nor shall we any longer utter the words "thine" and "mine." Let him who needs, take, and him who has, give. Surely God in His mercy will make the time short for us all, and for all there will be enough.

VI. As to the matter of Masses and services and rituals, there has been much dispute. There are those among us who believe it is presumptuous and useless to look to these things, since God has turned His face utterly from the world. There are those who believe it is impiety to turn our faces from God, though we are not within the reach of His eyebeams or the compass of His thought. Therefore, it is agreed in compromise that the following obligations will be fulfilled by the Abbot and Brothers of Saint Cyprian, so long as even one of them shall live:

Four Masses to be said at summer and winter solstice and at autumn and vernal equinox.

Two Masses and processions, one at Christmastide and one at the time of the Passion in spring.

It is agreed further that we will say no more Masses for the dead.

Inasmuch as we hold the shepherd's crook but feebly, and there is none among us who can claim the right or the will to take up the civil sword, there will be no more beheadings, nor burnings, nor shut-tings-up in sealed cells. Let him who trespasses these few laws which we have made (and they are simple enough to be understood by all) go up to the salt cliffs alone and there await his own death. For, even as it is inconceivable to give life after the Last Day, so it is incon-ceivable to take life away. Henceforth we will merely wait, chaste, without covetousness, and in peace.

He started and shook himself. He had fallen into one of his long drowses, had been seeing a vague image of the company of survivors walking away, solemn and chastened, from their first convocation, skirting in small groups the leaden sheet of water laid forever over the drowned turrets of Saint Cyprian's. Never —and now least of all, with the stranger in wait to catch him up—did he mean to be possessed by the thought of that Cathe-dral. Many were: Alain was a deplorable case. With a flap that shook the candle flames, he turned many pages over together and began to read one headed with another date:

The Feast of the Pentecost, or thereabout, in the year 4 after the Termination.
    Of the last days of the Abbot Benno, and his death, I, the chronicler Anselm, write these things which I saw with my own eyes.
    There are those who say the Abbot Benno died of the poison that was in the wafer. There are those who say his death was justly visited upon him because he made use of magic and the ways of wizards to bring down a revelation. But I myself believe he was tormented to death by a multiplicity of questions. Indeed, by bodily signs it was plain that his brain was burst by a crowding-in of questions. When he lay in death, my own eyes beheld the blue marks on the skin of his brow.
    These are some of the questions that harried the Abbot Benno to his death, nor has any man since found answer for any of them:
        I. If a person transgress against the new law and go not up of his own will to die on the salt cliffs, will those who drag him

there be guilty of violence, which is forbidden? Are they not, in will if not in act, the agents of his death?

II. If an idiot woman in the rankness of her desire draw on a lad of twelve until he lie with her, is she guilty in her witlessness? And is he guilty in his childishness?

III. Who is a child? One who has not yet passed the eleventh year. Yet if one say a child is eleven years and one day, and another say, no, the child is four days short of eleven, how is a man to pass judgment (time itself being finished) based upon a matter of five days?

IV. If a nun give birth to an infant and swear that no man has touched her, shall a just man count it a lie or a great wonder, since even so the Son of God was born?

V. If one take what is dear to another—a cup or a garment or a carven chair—and willfully smash or tear it in sheer wantonness of spirit, is it his right, since nothing belongs to any man?

VI. Shall a man be given his daily bread if he drink mead and sleep and turn his hand to nothing, leaving his wife and children to be fed by his neighbors, who themselves have little enough?

Buffeted by such questions on all sides and every day, the Abbot Benno denied himself what was granted to the commonality. He slept on the bare floor, went naked under a shirt of doeskin, and ate only bread. And he was so transformed by austerities and troubles of the mind that he became as one walking about after life had gone out of him.

This year at the time of the Passion there was a stirring of the waters within the basin of the island, and certain things came up from the bottom thereof, all of them holy: a small wooden crucifix, a cope, and a light box, also of wood, in which the nuns had in old times stored the wafers they made to house the body of our Lord.

These things were brought to the Abbot Benno, and he opened the box, and there were wafers in it, sodden and covered with scum. And he took out the wafers and laid them on a sill to dry in the sun, running to look at them between judgment and judgment by day and sleep and sleep by night, as though they had driven him mad. Then the eldest among the Brothers, seeing his mind so fixed upon the wafers, counseled him to bury them or consume them in fire, but he would not.

86

And, preaching in the fields in the week of the Passion, he spoke of them wildly, likening them to Noah's rainbow and saying they well might be a second covenant offered after the second Great Flood.

And on the day of the Resurrection, I myself saw him eat a wafer, corrupt and foul though it was. The eating thereof was not wizardry, but madness. For a man thus driven and put upon will seize upon anything.

I do not know whether he sickened with the corruption that was in the wafer or with scrupulousness because of what he had done. But he died within three days, and, to my mind, he would have died soon in any case, not of a wafer, but of exhaustion.

They have buried him in the churchyard, and set a cross at his head. But it is as if his grave were accursed: all men who pass it turn their eyes aside. At his feet is a thornbush, and yesterday it came into bloom. For this reason, I believe he has been taken up in the spirit though he was rejected in the flesh. May he rest.

The Abbot Ottric closed his eyes and wondered whether his daughter Liese had gone to bed. Probably not. Probably she was still sitting on the floor in the lean-to he had built against their house for her, nursing one of the sick beasts that their owners had given up for lost. Like his, her head was too big to go well with a short and sturdy body, and seemed bigger because of the curling of her black hair. Her eyes were round and gave her face a look of constant wonder. Her cheeks were high-boned and rich and flushed like fruit. Unpicked, and ripe for the picking. . . . What had summoned her was a creaking of boards overhead. Eustace was restless, Eustace was wandering about. Well, he would give thought to that business after the encounter with the stranger. Now . . . He turned over another fat sheaf of pages and skimmed page after known page until he came to:

April, in the year 34 after the Termination. Of the holy madness, and the burning of flesh, and the plague. I, the chronicler Joachim, write these things which I have suffered and witnessed. No man of a new generation will believe them. But if they were not, then the thirty years of my life have been a long dream.

No man has written here since my predecessor felt the flames in his hands and feet and vomited up his inwards and perished. Therefore I must make a page stand for a year. Nor can I ask God to help me in my labors. If any man had doubts before, it is plain now that God has departed utterly from Saint Cyprian's.

Came upon us in this accursed year the most beautiful of Aprils. Rain and sun alternated in due order and begot such greenness that every scar of fire and earthquake was covered over. Rainbows were suspended over the waters, and dolphins leaped out of the sea, and birds of fair plumage sang new songs in our boughs. Sure of a plenteous crop, we ground the remaining rye and ate much bread, and the dugs of the heifers were filled, and bees swarmed in the blossoming trees, and every man had a full stomach and a high heart.

It was our way in that April to be more and more together, since every man saw wonders and wished to tell his fellows: one how, in the graveyard, the dead awaited a present resurrection, for their breathing moved the sod, making it rise and fall; another how a blossoming pear tree became the Mother of God and bent over him and wept in pity for us all; yet another how at sunset a scroll of molten gold unrolled in the sky, bearing upon it in curious scarlet letters: "The Compassionate Angel Will Come." And as we nourished ourselves on food and on such miracles, the old yearnings came upon us, especially upon the young, so that hand reached for hand, and loving and begetting began again, and no man in his exaltation thought to say nay.

Indeed, it was as if the word of John of Patmos was fulfilled, for a new heaven and a new earth seemed to have been given unto us. All things were the colors of precious stones: pink quartz and sardonyx and amethyst, and blues that were forever changing, and with each change were more dazzling than before. Only, we ate somewhat less as the month advanced, for the taste of fish was in everything. And some in their hope and joy said this, too, was a blessed sign, for Leviathan had died at last and was given to corruption, and it was his corruption that tainted our tongues, but it would pass.

Until then our rejoicing had been pure, but now a fever came into it. Before, when a man recounted a miracle, we said, "Even so," and accepted his word; but now all followed after the teller and wrought with lies upon their own minds until they believed, or said they believed, they also saw the sign. So it was that ten talked with John the Baptist under a sycamore, and he blessed them and sprinkled water on their cheeks, and their cheeks tingled because the water turned to fire. So fifty came to me one evening with what they said was the egg of a marvelous bird, and I do not know to this day whether what I held was light and pulsed with life, or was a common stone. Nor could any man walk in seemly fashion, for the feet were benumbed, nor tell what it was he felt with his fingers, for all men's hands were afire.

Little by little, day by day, the visions departed. And men vomited and voided, and women aborted, and many lost their fingers to the second joint, and some were bereft of their ears and their noses, and many—yes, as many as a fifth of us—died.

And those who remained had a dull anger and a sullenness and a scorn for all things stripped of the magic of their madness. They spat upon the earth because it was paltry, and mocked the maimed with the parts they had lost. In rancor and spite, they did not bury their dead at once, but let them begin to rot, and kicked and hauled them into their graves, jeering at their corruption.

Yet the island bloomed with a greenness that had become terrible, and the balm of the night was heavier than the stench of the dying and the dead, and the weeping was loud, especially the weeping of women, because not one quickened womb could hold the child.

This autumn there is a great harvest with few hands to take it in. And the Brothers of Saint Cyprian have made a service of purification and penance, but only a few score came for absolution. The taste of the corruption of Leviathan is gone, but we carry our own corruption. For in our madness we have committed a sin that is the sin of sins, and not one of us can look another in the eye.

But hurry, hurry, the night is short. Press two decades into half an hour, as women press the fruit of a cherry bough into a little jar. Skim page after page, all telling of peace and plenty, since for years after the opulent and evil spring, all springs were opulent and good. Read how the old laws fell out of use, and many conceived, though some were left barren. Read how children were born with all their fingers and toes, and grew tall, and were splendidly arrayed. For the skills revived and the weavers wove and the carpenters sawed and all things for the uses of men were at hand, though no man thought now of things for the use of God, for He had turned away His face. Two decades and three abbots who all died between smooth sheets, and only two wonders to intrude upon the tranquillity:

February, in the year 53 after the Termination: One Gervaise, an old man, seneschal in the castle, came before the Abbot and the Brothers and told a strange tale. In his age, he sleeps but lightly, and one night he stood at a high window and looked out to sea. At the hour of dawn when the mists were heavy, he beheld a great ship heaved by the churned waters. And he said it was just such a ship as had visited Saint Cyprian's by the score in his youth. And many (the young especially) desired to believe him. And they clambered up to every roof and turret and looked north and south and east and west, but saw no ship.

So all pitied him as one who had formerly been stricken by the fiery madness. For a while they let him tell over and over what he thought he had seen: sails swollen in the blast like pregnant women, and masts and hull encased in ice, and a banner with a dragon's head. But by and by, seeing the young were still restless, the abbot bade him hold his tongue. Which he did, save only when there was mead in him; but that was no great matter, for he had begun to add such things as he could not have seen. And the young ceased to listen; and he, being heavy with years, soon died.

And:

January, the year 57 A.T.: There was an event of the preceding year which I, the chronicler Theobald, failed to record. I record it now because it was passing strange, and men born later and endowed with more wisdom may comprehend it better than I. There was with us a virgin, thin and pale, who from her fourteenth year wanted no traffic with men, but yearned with all her heart and beseeched the Brothers repeatedly that she be made a nun of Saint Cyprian.

Nor would she listen reasonably when it was shown her that there was no sisterhood, since during the fiery madness and the years of plenty all the women so devoted had forgone their vows or died. And she spent much time in the abandoned nunnery, though it was rat-ridden and filthy. And she tried with helpless hands (for she was sick

90

and coughed up blood) to make some little clean space in the chapel, before the crucifix and the statue of the Mother of God.

Then, overcome in her soul by the filth of half a century, and by terror of the rats, she could not go there, but went instead to a high place that jutted out over the basin of water at the middle of the island. From morning to night she sat there, and people fed her out of pity, and always she gazed at the water. For she believed that some change in the light would pierce the leaden surface and show her the roof and turrets of the Cathedral.

And one day in October, when the air was very pure, she stood up and went her way through the streets, and tears streamed down her face. And men and women asked her why she was weeping. And she said, "For joy immeasurable, for I have seen it through the water— the glory of Saint Cyprian's." And she came to the abbot and told him of it (with my own ears I heard her) and another Brother wrote it down in every detail, and the document was laid by. Though whether it is a holy document or a piece of madness, no man knows. In December, the water in the basin began to freeze at the edges. And she was tormented by the fear that the Cathedral would be utterly sealed up in ice. And by night she rose from her bed and left her house, and was never again seen by any.

Nowadays it is taken for truth that she lashed a rock to her body and went down from the high place into the water, that she might be with the Cathedral of Saint Cyprian. May she be given peace.

Incidents isolated and self-contained, like two pellets of hail in a garland of kingcups. The rest was green and golden—hardly a month without an occasion for a feast. Feast to mark the springing up of the wheat. Feast to honor a woman whose womb had yielded three at once. Feast for the blossoming of trees and the return of the bees. Feast of Saint Stephen, though few were at the services, most being at home, dressed in fine cloth and bidding guests to their tables. Much made of children here, and the joys to be had of children: how a lordly father had roasted an ox when he gave his daughter to a Brother; how a peasant mother was presented with an embroidered shift because she had borne eleven and all of them had lived.

And, as the old doted more and more upon the young, the young were drawn more and more toward each other and kept their own company. A merry fever of dancing seized them. They made their own dances, for the old dances were forgotten; and whoever made a new step or figure reigned for a week among his fellows like a king or queen.

February, 69 A.T.: This night as I write the island is ablaze with torches. All the maids and youths dance in the streets, whirling and shouting and waving kindled brands. The wind is still and the night is unseasonably mild. Yet they would dance if a hurricane such as came on the Last Day were blowing in.

He, Ottric, had danced once under the torches. Through the streets of the town and past the castle, where the young Alain stood at the window with Julianne, whom he had lately taken as his. Past the black ruin of the monastery, where the smoke of brands became for him the smoke of the first burning. Through the graveyard and over the grave of the Abbot Benno, where a thornbush tore at his ankles. Over the rickety bridge, with the basin on one side and the blank sea on the other, and torch calling up torch out of the inky water below. Not in his youth, when his bones were limber. Old then—forty-eight—in a lay brother's cassock, with white bristling whiskers on his cheeks and grizzled hair on his chest. For only then was he given the filled goblet of his manhood. His wife Berthe lay abed after a miraculously safe delivery, seeing that she was well past her fortieth year. While he danced with the young, she suckled their Liese, his first child. And what hands he grasped and what mouths he kissed in the fever of dancing—they made him shiver still with a dark bliss. A negligible falling-off in the days of plenty, when the highest among the Brothers took unto themselves not one but two or three, and hardly one maid could say she was a maid in truth when she took a man's hand and said: "I am yours from this hour."

Ah, well . . . He rubbed his nape and the small of his back. He was so stiff he would stagger when he set his feet on the floor—if ever he got to the end of the Book and walked out of this smoke-haunted place. Over his head there was a cry of anger and a thud: something hurled at a rat, no doubt. Brother Eustace had a horror of rats bred into him. An aristocrat, nephew to Alain by a dead young brother, one who had been slain with scores of others—he turned pages until he came to the place—during the Three Years of Blood.

Spring, 72 A.T.: I, the Abbot Hildebald, have no astronomer by to tell me whether it is April or May. I am a sinner, and if God's eyes were upon me, they would wither me as if I were a leaf in the fire. But He sees me not. Nevertheless men see me and know me for what I am: light of mind, hollow of heart, behindhand in all things, even in the keeping of this Book. For these reasons, after I have burned whatever I call my own in this monastery, I will give my crook to him the Brothers choose. Only, before I go, I will write briefly of the Three Years of Blood.

Who will understand it? That men should fall upon each other and murder and burn in a time of famine—this can be comprehended, for men are imperfect even with God, and God is gone. But that rage should rise out of peace and plenty, that hate should be the issue of ease and tranquillity, that men who have all things should make havoc because there is nothing for them to desire—that is monstrousness. Herein we see why Eve hearkened to the serpent and Adam ate of the fruit. For if she had had many children and had spun and woven and scrubbed she would have had no ear for whisperings. And if he had wrested his sustenance out of stony earth, he would have found a sour gooseberry infinitely sweet and would not have craved for heavenly fruit.

It is true that some of us had less and some more. When has it not been so? But all had enough to be full and sit with folded hands, and there was too much staring at what did not change, for we saw only the same island and the empty sea.

Two kinds there were among us, lords and peasants. All the Brothers, save only the peasant lay brothers, were accounted lords; and a few had become, like me (miserable sinner that I am), lords of great power. Now, a man would think the peasants would have fallen upon the lords, but it was otherwise. Arbitrarily, for the most trivial causes and on the most fantastical reasonings, lord fell upon lord. The Three Years of Blood came out of such quarrels as these:

I. In a procession, one stepped on the train of another's robe, and it was torn away and showed the other's buttocks in their nakedness. And he that was shamed came with a knife to the other's hearth, and stabbed him mortally before his woman and children, and no man touched him, not even I (wretch that I am), though he boasted of shedding blood.

II. A child tormented a mastiff, and the mastiff tore the cheek of the child, and the father avenged himself upon the dog, hanging it with a strong leather strap until it was dead. Whereupon every man of both houses got him a knife and there was common slaying wherein twenty-seven went to their graves.

III. A woman loved her husband's brother, who loved her not and spoke of her scornfully to a maid who waited in her house. And the maid, being spiteful and less than graciously treated by the woman, told her what he had said. Whereupon the woman made a feast for all that were his and her own, and put poison in the meat, and they ate and died.

In such manner, as fire moves from house to house in high gusts, hate went and kindled all, until those in the town barely dared to unbar their doors and those of the village kept themselves and the yield of the earth from the marketplace. So, in fright and starvation, ended the first of the Three Years of Blood.

Early in the second year, certain lords of one party went stealthily to the peasants and told them: "Kill such-and-such a one, and put the torch to his house, and we will give you land and make you as one of us." And I (accursed that I am) knew not of it, nor if I had known would I have raised a finger, for my own house was in jeopardy and I wanted only to be left in peace.

Who would have known then how it would be with our peasants? Mild as heifers they had been since the beginning, and under grievous suffering they had only lowed a little in their pain. But now it was as if seven decades of rage were stored in their thick sinews. They were more pitiless than the sea, once they had taken up the mace and the sword.

The Brothers who strove to stop them they killed and hacked to

94

pieces. As for the delicate women of the lordly houses—even frail children and aged dames—they stripped and wrought their will upon them, twenty men to one woman, and left them naked and close to death in the streets. Thirteen lordlings they hung up, heads down, and set fires under them so that the whole town smelled of the burning and two who saw it went mad.

And many of the peasants seemed mad, for they burned the standing grain in their own fields and set the torch to their own hayricks and ate and drank like swine while their children's bellies swelled up for lack of nourishment. Witless things they did: Calling to mind old affronts, they dug up half-corrupted bodies and burned them at the stake, and they sewed up a lordling in a deer's hide and made him hold up the antlers in his hands and chased him with lances through the town and slew him when he fell.

So (with no man safe, for they threw sheaves of burning straw soaked in oil of flaxseed through the windows) came to its end the second of the Three Years of Blood.

And black winter was upon us, and universal hunger, since most of the rye had rotted uncut and whatever was in the granaries made grey flour and foul-tasting bread. And two went into a cave to lie secretly together, and the cave was infested with bats, and they came out shrieking that devils were abroad, and no man would go near the place.

And many who were sick in those days with the old sickness, feeling their flesh aflame, took it that devils were in them. And one man added the madness of his visions to another's, until both the ailing and the sound said that the Prince of Darkness had sent his legions to take unto themselves whatever God had left in the abandoned world.

Whereupon all things ceased: there were no more burnings or killings. Each waited in horror for the devils to come and bear him to Hell. And none would fish on the sand beach because it was said an army of devils was gathered on the opposite shore in the forest.

Then spring came, but without ploughing and sowing, for each man said "There is no purpose in it." As for me (carcass emptied of spirit that I am), though I no longer believed in the devils I did not bestir myself. For I also took the sickness, with gangrenous sores on my feet and shins.

95

But there was among us a certain Brother Galbart, born in the same year as I, who had seen all this and had yet kept his youth. Fair and frank he was, straight of limb and back, with brown hair grown down over his forehead. And his mind was ample and quick, and he knew men and measured them, and he came often to the chapel of Saint Cyprian and read the Book.

And he went speaking comfort, first to a few listeners and then to many. He entered the cave and came forth with a bat in his hand and asked how it was that men should cower before a miserable mouse with wings. He summoned the people into the field and counted them to the number of four hundred and twelve (for many had died by violence and sickness). And he said that there was more than enough to feed so few.

Some he set to planting and some to building. And for a while many followed him, sowing plots and cutting down oaks for beams. But they were slow and he chided them, and his reproofs rankled. Others also took offense, Brothers of houses higher than his. And still others—and these were many—after the slayings and the burnings and the terror of the devils, had no appetite for such mean matters as cutting beams. And they murmured foolishness against him, knowing not what ailed them, how their souls were weary of the sky and the island, sick of summer and autumn and winter and spring. And one said: "I am irked by his hair and the way it grows down over his forehead," and another said: "His speech offends me, especially his parables." So one morning when he was chiding a mason a tumult rose around him, and one knocked him down, and another battered in his head with a building stone.

And a Brother of Saint Cyprian (not I, dog that I am) sat on the ground, and took his bloody head and held it on his knees, and kissed his mouth and wept. And the weeping spread, so that men fell on each other's shoulders and sobbed aloud, and a sound of mourning went like ripples from a dropped pebble to the very edges of the island. And all that were left after the Years of Blood came and knelt and touched his feet and begged forgiveness of his dead body. Not only for him did they weep, but for all to whom they had measured out death, and for the living death they had measured out to themselves.

So all in their self-loathing desired to be other than they were, and made division of their wealth. And I also have said I will no longer be abbot, and have asked them to choose another to whom I may give the crook. Their choice has fallen upon one Ottric, a peasant, but a prudent man untainted by sin. Let him who reads this Book believe that, though he is of common stock, he is a shepherd a hundred times more worthy than I.

"Pah!" said the Abbot Ottric, and spat across the reading stand, barely missing the Book. Nobody on the island galled him so much as this predecessor of his with his toothless self-condemning mouth and his wheedlings and his liar's humility. His crook and his obligations he had indeed handed over, but there were other things that had stuck to his fingers. Honey from the best hive, fruit from the best trees, three kids at the Feast of the Passion and five geese at the Nativity—surely the Brothers would give him such gifts for old times' sake. He had been collecting them now as a matter of course for—he turned to a blank page, took date from date, and glared at the result—yes, he had been collecting them for eighteen years.

And if I should die before him, thought the Abbot Ottric, he will come here to console the Brothers and carry off whatever he can, calling it a precious relic whereby to remember me. But not this onyx inkstand. Not that. That I will bury when I get my mortal sickness: for it is very old and belonged to the Abbot Benno, who sat here, even here on this high stool, in the time of the Termination—

But there had been no Termination—a thing he could not get into his head. There had been a crack in the earth, a flaw in the floor of the sea, an earthquake that shook the opposite shore, but no Termination. The strangers—the fat one who talked too much in the streets and the thin one whose ravings Berthe had brought home—they proved incontrovertibly what he could not accept, what reduced his mind to the leaden thickness of the water which hid the Cathedral: there still was a world.

And in that world and to that world—such was the purpose of his reading out this night—he must give his account. An unbelievable moment would come when he would have to tell the

97

representative of Princes of the Church in whose existence he could not believe how the flock had survived what it had not survived. And what sort of God could it be who would perpetuate such a shabby and pitiless jest for a hundred years? And what could he say, being what he was: a wedded abbot, a peasant, unlearned and old?

His eyes burned. He closed them and gave himself up to the churning dark. Ah, well, he had done what he could. He had looked through all of it but the final page—his page—and he would read that, and then he would take himself home to his rest. Only . . . Somehow he could not bear the sight of his own script. Before the coming of the strangers it had seemed manly and forceful in its crude unevenness, but now it looked mawkish —the hand of a fool, time's fool, God's fool:

May, 72 A.T.: I, the Abbot Ottric, will henceforth keep the Book. May I write little. The less there is to suffer, the less there is to write, and we stand in need of peace.

Here are the rules whereby we will live:

> I. The lords will dwell in the town. The peasants will dwell in the village. Each man will have a house, but no man will call more than one house his own.
>
> II. Land and the yield of the land will be held in common, and twelve of the Brothers appointed by the abbot will serve each year at harvest time to divide and dispense.
>
> III. What is in a man's house is his, and he may add to it what is given him as a free gift, or brought by his woman, or what he makes with his own hands.
>
> IV. He who murders, burns, or steals, his head shall be cut from his body with an ax (if any man can be found to do it) and his woman and his children shall be fed from the general store.
>
> V. The feasts and services shall be as they were appointed by the Abbot Benno in the year of the Termination.
>
> VI. The madmen and the ranters shall be shut up in cells, for we have seen enough.
>
> VII. Every man, including the Brothers, may take unto himself one woman. Should a man take another, let him fell trees and

make ten beams for every month he lies with her. Should a Brother have a concubine, let him walk in shame with the sign of his holiness turned upside down on his cassock. Also, let him do as the others in the matter of the beams.

September, 82 A.T.: This year the harvest passed all men's expectations. After the division, much remained, so all received an additional measure, and the Brothers sat together at a seemly feast. Also, thirty-four thatched huts have been raised in the village and nine new houses in the town.

June, 87 A.T.: Last night there was a slight quaking of the earth. Some huts were shaken askew, and a crack appeared in the turret of the castle. But the quaking soon subsided, and, because of the law against ranting, there was no great confusion.

January, 88 A.T.: The sickness of the burning flesh would seem to have utterly passed from us. It is now three years since any man has been taken with visions and raving or afflicted by gangrenous sores.

July, 93 A.T.: An isthmus has come out of the sea, a narrow way over the waters to the opposite shore. He who first saw it was taken into bondage for raving, and was shut up in a cell; but I went and saw with my own eyes, and he is set free. It is of rock, encrusted with salt and strewn with shards of broken vessels and pieces of sodden wood.

December, 97 A.T.: One said he saw a fishing boat far out, but when he was accused of raving, he disavowed his tale, saying first that he never said he saw it, and afterward that he must have seen it in a dream.

October, 98 A.T.: From the opposite shore, which all of us have taken to be uninhabited or the haunt of devils, came two monks this day, in cassocks, with two donkeys, and their names are Father Albrecht and Brother Thaddeus. And nothing can be made of it, and there is much wonderment, for they say they are from a city called Cologne. And, though Father Albrecht is sick even to death with the fiery sickness, Brother Thaddeus is sound in his mind. And he says that we are the ones who are mad, that there has been no end to the world.

He took up the quill and dipped it in the onyx inkstand. Surely the stranger would assert his right to see the Book. Laboriously, for his fingers were very numb, he wrote a final entry:

99

November, 98 A.T.: That which I, the Abbot Ottric, did here at Saint Cyprian's, hoping only that it would seem just in the eyes of my flock, I am willing to show to the eyes of the world and the eyes of God. The rules were made with too much harshness and administered with too much lenience. He who held the crook was an unlearned peasant, and his flock was a stricken flock and stumbled often, for it walked in the dark. But let this be said of mine and me: no man murdered or raped or corrupted an innocent child, not in the period of my charge, which has been eighteen years.

☩   ☩   ☩

Waking on that same bleak morning, Father Albrecht took stern satisfaction that everything had come clear at last. To make sure he would keep hold of it, he told it off: sick at the end of what had almost been an endless journey; put by some dereliction of his flesh into a state he must learn to consider derelict; carried unknowing into a castle, into this room; tended here for three weeks by the lady Julianne. If he felt a sense of loss now that such tending was over, that, too, was a falling-off. And fear of what he would see from the window was only the residue of an invalid's helplessness.

Somebody had pulled the arras across that window—he could tell where it was only by the whitish light that strained through the warp and woof of the threadbare cloth. He folded back the coverlet, moved to the edge of the bed, and let his legs hang over the side. The worn shift that covered him was spotless. It had doubtless been put on him and taken off, washed and hung up to dry a dozen times by the chatelaine. Probably it was she too who had come in while he slept after yesterday's confrontation and put his cassock on a peg on the wall. On feet reasonably firm he walked across a stretch of foreign floor and took down the garment and carried it back to the bed. There he peered at it and found it at once familiar and strange: clean, smelling of some dry scent, all the rents in it mended with intricate stitchery of a sort he had never seen before.

He dressed after the chaste manner of the monastery. Get the shift off the shoulders, slide the cassock over the head, have the smallest possible contact with nakedness. But this investiture, this putting on of his clerical skin and his old self, was somehow tainted. Why had she so ornately repaired the honorable wounds in his cassock? Why had she dealt with it as if it were a knight's rich robe to be laid by between festive evenings in a powder of dried flowers?

Where had she put his sandals? No matter—he started barefooted for the window. But he found himself light-headed before he reached it: he had to stop and rest at the table where he had seen them at their curious game of varicolored stones. He looked at the chair where her Alain had sat and rejected it, and let himself down into the other one, the one that had been occupied by the saturnine monk, the one of the inverted cross.

From there he could just reach a fold of the arras and pull it back, opening for himself a triangle upon the world. Keen grey light and a steady wind blowing in upon him. Land descending in a series of tawny humps like the backs of crouching beasts. A narrow beach and small waves whose grating he could hear even from this height. Beyond the beach, a lead-grey heavy surface of water that rolled back and forth and only here and there belied its molten metallic look by breaking into crests. He dropped the arras and laid his head on his folded arms on the table top. Two afflictions, inseparable, assaulted him: dizziness at the height and sick-heartedness at the desolation.

What kind of human life could maintain itself on such a barren close-cropped piece of the earth? Like lice on a dying beast . . . He recalled the bloated belly of Patches and found himself wondering what crawled on it now. As a sleepless man tries every way of arranging himself and finds each new way as intolerable as the last, he tried and dismissed thought after thought. What strength was left to him? Was there any flesh on him at all? The wood under his forearms, the wood at his spine seemed to be bruising him to the bone. . . . And what hour was it, and how long would he have to wait for food to be brought in? Who would bring it?

101

Perhaps the lord of the castle, perhaps some servant—certainly not the chatelaine. . . . Yes, and he had insisted that they bring him their abbot this evening, and now he could not even remember the abbot's name, though the rhythm of it—two syllables with the accent on the first—kept beating in his brain. Eilardt? Edric? No, it would not come to mind. And the scent in the folds of his sleeves troubled him, and now that he had looked out of the window he could not rid his ears of the grating and washing of the dismal sea.

What sort of sickness was it that, in its passing, robbed everything of splendor? In the dark shelter of his arms he remembered his first waking: it burned almost as brilliantly as the dream of Saint Pelagia and the Brother with the gentian eyes. The little stone counters, blue and grey and violet, her grass-green skirt, the hair of her monkish paramour, even the blasphemous yellow cross on the cassock of the other one—no hoard of ecclesiastical treasure, no Paschal procession of bishops in jeweled and embroidered vestments had ever had such richness. And her breasts that had brought to mind the milk of God's own mother, and her hand that had somehow made up for the pilfered alabaster hand found in the pond with Father Carolus. . . .

The door creaked, and he straightened. It was she. She stood for an instant staring bewildered at the empty bed. Then she stepped over the threshold and took on an enthusiasm out of keeping with her remembered ministrations. "Oh, so that is where you are, Father," she said across the length of the room. "Up and dressed! How fine!"

He nodded, not knowing what to say. The strange accent was no longer pleasing to him. He had to remind himself that it was not an affectation, that she was doing nothing to the language, that the language would naturally have gone its own peculiar way in the last hundred years.

"I came to ask you what I could bring you for breakfast. Alain is gone for the morning—otherwise he would have come." If she meant to imply that she knew he preferred her husband's services to her own, she showed no wounded sensibilities. She went on without pause, repeating with her strained eagerness how well he looked, how surprised she was, how she had never thought to find him up and about. A woman, like any other. Her dress, of a mottled and faded lavender, did not particularly become her. There was grey in her hair and a straight wrinkle between her brows. Her skin showed too pale against the cloth at her neck and wrists. There were hollows in her cheeks and faint blue markings under her eyes.

"What shall I bring, Father? Milk and bread? But now that I come to think of it, where's the need for me to bring anything? If you are strong enough to dress yourself, no doubt you will want to come downstairs. After three weeks in here"—she moved her head and made a little grimace to disparage everything in the room—"you will surely want to look at something else. Wouldn't you like to go down and eat at the table? What do you think?"

Could she be going on like that to hide a hurt? Not likely: the surface of her, now that he was awake and saw her with sane eyes, was too smooth to be penetrated by any such small matter as his rejection. She was the chatelaine, with a bunch of keys at her waist—keys that she fingered and jingled. She was the lady of Saint Cyprian's who would afterward relate with a light laugh how, quite unconscious of his queer ecclesiastical scruples, she had nursed him and fallen afoul of his holiness: *Noli me tangere*— oh, they were very rigid out in the world. . . .

"Yes, I will go downstairs, daughter," he said, and rose, glad of the dignity that accrued to him from the austere folds of his cassock and the stern carelessness in his untrimmed beard. A worldly woman. Herodias? No, why should he make her worse than she could possibly be? Because he must look, at best, like Saint John coming out of the wilderness?

"Good, Father. Then I will show you my castle—let me lead the way." She did, and he walked behind her into an unbelievable bare and ancient hallway whose masonry was appallingly raw. "To your left—the steps are here, in this tower. As you see, we have a very steep and treacherous flight of stairs."

Steep and treacherous indeed! For fear of dizziness, he could not

103

look long into the deep circular well of stone round which the staircase wound like a segmented serpent: old uneven steps going down and down, barely lighted by slits of windows that let in a grey shimmer from the sea.

She went ahead, keeping her shoulders high, never looking down. Her neck, slight like a child's, showed now and then when the loose locks of her hair fell apart. How old was she? Probably forty, not quite young enough to be his daughter. What age were they when they married here? Fifteen, twenty? No wonder she was so sure-footed: she knew her husband's house by heart, had been going up and down these steps for twenty-odd years. Downstairs with him to breakfast, upstairs with him to bed—

And he had almost stumbled, might well have fallen if he had not steadied himself against the bruising stone. She stopped and turned—she had heard him catch his breath. Her mouth was parted, and he half expected to hear the compassionate "Ah . . ." —incongruous with today's chatter—that still hung in his recollection. But she said nothing, only gave him a brief smile and went on down, courteously slowing her pace.

Out of the stairwell into a vast, dank, cavernous chamber. Doubtless the common room: a feeble fire on the sooty hearth, but then any fire would have been insufficient in this stony vacancy. At one end, two high windows through which damp gusts kept coming in, stirring the strips of arras and the rushes on the floor. Near the hearth, a board on trestles, several chairs set at haphazard angles, a book and some sheets of parchment strewn among the rushes, some leather cushions, a lute. What lay at the edges of the room he could not make out because of the dark.

She went to the hearth, picked up one of the cushions, and laid it on the seat of a carved chair. "Here, Father, sit down," she said, pulling the chair close to the board. Then, more loudly, over her shoulder, "Adele—Daniel—where are you? We need breakfast. Is nobody here?"

She called so offhandedly that he could not be sure she was calling to servants. In Cologne, in the great houses, servants were addressed with a punctilious consideration that only emphasized their inferiority. Nor would any lady there have been caught at what she was presently about: gathering books and parchment sheets into a heap, standing the lute against the wall, drawing up her chair so that she could face him across the board. "If I had known you were up, I would have put the room in order beforehand," she said, settling down. "They heard me, whether they answered or not. They will bring us something soon. They are old and slow—we let them take their time."

"I thought for a moment you might be calling your children."

"Children?" She propped her elbow on the worn, scrubbed wood and rested her cheek on her hand. "I have no children." She said it ruefully, then produced an exaggerated smile to cover the ruefulness. "But Eustace, Alain's nephew—in a way he is a child of mine. And Jehanne, too, and Liese—Liese is the Abbot Ottric's daughter."

So Ottric was the name; and everybody, even the abbot, coupled and bred.

"They will bring us a loaf, and some honey and milk. If there is anything else that you—"

"No," he said, "whatever is brought will be more than enough."

He was so ill at ease with her that he welcomed the coming of the servants, a man and a woman in drab fustian. Age had reduced them both to the same long-nosed, toothless, sharp-chinned inconsequence. Though at first he took them to be sister and brother, he somehow gathered that they were man and wife. So old that it made no difference: take the skirt from her and put it on him, and who would know? *His* beard had grown scant, and *her* chin sprouted white bristling hairs. As they laid the table, he saw them aim covert glances at the top of his head. They were probably wondering why such a short furze was growing there. The tonsure, like clerical abstinence, was probably considered a ludicrous aberration here on Saint Cyprian's.

Hot bread, tin plates, goblets, yellowed napkins, milk in a dented bronze pitcher—they set them out slowly and without ceremony with their wrinkled sexless hands. Three of the Brothers back in the Chapter House in Cologne had hands like a eunuch's: fleshy palms, padded and tapered fingers, fatty wrists. . . . Yet, though this servile pair gave rise to nothing but disturbing thoughts, he did not find the occasion less burdensome when they were gone. Lame conversation that had to be prodded and dragged: Excellent honey—but really it had a harsh dark under-taste. Fine milk—but it was blue and raw. A loaf fresh from the hearth was always a luxury—but he could barely get a slice of it down because he had suddenly remembered the fishy taste of the tainted rye on the shore.

Finally they were reduced to strained and shaming silence. The fire crackled, and the wind stirred the rushes. He heard her swallow and knew that she could hear him chew. He stared at the board, the napkin, the pitcher—anything but her face. And she was the same one who had come to him by night in God knows what disarray, had slipped her hand under the nape of his neck in the dark.

"Perhaps after breakfast you would like to walk a little in the garden, Father."

Blessed possibility of escape! "Yes. It is a long time"—he risked rudeness by asking for solitude, but was willing to take the risk— "since I have been able to give myself to prayer and meditation."

"You will have privacy. Nobody will be there."

She had said it with a lilt, no doubt with irony; and he did not wish to seem churlish. He groped after something with which to fill up the small time that remained to them, and had a jarring realization of how much lay between them: an uncharted forest, shipless waters, a century in which their forebears had not even known . . . "I was wondering—"

"Yes, Father?"

"A night or so ago—if I remember properly, it was the night before last—the lord Alain and another monk were sitting at the table near the foot of my bed, playing with counters. What is that game?"

"It was no game," she said in a changed, guarded voice. "They were making a model of the Cathedral."

"What Cathedral?"

"*The* Cathedral. The Cathedral of Saint Cyprian's. You see— But then, I am not the one to tell you. You will hear of it in good time from Alain or the Abbot Ottric."

"I am sorry if I—"

"Oh no, there was no harm in your asking." She had risen, she was moving away. "In fact, I am glad you asked. It would be better if they did not know you thought it was a game." Her skirt —there was some tension in the air that made him unable to raise his eyes higher than her skirt—trailed out of sight into a black corner from which she continued to speak. "They take it as much to heart as you take your prayers and meditations. I am getting a cloak for you, Father. The garden looks over the water, and it is sure to be cold."

She came back—it seemed to him in his bewilderment from a long distance—and held out a garment of doeskin. As he took it from her, he caught a strong whiff of the same dry scent that tainted his cassock. He sneezed—once, twice, thrice.

"It is the scent," she said. "Now *I* am the one to be sorry. It is unpleasant to you, and I have put it on everything. I hope the wind will carry it off. Perhaps you will scarcely notice it, once you are out in the air." She went, still talking, toward the portal, and he followed, afraid that he would sneeze again. "It is the only scent we have here—there are not enough flowers for drying, and what herbs we have we use for medicines. We make the scent from a weed of the sea. We pull it up with hooks onto the fishing beach and let it dry in the sun."

He could not help it: he sneezed again.

"It is not that you have a chill, Father?"

"No, no."

Her hand went up as high as her shoulder: she had meant to touch his forehead. But she bethought herself in time and stepped back, smiling her cool smile and jingling her keys. "Well, since

107

you are entirely recovered," she said, "I will go and see what they are doing in the kitchen-house."

✠   ✠   ✠

He pitied her that she should call such a desolate place a garden. It was the back of one of those crouching falls of land he had seen from his window—leveled off, divided by footpaths into flower beds, bounded on three sides by a tall tangled hedge and on the fourth by the rough foundation stones of the circular tower. Making a good show of monkish meditation by walking back and forth there was not easy: the barrenness made him feel raw and exposed, and the height threatened him with dizziness. Above the hedge which bordered the top of the cliff he could see only grey sky curdling here and there into white crests. At the foot of the cliff—how far down he did not want to know—would be nothing but the vacant beach and the waves.

Damp gusts kept coming at him. When he walked in one direction, they assailed his back; when he turned in the other, they confused his eyes and snatched at his breath. "O Lord, show me Thy mercy. . . ." But he did not finish, there was no comfort in it. No, nor in trying to rehearse the Rule of Saint Benedict, either, though that he should certainly do: he would need it at his fingertips when he talked with the Abbot Ottric tonight. To keep himself from being alarmed by the numbness and emptiness of his mind, he filled it with any stuff at hand: the bits of broken shells strewn over the footpaths, the dry infertile sods in the flower beds, the sparse stalks, black and sapless, some of them dead even before winter had come.

No, he was undone, too weak even for the minor tasks he had left behind him in Cologne. At the thought of the load he would be shouldering now, he let himself down onto a stone bench in the seaward angle of the hedge and covered his face with his hands. The chill of the stone went through his skin and crept up his haunches. The wind came through the black intermeshings of twigs and whipped his hair.

If he were to find himself as inept at this evening's council as

108

he had been at breakfast . . . But, sitting face to face with her, he had been exposed to certain peculiar bafflements: he had not, for instance, found a satisfactory way of addressing her, and that had made all the talk between them halting and strained. Because she had taken to saying "Father" with irony, he could not comfortably say "my daughter"; "my lady" sounded like the prelude to a knight's dallying; and it was unthinkable that a monk should call any woman by her name. Her name was strange—Roman, Norman, Lombard? Julia, of course, was Roman—Augustus's daughter, she that made her name a scandal and died in exile for her adulteries. Anne, on the other hand, was chaste and staid: Mary's mother, Saint Anne. . . .

"Hst!"

He started.

"Hst! Here, Father."

He turned around. The whisper had come from behind him. What he saw on the other side of the hedge—massive, bending toward him—made him think he must have slipped back into one of his feverish dreams. A woman, yes; but such height and bulk he had seldom before seen in a woman. The breasts, pale and soft with a mushroom's dead cold softness, were bared to the nipples. A goitre as big as an apple swelled out of the neck, strained against the skin, seemed ready to break through. He got up and greeted her—as he had learned, thank God, to greet the leprous and the sightless and the legless—with a serene Christian "God give you peace."

She tossed her head—a small one, made insignificant by the three protuberances that sagged beneath it, and topped with a crazy knot of brown hair. "Dreaming, eh, Father?" she said.

Should he draw himself up in ecclesiastical dignity at the effrontery, or wait in pastoral charity to hear more? He chose the latter, and forced himself to look her candidly in the face. On any other body, that face might even have been thought pretty: little rosebud mouth, small snub nose, dark birdlike eyes. "I do not believe that I heard what you—"

"You heard me." The mouth sneered, the nose twitched, the

eyes gave him a veiled and knowing look. "I asked you if you were dreaming—dreaming, *dreaming*." She shouted it in a high-pitched voice, and a bit of her spittle struck his cheek.

Ecclesiastical authority then, the straight back and the ungiving stare. "No, I was by no means dreaming. You interrupted me in my meditations."

She laughed. "So said the jay when they caught him sucking the yolk out of the robin's egg. I know your kind."

And then there are some few whom madness or the Devil put beyond the reach of priestly help. Such as these must be dealt with in harsh justice, even threatened with rejection until a time when a more gracious spirit enters into them. "You know nothing of me," he said. "I never saw you before."

"No? Not on a hot September afternoon in the arc between earth and heaven?"

"If you persist in talking madness—"

"Not over there across the isthmus? Not in the forest where trees breathe?"

He lost dominion over himself, could not keep from looking into the black, beady eyes. "Trees breathe?" he said.

"Yes, Father." She lifted a pair of bloated hands and held them in front of her. Slowly, at a pace he could not keep himself from remembering, she drew them together and apart, together and apart, together and apart. "Trees breathe." She spat it at him. "Just so."

How could she know? He was unmanned, transformed into a child, locked into the black room of the shut universe. There, through a knothole in the wall, an eye—half conspiring with him, half damning him—saw him more nakedly and more relentlessly than he had ever seen himself.

She stepped back a pace and nodded her topknot at him. "You see? Exactly as I thought," she said. "Oh, and what a heap of carded wool you have put over their eyes! Berthe has it that you are a carved saint, and the chatelaine says— But why should I tell you what she says? Go and find out for yourself."

110

He raised his right hand in a sign of warning.

She sneered and countersigned, drawing in the air in front of him a cross turned upside down. "And the fat Brother," she said, panting, "the tub of lard—he tells us you will lord it over us and rebuild the monastery and cleanse the nunnery and say which days are for feasting and who will go to bed with whom."

She was slavering in rage. If she reduced him to fear, it was with good reason. There was incalculable danger in the mound of white flesh: under the softness, hate coupled with a strong man's striking-power. "Listen, my daughter—"

"Oh, as to that . . ." She unnerved him further by stepping backward and down onto some level that lay behind the hedge and out of his sight. Now he could see only her little head, mocking him over the bare twigs, holding itself slantwise in lewd flirtatiousness. "Daughter, sister, mother, wife, whore—whatever you like, I am at your service. But there is one thing that you must understand: Lord it over us you will not, tainted as you are. I know what I know, and I will tell it in my own good time."

"What do you know?" He whispered it.

The head, too, disappeared. She was going down the cliff, toward the waters, and for an instant he thought that she might be some ancient horror come up at him out of the bottom of the sea. "That you have eaten devil's rye," she said retreating. "That you have done strange things with he's and she's. The marks of your doings are upon you. Who will listen to you babble about God?"

✠　　✠　　✠

The chatelaine hoped he would stay where he was: there was a great deal to be done, and his presence kept her from it. For three weeks, all her time, all her strength, all her thought had run into the business of tending him, and everything else had fallen into confusion. Yet when she was back in the common room she did not set her hand to anything. She paced the length of the chamber, thinking how the main meal must be ordered, how a cloth should be spread over the board to hide its nicks and scratches, how the rushes were giving off a sour smell and ought to be replaced. Then she sat down on the chair where the visitor had sat and fell to staring into the fire.

Adele came in with a long napkin and a cauldron of hot water. She made no move to help the old woman, only sat watching while the plates and goblets were immersed and the crumbs and spillings were wiped off the wood. How was it possible to be at the same time exhausted and restless? Every day now for three weeks she had been giving this poor soul a string of scanted orders in an urgent and inconsiderate voice; and today—though there was no excuse, since he was up and about—it would be the same.

"Adele—"

"Yes, my lady?"

"What do you think we should have to eat?"

"Fish? There are two excellent—"

"No, not fish. Alain is sick to death of fish."

"A stew?"

"I doubt Father Albrecht would have the stomach for that. Roast a goose, and skim off all the fat, and serve it with a light sauce—crumbs and herbs and vinegar will do."

"And won't you be needing something for later in the evening?"

For the council—yes, of course—but she did not want to think of that. Ottric walking in with his Berthe and his Liese—he could have listened to Alain, he could have left the women at home this one time. Anger and affronted pride at the threat to his authority, and he so uncompromising and stiff-necked that he called the merest courtesy obsequiousness—oh, she could foresee what sort of thing would go on here tonight. Nevertheless, custom called for a hospitable board. "A pudding—make a pudding and set out a dish of dried fruit. Yes, and cover this wretched wood with a tablecloth—I am ashamed of it." She could not ask for fresh rushes without offering to help. The sodden smell would have to be added to the rest of the occasion's miseries: she could not bend and sweep and strew—she was too tired.

112

"Why not go and lie down for a little, my lady? You look as if you had scarcely slept."

With wrinkles in my forehead and dark circles around my eyes. Every morning, older. How was it that Alain, unwilling to come away from his building or his reading, stayed up for hours longer than she and got out of bed as blithe as a boy and went off with Giraldus to the Fishing-Beach to look for stones? "What good would there be in that?" She deplored her voice: it had offered no thanks for the solicitude. "I would only lie there and think of all there is to do."

The old woman nodded and sighed and started for the kitchen-house with a pile of tin plates rattling in her hands.

Alone, she stared again at the feeble flames that licked the sooty back of the chimney. If the general clutter of her neglect were set to rights and the stranger no longer had any need of her, she supposed she would be able to settle into her daily round: it had been sufficient, at any rate, before he had come. . . .

She envisioned that life, the best of it, making a small safe music by jingling her keys. She peopled the place with the little company that had gathered there often in the evenings: Ottric and Berthe and Liese, Eustace and Giraldus and Jehanne. Winter gnawed with iron teeth at the edges of the room. Alain had to come away from his corner and kneel on the hearth to warm his hands. Chestnuts popped open in the hot ashes. Crabs and mussels, the lesser sweeter creatures of the sea, writhed on the embers as if they were still alive in their shells. Mead with honey, and the music of the lute outfacing the noise of wind-churned water. Oh, and her children had been with her there: Jehanne on one side, Liese on the other, and Eustace sitting on the floor with his round brown head on her knees. And their voices speaking out of a hundred such evenings:

Forthright voice of Ottric: "The Abbot Benno bore greater burdens than any of the Caesars."

Acid voice of Giraldus: "I want to hear no more of Him. When time was finished, His suffering was finished. This much good came out of the tidal wave: we do not have to torment ourselves any more over the five wounds in His body. The Termination took Him down from His cross."

Old mild voice of Berthe: "Count yourself blessed in a husband and forget about the children. An aged husband is a friend. A grown-up child is more likely an enemy."

Eager voice of Liese: "But what weight can be put on the words of the virgin Genevieve? Since she rejected the love of men and rejected it out of hand, I myself can only think she must have been mad."

Voice of Jehanne, broken by coughing: "There is no peace to be found in Scripture. I have read it, and I tell you, one thing cancels the other out. How, for instance, can you love your neighbor as yourself and refrain from committing adultery?"

Voice of Eustace: "Close your eyes and try to imagine a Termination. I myself cannot do it. I cannot imagine utter dark, utter cold, utter stillness, utter anything."

Voice of Alain: "Essence is primary and pure. Substance is essence that has somehow sickened. If God became man, then He must have sickened in the process. And the image in your sick mind of God made man is a thing twice sickened, twice removed."

Talk and more talk, and another round of mead, and reluctant departures. Somebody would always stay: perhaps Eustace, perhaps Giraldus, perhaps the orphaned Jehanne. And she herself, having provided bolsters and coverlets, went solitary to bed and fell into a light sleep eddied by questions until she heard Alain's footsteps on the circular stairs. So it had been, and so it would be again.

Or would it? She started out of her chair. It was as if all the rumors that flew like wasps these days around the island had come straight at her through the window. Not a day but somebody reported something else that the lay brother was supposed to have said: A new dispensation now that the century of isolation was over. Processions bringing holy water and relics across the isthmus, palmers coming on pilgrimages, the vacant waters crowded with ships. Villagers would swear fealty to either the abbot or the lord. What was fealty, and how was it sworn, and why should anybody get down on his knees to anybody else? Monks would live as brothers in a monastery, not under private roofs with women. A monk's child was a bastard—Liese? Eustace? Eustace's father had been a Brother of Saint Cyprian and a lord too—he had worn his cassock as well as his gold ring when they hung him up by the feet and burned him in the Square. Delvings, probings, stirring of an ancient earth that might well have monstrous seeds in it. Remember the Three Years of Blood, and let well enough alone. And how could Alain, with such a council impending, go off to the Fishing-Beach? How long had he been gone, and when would he come home?

In her agitation she went to his corner, and stopped a little short of it, reminding herself what harm she could do with her trailing sleeves. On another board laid across another pair of trestles was a model of the left tower of the lost Cathedral of Saint Cyprian, built of the blocks that he had fashioned with chisel and file out of stones brought back from his wanderings on the beach. The tower under construction, once it was finished, would be five hands high and two hands wide—no pegs, no binding-substance, stone exquisitely balanced upon stone. On the board beside it, the Book of the Virgin Genevieve lay open to a page headed "The Left Tower." A poor girl's ravings set down by a nameless monk just as they had come out of her mouth. She read without touching the page:

This tower was crenelated, and the stones I saw through the water were of a deep purplish brown such as is to be found in rich loam. And three courses of stones were smooth, and the fourth was carved with likenesses of shells and great fish and small fish and all the various creatures of the sea.

Yes, he was going to do that too. A little to the right of the book lay a stone on which he had been working with a needle. She picked it up, saw that the surface of it was incised with the shape of a cockle shell, and carefully put it back in its place.

And there was one course of the palest blue, such as is to be seen in the sky in April at dawn.

How long would it take him to find such a color? Did such a color even exist anywhere other than in the sky? But then, the purple-brown loam-color had also seemed to her impossible to find, and he had gotten enough of it to build two-thirds of the left tower.

Whether he would finish it was another matter. Often she had seen an apse, a nave, a chapel, an ambulatory taken down when it was almost at the point of completion. Something would be wrong that necessitated the razing: he had mismeasured the foundation or misinterpreted the book; some other piece of lore threw the word of the virgin Genevieve into doubt; sheer reason showed him that such-and-such an area could not hold an altar or accommodate a procession.

Tomorrow this too, for all she could tell, might be dismantled. And she had scarcely looked at it in her wild preoccupation with the sick man's needs, she had not given him what little he asked of her in this the most exalted part of his existence, had not found time to say "How beautiful!" She reached out and touched it, and drew back her hand. At the bottom was a thick layer of dust, and the thought of how long it had been standing there incomplete, how many nights he had labored over it, came upon her with dismay.

Better lie down a little—Adele had been right. She stepped away from it backward, wary of her hips and sleeves, turned, and started up the circular stairs. At the first window she stopped to see how it was with Father Albrecht out there alone. Not well, not well at all: Mechthilde the mad was leaning toward him over the hedge, and there was nothing to do but hope he would see at once that the unhappy wretch *was* mad. To rejoin the island to the rest of the world was an infinitely difficult business. She saw it as an almost futile effort to put together the pieces of a shattered crockery plate. All that was lacking to complete the day's exigencies was the interference of a woman out of her wits.

Yes, and Mechthilde had a way of saying what had the bitter savor of truth at the bottom of it. For instance, what she had said about Alain's quicksilver eyes. His eyes, of course, were grey, not silver. They did not slide about like drops of mercury; they only had their own way of eluding a direct and naked look. "You with your quicksilver eyes!" she had said behind his back when he refused to let her into the house after the mastiffs were dead.

Now, pausing in the upper hall between the two chambers— Father Albrecht's to her right, her own and Alain's to her left— she was undone by the remembrance of that death. Alain had laid the guilt of it on her shoulders. What kind of household was it where a madwoman could walk in and poison the meat in the dogs' trenchers, where the servants had so little fear of the mistress that they left the door unbarred? And the dogs walking round and round and panting and looking at her with filmed and bewildered eyes. Their tongues lolling, their heads stretched out—those heads that had always after supper come down heavy on her knees, wanting to be scratched and kissed.

That had been just before the coming of the strangers. Human suffering had suspended the grief over animal suffering. A speaking mouth had called out to her in the middle of the night, had kissed her hands. Somewhere within her was an awe, an unasking and all-giving reverence for the needs of naked agony; and here in this room—she had turned to her right without knowing it—for three weeks she had put that reverence to use.

Well, now it was over and done with. Wipe the rim of the metal goblet from which he drank at night. Gather up the squares of linen, the boxes of herbs, the pot of ointment, and put them into his emptied basin: he would not be needing them any more. Shake the bolster, tug hard at the sheet, erase the very shadow of his body from the bed.

Cross the hall and step into the other, the connubial chamber. Here, twenty years ago, such precious things as the lord of the island could call his own had been assembled to make her welcome. Crimson coverlet faded and changed in spots to a dull

117

purple. Carved chair from some drowned kingdom called Asturias. Little marble-topped table from another called Lombardy. Jars of quartz, and ancient glass for unguents, and the unguents dried. Jeweled boxes for powder, and the powder caked. Silver mirror turned on its face. All those weeks she had barely looked at herself, and never anointed or painted herself, and in those three weeks she had grown old. Only the scent still clung to her, and Father Albrecht did not like it. Would he stay on Saint Cyprian's long enough to learn how rare and blessed it was that anything sweet should come out of the all-obliterating sea?

Oh, bed . . . She drew up the coverlet and smoothed away the wrinkles. Some things would never change here, no matter what ships and processions brought holy water and relics. If, indeed, they were any different in that world which had come so disturbingly back into being. Perhaps there, too, women learned early what it was to be possessed and yet passed through as though they were shadows. Perhaps there, too, they waited for the all-revealing and all-reconciling word and heard only how a certain number of trees had been killed by blight or another old book had been unearthed in the scriptorium. Perhaps there, too, they looked up in hope and got only the random scrutiny of quicksilver eyes.

As she did now—he had come upstairs unheard and was standing on the threshold. He was happy, he had had good hunting, the leather bag at his waist was heavy with stones. There was sand on his long feet and in the folds of his cassock. The wind had stung his thin skin and disordered his hair. He stepped in, sat down on the edge of the bed, and emptied his finds over the spotted crimson cloth.

Three chunks the size of a fist, and several smaller pieces. She bent over to look, grateful that he should be offering her even this small share in what was singularly his own. But she was distracted by the smell of his hair: clean sweat and wet wind and sand.

"I think they will match, but I cannot be sure. Not until they are cleaned and dried," he said.

"Do you have others to match them with?"

"Of course—the ones I got yesterday from Giraldus."

He had shown those to her too, and in her hurt over the stranger's rejection of her ministrations she had forgotten. "Oh, yes, I remember now. But these seem somewhat greyer."

"They naturally would, laid out on this crimson."

"To be sure. If you think they will match, I am sure they will. You have a better eye for that than I do."

There was the usual pause, the usual groping after the next word. Surely somewhere there was a pair who never wondered what to say next, who filled up their silence with an embrace. He took one of the smaller pieces, wiped it on his sleeve, and held it up to the light. Strange that whether the rest of his day would be illuminated or muddied should depend on how much grey there was in a bit of stone.

"I stopped by to visit your nursling and found an empty bed," he said, examining the fragment. "Is he flown?"

"Only as far as the garden."

"What is he doing out there?"

"Meditating—praying. He wanted to be out in the air."

"He could get more of it than he needs in such weather." He picked up one of the larger chunks and polished it vigorously on the curve of the bolster. "Perhaps I had better go down and bring him in."

And suddenly she imagined herself striking his prize out of his grasp with the flat of her hand. Something had flared up, some unfathomable rage as nameless as that which had precipitated the Three Years of Blood. Because of the empty bed and the flown nursling? Because of the scent that had come to her out of his hair? Because of his slippery way of dealing with her? Only a fool could give credence to his excuse for escape: he was not taking himself off out of concern for the stranger's health; he wanted to go down and allay his itching anxiety over the color of his stones.

She had not so much as lifted a finger. She had only stood up straight to get her face out of the range of his look. But it was the

119

same now as it had been in the business of the mastiffs: her remorse for the thought was at least as great as it would have been for the deed—she felt it as a bruise on her heart.

"And you—what will you be doing for the rest of the day?" He was putting the grey-blue fragments back into the pouch.

"Oh, I suppose I will go out to the kitchen-house." She did not like her own voice, it was tainted by a kind of false childishness. "We will be needing something for the council, and poor Adele is so harried. I should never have asked her to make a pudding. I hope she has not started it, I would much rather make it myself."

☒　☒　☒

He must learn to eat, must cushion his bones with flesh against the shocks of this horrible island. If he could manage to eat no more than he had got down at this first nightmare meal, he would die of starvation.

The meat on the platter had been so gamy that he had not been able to forget its origin. Every mouthful identified itself as some part of a feathered creature murdered. The crisp of it, his favorite delicacy back in Cologne, had stuck to the roof of his mouth: seared skin of what had waddled and tried to fly.

Over the empty courteous talk of the lord and the chatelaine, he had kept remembering the talk of the madwoman in the garden. "So said the jay. . . . Devil's rye . . ." And, thinking of that, he could no longer use the bread as an antidote for the meat. "And done strange things with he's and she's. . . ." The gentian eyebeams of Brother Matthias streamed at him from the candle in the middle of the table, reduced the man-face and the woman-face to almost invisible ghosts, called up the probability that the sickness had done irreparable damage to his eyes.

His eyes—he had covertly closed first one, then the other to test them. They were not good, he could not really see. Try it again—but no, those two could see his face more clearly than he could see theirs, and would take his testing for an uncontrollable or obscene winking. He would have to wait until he was alone.

And, wretched as the day's doings in company had been, he was assailed by terror at the thought of isolation in the night. To be unable to sit down in candlelight and read himself into tranquillity before he slept . . .

"You have taken very little, Father," she said ruefully in her strange accent. "Well, perhaps later. There will be a pudding and dried fruit."

And now that she was gone—following the two ancient servants and the soiled plates and the stripped carcass of the fowl toward the kitchen-house—now that he was alone in the vast chamber with the one whom he did not know whether to call her husband or her paramour, the risk of being caught winking seemed of little consequence beside the fear of blindness. He sat in a carved chair on the hearth and covered first his right eye, then his left with his greasy fingertips.

Alain—he always heard the name as she said it, childishly pronounced, with a halt between the syllables—Alain was tending the fire. They were small sticks he was throwing onto it, sticks so light that they made no noise and barely added to the blaze. "You see how it is, Father: I keep forgetting," he said.

"What is it that you forget, my son?"

"That there is no need to be so niggardly. There are doubtless plenty of faggots in the world."

"Then fuel has been scarce here?" He did not desist from his testing, though his host had straightened up and was looking at him now. The yellow hair and the fringes of the fantastical cassock gave off frightening streamers of light.

"Scarce? Logs for the most part are not to be had—we burn only the dead trees. Driftwood, straw, rags past mending, handfuls of weeds and rushes—and if the winter is long and bitter enough, there is nothing left, we can only lie abed and shiver. Forgive me, I would not wish to intrude, but are you having some trouble with your eyes?"

Though it had been broached by the flat baritone for which he had no fondness, he was relieved to have it introduced. "Yes," he said, grimacing, "the sickness has left me with dimmed sight. It seemed to me while we sat at table that I was going blind."

Even in the dark and through the blur he saw the change that came upon the long thin-skinned face. The line of the lips was loosened, and the loosening was a lesser likeness of her "Ah . . .," a signal of quick compassion.

"And the worst of it," he went on, "is that I am afraid I will not be able to read, and only God knows what would become of me if I could not sit down at night in peace with a book. These thirty years, an hour of reading has been the end and reward of my day. If I cannot read, I do not see how I can sleep."

"Ah . . ." He had actually uttered it, though he could not, of course, give it her intimations or her grace. "I know how it is with you, it is the same with me. If I could not work with my little stones, I tell you I think I would go mad. But wait a bit, it is dark here, let me bring you a candle and a book and we will see."

He went to the table and picked up the guttering candle; he went to a black corner where candlelight lay briefly over what must have been a mirage—a purplish-brown tower some five handsbreadths high. Returning, he stood behind his guest, giving off the dry and reedy scent, and almost embraced him, holding the candle over his shoulder with one hand and, with the other, laying the opened book on his knees. "Now see if you can read. Perhaps you can, in a fair light," he said.

And so he could. Even the careless, hurried scrawl and the words that made no sense—he could make them out. Like a learning child, he read with his lips, first voicelessly, then aloud: "And the ambulatory was so broad that dolphins could swim up and down it seven abreast, and the pillars thereof were of—"

"Granite, Father. It is written very ill. It took me a long time to make it out."

". . . granite, blackish-green, with veinings the color of moss."

"Exactly so. You see, you can read it perfectly well."

"So I can." In his relief he took a deep breath. The scent was drawn in with it, and he sneezed upon the candle flame and put it out.

"May you meet a friend."

He knew it for a formula. Sneeze in Cologne, and you heard "God preserve you." Sneeze in Saint Cyprian's, and you heard "May you meet a friend." While the book and the lightless candle were being taken away, he considered an answer: "I have already met a friend who has given me back my trust in my sight." But he could not utter it, not without further thought, not to the chatelaine's paramour. And when he found heart and voice for it, the time was past: torches moved by the windows, knocks and voices sounded at the door.

Now he witnessed such behavior as would have been unthinkable at an ecclesiastical confrontation in Cologne. The room was suddenly hectic with voices and the light of torches: torches carried in by the visitors, torches brought from another room by the servants and the flustered chatelaine, torches passed from hand to hand and set at last into the rusted brackets on the raw stone walls. He rose, but nobody expected or even noticed that formality: apparently all of them were meeting friends. Alain was embracing a squat old woman whose face was eerily familiar—he could not imagine where he could have seen it before. Julianne stood with a sturdy girl on one side and a man in a rough fur cloak on the other; she was twining arms with them, pressing their hands against her breast. It was a while before her voice rose over the others, saying, "Daniel, take the abbot's cloak. And you, Ottric, come over with me to Father Albrecht."

The person she led to him through the noise and the flickering light was a grizzled peasant tricked out in some wild notion of churchly magnificence. The grey cassock fringed with scarlet, the scarlet cross embroidered on the chest, the big stubbed scarlet shoes—these would have been matters for laughter, along with the broad squashed nose, if it had not been for the grimness of the rest of the face. That face was resentful—no, affronted—no, hardened into a mold of implacable bitterness. The eyes under the rough grey eyebrows rejected him: there would be no winning them over with a show of learning or easy wit. He could only hold out his hand and say "Peace," and was the more undone when

123

the abbot, doubtless following some ancient usage, ignored the offered handclasp and closed blunt fingers on his forearm, well above the wrist. "Yes, Father," he said in a toneless bass, "it is to be hoped that you and I can remain at peace."

Chairs were brought up on either side of his chair, one for the little old woman and one for the abbot. As he let himself down, he asked himself what in his life could have prepared him for this. His sense of his own insufficiency grew as the others withdrew: Alain led the girl to the black corner where he had thought he saw a tower, and Julianne went off again to the kitchen-house with Daniel and Adele. Summon up the authority of a legate of the Holy Father, make amends for a blundering start. But before he could turn his head toward the abbot, the abbot's woman touched him lightly on the knee. "You know, Father," she said, her head tilted at him in mock reproach, "I really believe you have forgotten me."

"I do not quite—"

"Berthe, Father. I was the one who lent a hand with your nursing."

"Yes, of course." He saw the mild old face as it had come toward him at his call, a lock of soft grey hair plastered to the round brow. The fingers that were trespassing clerical dictates now by sending human touch through the folds of his cassock—they had tended him, he had grasped them in the exigency of his retchings. "I am deeply grateful for all your kindness," he said.

"No need of that, Father, my dear. You gave us no trouble. You were as easy to tend as a babe."

Swaddling bands, soiled napkins. And the Abbot of Saint Cyprian's sitting in archaic dignity, determined not to be the first to speak, staring straight ahead with stubborn eyes.

He cleared his throat and turned and said in a voice that seemed cold after the warmth of hers, "I hope the reverend Abbot understands how deeply I regret the long delay. If I had not been sick, I would, of course, have delivered my message to him at once. As it came about, I could only take heart in the knowledge that he would be visited by the lay brother Thaddeus."

"Of the lay brother Thaddeus, I have seen neither hide nor hair."

"If my—" he halted, wanting to say "servant" and bound by the Rule of Saint Benedict to use no such word, "if my companion has not yet stood on the doorstep, suing to see the reverend Abbot, it is only because he is sensible of his inferior rank, and in his humility did not wish to intrude."

"Humility?" said the old peasant. "His humility did not keep him from telling my brothers and my flock and my daughter what changes are to come about here, so that everybody knows what is possible and impossible, holy and unholy—everybody, that is, except myself."

The old woman patted his knee again and fetched up a sigh. By their three shadows lying long and distorted over the soiled rushes before him, he could see that she was slowly shaking her head. Peace, peace: the soft answer that turneth away wrath. . . . "Whatever the lay brother may have uttered in his ignorance," he said, "is not to be taken as proceeding from me or from the Bishop of Cologne or from the Holy Father in Rome, at whose instance I come. You and I, most reverend—" for an instant he did what he had known from this morning he was going to do: he forgot the crucial name and could recall it only by hearing the two syllables as they had dropped from the chatelaine's lips, "you and I, most reverend Ottric, will sit down like the brothers in Christ that we are and put our heads together." He faltered again, seeing by the shadow how far those two heads—his narrow aristocratic one and the other big one with the unkempt mane—were set apart. "If discrepancies in rule and dogma have occurred over a period of five-score years, that is only to be expected. We will find means of reconciling your ways and ours. Christian Hope, which Saint Paul recommends to us"—he saw her, crowned and smug and mawkish, on the new arras at the Chapter House— "assures me that any changes needed will be made amicably—"

"What changes does the emissary of the Holy Father have in mind?"

She had come back, carrying a dented bowl filled with dried

125

fruit. And while *that* monstrous infraction remained and could not be brought up—not now, not with the women here—what was worth speaking of, where could he start? "Your ritual and ours, for example—surely they can be brought into harmony. You are not Byzantines or ranters. We are twigs grown apart, perhaps, but twigs of the same branch."

"Sodom apples."

"What?"

"Your twig sprouts the grapes of the land of Canaan, and ours sprouts the apples of Sodom."

"But what are Sodom apples?"

"What was left on the boughs after the rain of fire—nothing under the skin but grit and ashes—"

"Ah, now, Father," said the old woman; and it was plain that she addressed him not as the one who carried the crook but as the begetter of her child.

"Hold your tongue, Berthe. This matter is between him and me. Let him tell me straight out—"

The growing ripples of their stress had gone to the edges of the room. Alain and the girl had started up with a lighted candle behind what had not been an illusion: there on the trestle there *was* a miniature purplish tower. And *she*, bending over the other board, arranging plates on the cloth—her long slight back had stiffened. "God knows, my brother Ottric, there is nothing I could wish for more than earnest talk without duplicity," he said. "Let us try to bend our minds to the question of the rituals—"

"What rituals? You should know from the start that we do very little here in the way of chanting and processions and waving censers and making shows and signs."

"Of course. I take that for granted. I see that you have only a little to give to God. You do not even have wood to keep you warm. I do not expect, nor would the Holy Father expect—"

"Whatever you expect, we are bound to fall short of it."

"Not at all, not at all. God does not ask for the impossible. What—really—is necessary in His sight? A fragment of bread, a goblet of water and a few drops of wine—these are enough to celebrate the Eucharist, and so long as the brotherhood and the congregation celebrate the Eucharist—"

The old man turned and looked straight at him through small, hard eyes. "And what is that?" he said.

"What is what?"

"What is this Eucharist?"

He could not answer at once, even though he saw that the Abbot of Saint Cyprian's asked in good faith. Beyond this wildly lighted room, he envisioned the dark island crouching in the water like a dumb fierce beast, and, around its haunches, further dark meaninglessness: the random heave of the sea. Yet surely the metal cup and the pure draft and the bread that had its own breathing soul . . . "You mock me, Brother Ottric," he said in his helplessness. "I cannot believe you could have forgotten the Eucharist."

"I tell you, nobody here has ever heard of your Eucharist!" He said it loudly, looking around, inviting the others to bear witness to their common ignorance. "Ask him"—he pointed at Alain. "Whatever there is to know, he knows, and he knows nothing about this Eucharist."

"Why should the reverend Abbot make a stumbling block of a word? You may know it by some other name—the Last Supper, the breaking of the Lord's bread—"

"We never heard of it. Have the goodness to tell us what it is. Who breaks this lord's bread?"

Well, then, he thought, like Saint Boniface among the Saxons, I am called to preach to barbarians; only, *he* had his fair countenance and his youth, and I am sour-faced and old. . . . He proceeded with the called-for discourse, stopping to translate Latin into the vernacular, going back to explain what should have been laid down beforehand, realizing at every step how ill he built, sensing their uneasiness. ". . . And the celebrant—that is, the monk or priest who acts before God for the whole congregation— he raises the chalice. . . ." They were not looking at him though

127

their heads were turned in his direction. ". . . And when the chalice is lifted and the Holy Spirit descends and becomes one with the wine in the cup . . ." No, not one of them could look him in the face.

Nor could he look directly at any of them, which was no great wonder, seeing that he had conjured up between himself and them a garish mosaic of Father Carolus lifting a bejeweled chalice and rolling up a pair of cheat's eyes. Go back to the roots, quote it word for word as it stood in the Gospels. But then, he never read the Gospels any more—the last time he had looked at the Passion according to Saint Mark, he had been assailed by a terrible fit of weeping and had walked about for days thereafter bewildered, holding the pit of his stomach because there was nothing there, because his whole body seemed to be floating around a core of emptiness. . . .

"And as they did eat, Jesus took the bread, and blessed it, and broke it, and gave it to them, and said: 'Take, eat, this is My body. . . .'" Matthew, Mark, Luke—which was it? "And He took the cup, and when He had given thanks He said unto them: 'This is My blood, which is shed for many. Verily I say unto you, I will drink no more of the fruit of the vine. . . . And from this day forth, whenever ye eat this bread and drink of this cup, this do in remembrance of Me.'"

"When was that?" said the chatelaine. She spoke to him as if there were no others in the room. "Was that just before he—"

She gave the pronoun no emphasis, and the one she called up with it wore no halo. Not the Son of God. Not ivory carved into angles of hieratic agony and fastened onto wrought silver. A man stripped naked and gasping out the last of it on a plain wooden cross.

"Yes," he said, as strangely careless as she was of the rest of them. "That was on the night before His crucifixion."

"And he asked us on the last night of his life to take bread and wine in remembrance of him?"

"Yes, in remembrance of Him. That is the origin of the Eucharist."

128

The Abbot Ottric pushed at some rushes with the stubbed toe of his scarlet shoe. "Then it is some sort of feast to commemorate Jesus?" he said.

"Yes, but the simplest of feasts. Nothing that will tax your poverty—"

"A ritual of some sort, with wine and bread?"

"With watered wine and little wafers—"

"Wafers?" He started out of his chair as if the word had scalded him. "Wafers! So *that* is your Eucharist?"

"By a wafer I mean, of course, whatever you have on hand to be sanctified. A bit of pressed bread would serve—"

"Yes, yes, I know. It was a wafer that the Abbot Benno ate when it floated up out of the water. Only there was nothing sanctified about it by the time he put it in his mouth. It was corrupt, foul, tainted—it drove him to madness and his death! As for him who tells us what to do in remembrance of him—think how kindly *he* remembered *us* in the time after the coming of Leviathan. Think how he remembered those who died of the flood and the fiery sickness, and the nuns driven mad by the biting of the rats, and the lordlings burned upside down in the Square, and Brother Galbart and his crushed head."

"But I am utterly in the dark about such matters. These are saints and martyrs of whom I have never heard before—"

"Saints and martyrs? They were Godforgotten wretches. Neither God nor the Son of God held one of them in memory in the fifty years after the Termination—"

"Termination? What termination? I do not understand."

"No, I see that. How could you understand? Here, come now, old woman, we must be on our way." He pulled her up by the elbow and turned her toward the door. "Whatever we say tonight will only confound confusion. If the emissary of the Holy Father sees fit to talk to me again, we can arrange a time and a place. But not now, not tonight. Only after you have read the Book."

Chapter III

*O*ctober, 98 A.T.: From the opposite shore, which all of us have taken to be uninhabited or the haunt of devils, came two monks this day, in cassocks, with two donkeys. . . .

To read it was to see it happen again, but at a great distance. He saw himself and Brother Thaddeus crossing the isthmus— very small and very clear—from an incalculable height, as he had seen the piles of building blocks laid out for the new town. But here there was no color, only the white of bone and the black of charcoal and all the somber greys between.

And, though Father Albrecht is sick even to death of the fiery sickness, Brother Thaddeus is of sound mind. . . .

If what he carries in his brainpan can rightfully be called a mind. . . . The day's second obligation had been distasteful to him when he wakened, and was downright intolerable to him now. "Once I have read through the chronicle"—so he had said in taking leave of Alain on the threshold of the monastery—"I will go and talk with my brother." Sit with *that* one, talking of those who had seen themselves for a hundred years as the world's trash, left lying about after the Termination, not worthy even to be swept away by the wrath of God?

And he says that we are the ones that are mad, that there has been no end to the world. . . .

He would have put it in just such terms. "Mad" was one of the words in his impoverished store, and he would not have thought twice before mouthing it, in his thick-hided complacency. The last entry in the book had been written with a spattering quill, every letter of it angular with rage:

He who held the crook was an unlearned peasant, and his flock was a stricken flock and stumbled often, for it walked in the dark. But let this be said of mine and me: no man murdered or raped or corrupted an innocent child, not in the period of my charge, which has been eighteen years.

Opening the smoke-stained door, he saw by the watery disc of the sun that it was not yet noon. The downward slope of the ground in front of him was so bleak and stubbled that he walked several paces before he realized he was walking over buried bones. A wooden cross almost covered by a thornbush stood aslant at the foot of a mound that could be taken only for a grave. "Benno, Abb't. R in P. 4."—there was room on the cross for that much and no more. Still, it was enough to bring him down on one knee before a relic not to be discredited even by Father Carolus's rolling eyes. "Benno, Abbot. Rest in Peace. The year 4 after the Termination." The thorn could not be the same, of course, would have to be an offshoot four or five generations removed from the parent bush. Out of some irrepressible need to grasp the intangible, he took hold of a twig and snapped it and found sap under the winter rind.

Other mounds were visible, provided they were looked for. Anselm, Joachim, Theobald, Galbart—dead ivy, twisted burdock, stripped stems of plantain and timothy. He could not attach these names to particular events: he had read too avidly and been assailed by too much. He kept bearing mindlessly to the right— "Bear right, and cross the bridge, and bear right again, and you will come to the village, where your lay brother is housed"—he kept bearing to the right between graves and stunted pines until it broke upon him that there was no need for him to bear in any direction. Why go in the year 98 A.T. to speak of the unutterable with a dullard? The day bore no legitimate date, had fallen out of the calendar of Christendom. And, being outside of time, it was as limitless as the foggy stretch of sky over his head. A small eternity, undivided by the little monkish lines of Tierce and Nones and Complines. . . . Since he had been directed to the right, he turned due left along the path by which he and Alain had come.

And now this island that had seemed so raw and tawdry not three hours ago was as subtle and varicolored as birchbark, though the mist-filtered light had scarcely changed. The wall of the monastery, seen at a distance, showed as rosy as polished shell under grey outcroppings of lichen and trails of dead vine. The castle of his hosts, set on the highest of four stony terraces, bloomed with vague iridescences. A curtain hung limp at a black window—had she come to that window to look at her new domain, a bride moist and warm and supple out of her marriage bed? He put down the mild stirring without too severely rebuking himself: in a time of healing, a man's returning vigor runs wherever it will.

Nobody about, and not because everybody had disappeared into the church. The drowning of Saint Cyprian's became a reality—like the Word made flesh—in the water that glinted at him as he walked: standing grey water visible between heaps of boulders and the trunks of small trees. That wan, unbelievable shimmer lay to his right. On his left, beginning sparsely and clustering more thickly as he went, were the ramshackle houses of the town. Sounds animal and human went up behind fences and shutters: bark of a dog, cackle of geese, a woman's voice singing what he took to be a lullaby, a man's voice shouting "Fish today. Fish yesterday. Fish tomorrow. Fish is not meat." Oddments of life laid out on the windowsills: a bone gnawed clean, a knife with a broken blade, a ring without a stone. Now the water had disappeared; there were houses on both sides of him; the path had become a cobbled street. A child called at him from a far window "God give you a good morning, holy Father" and other children took it up: "God give you" "holy Father" "a good morning" "a good morning"—grave at first, then hilarious, and at last not altogether acceptable, verging on raillery. He was glad to come upon a sudden openness, a rectangle walled on three sides with ancient masonry. It was paved with cobblestones and looked like a place of consequence, though there was nothing in it but the charred stumps of what had once been three enormous oaks. These, too—blackened by fire and moistened by fog—had a dark shimmer, a solemn gloss.

He went toward them, thinking one of them would serve as a seat: he had walked a good distance and stood in need of rest. But before he could commit what would have been a breach of propriety he saw that a young man knelt before the largest stump, touching it reverently—the ruined trees were plainly objects of veneration.

The monk—it was a young monk in a white cassock with no outrageous trimmings—stood up and bowed from the waist. He had a grace that no word could encompass except the unmanly and unsuitable word "beauty." So angels were painted against gold-leaf heavens, with cheeks that could afford to be sweetly rounded and skin that could afford to be delicately white because there was no longer any need to outface a man's challengers in a harsh world. He was beardless, shamefaced, apologetic for something—for an instant Father Albrecht entertained the wild speculation that he belonged to some secret cult that worshipped trees. But his "God give you a good morning, holy Father" came out in an innocent chorister's voice and carried no taint of pretense, no echo of the children's earlier effrontery.

"And you also, my son." He said it cordially. Though the boy's upper and lower eyelids were overfull and marred by marks of sickness or sleeplessness, the eyes themselves were frank and clear, of a deep greyish blue.

"You are Father Albrecht, come to us from Cologne?"

133

"Yes. And you?"

"Brother Eustace, of the Order of Saint Cyprian, and nephew to your host."

Here was a lordling, with the lordling's inbred skill for putting a stranger at ease. They strolled, they chatted, they talked of the castle and the fiery sickness and the fog, they walked all around the enclosure before they came again upon the three charred stumps. There Father Albrecht stopped, leaving a piece of courtly discourse unfinished, and asked, "But can you tell me what is the meaning of these?"

"*These?*" The grey-blue eyes stared at him appalled. The carefully tended hand—not yet quite formed and all the more vulnerable because of that—came down flat on top of the hacked wood. "These, Father, are the Burning-Trees."

"The burning trees?"

"That is to say, the trees from which the lords and the lordlings were suspended by their feet to be burned to death."

"Oh, yes, I—" He wished he had worn his cowl and could withdraw into its darkness. He blushed at his own ineptitude, he winced at his own cruelty, and did not know which of them he regretted more: it was as if he had closed his fingers on a flayed hand.

"My own father, together with the others. So I come here now and again—"

"To pray?"

But that had also been an inexcusable blunder. The young man lifted one shoulder in a strained shrug and arranged his face in a pained smile. "No, not precisely, Father. To . . . But then, it is hard to explain, and why should I burden you with it, sick as you have been and new as you are to this place?"

"But I know of it, I was reading the chronicle this very morning. Only, I never thought . . ." What he had never thought, what filled him with excessive and unseemly excitement, was that anything alive could be directly rooted in that past. "You yourself—did you see it?" he asked, knowing that his tongue ran on against his better judgment, and shocked to find that he wished these living eyes *had* seen it and could see it now, just as it had been, in ineffaceable recollection.

"No, I did not see it. I was in my mother's womb, and she saw it. They tell me she bore me before her time and died during the birth."

He made no answer. Moved beyond speech at the thought of a quickened womb convulsed by the past into delivering the present, he started blindly and gracelessly for the far end of the hideously sanctified place. It was the young monk who mended matters, coming up beside him in courteous fashion.

"They were magnificent trees, Father," he said. "There are no others anything like them on Saint Cyprian's. But afterward they were scarcely a pleasure to us, as you can understand. The grass, too—there was grass here, with a few flowers—they cobbled it over because the women could never get it out of their heads that the grass was flourishing on blood. Enormous trees—it took days to hack through the trunks with axes. Still green at the tops, too—it was a pity to cut them down. But, quite aside from the fact that nobody could bear to look at them, the fire had damaged the roots. Alain assures me that they never could have lived."

None of the others whom he met as he walked through the barren elevated stretches beyond the town—not the gaunt women nor the girls in faded smocks nor the laborers carrying their tools in leather bags—could exorcise the image of the lordling or the echoes of the wounding and shattering exchange they two had shared in the Square. Whatever the lordling had set in motion could not be stopped; indeed he had no will to stop it. On every side there were monuments, and whenever he came upon one of them he stood still and was aware that he was exhausting himself in some dark inner labor: he was forging links, making chains, trying to get the present fast bound to the past.

High up where the land narrowed between heaving sea water and the standing water locked into the great basin, he saw a flat sand-colored stone. There was a knee-high fence of woven rushes around it, a kind of dried garland with some of the rush heads still intact. Words had been scratched into the porous surface of the rock, and he drew near and read: "This is the seat of the virgin Genevieve." Yes, he thought, the one who rejected men and yearned after the glory of Saint Cyprian's, and saw it only once in the slanted rays of an autumn sun.

He walked to the inner edge of the rim of the basin and stared down at the smooth expanse, a veritable lake, its boundaries lost in brownish mist. Today if she had sat there looking, she would have seen nothing. . . . He drew back, partly because he was repelled by the leaden dullness some thirty feet below him, and partly because he was sure he was being stared at: he felt the shock of eyebeams converging on the back of his head. Turning, he saw her for an instant: mortally sick, hollow of cheek and chest, her collarbones bluish white. Before she dissolved back into the fog out of which he had fashioned her, she looked at him and then past him with Alain's elusive eyes.

And higher still, near a pile of beams that gave off the dank smell of drenched wood, he came upon another memorial, also garlanded. This time it was half of a tree that had been split lengthwise, lying solitary on a stretch of sand. Its legend had been burned by a brand into the pale and stringy wood: "Here fell Brother Galbart, slain in the year 75 A.T." A round head—how was it he could remember that?—a round head shattered by a block of masonry and pouring out its brains and blood. And the hands that he saw reaching under it, cradling it and lifting it up, were the veined hands of the chatelaine.

In his brooding he had wandered into thickening fog and sounds of lapping water. The Fishing-Beach, so named in the chronicle. He knew it by what little he could make out through the mist: damp sand strewn with mussel shells and starfish, black nets piled in heaps or trailing away toward the sea. He looked to his left into whiteness that sometimes thinned out enough to reveal boulders, or stretches of sand so wet that they shone like silver mirrors, or the shifting wash of the tide. And then he was not quite certain of his own senses, for a gap in the fog showed him land where there should have been only water: mud-colored cliffs furzed over with brush and leafless trees. A dizziness more of the mind than of the body came over him, made him fearful of walking on with muffled eyes. He stood up to the ankles in sand and waited until another rift in the milky film showed him the same image: he was looking across narrow water at the opposite shore.

That was the edge of the world he had come from—he knew it with dismay. Somewhere far back behind those cliffs he had lived out close to fifty years, and all those years were gone and nothing, and all that life was an emptiness, no more to be grasped and held in mind than confused doings in some half-forgotten dream.

And, since there was no substance to his life and no measure for his days, he fell into doubt that he himself had any being. It seemed to him that his pulse had stopped: he would not have been surprised to hear that he was dead. At this thought his heart set up such a commotion within him—wild, senseless motions like the struggles of a beached fish—that he gasped and clutched at his chest. Not dead, only forced to feel in his body his own mortality. Not gone from the world, only left in the world utterly alone. He walked again, to escape, to distract himself, through the cold drag of the sand, over crunching skeletons of creatures of the sea. He walked on, coughing to steady the lawless struggle under his ribs, until a voice said, "Take care, holy Father, the net is tangled around your feet."

A woman sitting on a boulder, with a fisherman's net jerked out of her hands, sliding out of her lap and down over her gaunt knees—he saw only that before he was horrified by what was tripping him. Black meshes, slimy, hideously festooned with fish scales, barnacles, and sodden weeds. He tried to step out of it, and could not, and had to stoop over and pull it away with his hands. Wiping his palms on the skirt of his cassock, he straightened and saw that she had gotten down from her boulder and was standing some twenty paces off, her back to the water. Between himself and her, on a low slab of rock, burned a blue and feeble fire.

"God be with you, my daughter."

She stood in need of Him, plainly. She looked like a drowned thing. Her black hair streamed straight to her elbows, her body was so thin that it did not fill her sheepskin coat by half, her legs were bony and streaked with waterweed. On first glance, he had taken her for a hag, but now he saw that, haggard as she was, she could not have passed her twenty-fifth year. There was something disquieting about the mold of her face. The brow was unwrinkled, the eyes were alert, the nose was narrow and somewhat aquiline. It was the mouth that marred the rest: in her, too, the jaw was set forward, though not so markedly as in Brother Matthias. Her nether lip hung down a little and showed that the lower teeth, white and canine, stood slightly in front of the upper ones. She made what he took to be a primeval form of a curtsy, keeping her legs together and bending both knees.

"A miserable day for you to be sitting out here in the cold."

"The nets need mending, and I am the one who mends them," she said.

He took a few steps forward and came to a stop, close enough to feel the warmth of her fire on his shins. And all at once he knew he was famished: he had put nothing into his mouth since dawn, and the moisture around him carried the smell of broiling fish. The source of the savor lay before him on an iron griddle in the flames: cleaned, strewn with herbs, the flakes beginning to fall away from the bone.

"That is a fine fish you have there, daughter."

She opened her mouth as if to speak and closed it without utterance, her hand over the protruding lower lip, like a child who has barely managed to keep trouble shut in. She had meant—he sensed it—to offer him a share, and had thought better of it. But why? There was enough to nourish three hungry men, and she was plainly here alone.

138

"It smells as tempting as it looks—"

"If the holy Father is hungry—"

"I am very hungry—"

"Then he will find a rock not far from here, and I will bring him the fish as soon as it is done, and he can eat."

He stared at her in wonderment.

"I thought the holy Father would rather eat by himself," she said, and bent and took hold of the dropped net, and held it over the lower part of her body, from her waist to her feet.

There was something in that gesture—abject and pitiably useless since the wide meshes could not cover her at all—which made him the more determined to stay and eat with her. Not because Christ had broken bread with publicans and sinners—that was a random monkish remembrance, a bit of historical data which had nothing to do with the fog, his solitude, his unsteady pulse, his lost life and the gone years. Only because his vacant spirit, seizing on her futile effort to cover herself as his empty stomach had seized on the savor of the fish, let him know he was still among the living, body and soul. "Leave your net awhile," he said in gratefulness, "and we will eat together here by your fire."

She curtsied again and set about the preparations: found two wooden trenchers and two knives in a heap of nets, and set two places, at first so far apart that talk would have been impossible, and then, thinking better of it, somewhat closer together. "That way," she said, "we will both get the warmth of the fire." The trenchers were scored and greasy, and scales from former meals stuck to the knives; but he was so absorbed in watching her that he barely felt distaste. There was in her bearing a kind of tight cheerfulness, the angular alacrity of those who cut the meat for others and go away afterward to gnaw the bones. Was she a serving-woman? Her lowered head, her careful steps, her elbows held close to her sides—these made it hard to imagine her sitting on a hearth with a husband or quieting an unruly brood.

"Do you come here often, daughter?"

139

"Yes, Father. The nets are old and frail—they take constant mending." She was stamping down the sand to make level ground for their trenchers.

"And while you are here, who looks after your little ones?"

"I have no little ones." He could not see her face; it was hidden behind the strings of her hair. "Eight I had, and all of them died at birth—no, nine." She stopped her stamping. "Whichever of the nine I forgot, may he forgive me. So many"—she went and stared at the fish—"after a while there is no keeping them separate one from the other. Remember one, and you remember them all."

"God rest their souls."

"It is kind of you to say so, Father. Since they came dead out of the womb, I suppose that was what they wanted—rest. But now the fish is cooked, and if you will sit and give me your trencher, I will serve you. Eat as much as you crave, it will not hurt you, even after the sickness." She went and came again, and he saw by the red streaks on her offering hand that she had thrust it into the fire without a thought. "And here's bread, too." She dragged an ill-shaped loaf out of a pocket in her sheepskin vest, and broke it, and laid the larger half of it before him. "Take, eat, it can only do you good."

Her hastening, broken speech was so like the irregular sound of water that, when she ceased, the lapping and swishing moved in and made a negligible thing of silence. Both of them ate avidly, giving themselves over to taste and smell; when her fingers were greasy, she rubbed them on her vest.

"An excellent fish, daughter," he said after long stillness.

"I did not bring it in. We have Giraldus to thank for it. He was out here fishing this morning, and he left me the best of the haul—he is very good to me. You will come to know him, Father—he is often at the castle. I, too, go up there now and again. I sew for the chatelaine."

"I take it you are skillful with the needle."

"Oh, yes." For the first time, she smiled. "That—" she pointed to the line of intricate stitchery laid over the rent in his cassock,

140

"that is my work. Julianne—the chatelaine—she asked me to mend it carefully, and I did my best."

"Your best is very good indeed."

"Oh, that is only mending. Sometime when I am at the castle I will come to you, if I may, and show you my embroidery. I know all kinds of stitches and make all kinds of things. Just now I am stitching a sea mew on a blue square like the sky—a little piece, no bigger than my hand. There is a stitch that comes out like feathers—but it is nothing, and I run on too much. I made a fish for Giraldus—"

"Is Giraldus a fisherman?"

"No, Father." She suppressed a spasm of laughter. "He is a Brother of Saint Cyprian. I should, of course, have said 'Brother Giraldus.' He fishes only for the pleasure of it—the more monstrous the creatures he takes in, the greater the delight. Last week he fell afoul of your lay brother. He sorted through a whole catch, and whatever crazy creatures he could find—sword-tailed, ratchet-finned, wry-mouthed, pop-eyed—he laid them out on the sand and invited Brother Thaddeus to come and see."

"Why did he do that?"

"Ah, it will sound worse than it is—he meant no harm. It was only that the good lay brother had been saying God made everything according to a high order and a fixed purpose, and Giraldus asked him what order and purpose he could find in such monstrosities."

Now it was he who had to suppress a laugh, and she took on the old rigidity, chastened by the severity that his effort had brought into his look. "I suppose you have been exploring the island, Father," she said more soberly. "You went to the monastery, I know—Liese told me so when I saw her this morning. Have you seen the seat of the virgin Genevieve?"

"Yes, and Brother Galbart's tree, not far from here."

"Then there is not much more for you to see, except—"she fell silent, put up her hand again to stop herself, and, seeing his waiting look, went on, "except the nunnery."

"Is the nunnery far off?"

141

"No, not really. Over beyond the dunes."

"Can you leave your nets long enough to take me there?"

"As to leaving the nets—I always have to leave them, they are never finished."

He waited while she got up and scraped the trenchers and gathered up the fishbones and put them into her pocket—he could not understand why, since not one morsel remained.

"But," she said after a long pause that he had deliberately refrained from breaking, "the holy Father has been up since dawn and walked a great distance and must be very tired."

"Thanks to you, I am warm and well-fed and rested. And I could not imagine going there in better company."

She gave him a disconsolate smile that reduced his last sentence to exactly what it was: a charitable exaggeration. "Then go with me, if that is what you wish," she said.

But to go with her was impossible. He might walk behind her or ahead of her, but she saw to it that they did not walk side by side, not for more than a step or two. She was so elusive in her hastenings and laggings that he almost took her by the arm, almost forgot the monkish admonition that to touch a woman is to beckon to the Devil. Once, when they heard voices approaching in the fog, she went so far ahead of him that he would have been lost without her footprints in the sand.

"My daughter—" he said, catching up.

"Yes, Father?"

Having nothing else to say, he said, "It occurs to me that I do not even know your name."

"Jehanne." It came out as if it had been wrestled from her. "There is the nunnery—you can see it—you can easily find your way now alone. Perhaps I—"

"Come the rest of the way, my daughter Jehanne. I would not even know where to find the portal or how to let myself in."

She sighed and went slack. Her face, with the peculiar set of the lower teeth, now that the vitality had gone out of it, made him think of a skull. Her steps were slow and her chin came down almost to her chest. Once she stopped to pick up the shell of a starfish and add it to the other queer things in her pocket.

"What will you do with the fishbones? Make needles of them?" he said.

"Oh, no." She answered him lifelessly. "On the way back to the village, I will drop them into the great basin."

"Why?"

She laughed, but the laugh was flat and strained. "Because of a fancy of Liese's. Liese—the Abbot Ottric's daughter—she thinks we owe the fish we eat a holy burial, close to Saint Cyprian's. The abbot does not hold with that, but he says we may do it if we like, since it hurts nobody, and it eases our minds."

He had no time to ponder the strangeness of that. He was walking on masonry that seemed to have cropped up suddenly under his feet—weatherworn blocks of dark stone. A wall had toppled here, but not far off there was an unharmed edifice, circular and startlingly solid, grounded as it was on sand and set against the shifting of the sea.

"Is that the nunnery, daughter?"

"All that is left of it—the round chapel. Here where we are standing now, there used to be cells and a refectory, but the earthquake brought most of it down, and some time afterward the rest of it fell in. There were walks and gardens here, so I have heard. But the sea came closer, and now, as you see, everything but the round chapel is covered up with the sand."

"Does nobody use the chapel?"

"Who would use it—and what for?" Her face was further marred by a kind of fretfulness. "It is three generations since there has been any sisterhood. The place is cursed with rats. Nobody comes here—almost nobody at all."

Since she would not move, he shrugged at the Devil and took her by the elbow. And was hard put to it not to draw away his hand at once: so Elspeth's arm had felt—skin and bones. But she—the welder's daughter—had been his fellow at least in the number of her years; and this one—the light-headedness, the stammering of his heart returned—this one was young enough

143

to have been his child. She sighed again and drew away from him and walked on ahead, going toward the big wooden portal with her shoulders down and her head bent. "The rats and the foulness and the dirt—" She did not turn. She laid her hand to the iron ring and pulled the door wide with a grating wrench. "Well, there it is, you can see it for yourself."

What they stepped into was an ambulatory that ran round the full circle of the chapel. It was a dusky place, with the masonry on one side of them and thickly set columns on the other, and such scant light as they had coming down from narrow slits of windows some twenty feet above their heads. Sand had crept in and lay over the flagstones; damp had crept in and given a cold sheen to the columns and the wall. The columns were slenderly fashioned from marble of a color to be found only in the rosy linings of certain shells. "But this is a beautiful ambulatory," he said. "I have never seen its like. Take me into the chapel itself."

She complied, but in a devious fashion. Instead of leading him through the main entrance at the back, she conducted him along the ambulatory and took him out at the front, so that his back was turned to what would be the glories of any chapel: altar and pulpit, choir stall and carven screen and crucifix. Yet even this view—a circular emptiness broken into three aisles by two more rows of the rosy columns, and relieved in the middle by a great hanging cluster of metal lanterns that seemed to be floating on the accumulated fog—even this view was exquisite. Nothing here had been cracked by a wrenching of the earth or eaten at by fire. Everything here could be resurrected, called forth out of its winding-sheet of grime. It was she now who held him by the elbow, urging him from the front of the chapel toward the back, pointing out this and that: jewels in the lanterns, elusive patterns carved into the flagstones, acanthus on the capitals, snakes and crouching lions on the pediments. "And now you know how to find it, Father, and you can come back another day," she said in a voice that was at once false and desperate, her nether lip trembling from her effort to sustain an affected smile.

144

He put her gently from him, and turned, and looked down the broad central aisle. Blessed Jesus, what glories in the transept! Tiers of murked splendor rising one above the other. A screen of pierced stone so light and intricate that the Bishop of Cologne would have marveled at its delicacy. Choir stalls carved with the overlapping wings of angels or of griffins. A pulpit springing from a column, like a great flower opened on a stalk. And, between a massive altar and a richly painted ceiling—he started as if he had seen a face without a nose. Between the altar and the ceiling, where the crucifix would hang, there was a bulging blackness, a hovering dark sack. Somebody had muffled the crucifix in fold on fold of filthy cloth.

"Who did that?"

"I cannot say—"

Not "I do not know." Not a forthright "I will not tell." Only "I cannot say"—the slippery talk of a wily woman. The falseness of her voice, the realization that nothing here could be known or depended upon was enough to make him yearn for the old ordered world—even for so wretched a specimen of it as Brother Thaddeus. "You did it," he said.

"I? Surely, Father, you can see for yourself that I could never do it." She went on ahead of him, into the fog, down the sand-covered steps. "I must part company with you here, unless you are going to the village," she said.

And, much as he wished to go to his lay brother in the village, he wished even more to be rid of her. He bade her a curt good afternoon and followed their footprints back to the Fishing-Beach and his own from there toward the castle, trying not to remember her hand reaching him the heaped trencher, or her talk, or the net spread over the lower part of her body. Whatever he remembered of her made him feel like a fool.

✠　　✠　　✠

Yesterday the ramshackle town, today the squalid village. The mud huts huddled to no purpose around what had once been

145

the centers of life: a good third of the bricks had fallen out of the back of the beehive oven, and the mill was useless—its wheel broken, its stones mossed over, its spring run dry. Even the poorest villages where he and the lay brother had stopped on their westward journey made a sharper division between within and without. Here, in spite of the raw weather, the doors stood open. Children sat on heaps of straw and played with things that should have been kept indoors—filthy leather cushions, battered pans; and geese and goats and conies kept disappearing over thresholds or into unmended gaps in walls.

The house of Andraeus and Angela was not hard to find, nor much when he found it. Somewhere between the mill and the oven he stopped to stare at two pigs, not knowing at first that they *were* pigs, with their razor backs and their lean dugs and their almost fleshless ribs—he had never seen an emaciated pig before. While he tried to fit them into their species, a girl of ten or eleven slid down off a haystack and came and tugged at his cassock and pointed at one of the wretched dwellings. "There, there—there is where he is," she said. Though she was fleshy enough, with full ruddy cheeks, he found her as disquieting as the pigs. It was her eyes, he thought, walking toward the stoop— they were narrow and bright and shaped like crescents above the raised chapped rounds of her cheeks. It was the cunning and the boldness in her look that had made him think she must be a dwarf, could not possibly be a child.

Brother Thaddeus sat alone at a table in semidarkness, his face laid pensively against his hand. How many days had he sat so, waiting? Many, many—his eyes kindled as he half started up from his stool. But, seeing no eagerness in the look of his superior, he sank back down and said nothing but "Peace."

"Peace, Brother." Father Albrecht seated himself on the near side of the table, which smelled of accumulated anointings with pease porridge and mead. "I am sorry to find you in such a miserable hut—"

"Oh, I chose to live in this hut, Father. I could have stayed in

146

the town—they offered me a place. But I am better off where I am, here with my own."

"—and glad to find you in good health."

"*My* health was never anything to worry about. What news I got from the castle—and they *did* send news to me now and again—made any trouble I might have seem very small. My hands were healed in a fortnight—I was hardly aware of them, my mind was on you. You see"—he held his fleshy palms across the board, "not a scratch, nothing."

A long look would probably have gratified him, might even have made up for the fact that there had been too little at the start—no handclasp, no embrace. But Father Albrecht could not fix his eyes upon the proffered hands, could only look away from them at a grey goose that had wandered in through the open doorway. "Why do you leave it standing ajar?" he said.

"Are you cold, Father? I could close it, but there are still some scraps of the morning meal for the beasts to eat off the floor, and the house-dame will soon be back. Still, if there is any danger to your feeble health—"

"My health is not feeble. I am completely well."

"Thanks be to God for that! When they told me you were mending—but it is over, there is no need to speak of it." He paused to hiss the goose back over the threshold. "So much needs doing here," he said with a sigh. "Until now I have held myself to such little things as teaching them their prayers. In that at least I have been diligent and reaped a modest harvest. Everybody in the village has his paternoster in Latin by heart."

"A very good beginning."

"It is kind of you to say so, but I have been sorely confused. They know, and they do not know—a person cannot tell where to start. For instance: they seemed aware that the Feast of the Nativity is drawing on, but what it means and why they should rejoice in it, they did not know in the least. There is no proper chapel, and I thought we might put a candle in every hut, but the wax turns out to be short and candles are out of the question.

So they come here on certain evenings to carve little things out of wood—sheep, oxen, a cradle. We sing carols while we work, though I am afraid they go about their caroling somewhat too lustily."

"Better lustily than languidly." His own voice was languid, and he made no effort to enliven it. "You are going about it just as the Holy Father Gregory advised Boniface to do back in the old days: Give them spiritual gifts before you impose deprivations upon them; draw them into Christian joy through the rituals and the feasts; do not disturb their lives too much—"

"But, Father"—he fell to grinding his knuckles into his cheek— "I am horrified at how much we will have to disturb their lives if we are to snatch them out of the Devil's clutch. Are they monks? Ask them, and they tell you they are of the Brotherhood of a certain Saint Cyprian—not that I have ever heard of such a saint."

"There *was* such a saint. He was Bishop of Carthage, and a martyr."

"Well, there you have another example of my ignorance. But if he was a bishop and a martyr, what in the name of Jesus would he think?"

"Think about what, Brother?"

"About the goings-on in this place. Imagine what it has been like for me to live under the same roof with a married monk and his wife and daughter. He wears a cassock, but he lives in a house with women. Only last night when I mentioned my feet were cold, she got up in her shift to bring me another coverlet—"

His mouth tightened and he tapped the greasy board. "There are other pressing matters for us to address ourselves to."

"Yes, but the large matters—such things as doctrine—I thought best to leave to you, I did not wish to overstep myself. And I cannot think what else—"

"Well, there is the mill, for example. It is completely out of use. And the oven is scarcely better—a good third of the back wall will have to be replaced."

"My father is in error about my skills," he said. "I am a woodsman. I am not a mason or a miller. I cannot build a brick wall or call a clogged millspring up out of the ground. Because a monk can tell a true ancient manuscript from a false one, that does not mean he can lay out a plan for a cathedral. But then, to the wellborn, I suppose all these things are lumped together—it is all serfs' business, common and the same."

Father Albrecht stared at the poor muddied world beyond the doorway and thought that the reproof was just. Scores had tilled his father's holdings on the other side of the Rhine; hundreds had worked the abbey lands around Cologne; and of that multitude he could recall perhaps a dozen faces, no more. As to what particular labors these nameless ones had been put to, how they used the tools that callused their hands and bowed their backs, he had never troubled to ask himself. "I am sorry to have given you offense, Brother," he said, trying to meet the small pained eyes. "I only meant that there were many ways to give them gifts—worldly gifts as well as spiritual ones. And we must give them much before we take from them what they think they rightfully possess."

"Well, it is the true spirit of Christ that moves you to be patient and charitable with them. You too have been living these three months in the house with a married host. I trust they gave you a chamber to yourself over there, a place where you did not have to waken to grunting and panting—"

This time it was not he who caused the lay brother to break off—the doorway was suddenly filled up with the ample, blowsy body of a woman. "Now, praise be to God our Father in Heaven!" she said at the top of her voice. "Two visitors at once, and both of them here at the bidding of our Holy Father in Rome! I never thought I would live to see it, and on a day when I have not even wiped the table top."

"This is Angela, our daughter in the Lord," said Brother Thaddeus with emphasis, plainly making the point that she *was* their daughter in the Lord, even if she was loud and fat, and wore her

149

hair in a slovenly topknot, and did not care that her dress was so tight it could not properly cover her breasts.

"God be with you, my daughter Angela."

"And with you, holy Father." Her small eyes, dark in the damp and freckled whiteness of her face, took him in only for an instant, turned at once to the lay brother for reassurance and direction.

"Here you have a good woman, Father. Three months now she has cooked and washed and scrubbed for me."

"Never speak of it, it was nothing. A bit more bacon in the pot, another shift in the cauldron. And you cannot know—" though she addressed the superior, her look and her fatuousness were for the lay brother, "you cannot know how he has raised us up. Give him a few more weeks, and he will make saints and scholars of us all."

"I am sure he has done—" He stopped just short of belittling it with a condescending "whatever he could." But even if he had uttered it, she would not have noticed. She was going on at such a pace in her blurred accent that he could not follow, could only make out disconnected scraps and patches of what she said: She and her husband prayed together with this good Brother morning, noon, and night. *Pater noster qui est in coelis.* This good Brother knew everything except how long it would take for the ships to come with leather for shoes, yes, and oranges and raisins. It was a pity that a grown woman like Isabelle was stupid enough to carve her sheep the same size as her oxen, but God would doubtless take it kindly, as it was meant. Her daughter Peppi— only wait until the holy Father heard her daughter Peppi. Ten years old, and learned in Latin! She went to the door and bawled the child's name.

He could not bring himself to look at Brother Thaddeus. A conspiratorial exchange of glances behind her back would not have been seemly: she had cooked and scrubbed for him, she was one of "his own." And then again he might be feeling more complacency than shame: his ease with this poor woman and his ability to put her at her ease were gifts of a minor kind. The two of them would have been merry and holy enough together—so Father Albrecht thought—if he had not broken in upon their good-fellowship.

Her Peppi came in at last—the crescent-eyed girl who had pointed him toward the hut—and dismissed the formalities of introduction with a shrug. She knew him, she said, meaning of course that she had spoken to him outside, but managing in some overfamiliar way to imply that she knew him well and what she knew of him was not unequivocally good.

"Recite the Pater Noster for the holy Father, duckling."

"What for?"

"What for? Why, to show how well you learned it from our good Brother Thaddeus." She had seated herself on the other side of the table to listen, so close to the lay brother that her arm—big and bare and freckled—lay over his cassock sleeve.

"*Pater noster qui est in coelis. . . .*" She had it by heart from beginning to end, but it was painful to listen. Her eyes mocked and teased and flirted above the fatty protuberances of her cheeks. Her body, too forward for her age—he saw the mounds that were sprouting under her shirt——jiggled up and down as if there was some seductive rhythm in the prayer that impelled her to move. He reproached himself for such thoughts—it was probably only that she needed to pass her water—but when she came to the end, he could not offer her appropriate praise. "Well done," he said, and knew he did not improve it much by adding, "very well done indeed." She stuck out her pursed lips and looked to Brother Thaddeus for better words.

He satisfied her wholly with a smile and a nod. She turned on her heel and would have taken herself off if her mother had not said, "Wait a little, the Devil is not after you. Say that other prayer for the holy Father."

"Yes," said Brother Thaddeus, "they have a little prayer here that nobody knows the meaning of."

"*You* say it." She pointed in her bold way at Angela. "You know it as well as I do."

"She cannot say it as well as you," said the lay brother. "When

151

you say it, it sounds more like Latin. Come, say it for Father Albrecht. He is very learned, no doubt he can make it out."

What she uttered, with bad grace, was so garbled as to be incomprehensible. It was a quatrain in barbarized Latin, without rhyme, though the first and third lines were identical. He asked her to repeat it, and she did so impatiently, and while he listened he saw the shape of the great grey quince tree in his father's orchard, not yielding itself to him completely, swathed away from him in swirls of snow. Snow . . . The chiming word that the child was uttering was the Latin for "snow." It was not a prayer —it was a carol for the Feast of the Nativity. Fortunatus had written it, a lamb among the wolfish Thuringians. Serfs had sung it under his father's window on the holy Eve. He and his brother had sung it together on the hearth. His mother had sung it while she polished the apples laid by at harvest to decorate the Yuletide board. What God had come to on Saint Cyprian's and in his own dried heart!

"Do you know it, Father?" asked Brother Thaddeus.

"Yes, you were right, it is in Latin."

"Blessed Jesus, he is even more learned than you!" the woman said.

"Translate it for us, Father."

The girl ran off over the threshold, and he was glad of it: she would have seen the stagnant water standing in his eyes. He said her verse flatly, afraid his voice would break:

> It is the time of snow,
>> Sparkling with earnest light.
> It is the time of snow,
>> The day when Christ was born.

When he told them it was more than five hundred years old, Angela struck her cheek in affected astonishment. He got up, in a desperate hurry to go away. A snowflake miraculously preserved on a lost island for half a millennium—he could not let them touch it.

He carried it with him out of the hut, over the stoop and the muddy stretch where the children quarreled and the geese squawked, past the oven and the ruined mill. When he was utterly alone with it in a stretch of stubble, he said it aloud to himself as it had been in the beginning, in pure Latin. Said it and felt nothing: could not see the quince tree, the apples, his mother's face. Could not fetch up out of the clogged darkness of his chest anything more than a short, sharp sigh.

✠   ✠   ✠

The wintry afternoon was far gone when the chatelaine walked into the common room. Automatically she counted the three places set out on the board and realized she had forgotten to mention to Adele that a fourth would be sitting down with them tonight.

Why she had forgotten she could not tell. The issuing of the invitation had been the only memorable incident in a whole day's emptiness. Her bird—as her husband called their guest in dry mockery of her finished tending and her useless care—her bird had flown soon after dawn. Was always flying now. Went to the village to work among the peasants with the lay brother. Went to the monastery to do she had no idea what. Went to the Square and sat on the roots of one of the Burning-Trees and spoke to all comers, probably about God. And came back at about this hour when the red of sunset touched the threadbare napkins and dented plates. Sat at table with them and talked of things as little known to her as the walled cities and undrowned cathedrals beyond the forest on the other side. Said how it was stupid for people to grind grain in querns: the millwheel could be mended, the millstream could be made to gush up out of the ground. As to the oven—there was no miracle about making bricks. Bricks could be made out of mud and—look at his shoes!—there was no shortage of mud on Saint Cyprian's.

It was a way of living, this looking forward to his coming back. Much had been sacrificed for the little that there was to

153

be gotten out of it: Ottric in his anger did not come; the younger ones waited until the guest had gone up to his own chamber for the night—they came very late when they came at all. What was left to her was so tenuous she wondered how she could put such value on it: only an hour of talk in which she never had more than a negligible part. There were his questions, to which her husband gave the exhaustive, circumstantial replies of one who forces himself out of courtesy to help too much. "How many souls would you say there are here?" Father Albrecht would ask; and a pigeon could be stripped to its skeleton before the host would arrive at the estimate of five hundred and fifty. But meanwhile she did not suffer so much from the strange aloofness that comes upon those who have been too close when the closeness is gone. She would look at his head, at the new silky hair that had grown over his tonsure, and wonder why he had not shaved himself back into monkishness. She could touch his hand in passing him a dish, and sit there saying to herself, "It was so, it happened, I really touched his hand."

What had she come to? Could a grown woman set store by such insubstantial things? Moving the three set places to make room for the fourth, she shrugged: it seemed she could. Could prefer an hour with Father Albrecht to a long evening with Giraldus. Could want unspoken awareness of her presence more than she wanted outrageous spoken gallantries, though both led to nothing. Could—she pulled her hand away from the plate and stepped back from the table because the old woman had come in.

"Is there something the matter with the way I set it, my lady?"

"No, no, not at all. It is only that there will be a fourth—I invited Giraldus—"

Adele fetched up a sigh of aggravation.

"I could not help it. He invited himself this morning when he came back from the Fishing-Beach with Alain. It is so long since he sat down with us, and he said either I had grown niggardly with the food or I did not love him any more."

"My lady may bid anybody she pleases to table," the servant

said. "I only wish she would think to tell me what she has done. See how it is: I have roasted a little side of pork—" She held her old hands apart to show the disheartening size of it. "And Brother Giraldus eats for two."

"I will eat next to nothing—I am not hungry."

"There is some fish left over from yesterday—it will serve for me and Daniel."

"Give the fish to me. I can say I am sick."

"Who would think of such a thing? It would only make a bad matter worse," she said, and took herself off with another sigh.

It *was* a bad matter, and the scant cut of meat was not the worst of it, she thought, going to a chair near the window and picking up her lute. She drew her fingers lightly and at random across the strings, and pondered the threats of trouble: Father Albrecht's piety—tepid and reasonable to date—might be goaded to fierceness by Giraldus's vaunting impiety. Whatever there was between her and the stranger was too precarious to outlast one sally that implied there was more between her and the fantastical Brother than there had been or ever would be. The loose fabric of the evening's peace could be torn by a dozen possibilities— suppose, for instance, somebody should mention the swathed crucifix. . . .

Alain came in and said, "Why are you strumming?"

She laid the lute back on the floor, and the hollow sound it made in slipping from her hand seemed a kind of defiance. He hated all unnecessary sound. It was as if his soul were forever listening for indefinable music—let a dog bark, and he was robbed of the almost-audible voice of God.

"Play, if you like. I have no objection to your *playing*."

"If I wanted to play, I would play. It so happens I have no taste for it."

Daniel brought in another plate, goblet, napkin. How withered and sexless he was, she thought, suppressing a shudder. Did he and the old woman lie back-to-back at night to avoid the acrid smell of outworn flesh, the foetid smell of sick breath? And the best she could hope for was to live to be as old as that and share just such a bed. . . . Now that she thought of it, she really was too sick to eat—sick of her mortality. And her husband stood by the hearth in cold blitheness and a clean white cassock, untouched by her thought. "We may have more here than we bargained for, with the two of them face to face," she said to ruin his peace.

"Well, so it is. Everything must be measured in terms of Father Albrecht."

She thrust out her foot in anger and jolted another sound from the belly of the lute. *Her* Father Albrecht was what he meant. Father Albrecht had robbed him of this piece of priceless silence and that piece of absorbing talk, and she was responsible for Father Albrecht, had conjured him through the forest, over the isthmus, into the castle, where he offered little, took much, spoiled all that had once been her distraction and her husband's delight.

"*I* did not bring him."

"I never said you did."

"*You* offered him shelter—"

"You are shouting, and somebody is at the door."

He? Could he have heard? No, it was blessedly only Giraldus. He came in, wearing the cassock with the inverted yellow cross. That, too, she had forgotten about; and once her heart had contracted at the sight of it she somehow regained her steadiness. Luckily the flurry of compliments could be tossed in a jongleur's display before the fourth came. "You have made a bad exchange, my lady. But why should I tell you? You will see for yourself soon enough. *He* is not a man to lie awake at night wishing himself a spoon in your hand or a plum in your mouth, not he. He may brush against you on the stairs and fire up. But he has his holiness, he has his God. He says a couple of paternosters and goes to sleep."

She encouraged it. Better it should glitter early and fall early away. Besides, she had not utterly lost her pleasure in it—she felt as if she were in a different body whenever Giraldus was in the room: she laughed, she stretched, her voice grew warmer, she walked and gestured with a new suppleness. And the arrival of Father Albrecht was not the crisis she had thought it would be. He knew Brother Giraldus—so he graciously said—by sight if not by name. The side of pork was somewhat larger than Adele had indicated in her aggravation. There was a dish of yesterday's fish chopped in with hard-boiled eggs and made savory with vinegar. There was talk of the craft of brick-making, and they ate what there was to eat with good appetites and in the quiet of a courtly truce.

The first charged moment came when they rose and shook the crumbs from their laps, and it came not from either of the two whom she thought of wryly as rivals in wanting what neither of them would touch. Her husband was the one who was out of sorts, annoyed with her now—ironically—because she had asked Giraldus to supper. If Giraldus had not been there, he could have stepped away from finished obligations, could have gone with a good conscience to the real business of his life, the model of Saint Cyprian's. As it was, since Giraldus was staying, Father Albrecht did not go. The corner where the tower stood remained in shadow, and Alain made plain that he did not mean to spend an evening talking of how to make bricks for ovens and mash for hogs. "Do you never grow tired of it, Father? I should think you would leave it to your lay brother," he said.

"To tell the truth, my lord, I have been tempted to leave it to my lay brother." He had seated himself in a high-backed chair on the hearth, and the rest had taken their places around him. Giraldus on a leather cushion on the floor, mocking subordination by overdoing it. Alain in the other high-backed chair, from which he could gaze directly into the far corner where he wished himself. She on a stool at an angle that allowed her to look over Giraldus's head and past her husband at the face of which she could never see enough. "Though my lay brother is a woodsman and has neither the mason's nor the peasant's skill, there is none of it that he could not do better than I."

"Then why not leave it to him?" her husband asked. "Do you feel yourself bound to bodily labor by your Rule?"

"No, no, not that. It is true I am so bound, as you say. But until this instant, I never thought of it. It is because there is something about them all—townsmen and monks and peasants—something I cannot make out, and it is only by being with them—so I think—that I will ever be able to understand."

She did not listen to the desultory exchanges that followed. She was wishing she might go with him into the village where bricks were being made, into the forest where acorns were being gathered in buckets and mashed up in bins. She wished she could see him with the sleeves of his cassock rolled up—she had not seen his arms bare since he had held them out to her in his delirium. Dry arms with stringy sinews, old before his time—why was it that *his* age carried for her no taint of disgust? And hers for him? Covertly, as if she had an itch of the skin, she ran her fingers over her throat. There were better throats in the village, full-fleshed and moist. . . . They were speaking of despair—he and her husband. Three or four times she had heard the word "despair."

It seemed—she learned it by more attentive listening—that the thing he could not understand was the general despondency. He had brought them tidings that the world had not been swallowed up at the time of the coming of Leviathan, that thousands of their fellows lived in towns and villages and walled cities, tilling the earth, raising up cathedrals, draining swamps, walking in holy processions, kindling hearth fires and candles against the night; and they still despaired. He had told them that the eye of God had not turned away from them, that they and all living creatures were still encompassed in the clear sight of God; and yet they despaired. He had said over and over that the Church of God waited like a yearning mother to receive them. That ships would come. That here, too, hymns would be sung and Masses said. Then—he looked straight at her, probably because he had met with inaccessibility in Alain and something worse in Giraldus—

he looked straight at her and asked, as if she could answer, "Why this despair?"

"I do not know, Father."

"But you feel it yourself, my daughter?"

Yes, with the line of my breasts subtly changing, with the flesh of my throat drying, with whatever I had of beauty wearing away and whatever I had of hope remembered only to make a fool of me—"Yes, Father, I feel it myself."

"If you can bring yourselves to listen to me a little longer," he said, not now to her alone, raising his voice and trying to draw the others in, "I will tell you what we say of despair over across the isthmus. It is written in the preachings of Saint Paul and set down over and over by all the Fathers who wrote in a time of darkness as harsh as yours: despair is sin. To close your eyes against the pure light of hope, to set your teeth against the bread of comfort, to thrust out your hand and push aside the chalice and spill the wine into which He has infused His blood—that is sin."

"If you will excuse a little plain speaking, Father," Giraldus said, "it is not their despair that surprises me—it is your notion that any of us, knowing what we know and living as we do, could be without despair." Because he was affronted, he arranged his sallow and mobile face in an ingratiating smile. Because he was about to attack, he lolled against the stool on which she sat and stretched himself out in indolent ease.

"How so, Brother?"

"I begin to think you have come to us out of a world made up of children—"

"If that is the case"—she watched him flush and struggle with his anger at the jibing tone, and she was moved by the quiet manliness of his self-mastery—"then it is all to the good. Christ himself preached that, unless we become as little children—"

"Little children," said the fantastical monk slowly, with the threadbare patience of one who lessons a child, "little children live on dreams. If you abuse them, they comfort themselves with visions of reconciliation or revenge. If you shut them up in closets, they think of being birds or kings. Little children, Father, get themselves through the common calamities of their lives by imagining a glorious life to come."

"They stand in need of such dreams. You will admit that it is a merciful God who teaches them to dream in their helplessness."

"Oh, I do not grudge them their dreams, Father. I only wonder what comes over Him that He should allow them to suffer in the first place—but that is not the drift of my argument. I only wanted to say: If your countrymen on the other side get through their lives without despair, it is only because they go on dreaming like children far past the proper time—they spin out the dreams of childhood until old age and sickness and the imminence of death close in and make it impossible for them to go on deceiving themselves."

"Yet there have been saints, Brother—I could name you a score of them—who have never experienced what you seem to consider the inescapable wretchedness. It is not unusual on our side of the isthmus to live cheerfully to a venerable old age and go tranquilly into the final sleep."

"I believe you, Father. I can believe there are such saints over there if you tell me so, but I trust you do not hope to find the likes of them on Saint Cyprian's. There is nobody here so saintly, so childish—so foolish, if I may say it—as to carry the delusions of childhood to the edge of the grave. Since the day of the tidal wave, all of us were born old, all of us sucked in the knowledge of doom with our mother's milk. Every one of us—but perhaps I go too far in saying 'every one.' There *was* the virgin Genevieve" —he lifted his long face and looked slyly at Alain—"but in my opinion she was mad."

"Ah," she said, trying to find the right voice for banter, and tapping him lightly on the head, "must you set us all at odds?"

Her husband gave her the look that meant he needed no help of hers. "Whoever thinks the woman who left us *that* was mad," he said, gesturing toward the corner where the glory of Saint Cyprian's was being refashioned out of varicolored stones, "is mad himself."

160

Father Albrecht disregarded the little exchange. Not, she knew, because it pained him to see her tap Brother Giraldus on the head, or to see that head settling more firmly against her thigh. Only because flirtatiousness and the virgin Genevieve and marital coldness were not the drift of *his* argument. "I grant you, Brother," he said, "that life looks bleak enough if you consider it as a thing in itself. God's pattern, God's order, God's intent—these can be clear to us only if we predicate a life to come."

"Do *you* predicate a life to come, Father?"

"I hope so, Brother. If I do not, then everything I have known —everything from the Christmas apple I ate in my childhood to the talk among us here—is petty and futile and adds up to nothing. I fervently hope I believe in a life to come."

"I, of course, do not believe in it, and no amount of theological discourse will convince me. I cannot feel what it would be like to live in that other life you speak of, and what I do not feel I—"

"But how could you feel it, shut up as you are in the flesh? Whatever we know in the body, we know by means of the body. What is ineffable and immaterial—as such a life would surely be—we cannot see or touch. The one thing we know of the life beyond the flesh is that we cannot know it while we are flesh, inasmuch as it is pure spirit, beyond bodily comprehension."

"If that is the case," said Giraldus in a voice at once wry and mournful, "then this ineffable being into whom I will eventually be transformed concerns me less than my most remote and unamiable kinsman. I mean, Father: he is not connected with me, he will not be myself. The self that I am here and now—nothing of it, so far as I can understand, could be preserved in pure spirit. If I were to go looking for myself on the other side of my death, I would expect to find less of me in pure spirit than in the little heap of bones left in my grave."

She stared down at her own hand, laid flat on the carved arm of the chair. The stiffness of its position—the palm down, the fingers extended—expressed her dilemma. Her hand could not exorcise mortality by stroking the hair on Giraldus's crown, could not reach out in mortal terror to her husband who did not want it, could not appeal to the visitor—since he would not look at it—in mortal love. She stared through the drying skin, through the flesh, through the tendons, and saw with a horror that made her bite her lip the jointed bones of her fingers lying in the earth. Rigid, still wanting. My need, she thought, will live beyond me in my skeleton. . . .

She came out of her terror to find the room still there. Hearth fire, candle flame, their shadows enormous and distorted on the rough masonry of the wall. And he speaking earnestly to the mocker, he saying that despair was not inevitable, that it comes upon those—and only those—who carry a heavier load of sin and guilt than any man was intended to bear.

"Ah, yes, that guilt," said Giraldus. "There you have another gift from your merciful God. One Augustine—we have him minus a page or two over in the scriptorium—he says we took our taint from Adam and Eve. But he was a sane man—very reasonable, really—he saw for himself that the matter could not be left at that, it needed further proof. If we want to convince ourselves that we are born sinners—so he wrote, I can show you the paragraph—we only need witness the depravity of the newly born. An infant comes into the world with a howl of rage, and thinks thereafter of nothing but itself. If it had teeth in its mouth, it would surely devour the unoffending breast."

"And you think there is no truth in that? I myself remember a little white scar on my mother's nipple—I thought of it the first time I read that passage in Saint Augustine. That scar was a sign for my salvation, even though the breast that carried it had been in the grave for years. With my milk teeth I assaulted—"

"And who gave you the teeth, Father?"

"You think to drive me into a corner like a rat." But he said it without anger, in a courtly manner, as if the two of them were playing at chess. "God gave me the teeth. All things are given by God. But if I grant you that much, I have not thereby made a punishing demon of my Father and Creator. If *He* gave me the teeth, He also gave me the recollection of the scar and the grace

162

to say 'O Lord, I am heartily sorry'—the grace to ease my heart through repentance and tears."

How little, she thought, he knows of women! Barren as she was, she had often envied others at their suckling, had watched in excited wonderment while the infant mouth went at the swollen breast as ardently as the bee goes at the flower. What was a scar compared to the drawing out of the fullness, the sweet sleepy shuddering? Ah . . . She yawned at the thought of it, and the yawn was out of place. Giraldus had taken away the weight of his head, had pulled himself up to speak his scorn of repentance and tears. And Father Albrecht was saying that the children of God on Saint Cyprian's could rid themselves of their despair by opening their hearts in confession.

"God knows," he said slowly, as if he were groping after words, "I am the worst of confessors. I utterly lack whatever spiritual gifts the good confessor should possess. And yet it seems to me as we talk together here that the most valuable thing I can offer you is to hear your confessions."

"What is it like—what do you do—I mean, what do we do when you hear our confessions?" She had not meant to speak. Her thought had unaccountably gotten itself uttered, and the others looked at her—Giraldus in surprise, her husband in disapproval, Father Albrecht in courteous attentiveness.

"Am I to understand, daughter, that you do not know the rite?"

"No, she does not know it," said Alain. "Nobody here knows of it. Nobody here has ever confessed."

"It is a simple matter. The penitent comes to the confessor wherever he may be—in Cologne he usually sat in his cell, but any place is acceptable, even a rocky ledge. The penitent comes to the confessor, and stops some five paces short of him, and covers his face with his hands. Having so done, he—that is, the penitent, says, 'Holy Father, I have sinned and I am heartily sorry,' and thereafter it is only a matter of saying aloud what sins have been committed or contemplated."

163

But why five paces off? She had learned circumspection, she had not uttered the question. She saw herself kneeling in any suitable place at a five-pace distance, cut off even from the sight of him, her nostrils drawing in the dry scent of her own hands. Holy Father, I have sinned and I am heartily sorry. I desire to drag you back into the fiery sickness. I desire to lay my tending hands on you in more than tending. I desire you to desire me. I desire to have of you a bruise on my thigh, a scar on my nipple, a sweet shuddering, an utter undoing, a measureless night of entwined sleep. . . .

". . . And, had the wisdom of the Church not departed out of Saint Cyprian's," he was saying, "all of you would regularly have been making your confessions."

"To whom would we have been making them?" her husband asked with the cool curiosity of an antiquarian.

"To the Abbot Ottric, more likely than not. Now that you bring it up, it would doubtless be better for the time being that we shared the duties of the confessor, he and I. He will hear some of you, and I will hear the rest."

What others will you hear? she thought. Liese, with those full hips and that luxuriant hair—will you look down at her while she tells you what she dreamed about Eustace? And Jehanne, and the peasant girls out of the fields, their armpits aromatic with their sweat, and the wives of the lordlings who try to outboast each other with the number of times their husbands waken them in one night?

"Quite aside from the holy Father's low opinion of his gifts as a confessor," said Giraldus, getting up, "I will not encroach upon his time. I have no intention of opening up my tainted soul to anybody else."

"Nor I, either," said Alain, "but not for his reasons. Only because whatever there is in me that could be released in confession could not be put into words nor comprehended by any man I have yet laid eyes upon."

"And you, my daughter?" He asked it in nothing more than

Christian kindness, and she loathed his Christian kindness, with its remoteness and its impotence.

"Oh, I will confess, Father. We are, as you say, in despair, and any remedy is worth the trying."

"Then you will come to me when your heart is so moved?"

"When my heart is so moved, I will certainly come. But I will come to the Abbot Ottric," she said.

☒   ☒   ☒

He had come with Alain as far as the Fishing-Beach and went on from there to the nunnery by himself. For days now he had been thinking that sometime soon he would have to stand and meet the assembled folk of Saint Cyprian's face to face. It was to be taken for granted that he would stand in a pulpit raised above the congregation, nor was there any other pulpit to be had but the grimed and carved glory under the crucifix wrapped in rags. To take Christ out of His swathings, to scrub away the accumulated dirt of a century—these were the first tasks. And, since Brother Thaddeus was occupied with gathering in the last of the acorns before the first fall of snow, he had decided to begin alone.

A preposterous decision—he knew it as soon as he was relieved of the company of his host. The pieces of threadbare cloth in the leather pouch slung over his shoulder and the buckets for sea water that he carried one in each hand were laughable, considering the enormity of what there was to do. For the first time, he asked himself how long he would be about it, and said aloud to the desolation of sand: "Years." As he walked through watery sunlight, he thought without self-accusation, with nothing more than mild surprise, that he had caught something more debilitating than the fiery sickness here on the island. His mind, like all the other minds, had been infected with some disease that distorted time.

Time here was infinite and infinitely burdensome. A single day stretched out to what seemed like a year in the living of it. Yet, once lived it contracted into what would have been an hour back in Cologne, except that no hour lived in the past had ever left behind it the heaviness, the density, the weight on the heart. Such hateful time was to be dissipated or destroyed. Destroy the afternoon getting the dirt off a stretch of flagstone, the panel of a screen, a patch of wall. Dissipate the evening either in the common room or in his own chamber, it made no difference which. Perhaps destruction would prove more bearable than dissipation—there was the nunnery, he would soon find out.

This time he entered by the main portal. She who had fed him fish and befooled him was not there to make futile attempts at distracting him from what hung high between altar and ceiling. It was horrible in its blackness and its blurred, wind-stirred outlines; it looked like an enormous bat with spread wings. That is the first thing to see to, he thought, setting the buckets on the floor. With *that* hovering over me, how can I put my mind on anything else? But pulling away the swathings would be no simple matter. Even if he stood on the altar—unthinkable sacrilege—the pierced feet would be out of his reach. Put something on top of the altar then. But what? Holy oddments suitable to his purpose came to his attention out of shadow: a reading desk that had once held a Bible, a ceremonial chair, a big chest carved all over with thorns and crosses—a reliquary, no doubt. He imagined himself dragging the chest, heaving it up. Suppose he could get it onto the altar—could he safely stand on top of it, would the wood crack and splinter, would he find himself standing up to the thighs in bones of deer, bones of dogs?

"A good afternoon to you, holy Father."

It was a familiar voice that sounded behind him. He turned and saw the lordling whom he had met beside the Burning-Trees. God could not have sent him a more welcome emissary. Weak sun lighted up the smooth brown hair and the beardless face and the grey-blue eyes with the purplish marks around them. The young man had come to help him, carried two more buckets, had a veritable halter of twisted rags around his neck.

166

"My uncle, your host, told me yesterday that you would be laboring here, and I thought you well might need another pair of hands."

"I do indeed."

The look, less blithe than it had been in the Square, left him and lifted itself to the crucifix. "Let me tell you first, Father, that I am very sorry about that," he said.

Then it was these unformed childish hands that had done the swathing. The excuse came along with the realization—no room for anger to crowd in between. Born in a year of suffering, nourished on suffering, so thin-skinned that every nerve was vulnerable to the assault of suffering—this Eustace had not been able to look at a suffering God. . . . He waited, and the young monk went on, raising his empty buckets in a gesture of helplessness. "Only, the holy Father must not think that it was done to provoke or distress him. The nature of the crucifix is such that— But it must be uncovered, and when it is uncovered, I believe my Father will understand."

"When you came—and it was very gracious of you to come— I was thinking that the rags must be taken away at once. Only I do not quite see how I can get up there—"

"Not you, Father. I am the one to do it. Something on top of the altar—but what? There is that chest—it would seem to be sturdy enough."

Whereupon, he went about the business with an alacrity that showed how eager he was to do his penance. He wanted no assistance: he dragged the reliquary in a moving cloud of dust to the foot of the altar, tried to lift it, could not get it off the ground, opened the lid, and said, unbelievably, "I think it will be lighter if we take out whatever is inside."

"Take out what is inside?"

"I think we must. What is it? Let me see. Something wrapped up in—why, look—in some very rich embroidered cloth—"

"Do not touch it!"

"Why not, Father?"

"Those are bones—holy bones—martyr's bones."

"Truly? How—strange!" He drew his hand away and wiped his fingers on his cassock. And mastered almost at once the quivering of his face. "Then, as you say, they must not be disturbed, we will leave them as they are. Only, I am afraid I will need your help to get it up."

"Certainly, my son."

They could have used a third in the heaving. The weight of the bones was the least of it: the wood itself was a handsbreadth in thickness, and there was a brazen lining, to say nothing of brazen hinges and locks. Yet there was pleasure in their laboring together and in their mutual bodily slightness; and they shared that pleasure, looking through dust and falling flakes of wood into each other's eyes. When their twin strivings had gotten the reliquary into place on the altar, they nodded at each other in admiration and complacency, and the young monk's face was enlivened by a cordial smile.

"The moment I catch my breath, I will climb up, Father."

"There is no hurry. Give yourself time."

Yet his eagerness for penance and absolution was such that he stepped out of his sandals and pulled himself up before his panting had subsided. His feet, standing on the ancient bruising design of thorns and crosses, were like his hands: blunt and white and strangely moving in their childishness.

By standing on tiptoe, with the grace of a dancer, he was able to catch at the first rag. It came loose in a spiraling scroll and showed part of what had been covered: a wooden crucifix, very old, the polychrome so worn away that there were only transparent streaks of white on the loincloth, only pinkish dabs where there should have been blood. Two more tugs, two more rags falling slowly, heavy with dampness, and he saw the crucifix in its entirety.

It was of a sculptors' vintage that he had no taste for. Whenever he saw such a one and was called upon to praise it, he could voice nothing but reverence for its age. The head—it was a flaw he deplored in human beings and found intolerable in images—

168

the heavy hanging head was out of all proportion to the spindly body. The big face, crudely hacked out, was made up all of downward lines. The mouth hung open and was pulled earthward at the corners, not by torment but by what seemed like a need to vomit. The eyes on either side of the gross Roman nose were bits of onyx, cold stones, devoid of hope, resignation, and pity, glaring at extinction with nothing but disgust.

"My son, I can well see—"

"Oh, yes," said the young man, stepping down as far as the altar. "I was sure you would see how it was the moment you laid eyes on it." He surveyed the vista in front of him with a cool and charming curiosity. "What a net of chains and lanterns and jewels can be seen from up here—you must come up and look." Getting a chill silence that was perhaps unjust—he surely did not realize that an altar should not be desecrated an instant longer than necessary by a pair of bare young feet—he jumped to the floor. "He did it because he could not endure the sight of it," he said, shaking dirt and splinters from the skirt of his cassock. "I am sure he meant no harm."

"He?"

"Why, yes, Father. Surely you did not think that I—"

"What he?"

"Giraldus. My uncle's boon companion and familiar spirit—"

Yes, and your aunt's, too. Lolling against her in firelight, resting his head on the flesh of her thigh. Mocking, condescending, expatiating as if he were the only man whose mind had gone down through the warrens of the earth and seen how little is left in a grave. . . . "*He* talks of childishness! What could be more childish than that?" He pointed at the heap of rags lying limp on the floor. "What an inane, puerile way for a grown man to deal with suffering—hide it away, muffle it up—"

"Ah . . ." It had some of *her* intonation but none of her compassion. "Now I have told what I never should have let out. And I only named him because I was certain my Father would understand."

"I understand well enough. Your Brother Giraldus does not

169

tax my understanding. His mind is shallow and vulgar, like the minds of errant clerks who believe themselves inordinately clever because they cast dice on the altar and invent obscenities to sing while others chant the hymns."

Eustace bent down, gathered up the rags, and began to roll the longest one of them over his hand. "No, Father, truly, his reason is not as simple as that. It is very complicated—so complicated that I cannot explain or even remember it. All I remember is that it has something to do with time. And if I may say so—" he lifted a chorister's face so open and blameless that it gave him the right to say anything—"if I may say so, whatever anger my Father feels where Giraldus is concerned should not fall on me. I had nothing to do with wrapping up the crucifix, and I was eager to unwrap it, as I am eager to do anything else my Father may ask of me."

Whatever strain there was between them was quickly drained off. By the time they had brought in four buckets of sea water and chosen the column closest to the pulpit as the proper starting point, their good-fellowship was renewed. They had not been long on their knees, rubbing away at the carved base, before it was clear that the young monk could not be in company without conversation, and much preferred to do his conversing face to face. Without stinting his labor in the least, he kept thrusting his head past the curve of rosy stone; and his look would have been more welcome if his elder had not been ashamed of his own awkwardness. Twice he skinned his knuckles. Once he dropped a sopping rag into spattering filth. The water was bitingly cold and his hands did not seem to be his own. "I make a very sorry show of myself at such work," he said at last. "I have lost my skill—if, indeed, I ever had any. I have done nothing of this kind since I was your age and a novice at my Chapter House."

"I would be happy to do all of it myself, Father. We could pull up that big chair, and you could sit close and bear me company."

"As I conjecture, it will take both of us a good six months to finish."

"Oh, we will not have to work alone. Others will come."

"Besides, I am obliged to do whatever bodily labor comes to hand—that is required by my Rule."

"I am immensely curious about that Rule of yours. Would it be improper for me to ask you what it was like—the way you lived in your Chapter House over on the other side?"

"Not improper in the least." But there was no fervor in his voice, and his face, vaguely reflected in the emerging brightness of the stone, showed some of the sickly drooping lines he had found unbecoming to the unmuffled face of the Son of God. "At this season of the year, the day would begin some three hours before sunrise, with what we call the Service of the Night. Turn out of bed by torchlight—" He had so little heart for it that he could not trouble to shape it into sentences. "Go to the chapel with the rest of the Brothers, just as you are, without washing or eating or drinking. Sing a hymn, hear three readings from the Gospel, say a prayer or two in unison. Sing another hymn, recite a psalm. Then, still on an empty stomach, back to your cell for reading and meditation. Then another service—Lauds—when the light begins to break. Then three more hours of bodily labor or copying or studying—still empty, still hungry. Then the main meal, of two dishes at this time of year—probably a porridge of lentils and a serving of fish or fowl—those, and bread, and one goblet of wine. Thereafter . . ." He was weary at the thought of the unvarying round, and his voice trailed off in his weariness.

"Thereafter?" said Eustace, thrusting his brown head past the column.

"Well, we are at Nones, and Nones is the half-day mark. Thereafter, much the same thing as before. Service, reading. Service, meditation or confession. Service, and another meal— vegetables and salad and bread. Prayers and readings again, and then sleep. If it sounds deadening to the spirit, it is only that, after thirty years, I follow it by rote. I can scarcely remember the order of it except in the doing," he said.

"But it is the very order that seems remarkable. Is every day so divided into hours, and does every hour have its specified use?"

"That is the intention of the Rule."

"And no monk of your Order rises from his bed and wanders to the window and stands there gazing into nothing in his half sleep, asking himself how he will spend the time between the coming up and going down of the sun?"

"It is not likely in the Chapter House. The abbot, the prior, the deacon—whoever is charged with the awakening of the Brothers—enters the dormitories or the cells saying *Deus gratius*, and everybody is up and about. It is a hard life."

"I see that it is hard, Father. But I see also why many have come to it gladly, and come to it from a lordly station, even as you did, back in your youth. I, for example, live more pleasantly than most. Many are kind to me because I was orphaned early— there is no door here that is not open to me, I need nothing, I come and go as I please. Many mornings I waken and think blithely how I will do this or that, and of these good days there are some when the blitheness lasts the whole day through. Yet there are others when—how can I tell you?—when it is as if my eyes were darkened by a yellow film, and everything I see is tainted, and there is only a hollow place, here—" He dropped his wet rag and laid his blunt soiled hand half on the pit of his stomach, half on the ribs that arched over his heart.

"My son, it is the despair—"

"Yet the word 'despair'—though it is a very apt word, and full of despondency in the very saying—is only a faint shadow of what I mean. And it seems to me, if one came with a torch and called me forth in the dark of the night to hymns and psalms, my eyes themselves might be changed thereby, and I might see another world."

"Many in Holy Orders have undergone such a transformation. I myself experienced in my novitiate such exaltation as I had not known before. Not that I would say once and for all that the life of the cloister is the best of all possible lives. Not that I can even be sure, if I could go back and choose again, it is the life I would

172

choose. Yet for those in despair, for those who know the heaviness and the emptiness—"

"The heaviness and the emptiness—how well my Father puts it! If I had not come to him here, the blitheness would have gone its way, perhaps in the late morning, perhaps in the early afternoon, and I would have fallen into the emptiness and the heaviness. This work, for instance—you cannot know what pleasure it is for me to rub away at this column and see it come clean. I am far less tired now than I would have been if I had wandered about all day doing nothing. And I feel a new hunger, also—a sort of hunger that would gladly content itself with lentil porridge and bread."

"An ordered life would seem the better to you because the Brotherhood of Saint Cyprian has been so long in utter confusion."

"You are right, Father. In fact, we can scarcely call ourselves a brotherhood. We do not eat together or pray together or lie down at night in one company. Each of us goes his own way, looking for such solace as he can find for his own soul."

"And a human soul, my son, is a very vulnerable thing. It needs peace and seemliness and hours of meditation in which to know itself and renew itself. Here you leave it naked to be buffeted about by every sort of contention and distraction, you expose it constantly to assaults from without. For instance, I cannot see—" he moved backward awkwardly, still on his knees, "I cannot see how you can be so unmindful of your soul's good as to spend whole days among women, serving them like squires, making merry for their amusement as if you were jongleurs. And some of them very questionable women, too—disturbing and unwholesome."

"If I may ask, what women does my Father have in mind?"

"There was one I encountered some time since on the Fishing-Beach. A mender of nets—"

"Oh, yes, Jehanne. But, Father, that woman is much to be pitied. She has had so many children—a new one almost every year—and all of them are dead."

173

"And where is the father of all these children?"

"There have been so many—who could keep the account? It is well known that nobody who asks is ever refused."

He got to his feet—it was foolish to go on washing what was already clean—and tried to convey self-possession by making smooth and regulated strokes over a new band of grime. "It is only natural," he said, "that you should pity this Jehanne. You are young, you do not know the sordidness of the life she lives, and Christ himself has given us a divine example in his compassion for the woman taken in adultery. But unless your dealings with her are the strictly circumscribed offices of the father confessor, your pity will not lift her up, it will only drag you down. Pity for the leprous sinner—no, I will go further, I will even say pity for the upright and the virtuous—must be reined in because it is a great softener of the judgment and corrupter of the soul."

"I had not thought of that." He, too, had gotten up, but he did not step forward.

"Think of it well, my son."

"Indeed, I will."

With that discourse concluded, he allowed himself a few harmless indulgences. He, and Eustace with him, abandoned the column and went rubbing and dabbing here and there after foretastes of other beauties: the screen was of alabaster, the ceremonial chair was fortified with strips of brass, the front panel of the altar bloomed with copper flowers. The flagstones promised a variety of revelations: one stone out of every four was carved with a delicate and intricate design, and, so far as they could discover, no two patterns were the same. They were sitting on the floor, admiring what seemed to be a spined and tentacled creature of the sea, when the main portal creaked.

"Has the door been blown open, my son?"

"No . . . I do not think so."

It was Liese, the daughter of the Abbot Ottric, coming in at the center aisle, and it was plain from the young man's blush that she was neither unexpected nor entirely welcome. She, too,

174

carried buckets and was yoked with twisted rags. "God be with you, holy Father," she said, and made the stiff primeval curtsy, and set her buckets on the floor in order to roll up her coarse brown sleeves.

"You see, she does not lose a moment," said Eustace with a false kind of eagerness. "And she has brought us rags by the dozen. Truly, Liese, this nunnery is full of wonders. We have found a marvelous monster here under the dirt. Come and look."

She came toward them—sturdy and not beautiful—with a firm tread. She bent from the waist to examine their find, groped after words that would carry enthusiasm, could light on nothing better than "All those legs sticking out. . . ." Nor was the talk any easier when Father Albrecht had asked—as he felt bound to ask—after her father. The Abbot Ottric's time was much taken up, she said, partly with building a wall to shelter the windy side of the house; and her speech was so halting and reserved that he knew the old man never mentioned him without animosity.

At her request, Eustace dragged the great chair over to the column which they had left unfinished, and she stood on the seat and dealt with the dirt that had been beyond their reach. Warned off by modesty from her swinging skirts and swaying hips, they went apart to wash the alabaster screen; but their talk was mindless and desultory now. In the long pauses, Father Albrecht knew that the "blitheness had gone its way"—somewhat later than usual, perhaps, but still too soon. And he was not sorry, nor did he think that either of the other two had any regrets, when their work was cut off by the swift coming down of the wintry dark.

✠   ✠   ✠

Within a fortnight, Father Albrecht was aware that some rough semblance of the ordered life had begun to shape itself out of the chaos of Saint Cyprian's. Plainly there were many on the island who, like Eustace, took satisfaction in a day divided into parts. Men and women of the town, gentlefolk and artisans to

the number of fifty or sixty, came after their noonday meal with
buckets and rags, ladders and high-legged stools, to work in
the nunnery, and remained at their labor as long as they had
light. Remembering the Holy Gregory's advice to the Sainted
Boniface, Father Albrecht came regularly to bruise his knuckles
and to praise. Censure was out of the question. The living holly-
berry wreath they made to adorn—perhaps to hide—the divine
disgusted face, the reedy scent they shook into reliquaries to take
away the sacred troubling smell were, he supposed, no worse than
the harmless indulgences that had won the Saxons over to the
Lord.

His own day had begun to fall into three parts—at least the
major portion of it when the sun was moving from the jagged
line of the salt cliffs into the level line of the western sea. In
the morning he went to the village and coddled the infant faith
of the ignorant, though he could not bring himself to flatter
Brother Thaddeus that the conjuring up of the millspring was a
miracle. At noon he went to the Square and sat on the roots of
the Burning-Trees and heard confessions; for it turned out that
as many as a dozen a day felt it was either fashionable or necessary to confess. "Holy Father, I have grievously sinned, and I
am heartily sorry. . . ." So far, he had encountered no hardened
sinners, and the penances he meted out were light and in line
with those assigned by the Abbot Benno in the first days of
timelessness. A bucketful of acorns gathered in a snow-powdered
forest wiped out every sort of evil thought or intent. Abstention
from meat and mead for seven days cooled fleshly lusts and
preserved the precarious store. Liars gathered firewood. The
covetous made bricks. "God is merciful. Go and sin no more."
In the afternoon he went to the Nuns' Chapel and took his place
among those who washed and dusted and polished and swept.
Sometimes they sang—words so blurred by time that he could
not make them out; and he left himself in ignorance because
they were very likely carnal words. But the music itself—melancholy and almost tuneless—gave him a kind of yearning pleasure,

176

especially when the voice of Eustace, a chorister in truth, sang a stave alone. These songs, and the thought of the chapel emerging out of its filth, and the recollection of the young monk's reedy tenor, haunted the only part of his day not ordered as yet: the time of emptiness and heaviness between the lighting of the torches and the coming on of sleep.

There was one vacant evening that might have been filled up. At the end of the usual dreary supper his host had urged him to stay since there would be company; and the chatelaine, cool and remote with him these many days, had added her request. But the naming of the guests had made meditation—or dreaming—upstairs in his own chamber seem the better choice: What pleasure could he take in Eustace if Eustace came with Liese? What had he—or the chatelaine, for that matter—to do with the mender of nets? As for Brother Giraldus, he knew too much of him already, and from day to day he was learning more from the penitents who knelt five paces off from him in the Square.

If the scandalous monk—to call him "fantastical" was to excuse him—had lived in the Chapter House at Cologne, he would have been mortared up in his cell and given bread and water through a feeding-hole lest other souls be tainted with his infection. He had had carnal doings with dozens—Jehanne was mentioned repeatedly. And, out of sheer perversity, he had even set up a fleshly and spiritual bond with the crazy goiterous Mechthilde. Many times the two of them had crossed the isthmus; and there, in the wilderness on the other side, they had intercourse with devils. Or thought they did and said they did—which was more than enough.

"No." He had uttered only the naked negative. If the lord and his lady had chosen to read reproof into it, that was all to the good. Nothing they guessed had dashed their holiday spirits. If they had actually said to him "Very well, then, one spoilsport the less," he could not have seen more clearly where he stood. He had climbed the stairs with her voice calling behind him—

not to him but to one of the servants: "We will be wanting plenty of chestnuts. You had better drag out another bin."

Yet, once in his chamber, he had not been able to execute his half of the mutual rejection by closing his door. He could not settle down to reading or to making notes for the forthcoming sermon, constantly intruded upon as he was by their noise. The barrenness of the castle made it singularly apt for carrying sounds: the lute could not have been more distinct if she had been playing it in the next room, and every voice was audible, though the words stayed just out of the reach of his ear. The decaying copy of the sermons of Saint Ambrose which he had lugged home from the monastery grew more remote and repetitive after every burst of laughter; and such random thoughts as he could summon up either floated away into a drowse or exploded when another handful of chestnuts burst on the embers of the faraway fire. He wrote a few words—rambling? sententious?—worthless, at any rate, and crossed them out, and tried to write others, only to find he had ruined his quill.

For a while he slept in his chair and had a dream of which he could remember nothing but a futile effort to climb a slippery and cluttered stair. For a while he tried to hearten himself by comparing past dangers with present comforts. He conjured up the white owl with the rodent trailing from its beak, and the dead Patches thrusting four legs into the air. Then he fixed his attention on the circle of candlelight, his own clean hands, the pitcher of water beside his bed. But the journey remained as unreal as some flat painting of Hell on the wall of a chapel, and what lay before him here and now had no more reality. Death was in the room as undeniably as it had been in the forest: candlelight, clean hands, and water notwithstanding, men came to their deaths. He got up, stepped out of his sandals, and walked as far as the stairwell. There he could hear that they were singing a round, and he was strangely moved that he could recognize each voice as it came in. Eustace's, the chatelaine's, a breathy voice that doubtless belonged to the mender of nets, a sturdy one that must be Liese's—neither Alain nor Giraldus took part in the song. He listened through three verses and would have listened longer if the chill of the stone floor had not benumbed his feet. God forbid, he thought, I should catch a rheum and put her to the trouble of more nursing. Go back, lie down, pull up the coverlet, get warm. . . .

He wakened at what seemed to him the hour of the Service of the Night, sure that every soul in the castle slept and convinced that he himself would not be able to go back to sleep. His candle had almost burned itself out, and the prospect of three more hours of blackness was more than he could tolerate. There were scores of candles to be had downstairs; and, carrying the little glowing stub in the hollow of his hand, he went to filch one for his use. But when he reached the entrance of the common room he saw that it was much earlier than he had thought: a great yellow fire still licked and crackled in the chimney place. There on the hearthstones, in post-carnival disarray, with her hair unbound, sat the chatelaine, her legs stretched out straight before her. She was quite alone and at her ease, feasting on hot chestnuts and licking her fingertips.

He seldom came upon a woman who had not prepared herself for his monkish scrutiny, and he wondered whether all of them were so loose and lithe, so careless and keen after their fleshly delights in their solitude. She did not see him at once, and when her eyes did come to rest upon him and his glowworm candle stub, she utterly discomposed him by doing none of the things he expected: did not pull her skirt over her feet, did not put up her hand to tidy her hair, did not move her body out of its lolling lassitude. "I see," she said in a downright belligerent voice, "that our merrymaking disturbed you. We made too much noise. You could not go to sleep."

"I heard nothing."

"Well, that is fortunate."

"My candle is almost gone, so I came to look for another."

"Take your choice. There must be a dozen of them hereabouts." She brushed some nutshells from her silken lap and watched him with cool unblinking eyes as he went toward a reading stand. But before he could reach the candle upon it, his own precarious flame went out. "There's a sorry business," she said with the same edge of anger to her voice. "Now you will have to come over here and take your light from the fire."

It was a taunt: he would be forced to step over her or reach across her unless she chose to move. Was she punishing him because he had rejected her offer of hospitality, or had she taken more mead than she could hold? The closer he came, the more in possession of herself she seemed. Her look was level; with a slowness that could only be deliberate, she passed the tip of her tongue over her lower lip. And, just as he bent to reach across her legs, she shifted her weight sidewise and drew them back, bending them at the knee. The movement—intentionally sudden, serpentine because of the shimmering cloth of her skirt—startled him into stepping backward a pace. "Here, light your candle and go back to your readings and your prayers. You have no need to be afraid of me," she said.

"Why should I be afraid of my lady?"

"You know the answer to that better than I." She got up and shook the remains of her solitary feast out of her lap and settled herself again, more seemly now and somewhat less self-possessed, on the stool in front of the fire. "Light your candle, Father, and go your way. But then again, do not light it and stay awhile. There is a certain matter of grave concern to me, though it probably means little enough to you—something that calls for a word between us two."

"Nothing that concerns the chatelaine could leave me—" The word "cold" was what he had meant to utter, but after a pause he said "unconcerned" instead.

"No?" Her voice was quieter and more rueful. Her eyes left his face and stared down at her own open hands.

"Considering how gracious she has been to me, how kindly she looked to my needs in my sickness—"

"Oh, as to *that*—" In a single word she disparaged and dismissed it. "Come, spare me a moment, not because you are my debtor, but out of the generosity of your heart. Sit down—"

She gestured toward the tall chair on the other side of the hearth, and he took it, still holding the unlighted candle, not willing to let it out of his hands though he knew she saw it as a proof that he was eager to depart.

"I am curious to know which of my guests was unacceptable to you, Father."

He thought for a little, weighing the lapsed brother against the incorrigible prostitute. And, strangely unsure as to which it was— if indeed it was either—he said, "Jehanne."

"Jehanne? Let me tell you something, though you will not believe it. If I were to say to her that you hold against her what I think you do—that she has had many children by many fathers— she would not understand it in the least. She would quote texts to prove the rectitude of all her doings."

"God in Heaven, what texts could she have to quote?"

"More than I can remember. 'Love they neighbor as thyself.' 'If one asks for bread, shall he be given a stone?' 'Much will be forgiven in those who have greatly loved.' "

"For her self-justification, she soils Holy Scripture."

"I would not argue so complicated a matter so late at night. You may argue it with her, Father, if you choose. One of these days when her heart so moves her she will come to you and confess. She was much taken with you when she broke bread with you on the Fishing-Beach."

Two recollections converged in his mind, and he did not know which one of them disheartened him and left him wordless: the mender of nets loading his trencher with flakes of broiled fish, or the chatelaine saying in incomprehensible spite that, when her heart so moved her, she would go to the Abbot Ottric to make her confession.

"So it was Jehanne that drove you up to your chamber?" she said after a long silence. "I did not think so. I thought it was Giraldus, or perhaps the Abbot Ottric's daughter."

"The Abbot Ottric's daughter? What would I have to blame in

181

her? For all I know of her, she is a dutiful, decent, well-intentioned child."

"So she is to *my* knowledge, and I have known her from her cradle. But if you find her dutiful and decent and well-intentioned, why would you wish to come between her and her friend?"

Have I come between them so soon? he thought, and almost said it. But if he had smiled, she had not caught him: whatever anger was in her had fired her to speak on and on in the young woman's praise. "What could I have done to make you think I wished to come between them?" he asked in her first pause.

"I do not know, Father. I only know that he kept dwelling on his disappointment that you were not one of the company, and he argued with Giraldus about obscure sacred matters that were well over his head. Liese made the best of it, as she always does, and went home early."

"But why do you lay the blame of it on me? It would seem that your nephew finds himself drawn not to me but to God. He would not be the first who found women a burden and a distraction in his gropings toward Heaven—otherwise the deserts of Egypt would never have been honeycombed with hermits' cells. And Saint Cyprian's would indeed be a Godforgotten island if there were not a blessed few among you who felt that their only true peace was their peace in the Lord."

"Let me make this much plain to you," she said, uttering each word separately, with strained deliberateness. "You will not find me rejoicing if my nephew proves to be one of that blessed few. If he found himself without the desires of the flesh, to my mind he would be maimed—more maimed than if he lacked a leg or a hand. As to the God who considered him precious because he was maimed—*Him* I simply cannot understand. Is He sick or mad that He should fill up his courts with eunuchs—"

"We are not eunuchs! We transcend the fire—we do not creep like worms underneath it. When the Sainted Origen thought to disarm the Devil by self-mutilation, his sentence was heavy. His disgrace and penance lasted for years."

"You need not shout at me and rouse the household," she said. "Besides, you are telling me nothing that I do not know."

Her reference was plainly not to the case of the Sainted Origen. Her eyes—neither shamed nor bold—reminded him that he had lain naked under her ministrations. In a fever, confessing what memories, rising to what lascivious dreams?

"But what my lady has said of God's servants is nothing compared to what she has said of God Himself. To conceive that He, the Maker of Heaven and earth, could be sick or mad—"

"What He made, He abandoned, or He left us to believe He did. Our disgrace and penance too have been heavy—we reckon them at a hundred years."

"But He is knocking now at the gates of your hearts—"

"That gives us a choice, and you should not judge us too harshly if we do not leap up in joy to run and bring Him in. He who returns after an absence is not so readily accepted as He who has always been there. Say what you will, He comes threatening punishment."

"Who has been punished?"

"None as yet. But how am I to know how He or His servants will deal with Giraldus or Jehanne?"

"The Holy Father Gregory charged Boniface to proceed with all mildness among the Saxons—"

"It bodes ill for us," she said, rising, "that you are forever harking back to names and precedents. How the Sainted Origen dealt with his fleshly desires, how the Holy Father Gregory advised one Boniface to dispose of the affairs of the Saxons—these dry bones from the grave of another age will help us no more than *that*—" She gestured in sorrowful contempt toward the black corner where the model of Saint Cyprian's stood. "Whoever heals us—if indeed we can be healed—must bring us a new dispensation, a new word. Such a word cannot be lifted out of a book. Nothing can bring it forth but the labors of a living heart."

He also got up, bemused, unable to judge which part she had stirred, the flesh or the spirit. He thought it might be well to follow whatever prompted him, to take one step forward—for she stood close to him—and kiss her on the brow. But the intention, held too long, lost its life, turned flabby and foolish.

"I see you still have your candle," she said. "Take your light and go your way."

"And you, my daughter?"

"There are a few chestnuts left. Will you have some?"

"No, I never eat at night."

"I do, when my heart so moves me. I will sit awhile in front of the fire and finish the rest. As for you, get such sleep as you can."

"God be with you, my lady."

"I am neither your lady nor your daughter. I have a name, though you never use it."

"Well, then, God be with you, Julianne," he said.

☙   ☙   ☙

Three weeks short of the Feast of the Nativity, the snow began to come down in earnest. It accumulated on the stumps of the Burning-Trees and lay in irregular white lines between the cobblestones. And Eustace and two of the other townsmen built a shed —unintentionally seasonable, with the peaked roof and raw beams of a stable—so that Father Albrecht might go on hearing confessions in the Square.

There he sat for two or three hours in the middle of the day, welcoming sinners, in quarters not entirely appropriate for the sacrament of confession. The shed was so small that the five paces between the listener and the speaker had to be cut down to three. Charcoal burning away in an iron basin gave a domestic cheer to the windowless darkness and brought out the pleasant smell of the wood, and other items made the place more like a secure haunt for the body than a cell for the spirit: a cheese in a net, a tin cup, a great sausage, a red napkin, a knife in a leather sheath, all hung from ancient nails driven into the new wall. He himself had brought ink and quills and parchment, hoping to make his sermon grow between confessions. But he and the lay brother had agreed to delay the sermon—the flock was to be nourished with a Yuletide celebration before he admonished and chastised it—and he hardly ever picked up the quill.

What time he had, he spent in a dreaming lassitude. Not planning, not thinking, allowing himself to fall back into the vacuous pleasure a child of three will take in a rhyme said over and over for his benefit. Eustace had sawed these boards, this tin cup had been given to him by Eustace. The red napkin was the chatelaine's present, and he never looked at it without thinking how, when nobody was by, she sat on the hearthstones with her legs stretched straight out before her and her hair unbound, and bit on hot chestnuts and licked her lips. Flames on charcoal were more blue and gentle than flames playing over wood. The sausage —it, too, had been sent down from the castle—tasted of herbs and onions and smelled of smoke. He would cut off a thin slice of it to chew on at the noonday hour, and afterward would wipe his mouth on the napkin, which smelled of that dry scent that no longer made him sneeze. The shed, more than any habitation he had known since his childhood, belonged to him; and whoever came to him out of the whirling snow visited him in his home.

"Father, I have grievously sinned, and I am heartily sorry."

It was the mender of nets in her lambswool vest and her rags. Melted snow ran down her cheeks and her thin chapped neck. Her feet were only encumbered and chilled by her torn, soaked shoes; they would have been better off if they had been bare.

"God is merciful, my daughter in the Lord. Come in."

"Come in" was a departure from the ritual, and was not entirely satisfactory. To "Come in" should have been added "and take off your outer garments," which he could not bring himself to say, though many shed their poor coats and cloaks without asking his permission. She rid herself of her vest, but not before she had dragged something—a scroll of cloth tied up with a cord— out of her pocket. "I would have come sooner, Father," she said, untying the string, "but I wanted to wait until I had finished this."

What she unrolled and laid across his knees was a piece of stitchery, like nothing he had ever seen before. On a dun-colored strip of cloth the length of an arm and the width of a hand, three sea gulls descended, one beneath the other, in swirls of snow. The design exalted nature without elaborating it or imposing upon it, and the workmanship put to shame the arras of the Deadly Sins and Cardinal Virtues that was the glory of Cologne. The entirety asserted itself only in a kind of whisper: white, grey, darker grey, and black on a quiet background of dun—the one real color was in the little knots of scarlet set like jewels in the six red eyes and the six red feet. "Where would you find such a beautiful thing?" he said.

"I made it, Father. It is made all of wool—all except the eyes and feet. They are made of silk."

"You made it?" But surely such a thing could not have been conceived by such a one, must have its real genesis somewhere else, on some ruined pediment or memorial stone. "And the design—where did you find that?"

"I made that also," she said without pride. "I saw the bird on the Fishing-Beach, and watched it for a while, and drew it afterward on the cloth with ink. I was weeks at work on it, and when the season changed, I added the snow."

"It is beautiful beyond belief," he said, but there was something in his voice that made what he said less a compliment than an admission delivered under stress.

"I am glad if it gives you pleasure, Father. I thought you might find a place for it in the Nuns' Chapel."

He flushed. In Holy Church, all gifts were acceptable, save only the earnings of the whore. "Where did you come by the cloth? It it a strange color," he said.

"Oh, it is only ordinary cloth—a piece of an old cassock. The thread is of no value, either—bits unraveled from worn-out shifts and smocks. The scarlet—but let me roll it up, I have gone on about it too long."

She rolled up in a moment what it had plainly taken her more hours than he could reckon to create. As she went down on her knees before him—somebody, perhaps the chatelaine, had given her full instructions—he regretted, as if he had lost them irretrievably, the swirling flakes, the delicate feathers, the strong and exquisite wings.

"Holy Father, I have grievously sinned, and I am heartily sorry."

"God is merciful. What is your sin, my child?"

She did not answer at once; the showing of her handiwork had left her a little flustered. Her hair had gone too long unwashed; it was stuck together by its own oil in ugly strands. The reek of it was familiar—dance, dance in a hot kitchen on a day of large wet snowflakes—the reek was familiar and mingled disturbingly with the reedy scent of the scarlet napkin that hung close to his face. Strange, he thought, how carnality rears up and flourishes when everything else dwindles and shrivels. "To name a sin," he said, "is to lift a burden from the heart."

"I have plenty of fish, Father, the best of the catch, and surely that ought to be enough. But a time comes around this part of the year when I have such a yearning after a goose that I can think of nothing else. When that yearning is on me, though I know it to be evil according to both my own heart and the dictates of the Abbot Benno, I go by night into any yard where there is a cackling, and I take a goose and wring its neck and carry it back to my room in the loft. Nor do I ask any others to share what I have taken. I carry it to the Fishing-Beach and there I pluck and spit and sear it when I am certain that neither Mechthilde nor Giraldus will come by. For the rest of the week I eat it until nothing is left but the bones—and them I bury in my shame under a rock in the sand."

Another wintry sin: black hunger. He himself had never known it, but he had often followed the dark whore Elspeth when she carried the slops home from the tavern. Walk softly in the room where her father hacked and wheezed. Walk warily, do not wake him, and—once the slops are stored away—reach for the fever and the moisture under the rags. . . .

187

"It is a great sin, I know, Father, and I am very sorry."

"Considering your need, it is by no means a mortal sin, my daughter. Refrain from stealing. It is better to beg than to steal."

"Do you really think so?" She lifted her chin, which had been resting on her crossed fingertips, and looked him earnestly in the face. "I ask because it always seemed to me that begging was worse."

"How so? Holy Church not only instructs the needy to ask for alms but explicitly requires the fortunate to give freely."

"Yes, but who gives freely? Myself, I would rather have someone steal from me than ask me for this or that out of my little store. A thief gives me the right to feel put upon—I can unload my heart by cursing him. But a beggar leaves me baffled no matter what I do. If I give, I am angry at him; and if I refuse, I am angry at myself."

He turned from her kindled eyes and looked at the rolled-up scroll of embroidery she had put on his knees. Surely, if she could bestow so much on a stranger, she could see how others might also make generous gifts; but he could not find the words or the voice in which to tell her so. Nor could he be sure that an argument grounded on the strip of dun-colored cloth would not lead them into some frightening and equivocal intimacy. "I can only tell you that Holy Church protects the beggar and condemns the thief," he said.

"Ah, there it is again!" she said, sitting back on her heels. "There it is—the confusion!"

"What confusion, my daughter?"

"The confusion of sacred texts—I see it wherever I turn. It is true—am I right, Father?—that we sin when we lead others into sin."

"That is assuredly so."

"Then how can I beg, if by begging I make another turn into a hypocrite and a liar? I do not expect you to explain it to me in the little time we have—no doubt there are others waiting outside the shed—and I know it is a great mystery. I will not steal

188

again, Father—that much I promise you. But I would rather do without the goose, at least until I learn how I can beg without bringing another into sin for my sake."

"The word of the priest is all you need, and I have given you that word," he said, and he said it with asperity. He wished he could bring this plainly incomplete confession to an end: he had fallen somehow into a nagged, erratic mood, and had neither the time nor the courage to do more than recognize its elements. Pity for the wintry sin of hunger, remembrance of that other wintry sin committed on a dirty cluttered floor, disgust at her oily hair, an inescapable awareness of her meager breasts under the cloth of her smock—he could not manage them all at once. It was good to have plain truth to fall back upon: the uselessness of arguing scruples with a whore. "Since our time *is* short, you would do well to confess your most grievous sin. Once that is rooted out, the other matters will be easier to dislodge. Come, tell me without restraint, trusting in God's compassion, what it is that lies heaviest upon your heart."

She looked puzzled, tightening her ill-formed jaw and frowning so hard that a long vertical wrinkle stood between her straight black brows. "Threads of various colors are hard to find on the island," she said after a long silence. "I steal thread for my stitchery. I take it from a cloak here and a skirt there—wherever the color draws me. That scarlet in the gulls' eyes—I took it from the silk veil of a lady who was kneeling in meditation at Brother Galbart's cleft tree."

That speech was enough to turn his restlessness into annoyance, a physical irritation that made him feel as if he were locked up in the warm shed, the confining chair, his hot and nagging body itself. "As I have told you, it is a sin to steal. But I have reason to believe that stealing is the least of your sins," he said. "If your craft requires threads of strange colors, surely you could find dyes. I have heard, for instance, that very fine dyes can be trodden out of the bodies of certain creatures of the sea."

"Father!" She shook away the dank strands of her hair to look

189

at him through chiding eyes. "Surely you would not trample the body of a creature to crush its color out of it. That is terrible to think of, that is dealing with a living creature as if it were an unfeeling, lifeless thing. Surely you would never—"

"I myself have never done it, nor had the occasion to do it. I have only heard or read somewhere that—"

"I beg you, Father, never think of it."

"My daughter, we are stumbling over trifles, and our time is running out. Why do you refuse to confess what I already know?"

"That I say foul words when I am angry?"

"That you do foul things when you are lecherous."

"Foul things?"

"Yes, as you well know. Things that make a pigsty of your body, which is the temple of your spirit."

"With devils, on the other side of the isthmus? I swear to you, Father, I have never crossed the isthmus with the other two, nor eaten what they have eaten, nor had any doings whatsoever with the fiends—"

"What have they eaten?"

"No, truly, Father, that I will not tell. Send me out of here unforgiven, but I will not blab to you. I do not have a loose mouth like Eustace. What *they* do is for them to tell you. But of this you may be certain: I myself have no doings with devils, only with mortal men."

"Then it is true—you lie with many?"

"Yes, surely—"

"How many?"

"That would be hard for me to tell."

"But that is—" He stopped just short of saying "monstrous," and looked away from her eyes, and found himself staring again at her insufficient breasts, the more provocative for their childishness. "Lechery is a much more grievous sin than theft," he said, sitting back in his chair. "Only after a solemn pledge made before the Lord can flesh be joined to flesh to fulfill the cycle of procreation."

190

"Ah, Father, who would give me such a pledge?" She let herself back on her heels again and invited him to look at her poverty as an object of desire: thin neck, protruding collarbones, flat chest, belly gone slack with childbearing, meager thighs. "I am not such a one as could ask for bed and board and ring in exchange for what I have. Nobody would give me a pledge, as you can surely see."

Dark triangle between those thighs, moist and feverish—he put the thought of it down and forced himself to dwell on other matters. "You must not despise yourself. He who despises himself insults his Maker," he said in a voice that was not his own.

"If God is our Maker, then He is very careless in His handiwork. Some He makes beautifully—but there are others on whom He does not trouble Himself to use much skill. I know what I am, and I do not ask for much. If there are those who can find nobody better than me, they are welcome to me and my blanket—"

His heart was pounding so hard that he thought she must surely see it. He turned his head to one side to avoid the sight of her, and breathed the dry scent of the napkin that hung close to his face. "I will not threaten you with the everlasting fire you fan for yourself every time you share your blanket—we will speak of that at another time," he said in a shaken voice. "It is enough to tell you that the whore and her fellow sinner, here and now, are utterly wretched. They are worse than beasts in their coupling, and when their coupling is done they rise up to loathe each other and themselves, sick of the world, deathly sick at heart."

"Do you think so, Father? It may be so with some, but I can truly say that it has seldom been so with me. If it goes well—and why should it not go well if the man is in need and the woman gives freely?—I am always the better for it. The aches go out of my body, the worries that have tormented me go away, and I turn over on my side and go to sleep."

And I? he thought. If such sleep was not my portion, was the blame with me or with Elspeth? Was my need puny and despicable, or did she wring the strength from it with her avidity? A giving woman, sitting on the hearth, with her body stretched out and the light of flames playing over it like fingers. . . . A giving woman, sitting back on her heels, unaware that certain strips of bony whiteness are visible through her rags. . . .

She was going on about those who came to her by night: peasants who thought their bodies had been exhausted in the fields and were amazed to find them revived under her touch; ageing townsmen whose wives submitted unwillingly and with disdain; boys who were afraid and awkward and needed praise as much as they needed relief. Now and then a drunkard, now and then a clown, now and then somebody who did not know the difference between rage and lust. But for the most part, whether they said so or not, grateful. . . . "But the shed is getting very hot, and I am afraid the holy Father is not well," she said. "Let me go and get some snow in the tin cup."

"No, my daughter, stay as you are. It will stop."

It was a lambent wheel in which every object within sight blurred and turned round at a fearful speed—the napkin, the sausage, the grained wood, her frightened face. The wheel slowed, reversed itself, moved still more slowly in the opposite direction, stopped, and took itself blessedly out of the range of his vision in lines of wavering light.

"I could open the door, Father."

"No, it is gone, I am well enough. But you, my child, you are very sick, most gravely sick in the spirit. You sow sin right and left, repeatedly and without repentance, and the fruit of such sin can only be death."

"Ah!" She sprang up as she uttered it. "Never tell me that! Never say it is because I lie with many that all my little ones die!"

"It is not I, but you, who have said it. If the thought has come into your mind, it may well be that God has put it there, bitter as it is, for your eventual healing—"

"Then He is cruel, and I want none of His healing."

"Beg Him to tear such blasphemy out of your heart!"

"I do not beg, Father—I have told you." She stepped away from him without turning, and he would have risen if it had not been for the scroll of cloth lying across his knees. He could bring himself neither to take hold of it nor to let it fall to the ground; and while he sat confused and helpless, she reached behind her, opened the door, and stepped backward over the threshold, unforgiven and unblessed. "Wait a little," he heard her say to somebody who waited. "Give the holy Father time to recover himself."

He needed time—it seemed to him that there would never be time enough. It was the overwhelming size, the grotesque and indefinable shape of his task that she left him with when she closed the door. That task was like a palpable presence, crowding against him in the hot closed space, contaminating the air, making him gasp for breath. Sweat stood on his forehead, and he did not dare to wipe it away with the scented napkin, and in his agitation he almost used the strip of stitchery instead. "No, it must be quenched; wherever the fire burns, it must be quenched," he said in a whisper, sinking back onto his chair. "I must write the sermon now, at once." And he actually snatched up the quill and wrote the first sentence—"My children, I am sent to tell you that the death by water is as nothing beside the death by fire"—before he knew where he was and composed himself enough to call the next penitent in out of the snow.

✠　　✠　　✠

"Things being as they are," said the Abbot Ottric, "I do not want you dragging along with me."

His daughter Liese dropped her cloak onto a stool and put down an impatient sigh. "You are probably right. Maybe others besides the lay brother will come to conduct you. Maybe it will be a kind of procession—in which case a woman would be out of place."

"Propriety is not the question. I am not concerned with what they think about propriety."

"No, of course not." She could see she had only made him angrier, and he had been angry enough to begin with, treating the evening meal with rough contempt, scraping his tin plate with his knife, spilling broth on his good cassock, cursing the cassock and cursing the broth. The mild old mother stopped in the business of clearing the bespattered board and, by way of warning, tapped her forefinger on her lips.

"A fine procession! A procession for an ox led out to be knocked over the head."

"You always make the worst of it," she said, refusing to look at her mother. "Whatever he does, you take it amiss. He sends to invite you to his first sermon, and you say it is a command. He has Eustace tell you there will be a ceremonial chair for you on the right-hand side of the pulpit, and you say he is putting you there so that everybody will see your disgrace. He promises to send his lay brother to bring you in state to the Nuns' Chapel—"

"That dolt!"

"He has no better."

"I would rather go by myself."

"Then go, Father. Go now, before he gets here. When he comes, I will make some sort of explanation. If he is alone, I will go with him—"

"I do not want you going with him."

"Whatever you wish—"

"Whatever I wish!" There was pain under the taunt, and she ached the more because, now that she had seen a real churchman, he looked ridiculous in his gaudy cassock and big shoes. "You know what I wish. I wish you had decided of your own will not to go at all." He went out and slammed the door.

She waited until he would be well on his way before she wrapped herself in her cloak and set out in the snow, through the mud and the gathering dark. Avoiding the crowd that were quenching their torches at the entrance to the Nuns' Chapel, she went in and found a spot toward the center and near the back. Nothing had begun as yet: there was only stern emptiness in the pulpit, the

194

ceremonial chair, the choir loft. The beauty of the resurrected chapel in the pale wash of candlelight did not much move her, distressed as she was about her own uncomeliness. Mud on her clogs, the old brown dress, the worn brown cloak—if devotion to her father had not been strong enough to keep her at home, it had forbidden the smallest touch of finery. Those whom she knew—Julianne and Alain, Giraldus and Mechthilde, the Brothers of Saint Cyprian who ate at her father's table, her peasant friends—she did not stare at long for fear of bringing their looks to bear upon her plainness and disgrace.

Stare then at the crucifix, overhanging everything, horribly visible between the chains of the lanterns. The garland that had crowned the incarnate God had withered and shrunken away from the big, sick face. The final hour—all she could think of, looking at that, was the final hour. And one known face after another superimposed itself upon that mask, taking on its lines of horror and disgust. Her father, whom she had offended in his time of need, hung there sick unto death in his rage and degradation. Giraldus hung there, his wide, loose mouth fallen open, hideous now that it could not manage even mockery. Eustace hung there, with two faces, one laid on top of the other—the real face and the holy face, both of them terrified. Cold as she was from the long walk in the snow, sweat started from her armpits and trickled down her sides. All of them would come to this, yes, and she herself—

Alleluia! Alleluia! Alleluia!

The strange word thundered out, threatened to split the chapel and her head. It was not only she—many of the others in front of her half got up. And then sank down again, seeing that the noise was human, had been uttered by ten mortal men—Eustace among them—who had come soundlessly into the choir loft.

Pater, Filius, et Spiritus Sanctus!

The old pure Latin, she supposed. One of the monks seated in front of her said to his wife in a whisper, "Father, Son, and

Holy Ghost." She could not listen to the rest of the chattering; her father, escorted by Brother Thaddeus, was stepping out of the shadowy ambulatory and moving toward the ceremonial chair. He looked just as he had looked when he left the house—enraged, disordered, crumpled—though the candlelight dealt considerately with the stain on his cassock: nobody who was not looking for it would know it was there. With strained obsequiousness, the lay brother waited until he was seated, then bowed and stepped backward into the dark from which he had come.

Alleluia! Alleluia! Al-le-lu-ia!

On the last shattered and lengthened repetition of the alien word, Father Albrecht manifested himself in the pulpit that jutted out between the feet of the crucified Christ and her father's grizzled head. Backs straightened, necks stiffened, chins tilted. He laid some sheets of parchment and his two white emaciated hands on the slanted stone edge of the pulpit. As he stood waiting for the choir's last echo to fade out, he did not seem like one born of woman and grown out of childhood. It was more as if a stone figure had been briefly given the semblance of a mortal man. It was as if, once he had spoken, he would escape all questions, consequences, responsibilities by turning back into stone.

My sons and daughters in the risen Christ:
I am come to tell you that the death by water is as nothing beside the death by fire.

His voice was low—there was a general slanting forward to hear it. She did not know the townswoman on her left or the bearded peasant on her right, but the three bent forward at once, bound together in the same rigidity.

This I beg of you before I begin: Do not go out of this chapel tonight saying among yourselves, "He cannot comprehend our desolation, he does not know what it is to have lived after the coming of Leviathan."

Neither God nor my abbot in Cologne would have sent me out to you if I had been dull in my wits or hardened in my heart. I have read your Chronicle and lived in mind and spirit through your tribulations; nor is there one of your ancient calamities that has left me unmoved.

Saint Cyprian's was surely afflicted. A land of plenty was turned into a wilderness of mud and ruins. The drowned were counted in the hundreds, and a great Cathedral was lost.

But as much and more was the lot of Noah, who saw the whole earth transformed into a watery waste and did not grieve and languish, but lived to see the bow of the covenant in the sky and to take the sprig of olive out of the beak of the dove.

Herein lies the curse of Saint Cyprian's, passed down from generation to generation: since the hour when the tidal wave broke in upon you, you have given yourselves over to despair. Who but the despairing would say of a tidal wave: "This is the end of the world"? Who but the despairing would believe, because one peninsula was sorely ravaged, Doomsday had come? Who but those utterly devoid of hope would count five hundred dead and be convinced that his Creator had wiped out the whole race of man?

He paused and looked at them as if to ask what they thought of that. His eyes—blank to all because they fixed on none—summoned them to a hard reckoning. They—yes, and all their remembered dead—stood convicted of delusion and reduced to foolishness. It was clever of him, she supposed, to cite Noah as an example. But what was Noah to her and hers except a reproach?

The sin of despair is a heavy sin, my children. Yet even in their guiltiness God did not desert the people of this island. Though in their error they brought the end of time and the darkness of Doomsday down upon their own heads, they might still have lived out their lives in somber peace in the twilight they had imposed upon themselves.

Dwelling among them was their Abbot Benno, whose history I have read and whose grave I have visited. Had they lived according to his mandates, sharing all and enduring all, they would have been sinless. No, more than sinless—they would have been saints; and I and my lay brother coming to this unpeopled place and reading what he had

197

written in your Book would have called every foot of desolation holy, as holy as the catacombs.

But even the Abbot Benno, for all his wisdom, betrayed his saint-hood. Turning his back on the spirit, he fell into infinite confusions over the letter of the law, indulging a little here, retreating a little there until he had no firm ground to stand upon. Quibbling, sophistry, infirmity of faith and purpose—these were the sins of the Abbot Benno and the roots of his madness. In madness he ate the foetid wafer, betraying God even as Eve betrayed the Creator when she tasted the apple. And there is no such thing as a blameless death for one whose body dies poisoned by what is forbidden by God.

And now he was brought to a stop by two noises. Her father, red in the face at the affront to the Abbot Benno, hitched forward with his chair, making the feet of it grate along the flagstones. And the madwoman Mechthilde let out hysterical laughter so loud that everybody turned and looked at the bobbing knot of hair on top of her head. Some said "Hush!" in whispers. And—simply because the preacher was vulnerable in his waiting—Liese saw in his spare and melancholy mouth a new comeliness.

In my youth, when I was a novice and did my first readings in the Old Testament, it seemed to me that the most blasphemous words ever spoken were the words which Job's wife sought to put into her husband's mouth: "Curse God and die." Yet now, here among you on Saint Cyprian's, I have seen that words more dreadful and more blasphemous still can be thought and acted upon: "Curse God and live."

Think of it, I beg you: Curse the Creator, murmur in your heart unceasingly against the Creator, and yet nourish yourself to satiety on His Creation. This is the sin of sins, and of this utter depravity I accuse those whose blood you carry in your bodies and will pass down from generation to generation unless you repent.

God is long-suffering. So He proved Himself after the death of your first abbot. Whom He loves, He chastens; and His scourge fell heavily upon you in soul-sickness and famine—so heavily that I wonder much how the will to sin could have lived on in flesh so scourged. But His chastisement did no good.

For a spring came when, out of disgust for your obstinacy, He withheld His punishing and cleansing rod. He gave you your Eden of strange birds and balmy airs. He gave you rich crops and hung your trees with heavy fruit. And then, then—go read of it in your Chronicle, where it is written to your everlasting shame—you thought not once of His laws but only of yourselves. Cursing God, you lived—go read of it, how desire was born again and the nights were warm and sweet, and hand crept out toward seeking hand. Having survived the death by water, you entered by your own will, still cursing God, into the death by fire.

Now I would not have you take what I say hereafter as an interdiction against all carnal union. The man goes in unto the woman for the begetting of children—so God has ordained—and he who takes his pleasure within decent bounds and rises betimes to worship God and labor with his fellows, he incurs no blame for his transitory delight.

But whosoever shuts out God and the suffering world and makes the doings of the flesh the single object of his days, he puts upon love an insupportable burden, a burden far heavier than God in His wisdom ever fashioned it to bear. Believe me, my children, when love is torn out of the fabric of our life, when there is no life left but the life-in-love, the lover is doomed to say on rising from the beloved's bed: "Is this, then, all? Surely there must be more than this." The conjunction of flesh in a world without God and loving-kindness is no more than the coupling of beast with beast; nor has there ever been a lover who has not in the end found it so. For man, whom God made only a little lower than the angels, can never be satisfied with a beast's nourishment. His soul, in its anger and its bafflement, will surely turn in fury and loathing against the creature of whom it has asked too much. Searching here and there, trying one means and another, increasing its fever and lacerating itself in unappeasable desire, it will come at last to see every living being as an object of cruelty and lust, a contemptible thing on which to avenge itself.

He paused to turn a page and wipe his mouth, and in the short silence a drowned thought emerged into her consciousness. Once, long ago, perhaps in her tenth year, she had loitered on the Fishing-Beach to watch two boys roasting a crayfish alive. Kneeling on the sand, seeing the creature writhe among the flames, hearing the boys' exultant shrieks, she had felt such a surge of fever to her secret parts as she had not known again until she dreamed of

199

lying in Eustace's arms. Cruelty and lust—they were conjoined, he knew whereof he spoke. And she, doing equivocal penance by tending sick beasts—she was his living proof.

These monstrous yearnings can never be quenched. They can end only in the death by fire. Some of you have seen it with your own eyes, and the rest of you can read of it: the rending of all human bonds, the overturning of all laws, the perverse delight in the inflicting and undergoing of pain which you call by an awesome name—the Three Years of Blood. Your souls murmur against me that I should bring it back into your minds. "Why dwell upon it?" you say in your corrupted hearts. "We have outlived it, it is gone." But God has sent me to tell you that His wrath is only withdrawn for a little while. And, unless you change yourselves utterly, it will come again.

Next year or the year thereafter, other lordlings will be hung head-down from other Burning-Trees. Next year or the year thereafter, the brains of a new Brother Galbart will pour from his shattered skull. Yet a little while, and the flames will leap from roof to roof, and the dead—contemptible because they can no longer be tormented—will lie unburied in the streets, and the stench without will be as strong as the stench within. Then those who are left to creep about in the ruins like ants in a burning brand will bewail the day they were born and curse God and die, having known to the full what it is to curse God and live.

A young peasant cried out, and an old woman whimpered. She herself began to shiver in terror, and could not stop because the chapel was so cold.

But wait a little, my children. I have shown you what you have been these last hundred years. Let me show you now what you were in a better day, before the tidal wave came and despair swept in with the waters, and your forefathers, in their ignorance, believed that God's wrath had spurned them, leaving them solitary on earth after the day of doom.

Then men knew this island for what it was and will forever remain: God's possession, held in fee for Him by the holy Order of Saint Cyprian.

This chapel—the only perfect remnant of that ancient splendor—

was never intended for your use or mine. It belonged to the chaste sisterhood whose serenity so drew the virgin Genevieve that, inasmuch as it was no longer to be found in life, she sought it in death. Brides of Christ, devoted sisters to all suffering mankind, they came here in their decent veils to praise God and intercede for erring mortals at His footstool in Heaven. The ruins of their dwellings go down to the edge of the earth, on the margin of the western sea.

Their chapel remains, yes; but who can enter it, even in its newly purified state, without grieving over its emptiness? For it is empty, my children, though we crowd it to its portals. It is empty of the holy life it was builded to contain. You know nothing of that life. Things have come to such a pass here that not one among you knows what it is to live in a holy order, as a member of a sisterhood or a brotherhood.

She looked at her father—flushed face, slumped shoulders, hands closing and unclosing on his knees—and looked away at once. He had been shepherd these last eighteen years, and a good one, too, according to his lights; and there he sat in the ceremonial chair, taken to task under everybody's eyes.

Reason and mercy alike forbid me to reproach you that you have not lived the communal life under one roof. When the Abbot Benno dispersed you, your souls' home was in ruins, and he could not do otherwise. But you have sorely fallen off, you have grievously transgressed in other obligations. And I—sent as I am to amend your errors and restore the ancient purity—will sin against you if I further delay the hour of your reckoning.

My brothers—for all who wear the cassock are indeed brothers in the living Christ—it is not only that you have let this island, where every clod of earth belongs to God, slip out of His hands and yours into the secular world. It is not only that you have neglected to raise your voices in intercession for the sins of Christendom, that you sing no psalms and no anthems, that you have utterly forgotten the services of the day and the services of the night. It is not only that you live no longer according to the law of poverty, but say of houses and land, and such earthly treasure as must be devoured by rust and moth: "These things are mine." It is not even that you have let yourselves sink, flesh and spirit, into a morass of sloth, neither reading nor copying nor meditating on the Scripture and the Commentary, nor yet laboring in the sweat of your brow.

It is that you—monks though you are and sworn to chastity—have carnal doings with women, share your beds with women, sow unlawful seed in women to the begetting of bastards and the confusion of the intentions of Holy Church and God. He who lies with a woman is not and cannot call himself a monk and a Brother. And a woman who lies with such a one is not his wife—no, and not his concubine—but a snare laid for him by Satan, a vessel of spiritual poison, with less claim to heavenly mercy than an impenitent whore. Wait, wait—do not murmur, do not start out of your places—hear me to the end. Whom the Lord loves, He chastises. And if you reject the first stroke of His rod, you also reject the treasure laid up for you in His love.

He sees all and is merciful. He knows what I have come to see plainly: that you do not sin in arrogance, but out of ignorance. If He said in the last hour of His mortal torment, "Father, forgive them, for they know not what they do," will He say less of you who err blindly, groping about, as the Abbot Benno wrote, in the dark?

I am sent not to cast you out, but to gather you in. I am sent not to wreak vengeance, but to put this island back into the open hand of God. He cannot wish to number among His elect any who have taken His vows grudgingly or under constraint; and, so far as I can make out, you were born in the Brotherhood, you have not even taken vows.

Therefore I do not hold you to what you have not sworn, nor do I ask you to commit your souls either to the world or to the Order of Saint Cyprian without due meditation. It is only right that you be given time, that a new crop be sown before we meet again and you declare yourselves. Bear with me a little longer that I may tell you between what and what you make your choice, and thereafter you may depart, each to ponder the matter alone.

Whosoever after the next sowing chooses to remain within the Brotherhood and hold the island in fee for God and Holy Church will live thenceforth according to these rules:

> He will pray assiduously for all Christians, saying the services at the appointed hours and lifting up his voice daily in penitence and praise.
>
> He will labor in the sweat of his brow to restore what was rav-

aged by the waters, to bring the soil to yield its former abund-
ance.

He will labor with his mind and spirit to lay up holy wisdom and
enlighten the ignorant.

He will renounce all worldly possessions, calling nothing his own
except what he needs to cover his nakedness.

And, from the instant he enters the Brotherhood, he will put his
woman from him and reject all commerce with women, knowing
them no more as snares for the flesh and breeders of sinners, but
only as chaste sisters in the spirit.

I know there will be some here among the daughters of Eve who
will be called, like the virgin Genevieve, to come into the sisterhood.
Let them also ponder these matters in their hearts, for a chamber will
be prepared for the day of their coming. The scattered stones of their
place of peace will be raised again one upon another, and their lights
will be rekindled at the edges of the earth.

I do not wonder that your spirits are still disquieted. You would
know—and rightly—what is to be the portion of those whose souls
are worldly and cannot be rooted up out of the world. For them, too,
provision will be made. Ships will come in due time to carry them to
some new town on the other side of the great forest, or to some ancient city like my own. There the alms of Holy Church will sustain
them until such time as they have found a means of sustenance for
themselves.

They whispered, they murmured, they turned appalled faces
upon one another. He waited until the first wave of their protest
had crested and fallen away, and then he spoke to them slowly,
in the voice of one who is not to be gainsaid.

So it is, and so it will be. Meditate upon it until spring, when
we will meet again in this same place. Having said so much, I have
no other word to speak, save only to bless you in the name of the
Father, the Son, and the Holy Ghost. Depart in peace.

The choir withdrew, singing repeated *Alleluias* above the tumult
in the congregation. When Eustace had passed out of her sight,
she turned back to the pulpit and saw that Father Albrecht too

was gone. Once she was on her feet, she found it almost impossible to make her way in the press: they were crowding toward the center portal as if, by getting out of the chapel, they could wrench themselves free of what he had said. One cursed another for blocking his way, one stopped beside a pillar and began to weep; one caught his neighbor by the sleeve and asked earnestly, desperately, "Is it possible? Did I hear him aright?" Outside, the confusion was increased by the lighting of torches: the orange flames swayed and fluttered this way and that, the air was thickened with resinous smoke, and she found it hard to catch her breath. She struggled out of the crowd and leaned against the trunk of a tree, and thought how calmly Eustace had taken all of it. Fearful of meeting him, unready to hear what he might say, she stayed in the shadow while others hurried by.

Pieces of their frantic talk were flung up like spume in voices she knew but could not identify: "But I know there is sin in me—it comes up in my mouth like vomit." "To live in an alien land, on the alms of strangers!" "You need not put me from you, I am not one to wait your bidding." "Is it possible that we could have gotten three bastards?" "I will never depart—it would be better to die." I, too, she thought, am a bastard, the Abbot Ottric's ill-born daughter. . . . And only then did she see the desperate case in which her mother and father stood. How could he put the gentle old woman from him in her age and her sickness? How could he pack her onto a ship and send her utterly out of his ken? How could he go with her, how could he resign his crook to another shepherd? No, she could not think—not of them, not even of herself and Eustace—not with the wild voices assailing her ears and the flames streaming past her eyes. She moved farther back into the shadow and covered her face with her hands.

"Liese—"

In her confusion she took it for the voice of Eustace. But it was not he, it was his kinsman the lord Alain who stood with old Daniel bearing a torch on his left and the chatelaine on his right.

"Shall we light you home, Liese?"

"No, no," she said, repelled that his long face was as composed as the one she had watched in the choir loft. "Others will go my way—I will follow their torches."

"Are you ill? Have you and your father fallen out?"

"No, not ill—and I do not know where my father is, there was such a press."

"Yes, it would be hard to find him. What do you think, Julianne —shall we send Daniel up with her to the Abbot's house?"

"I do not need him. Truly, dear lady, I do not need him. I would rather go by myself." She addressed it to the chatelaine, and in so doing looked at her, and knew that she had not spoken because she could not find the voice to speak. Her face, chalk-white against her crimson snood, was not—could not be—her beautiful and gracious face. Her mouth was without color, and she glared at her husband in frozen rage.

"I think, Daniel, that you should—" But he did not finish it, his lady broke in.

"Will you stop plaguing her?" she said in loathing and contempt. "Are you too buried under your own concerns to see that she means what she says? God knows, you set enough store by your own precious solitude. I would think you had the wit to see that others, too, might sometimes wish to be alone."

Chapter IV

*T*he Abbot Ottric had never had the gift of patience. In the twelve-day stretch between the sermon in the Nuns' Chapel and the first word he had from Father Albrecht, his temples began to throb and the veins came up purple on the backs of his hands. To wait at home for a summons only aggravated the insult. So, though the weather had turned bitter and the two women never stopped begging him to stay by the fire, he left the house as soon as there was light and worked all day in the village on the ruined mill.

He worked in part to mock the drivel about laboring in the sweat of your brow. It was no small accomplishment to bring out a sweat when the air struck into your lungs like slivers of ice. Once the sweat came, it came in a drenching wave—he doubted the holy Father could do as well himself. Light-headed, bleary-eyed, miraculously warm, he would sit down on the frozen bank and watch the landscape shatter and take shape again with every pounding of his heart. Then when the line of hayricks and hovels and filthy yards had settled back into drab solidity, he would heave himself up and return to the business of dislodging vine and lichen and dirt from the big stone wheel, and to another imaginary confrontation with the stranger who had poisoned the island.

Nothing in his lived life was as real as these imaginary confrontations. At first he saw them happening in the common room of the castle, with the chatelaine holding up her spread palm to stave off chaos and Alain retreating behind his everlasting stones. Then the news got about that Father Albrecht was trying to prove himself as good as his word by renouncing luxury and taking up bed and board at the monastery, and the scene of their encounters had to be changed. Not to the monastery—he could not bear that: the image of the stranger walking around in *his* chamber, sitting on *his* stool, dipping a quill into the Abbot Benno's inkwell stopped all thought and turned the beating in his temples into a terrible pain in the head. After that, he transported their quarrels to the Nuns' Chapel, emptied of the congregation at some weird hour of change—night passing into day, day passing into night. He sat where he had really sat on the evening of the sermon, in the great ceremonial chair; and the holy Father stood where he had really stood, behind and above him in the carved pulpit; and, though they spoke to each other, both of them hurled their talk in the same direction, over the vacant benches, down the echoing aisles.

"I have disposed of the inkwell," said the voice of the stranger.

"Why?" Two candles had already gutted themselves into smoky dark, and now three or four more went out.

"Because the inkwell, and everything else that belonged to the aforesaid abbot, including his bones and his thornbush, spread pestilence. He died in sin."

"He died for the flock, which is more than will ever be said for your Holy Father in Rome with his rump on a cushion and his feet in velvet shoes." He thought he had made a furious sound by scraping the legs of the chair across the flagstones, and found that the noise had actually come from the smaller of the two millstones—it had budged a little at last.

"Quibbling, sophistry, infirmity of purpose—these were the sins of the Abbot Benno," said the voice above and behind him. "Also the roots of his madness."

"If he had been mad, the thornbush would never have blossomed. Read the Book."

"In madness he ate the foetid wafer, betraying Christ even as Eve betrayed the Creator when she ate of the apple—"

"You and your analogies!" He exulted that he could use such a learned word. "You and your false analogies!"

"*Ibi, sibi, tibi, in viaticus daemonicus, corpus Christi* . . ." A whole string of incomprehensible Latin came from the pulpit and wove around the chapel like the smoke from the quenched candles. He did not listen: he marshaled up his argument.

"Are you finished?" he shouted when the voice failed and the holy gibberish stumbled. "If you are finished, let me tell you that Eve's apple and the Abbot Benno's wafer have nothing to do with each other. Eve ate in luxury to fatten her breasts and anoint her secret parts. The Abbot Benno ate in despair in order to find an answer for what has no answer—not then, not now, no matter what you think. The likeness is that the two of them opened their mouths and chewed and swallowed. The difference is that she ate life and he ate death. Since the difference far outweighs the likeness, you are guilty—"

"*Pater et filius—*"

"I say—" he said it so violently that the spittle of his rage fanned out and quenched the last candle, "I say you are guilty of a false analogy and an itch for the chatelaine and a wandering eye for the little lily-fingered Brother. Your jack still jumps under your cassock, and in more than one direction. I'd lay my life on that, *in spiritum sanctum.*"

This was only one of the clashes he carried out in his mind with the hatefully unreachable stranger. There were others about different matters and in different places. There was that time in the hut built in the Square for the convenience of penitents and confessor when he jeered at confessions: to think that God would listen to such trash—imagine running like an old woman who has to tell somebody how she did or did not move her bowels— surely there were some things a decent human being kept to himself. And once, just before the summons came, in a time of heavy sweating when he could not tell whether he was awake or asleep, it seemed to him that they met on the bridge, and the holy Father said courteously, "Where are you going, reverend Abbot?" and clever and polished Latin came out of his own mouth in reply: "*In locus simulate tibi, in gravum meum*," which is to say: "The same place as you are, into my grave."

So when he was told that the lay brother had been to the house to ask him to call at the monastery, he shrugged. His rage had long since had its feast, its fire. "I will go when it suits my purpose," he said, and spent another day at the mill, and yet one more day lying abed to ease the swelling in his legs and feet. It was a full fortnight, then, after the sermon in the Nuns' Chapel that he saw his adversary and usurper again, in his lived life, in the world as it was: a world bled out, strangely distanced and muted, neither bright nor dull, neither warm nor cold.

While he waited—he could not even stir up anger that he had to sit and wait—he looked at the chamber which had once been his and admitted without feeling that the changes were for the good. The three bearskin rugs had been shaken out and brushed and spread. The floor was spotless. Certain marks that might have been filth and might have been smoke stains had been scrubbed off the walls. The orderliness of the reading desk impressed him most: the slanted wooden counter was paler and sleeker than he had ever known it to be, the ragged edge of the Book was lined up precisely with the sharp edge of the counter, and the Abbot Benno's onyx inkwell, cleansed of its scum of ancient ink, showed veins and spottings he had never seen. He entertained the notion of going over and taking it in his hand, but knew at once that he no longer cared for it enough to pull his body up out of the chair.

Did not care either, though he duly noted it, that there was a difference between Father Albrecht envisioned and Father Albrecht seen. The actual man was frailer, yet more impressive. Though he preached the letter of the Benedictine Rule, he had oddly stopped applying it to his person: as he stepped into the room, the seaweed scent of Saint Cyprian's came with him; his hair hung almost to his shoulders, and his tonsure had grown in. "Forgive me, reverend Abbot—I would not have kept you waiting if they had told me at once," he said. "I was in the scriptorium with Brother Eustace when . . ."

He did not hear the rest of it. He considered the strangeness of his own feelings at the naming of Brother Eustace. He had asked for nothing better than the present arrangement: Brother Eustace with his nose in a book in the scriptorium and Liese left once and for all to get over the foolishness. Still, there was a surge of annoyance at the stranger whose courtliness had drawn the young man's lordly blood away from peasant suppers and herb brews and sick sheep.

". . . So I have long been looking forward to your visit. I would have thought you would come long since to claim what you surely know is your own."

Father Albrecht plainly meant this place, this chamber. But he did not know it for his own, no matter what the speaker might believe. It had receded, was far away, like some little Jerusalem off in the corner of a carved Nativity, small and remote behind manger and kneeling kine. He looked down at his own knuckles, swollen and cracked with the work at the mill, and shook his head.

"Ah, but you must not reject what the Lord has given you and His servants have made ready—"

He forced his eyes to take all of it in: the seemly reading desk, the washed walls, the scrubbed floor. "It is very orderly now—a different place altogether," he said out of courtesy.

"I can see how your wife's feebleness would keep you at home for yet a while until other arrangements can be made—"

He shrugged at his wife's feebleness: she somehow managed to drag her aching bones from one place to another while he hacked at stone and tore at lichen. He shrugged, and knew it was the wrong gesture, seemed crude and heartless. It was wrong, too, that this emissary of the God of the unforgotten should be standing before him while he sat. He began to pull himself up.

"Sit, reverend Abbot—" There was shock in the raised voice.

"You also, Father, sit you down. I am tired—befuddled—I forgot myself."

"I thank your Reverence."

But Father Albrecht was no less formidable once he was seated; indeed it was harder to encounter him on the same level, face to face. Plainly aware of the stress, he fixed his veiled eyes on the bearskin rug and got on with the business: "For the time being, we would rejoice to have the shepherd with us an hour or so each day, to direct our efforts at rebuilding, to give spiritual nourishment to the Brothers, to pray with us now and then. A week hence, he may find himself staying all day. Thereafter, before the time for the decision comes, he may well see the monastery for what it is to the monk—his true heart's home. Very likely it will seem to him then that a visit elsewhere, an hour in his house or in the village, is a grudged exile from peace."

"You mean, stay here from morning till night?"

"If we rebuild and refurbish—if we reinstitute the orders—Matins, Nones—"

"What would I do with myself?"

"Many things that are properly your charge, things that I deal with now in your name, beyond my own authority. You, not I, should be confessing the Brothers—"

"Excuse me, holy Father, I cannot confess the Brothers."

"Why do you say so? The ritual of the confessional is simple, I could teach it to you in the time we have been sitting here—"

"It is not that. I could probably learn it if I put my mind to it. But I set no store by confessions."

"No? And can you tell me why?"

There was a maddening condescension in that. "And can you tell me why?" was a thing for the male to say to the female, the elder to the child. "Yes, Father, I can tell you why." He heard the rasping edge of his own voice sawing away at propriety. "To my mind, a man who commits a sin commits it once and for all, beyond undoing. I cannot take away a sin any more than you can call the Cathedral up out of the waters or give life back to the dead. What is, is."

"Do not discount God's mercy, reverend Abbot, no, nor the miracles that have been wrought in the name of the Father and the Son and the Holy Ghost—"

"*Ibi, tibi, sibi*—"

"What did your Reverence say?"

"Nothing. Nothing beyond what I have said already: I set no store by confessions."

"Then we will speak no more of them, at least not for the present. Though the world without them—" he raised his eyes, mournful and startlingly naked, "the world without them, as I see it, would be a very hard and barren place. Think how it would be with this earth, reverend Abbot, if every time a man set his foot on the face of it the footprint remained. Nothing to wash it away, nothing to soften or efface it—no rain, no rivers, no springs—though I know you are about to mock me, you are on the point of saying: 'And no tidal waves either.'"

"So I would have said if you had not said it for me." Unable to sustain the steady look, he went back to staring at his knuckles.

"But it is not as if confessions were your only duties. For months the chronicle has remained untouched. You must begin again where you left off, and how can you write of the changes that are coming to pass if you are not here?"

"I will not be writing anything more in the Book, holy Father."

"But why?"

"I am not a scholar, I do not know the pure Latin of the great cities." He overrode the courtly gesture that belittled inflections and spellings; he raised his voice until anybody in the next room could hear. "I am fit for only one service, and I have already laid my hand to that. I bow to Saint Benedict, I labor in my sweat, I am mending the wheel at the mill—"

"Dear brother in Jesus, so I have heard, and I am sick at the

212

thought of it. That a man of your years—yes, and the shepherd of the flock—should be doing such work in this bitter cold—"

"I am not so very cold, holy Father. Our hides are different, yours and mine. You shiver at the first frost, the ox shivers at the first freeze, and I fall somewhere in between—"

One thin hand, still blue at the fingertips with the marks of the fiery sickness, reached out as if to touch him on the knee. Reached out, but did not touch; and whether it was squeamishness or fright that made it withdraw, he did not know and did not greatly care.

"You must not read me any lessons. I am no child, holy Father. Look, you are not young, but I could have begotten you if I had been at it as early as I should," he said, getting up out of the chair. "God may have sent you to read lessons to the people of Saint Cyprian's, but my eighteen years as abbot here have put me beyond it: I am not at your beck and call—"

"God bear witness that the furthest thing from my mind was to read any lessons to your Reverence—"

The voice was stricken. Perhaps the face also—he did not stop to see—rage gave him strength to stride past it to the door.

"Do not go in anger, I earnestly entreat you. What am I to say to the flock? What can I tell the Brothers?"

He waited until he had passed over the threshold into the vestibule with its newly polished pillars before he turned and said, "That is something you will have to fathom out. That is no longer any concern of mine."

✠   ✠   ✠

Six days had gone by since Father Albrecht had laid down earthly and heavenly law from the pulpit in the Nuns' Chapel, and in the interim little by way of speech had passed between the lord of the castle and the chatelaine.

Probably she had been the one who first fostered silence. As soon as their guest took himself and his few belongings off to the monastery, she had set diligently about a dozen neglected household tasks;

213

she did not want to hear again that her bird had flown—far this time and for good. But after the sermon it was another matter. That her husband should sit day after day burying himself in the Book of the virgin Genevieve, as if no preposterous future had been proposed, as if no unthinkable choice hung over their heads—it was enough to drive her to distraction.

And on the fifth day, when a solemn Brother came to the door with his finger laid across his lips and handed her a piece of parchment, it seemed that fate and old custom had taken up her husband's cause and were conspiring against her. "The Abbot Ottric is no more. We found him dead at his labor, in the ditch under the mill wheel"—such was the written news. Once she had read it and communicated it to the rest of her household, she was bound, like everybody else on the island, to hold her peace. Inasmuch as Masses for the dead were forbidden, it had been agreed among the children of Saint Cyprian's that they would honor a departed shepherd by sharing his silence while he still lay among them, waiting to be put into his grave.

He killed him, she thought. As surely as if he did it with his own hands, he killed him. Put him in a ceremonial chair in front of the Nuns' Chapel and disgraced him under our eyes. Sent him to labor in the sweat of his brow. Swelled his old heart until it burst. . . . And her own heart swelled with what she could not utter, so that she felt it beating in her throat and her ears. And all the while, Alain sat in the common room, swathed in silence, protected and sustained by hallowed, ancient silence. Death and mourning had never called up in him anything but constraint, and this prescribed silence justified him in doing what he would have done in any case.

She herself could not grieve as she wished she could: her first shock and sorrow were meanly pecked away by the annoyances of the day as it wore on. Miserable supper of cold apples and colder fowl. A stretch of night to be walked through on the way to what had once been the Abbot Ottric's house. Apprehension over seeing a corpse, over staying with a corpse in a little room. There had been a thaw at noon and another freeze as soon as the sun went down, and now the ground was so slippery that she had to cling to her husband's arm all the way. Though they had come early, there were half a dozen torches, whose carriers were already inside, stuck into heaped snow near the path, and other torchbearers stood outside, waiting their turn to go in. *He* was not among them, nor likely to be inside, either, and she was glad of it—or so she told herself. Considering what had passed of late between him and the dead, he would come later, when the press would be greatest; he would come after she was gone. And, knowing her thoughts were not with her husband, she relinquished the support of his arm out of scrupulousness. Not that it made any difference to him one way or another: his quicksilver eyes followed the comings-out and the goings-in and never once settled on her face.

Two peasants. Three goodwives from the village. An old man with a child. Some weeping, others with the cold tears standing withheld in their eyes. Though she tried dutifully to call grief to the surface, when it was their turn to step under the lintel she had not summoned up a single tear. After the streaming red and yellow light in front of the house, the darkness inside it—custom permitted neither candles nor hearth fires—was like blindness. She dared to move only in her husband's wake, plucking and holding on to a fold of his cassock. To the right, warily, in the little space between the wall and the bier. Up to the head of the bier, where Liese and Berthe sat on the floor. She bent over and kissed them on their foreheads: Berthe's cold and damp, Liese's dry and feverish. And back down now, between other mourners sitting cross-legged on the rushes, according to the ancient use. The door opened to let one out and another in, and in the sudden accession of light she counted only two cassocks besides the one she clung to: Eustace's white one over by the fireless hearth, and Giraldus's russet one, farther off, with the inverted yellow cross. Dark again, and Alain sat down, and she knew that they had settled near the bottom of the bier, close to Ottric's dead feet.

It was those feet that she saw first on the next brief opening of the door. They were yellow as wax, with blunted toes and ingrown nails, and she tried to put down horror by thinking how far they had carried him, on what errands of stern obligation and unceremonious charity. But she could not get on very well with that: her mind skipped over to the red shoes he had worn on the evening when Father Albrecht had discoursed on the Eucharist. Precious shoes, precious abbot's cassock, not to be laid with the poor corpse in the earth, but to be handed down to his successor— which was foolishness now, since proper shoes and all the other churchly trappings would be coming over in ships from the other side, and it was a pity to put him barefoot, in a threadbare shift, into the cold ground. . . .

Streamers of light again, and somebody else—only the goodwife Angela—stepping in, a shadowy shape topped with tousled, aureate hair. Next time, look at his face, she thought, and waited a good quarter of an hour before she was given the chance. A mask in the wavering yellowness—a big flat mask with fury written all over it. Nothing that had been done for it, not the weighting down of the eyelids, not the arrangement of the coarse, curled locks around the cheeks and over the forehead, could hide the fact that the Abbot Ottric had died in a rage. Let *him* come and look at it, let *him* see what has sprouted out of his holiness, she thought. And, as if she had conjured him up, at the next opening of the door, he was there on the threshold with a forbidden candle in his hand. "Dearly beloved, my children in Christ," he said.

His light invaded their darkness, his alien accent broke in upon their ancient stillness—but only Giraldus had the temerity to say "Ssh!" He chose to ignore it—or perhaps he had not heard.

"We are gathered together," he said in a quiet voice that was an affront only because it *was* a voice, "to pray for the soul of the Abbot Ottric, and to commend him to God and to God's everlasting peace."

The dank cold of the night was coming in behind him, and somebody got up and shut the door. The flame of his candle almost went out, then steadied itself and cast a small area of light that included little: his face covered by the cowl, save for the nose that turned to the right at the tip—that and the chest of the corpse, wide as a bull's, over which he stood.

"Even the least of the flock, even a stranger and a late-comer such as I, knows how it is with the sheep when the shepherd is gone. Therefore I have come to offer you such comfort as Christ our Redeemer and Holy Church—"

"We do not want it." Giraldus, speaking in an audible whisper out of his black corner.

"Ah . . ." said Liese, like a sleeper sick and in pain.

"And there are comforts for the living as well as blessings for the dead in the service of the Mass, which I am bound by my Order and my mission to say for my brother in Christ who lies sleeping here."

"Say it elsewhere." No whisper this time. "Our custom is otherwise. We are committed to share his silence and darkness, and you intrude upon us."

She was conscious that the silence hallowed by a hundred years was dribbling away in babblings and whisperings, but still more conscious of *his* stricken face. His mouth twitched as she had seen it twitched by the pangs of the fiery sickness, the candle jerked in his hand, and she felt no satisfaction in seeing him undone.

"Oh, now, truly, Giraldus," said the strident, good-natured voice of Angela, "is that a way to talk to the holy Father, who has come out of the kindness of his heart to say for our abbot just such a Mass as would be said for the Holy Father in Rome himself?"

The lord of the manor stood up. "Let us not loose contention in a room where mourners sit," he said. "Though two customs are at odds here—the custom of Saint Cyprian's and the custom of the other side—we need not quarrel over it at a wake. It should be settled reasonably and peaceably, according to the will of those most concerned: the wife and the daughter of the dead. What is your will, Berthe? You knew him the best and were with him the longest."

"So I was," said the old woman. "Forty years, day and night. But that is all gone now, and he is gone, and, one way or another, what difference can it make to him or me? Let the holy Father say the Roman words, if he sees it as his duty. I am sure he means it for the best, and what can I lose more than what I have already lost?"

"No, Mother." Liese stood up and came into the candlelight, face to face with Father Albrecht, with the bier between them. "I will not have it, because he would never have wanted it so. He was my father as well as her husband, and I saw how it was with him under the old law and under the new. Before you came, holy Father, he prospered as well as anybody prospers here. But he had a bitter end—confusion and disgrace and labor beyond his bearing. If my mother says it makes no difference to her one way or another, she does not mean it, she only wants to keep peace. To me and to all of us, it makes a great difference, so I beg you to let us alone."

"Let it be as you say, my daughter." He lifted his hand to make the sign of the cross over the bier, and for the first time the chatelaine knew that his eyes had found her on the edge of shadow. She had shaken her head to warn against the sign, and his hand came down, lifeless as a bird stopped in midair by a stone. Some watcher outside, wondering at the voices, opened the door to see what strangeness had come to pass, and the candle went out. "God comfort you all. I also grieve for him," he said, and stepped out into the cold.

☩   ☩   ☩

She lay in the great bed that was as good as empty, and kept telling herself not to move. He who lay sleeping beside her had been kind to her on this wake-night after his own fashion: had not invited Eustace back with them to the castle, had stayed less time than usual sorting his stones downstairs, had heaped three coverlets on her side of the bed when she complained of the cold. But even Eustace's company would have been better than this loneliness; even the clicking sounds from his corner downstairs would have been more comfort to her than this stern deep-breathing silence; and the covers were a damp weight pressing down upon her body, becoming as she moved into dreams the earth filled into her grave.

Twice she had slipped in sleep into the place where Ottric would be tomorrow and forever, and now she did not dare to close her eyes. She fixed them on the arras drawn across the seaward window: its shabby warp and woof were visible in the light of the moon. There was movement too—an undulation and now and again a billowing. She stared until her eyes went blind with staring and then made use of her ears to assure herself that she lived. Only the living could hear the wind, the grating of stones dragged back and forth by the wash of the tide, the crash of a great wall of water far out at sea.

Another sound too—something, somebody in the garden. "Alain," she said.

He drew in a long breath and let it out on a sigh. Even in his sleep she was mainly a cause for sighing: Are you there again with all your needs and wants? Will you never let me alone?

Well, sleep, she thought, and sat up, and turned the coverlets back at the corners. Somebody *was* in the garden—sound of gravel crunched under pacing feet. She knew what she hoped, and named against her hopes the ones who might be walking there: Jehanne too desolate to stay in her hovel and too shy to knock, Eustace with a gnawing conscience, old Daniel worried in his dotage about prowling devils, Mechthilde looking for food. . . . She got up, crossed the room barefoot, drew back the curtain and saw bleakness—churning water, jagged cliff, barren garden. The emanation of the moon—she could not call it light, filtered as it was through fog—showed her the top of his head where the hair had grown back short and fine. Do not go away, old man with an infant's vulnerable pate, she thought. Wait a little, and I with my faded hair and shrunken breasts will come down and let you in.

Halfway down the stairs she realized that she was almost naked. Old fur cloak—she snatched it out of the closet at the foot of the staircase and put it on. The room was in appalling disorder: the servants had used their grief as an excuse to leave the supper-time board still spread, the fire unbanked, the leather cushions strewn about. She undid the latch, opened the door, swung out with it into fog and frost, and said his name. He turned in his pacing, but there was nothing for her in the monkish blankness of his face. "Come in, holy Father," she said, suiting her voice to the meaninglessness of the event. "I believe there is something left of the fire."

He came with so little hesitation that she wanted to laugh at herself. She, not he, felt the replacing of the latch as an embarrassing significance. She, not he, paused at the entrance to the great hall, not knowing what spot to choose. He rejected the hearth and went straight to the cluttered board. Very well, she thought, we will keep good solid wood between us; and she went round to the other side. "Sit down, if you can bear the sight of these crusts," she said, and seated herself.

"I hope I did not waken you, my lady." In settling onto the bench with his back to the fire, he gave her one of the quick and churchly glances which were all he had had for her since his departure, looking intently for an instant at her forehead and avoiding whatever of her person existed below the level of her brow. "It never came into my mind that you would have gone to bed."

"It is very late." Foolish to pull at the fur cloak, to try to keep it from slipping away from thigh and shoulder. "We left the wake early—we came away to make room for others—Alain is asleep—"

"As I remember it, you kept later hours when I was at the castle."

"Now and again—on certain evenings." If he had recalled the evening of roast chestnuts and mild dalliance, he did not show it. He was staring down at a tin plate filled with curled apple peel and a brown chewed core. "But tonight both of us were very tired."

"Then I *have* wakened you, though I did not knock."

"No, really, I was awake, I could not sleep."

"I took it that you would surely be up, like everybody else on Saint Cyprian's, or I would never have stopped by."

"Is everybody up?"

"Yes," he said with bitter emphasis.

"Grieving over the Abbot Ottric's death—" The words and her own voice sounded false and vacuous in her ears.

"Just so. Grieving over the Abbot Ottric's death—and laying the blame of it on me."

If that is his tune, let him do the singing, she thought; I have gone far enough in making a fool of myself.

"Laying the blame of it on me, as if it were all my doing, though plainly he brought it on himself through his own ignorance and stubbornness."

And you came, she thought, not for my comfort but for my husband's support. . . . That he would have had it, too, galled her into sitting tall and staring back at his forehead and letting the cloak slip and slide as it would. "I do not know how it is on the other side of the isthmus," she said, "but here on Saint Cyprian's we wait to speak ill of the dead until they are in their graves. When you have taken his abbot's crook unto yourself—when you have set to rights what matters he could not manage—then there will be plenty of time for you to speak of his stubbornness and his ignorance."

"I do not want his abbot's crook or anything else on this island—"

"You have made that plain enough."

"I was sent to this island to bring it back into the fold. Once that is done, I will depart and leave to others the arrangements and dispositions of . . ."

She did not hear, she could not listen. Her heart had begun to beat violently at the announcement of his going. She toyed with a crust to hide her consternation, and had to drop it at once lest he see by the shaking of her hands what devastation he had wrought.

". . . back in my Chapter House in Cologne, from which— seeing what came about tonight—I should never have come. In my cell, by the grace of God, I mean to spend what little of my life is left in peace."

"Forgetting us utterly?"

Even her stricken voice did not make him raise his eyes from the plate. "It is useless to brood over what is finished and done with, even when we wish it had been done better," he said. "Besides, I have not committed such atrocities as you and the rest here seem to think. The Abbot Ottric lived to a ripe age, and in a time of change God shows His wisdom by giving the Brotherhood a younger shepherd—"

"And it is nothing to you that he leaves behind him a daughter whose lover you have taken away, and a poor old woman—"

"We have spoken of the daughter on another occasion. As for the old woman—"

"She is nothing to be concerned about? She can be put out of thought, thrown like an old crust onto a garbage heap?"

"That is not so, I have no such thought," he said. "The truth of it is, I have thought more than you know about the old woman—" There was a working and a pulsing in his neck; he raised his hand in an awkward gesture toward his throat and then let it fall open and palm upward on the soiled cloth. "You may remember, that evening when they first came here, she touched me. I think she touched me on the knee. She touched me, and I did not forbid it"—he paused, trying to steady his voice—"though I and my kind have foresworn all touch—"

Seeing that weeping had come upon him beyond his mastering, she laid her hand on his and left it there, though his fingers did not stir.

"It was no small thing that she should touch me—no woman had touched me, not for twenty years—"

What is he that he could have forgotten it? she asked herself. If I can never wash my hands of the knowledge of the secret places of his body, nor deliver my nostrils from the mingled smell of the ointment and his sweat, nor blot away from my eyes his arms held out and his ribs rising and falling in his fever, nor stop my ears against his voice crying out to me, "Come, come—"

222

She felt his eyes upon her, and not on her forehead. In the long look that was between them, one swathing after another fell away —first anger, then pride, then shame—until she knew him in spirit as she had known his body in its vulnerable nakedness. And she surrendered herself as freely to be seen, her face still and stripped beyond a smile or an utterance.

"Come," he said, rising. "What are we doing with this table between us?"

Three times they had each other then: once for the slaking of desire, once for the richness of full knowledge, and once in aching tenderness because the light was showing at the window and they must go their separate ways; and now she was the one who wept. He brought her her shift and wrapped the cloak around her. "I will not leave you wondering if I will come again," he said. "Be sure I will come. Nothing could keep me from it."

"Nothing? Truly?"

"Nothing this side of death."

✠   ✠   ✠

Never in all his monkish days had Father Albrecht found so much advantage in the monastic life. Now that he had rid himself of one of its three primary strictures, he saw the other two as downright blessings. With chastity out of the way, who could murmur against obedience or complain about poverty?

If he had not accepted the yoke put upon him in Cologne by his abbot, he would never have known the surges of love or the still pools between them, would never have stretched out on his back with his head in her lap and made a ringlet of her hair around his finger, would never have dredged up unsuspected riches from his past and turned them into words and given them into her keeping so that his union with her was also his own resurrection. In obedience to his spiritual father, he had exchanged a candle butt and a little circle of light in which to read about the dead for the stored autumnal sweetness of her body and the winnowed harvest of her thoughts.

Nor could he fail to recognize that this fulfillment was the fruit

223

of poverty. The white birch tree that moves and beckons does not flourish in the opiate South; there is a singular savor at the core of a winter apple; purer honey drips from the comb in a land where the flowers are small and few. This starved island and her starved life and his Christian starvation had fused to work a miracle of austere alchemy. Once in this century, only between him and her, only on Saint Cyprian's . . .

On days when he could not see her—and nine of the fourteen since their conjunction had passed without that blessedness—he meditated on Saint Cyprian's. It was a strange kind of meditation. Back in Cologne the mad brother who was forever tormented by the possibility that a crumb of Christ's body might find its way into the belly of a rat had sometimes gotten respite by meditating on the Virgin Mary's womb. He had not understood it then, but felt kinship with it now. Divine spirit entering into a red coagulating mass and thereby making all red coagulation holy—something of the kind, something connected by no strands of reason to this island, this peninsula in the western sea. Blank beach, tawny cliffs, hungry land, ravenous water—her spirit had entered this and no other place, had compounded only here with time and mortality. Here he lay beside her, her lover and her twin, a spirit accumulating a body, aware and not caring that the only birth out of such a womb is a birth into death.

Between the times when they met wherever they could—at the castle if Alain was on the beach, in a crypt under the Nuns' Chapel ostensibly on a search for the bones of a martyr, in the booth in the Square on the pretense of a protracted confession—he meditated also on the name of the island, as all monks meditate on the Holy Name. As her hair had two colors—the silver of a veiled sun in one light and the dry gold of wheat in another—"Saint Cyprian's" had two meanings. It was named, of course, after that martyred Bishop of Carthage whose bald and reverend head had fallen under a Roman ax in Valerian's persecution. His green marble likeness stood in the entrance of the monastery with outstretched hands whose emptiness was eloquent. In the blackest years of Holy Church's history he had given all he had—a great fortune, a patrician's ease and power, a scholar's mind, that bald frail head itself—to his Carthaginian flock of the Lord's sheep. *Caritas,* charitable love for the lapsed and the sinners and the poor, was a word often in his letters and on his tongue. His rhetoric had flowed as cool as silver water over the fire of schism and put it out. Thascius Caecilius Cyprianus, Saint Cyprian . . .

But how had he come by his patronym? Had his forebears gone to Carthage from the Isle of Cyprus, where Aphrodite the Golden sprang out of the genitals of Chronos, a red coagulation on the floor of the southern sea? Saint Cyprian with his empty hands spread: I have given everything. The Cyprian with one hand over the mound of Venus and the other across her breasts: I have everything to give. The Saint and the goddess could become one— perhaps in his union with the chatelaine had already merged into a new thing in the world.

A reborn body does not ask for much. Somewhere he had read —and he pondered it at the risk of sacrilege—how the risen Christ had accepted some small nourishment: a fragment of fish, a bit of bread. Anything more than the fare of a deprived brotherhood would have been too much. He sat at noonday at table in the refectory with those seven Brothers who had made their choice early, and felt himself attended by a goodly company. God's promise of plenty to the children of Israel was fulfilled in him with a single egg, a scattering of dried herbs, a coarse rusk. The reader for the day uttered the hot desert phrases over the sigh and rasp of the northern wind—"I am the rose of Sharon, the lily of the valley." And when I have eaten this last morsel, he thought, I will go and walk on the dunes in prayer and meditation.

"Father Albrecht—" It was Brother Thaddeus, coming toward him down the length of the board now that the meal was over.

"Yes, my son?" He had miscounted. There had been eight, not seven, with him at table. The Brotherhood of Saint Cyprian, if he included himself, now stood at nine; and the one he had omitted was the fat lay brother who had come with him across the wilderness.

"I know how heavily burdened you are these days—"

225

It was not true. He had never carried his duties so lightly. Problems that would have gnawed at him for weeks he disposed of now with immediate solutions. Even his handwriting was more swift and sure: twenty pages of Cyprian's *Discourse on the Lapsed* done in a week, and every one an impeccable page.

"But there is a certain scandalous matter I am sure you would wish to hear about—"

Why would anybody think he wished to hear about such things? "Is it urgent, Brother?" he said.

"Not so urgent, Father, that it cannot wait until you have had your daily consultation with Brother Eustace."

It galled him, too, to hear his casual wanderings into the scriptorium transformed into "daily consultations" by the lay brother's jealousy. "Brother Eustace does not need me, he has his work laid out for him," he said.

"Then, if you could spare me the time for a word or two—"

"As many as you like. Sit down, Brother." The refectory was empty now, except for one new Brother who had stayed to scrape the plates, and he would soon be gone.

"I thought we might speak in private—"

He got up, jarring the table. "How is it, my son, that you can never make the simplest request outright? Come along, come along—it is no great matter for a member of the Brotherhood to ask to see me in my cell."

But in saying "my cell" and moving toward it in proprietary haste, he knew himself guilty of a presumption that his follower was luckily too thick-headed to note. He was not the abbot here, had not—as *she* had said in the bitterness before the ecstasy—snatched the shepherd's crook out of the dead hand. These washed walls, these bearskins, the Book and onyx inkwell on the reading stand—they were his only until a new abbot was duly elected to take the peasant-Father's place. Not that he could allow himself to think about a time when he would be going away: to brood on that would be to press too hard against the delicate membrane, the refuge in which he had enclosed himself. He chose to sit on the high stool more to assure himself that he belonged there than to assert his authority. As for the lay brother—he let himself down, put off and resigned to repeated puttings-off, on a bench that stood six paces away against the wall.

There was not much room for his big body. He sat on one end of the bench because the rest of it was a clutter: the embroidery of the three sea gulls folded up into a square, the scattered pages of the sermon, the butt-end of a sausage, a scarlet napkin—all of them brought here from the confessional booth near the Burning-Trees. *She* had collected them and handed them to him after a long, cramped, laughable round of pleasure; since he had taken up his quarters in the monastery, she said, why should he leave his possessions behind? And what could he do but take them with him? And, now that he had them here, where was he to put them? The one possible receptacle and hiding place—still unthinkable—was a chest believed to hold a comb and a shift that had once belonged to the virgin Genevieve.

"Believe me, Father, I am not here to trouble you with a trifle. But yesterday when I visited the house of the Abbot Ottric, I became aware of a most unseemly situation." He was doing his best to keep his eyes off the unseemly sausage.

"What was that?"

"Liese—the daughter—is out of the house all day long. Instead of taking care of her mother, she has gotten it into her head that she should be mending the big wheel down at the mill."

"Well, that I can understand, Brother. She is, as it were, 'about her father's business.'"

"Yes, that is true enough, but who do you think she has brought into the house to take her place?"

He saw that he would never hear the end of it unless he showed the proper interest. He dragged his look away from the trophies that cluttered the bench and fixed it on the round, excited face. "Well, then, who, Brother?"

"The whore—bless me, now that I am most in need of it, the name has slipped utterly out of my mind—the dark whore—"

227

He was on the point of saying "Elspeth?" and barely managed to say "Jehanne?"

"Jehanne, yes. She and no other. Where, except on this island, would a prostitute sit at an abbot's table, dust and wash and handle an abbot's belongings, sleep under an abbot's roof?"

"Only on this island, as you say, Brother. But, once we have said so much, we must also say that the islanders themselves may not see in it any cause for offense. Perhaps they never considered their abbot's house a holy place. Perhaps it was hallowed for them only so long as he lived in it. Perhaps—"

"But that the girl should bring home a whore, Father—"

"Perhaps she was the only one who could come."

"No, on the contrary. Any number of women would have gone to them. The goodwife Angela, for one."

"But they are grieving. The goodwife Angela, for all her virtues, might have been hard put to it to temper her cheerfulness."

"And her cheerfulness would have been less painful to them in their grief than the sight of a whore? No, Father, that is a hard thing for me to understand. You should see her, you should go to that house and see her."

He conjured her up as she had been when she walked out of the confessional, leaving him there with his pounding heart and his turning wheel of light. Head down, sheepskin vest hanging loose and damp on her starved body, unforgiven and unblessed, going back into the snow out of his little cubicle of warmth, yes, and without hope of any share in such warmth as there might be in Heaven. . . . "I have seen her, Brother. She is ill-clothed and wretched."

"Ill-clothed? Her clothing is such that she would be better off not clothed at all. A hole here, a hole there, a tatter in back, a tatter in front. Whichever way she turns, something reveals itself, and a person stands with his heart in his mouth wondering when it will be the stinking pit of Hell itself."

"Is that what you call it?" The outrage to the poor girl's womanhood, spied upon and found out and disparaged by the very eyes that avidly sought after it—

228

"What am I to call it?" The lay brother pressed his knees to-gether under his cassock and went red and sweaty in the face. "So I have heard it called in a hundred sermons. A pit—and whoso-ever enters into it is dragged down to Hell."

Call it otherwise and enter into blessedness. Call it a sanctuary for hallowing and crowning. Lift up your heart to know that every woman carries such a sanctuary with her wherever she goes—car-ries it under faded silk, under a nun's white woolen, under rags. Rejoice and be exceeding glad that whoever enters there, if he has the grace to make himself welcome, is welcomed with unguents and incense and transformed into God's anointed, a king of kings.

"What would you have me call it, Father?"

"Why must you call it anything?"

"I am—as I have confessed to you over and over—much beset by the sin of lechery. I cannot fail to see what is put before my eyes. If I spoke grossly of the woman, it is because she is a pros-titute."

"Read the Gospel and see what the Lord said of such a one: 'Much will be forgiven her, for she has loved much.'"

"Did He say that? It is a hard text—"

"But well worth pondering. Now, as to this matter of Jehanne, I will not meddle in it. She can do no harm to Liese, much less to Berthe; she is there at their bidding, and I would be gainsaying or reproving them if I were to ask her to go elsewhere. She herself is giving Christian service to the afflicted, and Holy Church would say that she could not be better occupied."

"Well, if such is your judgment, Father." He got up, rueful and unwieldy, and started for the threshold, but stopped there to sigh over the ruin of his good intentions. "Whatever I do, I always manage to provoke your displeasure. How can I bring myself closer to a state of grace?"

Grow a beard, put away childish things, eat less, find a woman —so he thought as he got down from his eminence. And good humor worked like a leaven in him, making it possible for him to lay his hand on the big shoulder, and smile. "To displease me and to fall out of the grace of God are scarcely the same thing,

229

Brother," he said. "Pray for all sinners, including me. I will see you at service and listen for your good strong bass in the *Alleluia*. Meanwhile, peace."

Once the door was closed, he went to the bench and picked up the piece of stitchery with the sea gulls. He had no longer any question as to where it belonged; after unfolding it and shaking it free of dust, he laid it on top of the chest sacred to the virgin Genevieve. A proper cover for the worm-eaten wood—he stepped back and admired how the eyes and the little red feet glowed like rubies out of the dun-colored cloth.

The script of the sermon he had given in the Nuns' Chapel—that too should be laid by in some apropriate place. He got the parchment sheets into order and carried them to the reading-stand; but, once there, he did not know how to place them in relation to the Book. On the Book? Unthinkable—on top of it they had the air of superseding it. Inside the Book? No, scarcely—something as disturbing as the after-odor of bad cooking clung to the sheets in his hand and would somehow dishonor the smoky smell of the bound pages. Where, then? For an instant he thought of crumpling them up and throwing them onto the hearth, but that was mad: here was a document that belonged to the Brother-hood, a statement that the next abbot would be certain to re-quire. Under the Book then. He raised the heavy volume at a slant and pushed the sheets in under it, let it come down on them, and was inordinately pleased to see them go completely out of sight. Yes, he thought, wiping his hands on his cassock, exactly the right place, under the Book.

But somebody was standing behind him. Mechthilde—the one that everybody called a witch—and how could she have insinuated herself into a monastery, and why would she be standing in his cell? He had seen her only at a distance since she had reviled him over the hedge; and the nameless guilt she had called up in him then assailed him again, though her face had undergone a total change. All hate and rage were gone from her, and in their place was a sickly look of adoration, a sweet and maudlin devotion that melded all her little features into one mass of crinkling fatuity.

"Father! Dear Father!"

He steadied himself against the reading-stand. "What are you doing here?" he said, more affronted by the adoration than by the intrusion.

"Only what I have been wanting to do ever since you spoke to the damned from the pulpit in the Nuns' Chapel: I am looking my fill at your holy face."

"Look beyond it, my daughter. It is a sin and a confusion—" He did not finish the formula about the dangers of mistaking the earthly wick for the heavenly flame. He himself could no longer clearly distinguish between the two; besides, the woman was mad beyond the comprehension of metaphor.

"Just as you say, Father: sin and confusion. Nothing here, nothing any more on the other side, nothing in the whole world, drowned or not, nothing but sin and confusion."

"You must keep a firm heart, my child. You must—"

"Have you ever seen a jellyfish, Father? My heart goes to nothing, like a jellyfish." Her face became the unwrinkled, tormented face of an infant whimpering in an evil dream.

"It is a sin to give yourself up to despondency. A Christian clings to hope—"

"What hope, Father? If you sent Jehanne away without forgiveness, what hope can there be for someone like me?"

"Christ died for your redemption—"

"I don't know anything about all that. But you, you—"

"I am only the earthly shadow—"

"There is no shadow on you, Father. No shadow and no stain."

She took a few steps forward, knelt down, and hid her face in the folds of his cassock. The rank smell of an animal too old to clean itself came up from her hair and garments, and he had to resort to the old frozen stiffness to keep himself from snatching the cassock out of her clutching hands. "You must not grovel—you must not give yourself up to the sin of despair, no matter what other sins you may have committed—"

231

"May have committed? I have committed every sin you can think of. I am as bloated with sin as the dark bug on the bed-clothes is bloated with blood—"

Only the reading-stand, pressing hard against his back, kept him from moving out of her grasp; but she had felt the impulse, and she threw her arms around his rigid knees.

"You will not ask me to confess, not yet," she said, sinking her fingertips into the flesh of his legs. "It is enough that I soil you with the touch of my body. My soul is filthier still—I will keep it to myself until I have wiped it cleaner. Give me a time of general penance—a month, a year, whatever you say. Only let it be hard and long, only let me come here and labor in your sight for my salvation. Whatever anybody else would be loath to touch—your undergarments, the bucket you fill in your cell by night—let me wash it. I am too foul to lay a hand upon the meanest leavings of your holy life, but give them to me nevertheless."

He could do no more than utter a formula by rote. "No sinner who asks for penance is ever turned away without it," he said.

"I knew, dear Father, that you would not cast me out—"

"It is God, not I, who takes you in. Inasmuch as you call me your spiritual father, you must see also that it is for me to choose the manner of your penance, and the length of it, and the place."

"Only let it be long, only let it be cruel, only let it be—"

"Twenty paternosters every morning. You know the Pater Noster?"

"Oh, yes, I learned it in your pure Latin, I learned it from Peppi. But twenty paternosters, Father—"

"Wait, I have not finished. Twenty in the morning and twenty at night."

"But if you knew my sins you would see that even a hundred paternosters—"

She longed for the whip—not God's, but his—across her writhing shoulders. "Repeat them on your knees," he said, desperate to be free of her. "While you repeat them, grind your bare knees into the ground."

"Dear Father!" She snatched his hand and covered it with

232

kisses, and he could get it loose only by closing it around her wrist and dragging her to her feet. "Here—can I say them here in your sight?"

"By no means. Never—I charge you in the name of Christ the Lord—never set foot over the threshold of this monastery again."

"In the yard, then, Father. Out behind this building, among the beasts." She said it blithely, taking his answer for granted, nodding like a child who anticipates assent, smiling her sickening smile.

"If that is what you wish. Go now. Peace."

As soon as she had closed the door behind her, he went to his basin and plunged his hands into water up to the wrists. Maggot, he thought, blind worm that feeds on the festering wound of our mortality. . . . Then he saw that what he had taken up to dry his hands on was the scarlet napkin, the one that had come to him from the castle, carrying in its warp and woof the touch and scent of the chatelaine. She also—so he thought, holding it against his face—wore undergarments that took on the smell of her mortal sweat, left mortal droppings in a bucket in the chamber where she slept. Nor would he have had her otherwise: being himself flesh suspended for a little while in the womb of time, he had no longing for the state of angels who neither marry nor are given in marriage. It was no cause for revulsion that the sanctuary was established in a raw trench near the place of dung; it engendered in him nothing but compassion and tenderness.

There was no longer time for a walk on the dunes. He folded the napkin, smoothed down the new crop of unruly hair that covered his tonsure, and went to the chapel for the first service of the afternoon. There, in the smoky smell that would never be gone from the Monastery of Saint Cyprian, he conjured her up, all of her, without shame or scruple; and his *Alleluia* came strong and tremulous at once out of the fullness of his grateful heart.

✠   ✠   ✠

Whenever the chatelaine and her lover went their separate ways, he went with reasonable cheerfulness and she went troubled. In the first weeks of their union, she took it that his love

233

was less than hers: he, too, would someday pass through her as if she were a shadow; there would be a time, if he remained on the island long enough, when he would no longer care for her at all. Then she realized with joy and fear that his hunger only multiplied with the increase of her bounty. He came to her oftener and with greater risks. He left signs for her in the sand on the dunes, gazed fixedly at her from the pulpit and the choir loft, stopped her in the street on thinner and thinner pretexts. And still she had no peace.

She knew then that the difference in their leave-takings had nothing to do with what was between them, rose solely out of the difference in their destinations. He left her to be with her still, to brood upon her. She went to Alain.

And the breaking of faith with Alain had been the sorrier shattering of the two. What had fallen out of his hands was vague, intangible—a mere law of God. What she had broken was palpable, familiar, made dear even in its barrenness by years of use. Whether her husband knew it or not, she had betrayed him and wounded his pride. Every kindness he offered her—and it was strange how many she could count now that she no longer wanted any: an arm held out to her on a slippery path, a fire kindled when she shivered, the best cut of the meat laid on her plate at supper— every kindness was a bruise on the heart.

So, on days when she went out to look for the beloved and returned without a sight of him, she was rewarded with a sad serenity; at least for that one day, she had been innocent. Coming home late in the afternoon under a sky heavy with clouds, from a visit with Jehanne and Liese and Berthe, she stepped into the common room with more ease than if she had found *him* sitting on one of the ruined benches in the cemetery or loitering on the bridge. Nobody was in the big chamber: she could hear her husband moving about upstairs. Warming her hands at the hearth, she took muted pleasure in the neatness of the room and remembered with regret the orderliness of their shared nothingness, the quiet of her twenty-year-long sacrifice.

234

But Alain was staying up in their bedchamber overlong. Old Daniel came in and lighted the candles, smells of broth and seared meat came in from the kitchen-house, and still he did not come down. Perhaps he is not well, she thought; and knew that she saw her own doings as a sickness that might infect him. Distressed now, as distressed as she would have been if there had been a meeting and more than a meeting, she smoothed her hair and skirt and hurried up the stairs.

What she found when she walked in was her husband moving about with unusual energy through unaccustomed clutter. All the available surfaces were hidden under a confusion of things: hose and shoes on the seats of the chairs, belt and sheathed sword and leather doublet on top of the table, his scented robes, his cloak, his undergarments laid out on the faded crimson coverlet. Hearing her come in, he nodded but did not lift his eyes from a nightshirt he was folding. "What in God's name are you doing?" she said.

"Assembling my possessions." He said it casually, without turning in her direction. He knows, she thought, and advanced toward him and against that thought until only the bed was between them.

"But why?"

"I am leaving this chamber to you. You are used to the place, and you sleep less soundly than I. Wherever I lie down, I sleep soundly enough."

"But where will you be sleeping?"

"In the guest chamber. I have carried some of my belongings over there already."

He does not know, she told herself. There are other rooms; surely, if he knew, he would never lie down on *that* bed. "But why, Alain? Have I been having nightmares? Do I disturb you? Have I been talking in my sleep?" Long ago, some five years into their marriage, he had threatened to sleep elsewhere because she whimpered and cried out in the grasp of evil dreams.

"No, nothing of that sort. Nothing, truly."

"Then why?"

235

He did not answer. He had made a toppling heap of shifts, shirts, doublets, and napkins, had taken them up, and was carrying them past her, securing them with his chin. She could not see his face as he went by her, covered as it was by his silky hair. "Why?" she called after him into the hallway, and heard how her voice was distorted by her fright.

He stepped back, empty-handed, and busied himself with gathering a second load: the robe in which he had come to her on their marriage night, a smock whose sleeves she had adorned with an inept version of Jehanne's stitchery, a pair of soft boots whose every crease she knew by heart. "Why should you distress yourself?" he said. "Put a feather pillow against your back, and you will be as warm as ever." His tone was flat and even—there was nothing in it to tell her whether the smile that curved his thin mouth was there to cover a moment's uneasiness or rose in spite of him out of cruelty.

"Alain—"

"Sit down. You look tired."

"I have no reason to be tired. All day I did nothing. I was sitting with Berthe and Liese and Jehanne the whole afternoon."

"Sit down, nevertheless." He pointed to a cleared spot on top of the bed, and she let herself down onto it, unstrung. If he knows, she thought, better that we speak of it now. To lie here alone, night after night, wondering whether he knows or does not know . . .

"I will be back in a moment. I only want to put these doublets into the other chest."

"Wait. Why are you moving—why would you want to leave this room?"

He laid his armful over the back of a chair and came and stood in front of her. His quicksilver look passed over her face, and she could not sustain it: she turned aside and played falsely and foolishly with a moth-eaten glove that happened to be under her hand. "Why should it concern you? We are many years married, we are no longer young, there is not all that much between us," he said.

236

"There is still the—the companionship."

"Oh, the companionship. Yes, the companionship. Well, that is my fee, my monk's dower, as it were—whatever it is that is paid out to the Brotherhood when a man takes his vows."

"I do not know what you are talking about."

"No? Surely you have learned from Father Albrecht, among other things"—he put no emphasis on the last two words, only followed them with a short pause—"that every monk brings to his Chapter House a certain fee—"

"I know of that, yes. But you are not moving into a monastery —you are moving into another room."

"I am moving, in a manner of speaking, into my own monastery. We were told, as you may remember, some weeks ago in the Nuns' Chapel that it was incumbent upon each of us to make his choice between God and the world. So I have made my choice, but according to my own lights, not according to *his*. I hereby—" he took up the armful of clothes again and slung it over his shoulder, "I hereby renounce the world. Henceforth I am God's man in the guest room. The Holy Father in Rome and the Bishop of Cologne and their emissary notwithstanding, each man has the right to dispose of his own soul, and this is the disposition I have chosen to make of mine."

She sat on the side of the bed for a long time, waiting for him to come in and pick up another load. But he did not return; and after a while—whether to spare her further waiting or to shut her out, she could not tell—he closed the guest-chamber door. Even then she was not certain that he knew, would never be certain unless she asked outright and got an answer. Nor did it seem that he would soon give her occasion for asking: downstairs—she took note of it now for the first time—only one place had been laid on the board, and his books and parchments and writing-quills were gone.

He knows. . . . He does not know. . . . She pondered it until old Daniel brought in the food, and after the first mouthful, she found it hard to swallow more. In the shadowy corner where the replica of the drowned Cathedral stood, some subtle changes had been wrought. The tower had been placed on a plank, doubtless so that it could be carried upstairs in one piece; and the clutter of varicolored stones that had brightened the table as long as she could remember was also gone. Seeing that desolation, she could not get down another bite: she pushed aside her plate, put her head down on the table, and wept.

✠   ✠   ✠

On all the island of Saint Cyprian's there was no drearier spot than the one in which Liese had chosen to spend her days: mud underfoot, the great broken millwheel curving like a bludgeoned skeleton between her and the yards and hovels beyond, and overhead a grey-blue sky heavy with rain. The weather had turned unseasonably warm; and a smell blown in from the sea, as if the creatures at the bottom of it had stirred and were giving off the scent of their hidden lives, brought back spring's yearnings without spring's self. Eustace had been here two days ago to intensify the poignance of those yearnings—remembrance of a walk on the shore when the sand had been warm to the soles of their bare feet, remembrance of climbing up together to pick the first green herbs out of the crevices in the cliffs. Eustace had been here, not on any errand of his own: naturally, on behalf of Father Albrecht. And, though that visit had brought her nothing but recollections that she could not use, she had paid for it with the only thing she valued still: her solitude.

Oh, the way he had of talking a person into whatever he wanted! In anybody with less grace, it would have been sheer brazenness. Hammering in one of the pegs that her father's hands had made, she could not exile from her mind that smooth face her father had despised, talking away as cheerfully as if she had never been anything more to him than Angela's Peppi's cat.

The holy Father was too kind, too indulgent. He had fallen into an intolerable situation out of the goodness of his heart. Only he would have given in to Mechthilde's importunings. Only he would have given her permission to do her penance—twenty paternosters, morning and evening—in the monastery yard. Her presence there was not to be put up with, that much was certain. She fell upon the holy Father and kissed his hands in all his comings and goings—he could not step beyond the gate without her tagging behind. The Brothers were scandalized; even the beasts were disturbed: the best grey goose had stopped laying, and the donkey Asmodeus had kicked at her and barely missed her head. Yet simply to send her packing was out of the question: the holy Father would never be guilty of such unchristian callousness. It had come into his thoughts—and he would not, of course, make the slightest move without the express permission of Liese, his daughter in Christ—it had come into his thoughts that Mechthilde would be much more profitably occupied at work at the mill.

So there she was, not twenty paces off, on her knees in the mud, saying her paternosters and pulling up roots and moss, breaking in upon the stern silence of mourning with insanity and obscenity:

"Liese—"

"What is it now?"

"Did the Blessed Cyprian have a prick?"

"What?"

"Did he have a prick—the Blessed Cyprian? I saw him in the entrance, made out of some green stone or other, but his robe comes down to his knees, and it was impossible to make out."

"Why would you ask me a thing like that?"

"You are an abbot's daughter. I thought if anybody would know, you would."

"He was a man. I take it he had a member, like anybody else. You talk too much, Mechthilde. Say your paternosters and let me alone."

She wished she could have brought herself to deal more charitably with the poor creature. Mechthilde, too, was a woman and felt the yearnings of spring in the moist air. Mechthilde, too, hankered after what was not for her having, though the canticles she sang out to Father Albrecht between her paternosters were scarcely human, were more like the lowings of a heifer that needs

239

to be bred. And her miseries were multiplied by the fact that, since the night of the sermon, she had not crossed over to the other side. Some dim flare-up in the chaos of her brain had shown her that they did not go together—the love of the holy Father and the eating of devil's rye. To live without it was hard for her: fits of gnawing deprivation seized her—she would clutch at her belly and rock from side to side, whining; she would claw at the nape of her neck and knock her forehead against stones.

"Listen, Liese—"

"What can I do but listen?"

"There is a woman-smell, like the smell of a fish—"

"Not if you bathe yourself. Really, now that the weather has turned, you should sit in a tub of hot water."

"If the woman-smell is the smell of a fish, what is the smell of a man?"

"Is it a riddle, or am I supposed to answer in earnest?"

"Oh, answer in earnest. I want to know."

"But how can I tell you? It is different from one man to another." She tossed the hammer onto a heap of uprooted moss. The peg was in place, and before she reached for another she let herself breathe a little, wiping the sweat from her forehead with her sleeve. The scent of her father—let no sick thoughts of the grave take the remembrance of it away—the scent of her father had been a mingling of the smells of humble and innocent things: wet stones, wood-shavings, March earth turned over. The scent of Eustace was the smell of washed linen and candle wax and dried seaweed and ink. . . .

"Liese—"

"Wait a little, I am thinking."

"Look, Liese, look who is coming."

She lifted her head and saw through the bare wooden bones of the wheel somebody walking toward them down the main lane of the village. Nobody that she wanted. Only Giraldus in his mud-spattered russet cassock. Yes, and moving with the loose lurching gait that meant he was coming back from a bout of it over on the other side. As he drew closer, she saw more signs: the eyelids so swollen that the eyes were mere liquid slits, the ripe lower lip hanging, the arms and hands flailing as if he were pushing his way through water. "Oh, God!" she said, turning her back to the wheel and her face to the madwoman. "Now you have brought *him* down on my back. Am I never to have any peace?"

"How can you say that? It is none of my doing. He is crawling with sin, and if he touches me I will have to double my paternosters. Besides, I liked it better the way it was—so much to talk about and nobody here but us two."

There was no chance of avoiding him. He had sighted them, and he let out a long, indecent whistle. She counted the pegs—there were seven left, and she had them all. Having stored them in the pocket of her skirt, she sat down, angry and unresigned, on one of the big stones that edged the mill channel.

"You had better not sit close to me," said Mechthilde. "I, too, am crawling with sin."

"It is not the sin, it is the smell. Tell Eustace to tell Father Albrecht that you cannot come here to say your paternosters tomorrow unless you scrub yourself from head to foot tonight."

"I will, if I remember. Sh! Close your eyes. If we close our eyes, he may not see us."

He came up behind them, bent over between them, and embraced them with both his arms, knocking their heads together. He had had far too much devil's rye, had plainly been taking it for days: his fingernails were blue and his fingertips were cold. But he was less aware of his bodily afflictions than a man far gone in wine. He squatted down cheerfully between them and let his legs dangle with theirs into the muddy ditch. "What an edifying world to come back to!" he said. "Everybody occupied with the work of the Lord."

"I have said six hundred paternosters, and I beg you not to touch me. How many paternosters did I say today, Liese? Fifteen so far, do you think?"

"You cannot expect me to keep count for you. I have other things to do."

"Indeed she does, Mechthilde, and you must not interrupt her.

241

The mill wheel must be mended if the holy Father is to be pleased—"

"The holy Father has nothing to do with it. He never told me to work on it. Nobody told me—I thought of it myself, and why I thought of it I do not know. I wish, Giraldus, you would take her elsewhere for a little while at least."

"Yes." His long fingers played out some rhythm, tapping on the penitent's doughy thigh. "What do you say, Mechthilde? Shall we go elsewhere? Back in the old days we went elsewhere often, and it was merry enough, for you as well as for me. The place is the same as ever, the rye is still standing. Gold it is, though somewhat faded, and there are enough little purple bumps on it to send the two of us to Heaven for the rest of the year."

"To Hell, you mean," she said, striking his tapping hand away.

"Well, call it Hell if that is more to your liking. But watch out for my fingers. I have been eating every day, and my fingers are on fire."

"You know it is Hell. How else would you have had the witch back among the fallen trees? All witches are in Hell, and wizards with them. I had a wizard with a horn in the middle of his forehead."

"So you did. Look, I have brought you a present." He reached into the leather pouch that hung from his belt and brought out a strange handful: three bits of stone of various shades of yellow, a mandrake root, and four of the rye seeds slimy to their tips with the purplish blight.

"It was good of you to bring them," the madwoman said with a sigh. "But I do not want them, I cannot take them, I am undergoing my purification. Here"—she plucked them off his palm and threw them into the ditch—"I renounce and sacrifice them in the name of the holy Father and Christ my Lord."

"As you wish, but leave these other things alone. The stones are for poor Alain, and the mandrake is for me."

"What would you want with a mandrake?"

"I have not made up my mind as yet. Maybe I will burn it on a spit. Some saint or other was burned that way, roasted on a spit,

242

first on one side and then on the other. Or maybe I will crucify it. Yes, what do you say, shall we crucify it now? Liese, hand me a couple of sticks and we will have a crucifixion."

"I will do nothing of the kind," she said. "What is this craziness you have about crucifixions? First, the one in the Nuns' Chapel is so terrible you cannot bear to look at it, you have to wrap it up in rags. Then you find a mandrake and want to make a crucifixion yourself."

"Ah, well, things have changed in the meantime. Say simply that we have changed in the meantime, the island and I. Surely, Liese, this last fortnight you too must have noticed a change?"

"This last fortnight I have been mourning my father, and anything *you* notice is not to be taken to heart. If my father had lived, he would have locked you up until you were yourself again—"

"And a very good way of dealing with me it was, my girl. While your father held the crook, a man was locked up until he was sober, or he felled trees until his member shrank out of sheer weariness. It was a commendable rule: sin, punishment, and a fresh mind for sinning all over. According to my lights, next to the Abbot Benno your father was the greatest of all the abbots of Saint Cyprian's. 'Nothing,' said the Abbot Benno. 'Everything, with a decent conscience,' said the Abbot Ottric. And I will go along with either one of them. What I cannot stomach are the shilly-shally asses that eat of two bales of hay and thereby put a crick in their own necks and the world's."

"Do you mean me? I have a crick in my neck," said the penitent.

"So would any toad that stared up at a yellow finch day and night. But I am sorry if you are wretched."

"I would not say I am wretched. It is only that I could not call myself happy."

"Ah, well, there are very few left on Saint Cyprian's who could call themselves happy. You, Liese, are you happy?"

"It would be a sorry sort of daughter who could dance before the earth had settled on her father's grave. What do you want of me? I came here to work and mourn, and first I am saddled with her, and now with you. Talk your crazy talk to her, and let me alone."

"Forgive me, my poor girl, I know you are very unhappy." He stroked her hair, and she did not push away his hand, partly because she knew how his fingers suffered from the fire that left them cold, partly because there was real tenderness in his touch. "But then, which of us is happy? Look at me—am I happy?"

"I would be hard put to it to say," said Mechthilde, "you are so bloated with the rye."

"Your mother, Liese, is she happy—bereft of her husband and plagued with visits of condolence from the reverend Brother Thaddeus, Christ's most exquisite comforter? Jehanne could scarcely be called happy—all that good-fellowship under the bedclothes dampened and soured by a bad conscience—"

"Look, Giraldus," she said, fondling the wooden pegs in her pocket and turning her head aside, "nobody has touched me since my father's burial, and if you go on stroking my hair I am going to weep."

"Weep, then, it will ease your heart. There is plenty to weep over, God knows. Could you call the Brothers happy, running as they do between home and the monastery and getting themselves reviled at both ends of it? The goodwives could hardly be considered happy—a flock of uncloistered nuns, and a good part of them with bastards in their bellies—"

"It is very strange," said Mechthilde, "that I never carried a bastard. Do you know what I think? I think it was a portent of God's special affection for me. I take it as a sign: though now I am rotten with sin, in the end I will be pure as snow."

"Pure as snow. Laid out in Heaven on a bed of spotless linen, waiting for an archangel with a fiery prick," he said. "Say your paternosters and count on your reward. I am occupied, I am talking to Liese."

"You need not talk to me. I wish you would go home and sleep until you wear some of it off. The things you say are not much in the way of consolation. Some here are happy, surely. Angela, a few of the Brothers, Alain—"

"Alain? Oh, come, you will have me laughing, and my throat still aches from my last bout of vomiting. There are only two happy ones on this island: Father Albrecht and the chatelaine."

Father Albrecht and the chatelaine—it was so, she knew it in her body. Like a deep-sea creature in a time of thaw, her heart stirred and turned over. The icy casing of anger that had sealed it against the stranger from the other side melted and was gone. That these two should come together was right in itself and also a kind of covenant: if it was so with them, then rightness was possible even in this Godforgotten place of mud and grieving.

"And can you tell me any reason," said Mechthilde with haughtiness, "why the holy Father should not be happy? If anybody deserves to be happy, he does. He is deep in God's grace."

"Deep in God's grace, as you say, my dear. And also deep in the chatelaine."

He had not gotten it out of his mouth before the fatty bulk of the madwoman heaved up and got behind him. "Fucker of devils!" she screamed, and brought both fists down on his head. "God will fix it for you, wait and see! He will crucify you on a dung-heap with a molten nail up your ass and your jack tied in a wasp's nest. Yes, and I'll go to Hell to see it—let me see that in Hell and I piss on Heaven!"

"Oh, God, Liese, get her off, my head is bursting."

But she broke and ran, still shrieking, toward the village, with her hair undone and flying behind her.

"Listen to her," he said, rubbing his crown. "Now it will be nothing but 'dung' and 'piss' and 'fuck' all the way to Angela's— think what such talk will do to Peppi's innocence. In the old days, I would have marched her to your father, and he would have put her under lock and key. But the way things stand now—"

"Go after her, Giraldus. I am afraid she will do Father Albrecht some harm."

245

"Not she! She will never do anything—she lets it all run off into ranting."

"Nevertheless, I am afraid—"

"Put it out of your head. What could she do? And what difference would it make? We would all be better off if he were dead."

✠   ✠   ✠

Spring, 99 A.T.

Or, according to time in the world, the third day of the month of March in the year A.D. 1101.

I, Father Albrecht, Emissary of the Holy Father in Rome, and of the Bishop of Cologne, and of the Abbot of my Chapter House in that same city, write these things in the Book of the Island of Saint Cyprian's.

As to the matter of the date: Knowing that all conjecturings of days and years are faulty, and seeing that time itself is only one dream that we dream in the womb out of which each of us must be born into death, I enter here both the time of the island and the time of the world. Also, be it noted that I leave it to the Abbot Ottric's successor to decide which of the two calendars will henceforth be kept in use. For I am in no wise the holder of the shepherd's crook, nor have such decisions as I have made yielded fruit so sound that I may say the grace of God is upon the work of my hands.

As to the matter of the long hiatus: Let it be upon my head that nothing has been written herein since the Abbot Ottric laid down his quill somewhat less than five months since. Vain with the last and most foolish of mortal vanities, eager that men should say of my bones "They are honorable," I have refrained. For my blood rather than my mind said secretly to me of my doings, "They are not altogether honorable." Nor will I know in any accounting this side of my death whether I have done ill or well. Like the Abbot Benno—whose soul God rest—I and what I have done here will be judged according to what shoot or seed takes its lodging by chance on my grave. I write herein, then, that I have erred much and can lay no claim to perfection.

As to perfection: Though in the world on the other side of the

246

isthmus men strive mightily to attain it, the children of Saint Cyprian's have so wrought with me—and I rejoice in it—that I no longer believe in the possibility of perfection, nor myself seek it, nor wish others to seek it as their salvation. With perfection, whatever is born of woman would be repellent to the soul and obliterate love, for nothing can be truly loved that does not contain within itself some element that is to be forgiven. It is for this reason, I take it, that the gods of the pagans, whose alabaster flesh was chiseled out for their worshippers as blank and smooth as an egg, had no power in a time of misgiving to sustain the troubled minds of men. And we now in the world do ill to shadow forth in paint and stone Christ Militant and Christ Triumphant. Darkness is upon us, and He can serve us best with the bread and the wine, the flesh and the blood.

As to my charge upon this island: It would be foolish for me to enter herein what I have charged them to do in this place. All of that is made plain by the sermon I preached in the Nuns' Chapel, soon after the Feast of the Nativity in the preceding year. A copy of the sermon lies under this Book.

As to the above-mentioned sermon: There is a time between night and sunrise which is deceitful and strikes terror into the heart. Men knew what they did when they named it the false dawn. In such a time, between my soul's darkness and its true dawning, I wrote the sermon, and there was terror in me, and all the works of creation were made leprous and livid in the lying light and distorted by the sickness of my perceptions. Would I had never written it, or, having written, never uttered it abroad, thereby infecting many innocents. But I have written it, and it is the property of the Brotherhood. I have drawn this night one vertical and one horizontal line across each page of it. And those who come after me may see those lines as their souls choose, deciding for themselves what I do not know: whether I meant to strike it out or wished it to be read henceforth through the sign of the cross.

✠   ✠   ✠

The two only happy ones on the island had been lying in the same bed since midnight, and now it was almost dawn. The bed was narrow, and pushed into the corner of a narrow room in a

247

hovel, and he lay on the harsher side of it with his naked back against the wall. Behind him was the hardness of quartered tree trunks, splintery and chilly with the winter's accumulated cold. Before him was her warmth and softness, willing his will before he himself knew he willed it; her hands finding the places that ached with a dumb longing, her mouth pressing the hollow in his throat that knew only now how much and how long it had been yearning, her feet like small animals with a life of their own visiting his feet.

They had slept only by snatches and never both at once. Something in the way she had borne herself tonight—not fear, but a muted grief—had told him there was need for watchfulness. Now she slept with her hand on his thigh and her nipples touching his chest with every breath, and he was the watchman: the bolt of the door had rusted away and never been replaced, there was no way to lock the door.

Jehanne's room—a whore's room passed on to them by an abbot's daughter. She had told him all he needed to know yesterday morning in the monastery graveyard: We have a place, Jehanne stays all night with them now at the abbot's house, the room is unlocked, we can come and go as we please, it was Liese who told me so. As she delivered the last fragment of her news, her eyes had filled up. That Liese should have guessed their need and hurried to supply it—this kindness was as great a gift for her as the place itself.

On coming here this evening, she had tried to give the room an air of permanence, had brought with her under her cloak a bag of the dried seaweed scent and had strewn it about, saying this was one way of turning the room into their love's home. He had regretted the lack of eagerness in his own response. His failure to give her little ceremony its due had nothing to do with whose room this was or what others had met there for what sort of encounters. It was only one manifestation of the nervelessness that had been upon him since they had first come to each other. He could not think in terms of time: the terms of time, past and present and future, so available to everybody else, had eluded him —or he had eluded them—these many days. Now in the alien darkness, listening to her breathing and drawing the warm morning scent of her in with his own breath, he tried to force himself back into time, to think, without detaching himself from that which is, of that which will be.

What will be? A choice will be made by the children of Saint Cyprian's in the time of the spring sowing, and icicles have begun to drip, and with every breath she takes she has one less breath to draw beside me in the womb of time, and I also—going breath by breath—and, though every man finds it hard to conceive of lifelessness within life, it is easier for me to believe in that than to know I will depart. . . .

A mouse scuttled across the floorboards, and he thought of its little life closed up in its little skin. Beware the cat. Beware the sleep that leaves us vulnerable. Beware the hostile eye peering through a knothole into the closed universe. . . . He started up with a loud crack sounding in his head and shook off lethal drowsiness; and she sighed and made a contented sucking in her dreams. "What time is it?" she said.

> It is the time of snow,
>> Sparkling with earnest light.
> It is the time of snow. . . .

He also moved his lips, chewing on a winter apple. That was in the past. Her half-open mouth satisfying all ancient hungers— that is in the present. The future is Brother Thaddeus mounted on Cicero and leading Asmodeus by the bridle. Brother Thaddeus carrying a letter to the Abbot at the Chapter House in Cologne: "Reverend Father, I have done such-and-such, according to your dictates, and I inform you hereby that I myself have taken the shepherd's crook—yes, and out of a dead man's hand. Henceforth I am the Abbot of Saint Cyprian's, and will remain on this island. . . ." I will not depart, I cannot depart. . . .

No, never, let me die while I am at it, body and soul. One

touch and she was on her back, open to receive him. Deep, deep, and even deeper than ever before, and there, there, and none too soon. But late enough for her—always, for her, late enough: she issued on waves of laughter out of sleep and the spasm at once, saying, "Oh, glorious, oh, wonderful, oh, glory be to God." He stayed long, too spent to support his own weight, the whole weight of him and his life welcome on her body. When he was back on the pillow, he could see as well as feel the errant, joyous movements of her hands over his face, and knew that the light he had for seeing was the whitish premonition of the dawn.

"I must go now. They will be getting up for Matins."

"Yes, I know. You go first. I will wait a little and remember it."

"Only, be careful not to fall asleep."

"No, no chance of that. You have wakened me well, I am wide awake." She sat up to make way for him, but did not let him go at once, drew him back as he stepped aside and pressed her face against his belly. "Like bread," she said. "It smells like bread."

"I love you."

"So it seems. You do not need to tell me." She watched intently while he put on shoes and cassock, and that and the unaccustomed place made him awkward in his dressing. "But I am glad you told me, nevertheless," she said as he closed the door.

The world was more wintry than he had expected. Hoarfrost lay white over the hard refrozen edges of things—the thatch that roofed the hovels, the ridges of mud, and the stones and rubbish in the lane. Light grew in the sky as desire grows in the flesh, a rising pulse, a steadier and faster throbbing: grey, white, rose interchanging and interpenetrating through racks of mackerel clouds edged in a bleak diluted gold. Oh, glorious, oh, wonderful, oh, glory be to God—he remembered it, walking past the mill-wheel. An instant in the past, really, but he would not let go of it. Oh, glorious, oh, wonderful . . . The sun was rising red out of the moving waters when he crossed the bridge. In the cemetery the frost on stone and barren twig and brittle blade glittered and was roseate. Here he stopped among the graves; it was here that he always stopped to compose himself.

He had come back like this so often that he knew what he would say if he encountered one of the Brothers by chance: A restless night, a need of air, up betimes for a solitary walk and an hour of meditation. He had even prepared himself to see a watching face at one of the upper windows, looking down at him with knowing eyes.

But not *this* face.

Suddenly materialized out of God knows what or where. Straight in front of him. Crazy knot of hair above, goitre straining out below. And the pretty little features pulled awry with rage and loathing, and the massive arm up, and a knife in the hand.

"My daughter in Christ—"

"Hypocrite!"

She thrust at him full force and missed him. He ran from her toward the entrance, and she was after him, in and out among the stones. He got to the door, reached for the latch, never got hold of it. Cold, not to be believed, a blade and pain sliced the skin at the small of his back, went slantwise into whatever was vital and mortal inside. He staggered and fell backward with his arms stretched out and waited for the knife at his chest. But she saw what he felt—the sticky warmth spreading around his hips—and she flung her executioner's blade down beside him and fled.

Mackerel clouds, still pulsing and glowing. Oh, glorious, oh, wonderful . . . How long does it take before the final darkness closes in? Who will be the first to come out by the portal and find me cold?

Chapter V

*I*t was by the pain that he came to know he lived. Pain had been the first awareness, the one throbbing point of light in the universal dark. There, in the small of his back, a little to the right side—a fiery pulsation radiating out to his boundaries, to the skin of his scalp and the tips of his fingers and the soles of his feet. As the pain spread outward, he repossessed himself; and when the self was completely known, the awareness did not halt. It went unbelievably beyond what suffered; it took in his cell—no, the Abbot Ottric's cell. He lay on a narrow bed made up on two trestles, just as the Abbot Ottric had lain—only, he could move his fingers and flex his knees. One bearskin lay on the floor and the other was spread over him, probably because, along with the fire, the pain sometimes glinted ice cold. Persons whose legs could bear them wherever they liked came and went, throwing enormous shadows on the wall.

Brothers. The times became more frequent when he could attach names to their moving masses: Brother Andraeus, Brother Jonas, Brother Eilert, Brother Rudibardt. . . . Utterances, too—he could understand and sometimes even nod in answer: "Ah, I have hurt you, but if you always lie one way there will be bedsores." "Dear Father, for the love of Jesus try to swallow one more bite of bread." "That is the redbird whistling on the windowsill—the first sure sign of spring."

So it had been day after day and night after night, and many had come to him, but never she. Doubtless what kept her away was the rule: No women in the Chapter House. Yet why that rule should hold when so much else went unobserved, he did not know. If they could haul an adulterer into a monastery and make up his bed in the abbot's cell . . . If they could go on calling him "holy Father" . . . If they could bring the Eucharist to his pillow to be blessed . . . Once or twice it occurred to him that they might be ignorant of what had come about. But several days back and repeatedly since then he had heard Mechthilde ranting outside, and nobody in his proper mind could see anything but his guilt in her violent protestations of his innocence.

Not she but a terrible dream had awakened him that night. In the dream he had both been and seen himself lying dead at the entrance in the snow. In contrast to the images available to his blurred waking sight, the dream-image had been fearfully clear: the blood around his hips black and congealed, his mouth hanging open so that the lower gums were visible, his hand lying palm down beside the knife, wax-yellow against the glittering white, the nails a purplish blue. That is the reality, he thought, sitting upright. I am dead and still lying unburied in front of the portal—all the rest is a dream-in-death. And warily, like a child that does not want his parents waking, he got up and staggered to the window, supporting himself against the wall, stirring up the life-giving pain. Nothing lay at the entrance—not even the vaguest shadow of his prone body. New snow had fallen, bluish in moonlight. Oh, glorious, oh, wonderful—and pain was the remembrance of desire, and desire rekindled was pain, and where was she, under what duress, looking through what window at the glistening night? Before getting back into bed he urgently made water in the first thing at hand—the basin in which he usually washed himself. Something prompted him to hold the filled, warmed basin in the moonlight, and what he saw in it was the color of red wine. Shaking now because the stabs in the small of his back were almost unbearable, he emptied the basin into the bucket and hid the bucket under the bed. If he was the only one who had seen it, it might be some trick of the eyes or another dream. Whoever else saw it would give it authenticity, would turn it into another threat: blood finding some strange and unseemly passage through the tangle of vitals and issuing through his shrunken member—a new assertion that there was no escaping death.

After that, the madwoman's ravings took his mind off grimmer matters. She ranted in the courtyard some way off, to the cackling of geese and the stomping and whinnying of Asmodeus. Her voice, now that it was detached from her person, had a lilt to it, had, like her features, a certain prettiness. She began with an imprecation. Damnation and utter destruction come down on devil's rye.

Eat it, and you had carnal doings with fiends. Fiends rammed their things into all the openings of your body—spurted their filth up into your womb and down into your throat. And wherever it landed, it festered. Festered until you were a walking putrefaction. Swear in the name of Jesus and for the holiest man on earth to do without it, and you were in an even sorrier case. Wolves gnawed your vitals, vultures clawed the back of your neck, feathers of dead finches clotted in your stomach so that there was eternal retching and vomiting.

And when you were at the mill, saying your paternosters and doing harm to nobody, who came by? Giraldus, bloated and bleary in the eyes, with his thing-of-things as thick as a snake under his cassock. With blasted seeds to tempt you—yes, and infernal lies. Who but a wretch rotted by devil's rye and sick to death without it would believe that Father Albrecht rammed his thing into the chatelaine? Or that the chatelaine—so pure, such a free dispenser of charity—would spread her legs and let him in?

"Go elsewhere! You have brought me to such a pass a pig would serve my purpose," a Brother shouted from an upper window.

"Only tell me how it is with the holy Father. Is he done for? Have I killed him with the butcher's knife?"

"No, you have not killed him, he is not dying." It was another voice, older and wearier. "He needs rest. We all need rest. Go away and let us sleep."

The world of beasts ushered her out with intensifying noise: grunting, neighing, flapping of big earthbound wings. He was neither dead nor dying—the third voice had given him that much assurance. But she, the beloved, conjured up for them here in all her vulnerable nakedness . . .

The pain flared up and burned away guilt, thought, remembrance. The pain died down, flickered, became a slow breathing of light over embers. Not bad, less and less night by night, there was nothing lying out there at the entrance, he could go back to sleep.

The lay brother Thaddeus was the first to come visiting in the morning. He had been in and out before on occasional services and errands; but today, since the vagueness had diminished, the bulk of him was clearer there at the bottom of the bed: he had changed, he had changed considerably. There was an old wives' tale about a boy who had grown into a giant while all his brothers pined and dwindled—some business about a magic power to appropriate from others their strength and blood. Sitting propped against pillows, staring at the wine-colored rim left in the basin and at his own dry and withered hands clasped on the bearskin coverlet, he could not utterly rid himself of the notion that Brother Thaddeus had somehow assimilated what he himself had lost.

"God be praised, Father! If you are not quite yourself as yet, you are certainly much closer to it than you have been these last two weeks," he said.

"My mind is clearer." Clear, but slow and stubborn, set on going its own way. It refused to assume the burden of conversation; it insisted on examining the lay brother as if he were an object, a new chair or a table, set down in the room. Not really any bigger—that had been another of the feverish illusions. More muscle controlling the fat; a straighter backbone; a little beard—yes, that was the crux of it—a short new beard, more bristly than

255

the hair on his head, sticking out assertively from his chin.

"Did you spend a restful night, Father?"

"Reasonably so."

"I am glad to hear it. And somewhat surprised, to speak the truth. I myself hardly closed my eyes—I never heard such a clamor."

To avoid further talk of the clamor, he asked for a goblet of water and immediately regretted his tactic: Brother Thaddeus, in handing him the goblet, saw the basin and clucked his tongue. "So the wound is still bleeding a bit?" he said. "Then you will have to lie abed a while longer, and I will have to stay here at the monastery and leave the village to Brother Rudibardt. You have no idea how ignorant they are of the practices of Holy Church—they bring me some question or other at every turn. I can imagine how often they must have troubled you, asking you about this and that."

"They have not asked me anything, so far as I can remember. Give yourself due credit for bearing the entire burden alone."

The lay brother bowed without irony and seated himself without permission on the stool at the foot of the bed. "There is, however, one matter that I cannot take upon myself. I thought I would stop by this morning and ask you what you think. Mechthilde—the crazy woman—she must not be allowed to go on ranting out there. The things she says—and on the very property of the Brotherhood!"

"What would you have me do, Brother?"

"One word from you, and I am sure they will put a stop to it."

"What kind of stop? She is out of her mind—nobody can chide her into silence."

"Some of the Brothers keep saying that the Abbot Ottric would have had her under lock and key."

"Well, the Abbot Ottric is dead and gone, and I am not the abbot—nobody is the abbot. If you came to ask me what I think: I think she should be let alone."

256

"Oh, but if that is your position, it is only because you have not heard her. There is nothing—absolutely nothing—that she will not say. Every one of us is at the mercy of her tongue."

"You are not telling me anything I do not know." It was driven out of him more sharply than he had intended by a twinge in his back.

"It would be only circumspect to—"

"I will not lock her up out of circumspection. I have no circumspection left. What is it to me what anybody says? You asked, and you are answered: Let her alone."

The lay brother stood up, bereft of some of his new assurance, perhaps by the voice of authority, perhaps because the anger had not masked the pain. "It was bad judgment on my part, Father," he said. "You are not yet in a state to deal with any of these things. For the time being at least, we will let it stand as it is. When you are better, in another week or so . . . But by that time she may well be ranting about something else."

A long silence, somehow intensified by the meticulous orderliness of the room, hung between them. It was he himself who broke it, troubled by the thought that he could not be as aggravatingly certain as usual that he would be seeing Brother Thaddeus again. "I hope you will forgive me. I am too easily set on edge. As you say, I am not entirely myself."

"No, to be sure, how could you be? You must put all your mind to the business of getting better—it was my foolishness—"

"Not in the least—"

"—so that it can be as it was, and you can go on hearing my confessions. I will leave you and come again when you are more rested. Peace, Father."

"Peace."

A little later, when full morning sun was lighting up the crimson napkin on the bench, Brother Jonas came in with the morning broth. An old man, crippled in the hands and bent in the back, but mild and cheerful and quite content to fill up the tag-end of his life with the doings of the single day. He chattered on

257

without the smallest sign of strain or embarrassment: They were to have fish today at noontime. Brother Eilert could not sing in the chapel—his rheum had settled in his throat. The holy Father would be delighted at the progress they were making in the scriptorium—the epistles of Saint Ambrose were almost complete. . . .

The scriptorium—Eustace was up there among the inkwells and the sheets of parchment, had been only a staircase and a few steps away through all the days and nights of tormented conjecturing. But, unlike the other members of the Brotherhood, had never set foot in this cell, not since the morning of the mackerel clouds and the knife.

Brother Jonas was wiping the basin with a wet rag. That he showed no concern over the stain was irrationally heartening, furnished the courage for taking the necessary measures at once. "I would be grateful for a visit from Brother Eustace," he said.

"Certainly, Father. I will go up now and ask him to come at once."

But there was a long lapse thereafter. The sounds of the monkish life—poignant and distant and somehow related to noises other children had made at their play when he had lain abed as a child—told him how much time was passing. Tin plates and the voice of the reader droning away in the refectory: "I am the rose of Sharon, the lily of the valley"; the whispering silence of the hour of the confessional; a service he was too drowsy to name; a chanted psalm . . . He let the cadences carry him where they would, and they carried him toward sleep.

At the first creak of the door hinge he was awake, confused and wary as a hurt animal, wary enough to pretend that he was asleep. Through the narrow slits he made of his eyes, he saw the young monk stop on the threshold, looking reluctant and aggrieved, saw him shrug in a way that was at once brash and pitiful, and turn as if to walk out again.

"Brother Eustace—" His voice cracked, his mouth was dry, he cursed himself for drowsing away the time in which he could have charted out the interview.

258

"Peace, Father. I thought I would come back later. I did not want to break in on your rest."

He came without eagerness and seated himself on the stool. In his white cassock he looked singularly young, frail, and forlorn. And, as if he realized and hated his own vulnerability, he hid it under the cool little ways of the aristocracy. Stretched one leg out before him. Set the heel of his other foot on the rung. Poised his head with conscious grace.

"It is a long time, my son, since I have seen you."

"Two weeks." The sparseness of the statement and the flatness of the tone conveyed a melancholy pride. Two weeks, and he had waited until he was sent for. Two weeks, and he had not given in.

"I have missed you, Brother Eustace."

"Truly?"—which meant only that he did not believe it. But his breeding would not allow him to take satisfaction in an awkwardness of his own making. He called up the poor ghost of his usual fluency to relieve the stress: He had inquired every day, had heard better and better news, was particularly glad that the pain was less. He had lighted a candle in the chapel—Brother Thaddeus had said it was a thing to do. He had sent dried plums and a new pillow case—would have sent flowers if there had been any flowers. . . .

If there had been any flowers . . . A reliquary opened thirty-odd years ago in the presence of the abbot and the deacons and the elders. White hand of Saint Ursula, incorruptible. The scent of roses spreading out over a plague-stricken city, though streets and fields were buried under three handsbreadths of snow. He remembered the yearning after fleshlessness that comes of making ill use of the flesh, the longing of the spirit to be disembodied—spirit too young and wild as yet to know that disembodiment and obliteration are one and the same. And always, unto the third and forth generation, some wizard there to put that time of youth's sickness to his own use, to twist out of that sickness a proof of his own unearthly powers. As Father Carolus was to me, so have I been to Eustace; and so will Eustace be to some other not yet born in the womb of time.

259

The young monk stroked down the folds of his cassock. "Was there some particular business my Father wanted to ask me about?"

"No, nothing."

"Everything goes on apace upstairs. I am copying the very last epistle of Saint Ambrose."

"Good." He reached for his goblet and took a draught. There was no magic in it—a taste of cold, wet metal—nothing more.

"Then let me give you such news as I have." It was a gallant offer made in a courtly voice. "Not that I have much to give— these days I am never anywhere but here and at the castle. You know what passes here, and at the castle it is much as always— quiet and cold. They have run out of firewood—that happens almost every winter. Jehanne and Liese—Giraldus, too—go up there sometimes in the evenings."

"How is it with my lord and my lady?"

"Oh, she is well enough. He is the one to be concerned about."

The faint trace of irony that put its edge on the careful voice reminded him where the blood relationship lay: Alain's brother, not hers, had sewn this seed before he hung head-down from the Burning-Tree.

"Alain is not ill, I hope?"

"Oh, no, not ill—only somewhat troubled. He has taken his cathedral up to his chamber, and he works on it there. He says his chamber is his monastery."

"There is nothing strange in that. Hundreds of the early fathers went into the desert and lived in solitary cells. Saint Anthony, Saint Jerome—I could name them by the score. Such a cell was considered even holier than a Chapter House—they called it a hermitage."

"Truly? I must mention that fact to Brother Eilert—he and I have been arguing whether such an arrangement is acceptable according to the Rule. In fact, now that he has come to mind, I remember that I promised to meet him—he is doubtless wondering where I am. We two are working on an *Alleluia* and mean to have it ready for Vespers. We pray for you, all of us, every day, Father, at all the services. Look after yourself and come back to us soon. I must be on my way now. Peace."

Once the door was shut, there was the late-afternoon quiet of the time of meditation: footfalls and whispers too faint to come through the wood. He had a place in their world—which was strange, since it had no place in him. They prayed for him at all the services, and that was hard to take in, since not once—not when the blade drove home, not when the pain spread out, not last night when the urine showed wine-red—not once had he prayed for himself. If God, with a wisdom or a carelessness that passes understanding, had created the lot of it, He had since withdrawn and let it unfold after its own manner: womb of time, enormous flower, contracting and dilating with its own rhythms, dyed in its own colors, emanating its own warmth, nourishing as long as it chose and casting out whenever it would. Still enclosed—and grateful for it—in the All that is in spite of Nothing, he let the ones on the other side of the door lift up their hearts to the Father and the Son and the Holy Ghost. His was where it had been since he had first known his mortality. His was in the lap of the chatelaine.

✠   ✠   ✠

"There, now, Father, we have finished it," said Liese, and gave the closest spoke a shove, and watched the mill wheel, black against a sky smudged with fog, make its first half-turn in a hundred years.

Nobody else was there to see it. Since the knifing among the graves, she had been left in peace. No Mechthilde—she could not be budged from the courtyard at the monastery. No Giraldus—he was up at the castle, shivering and burning through the aftermath of his bout with devil's rye. The wheel creaked to a standstill in utter silence—there was not even the usual clinking of bricks over at the oven. Whatever headway the Brothers had been making there had stopped three days ago, after Brother

261

Rudibardt, with a handful of dried monastery plums, had wheedled little Peppi into coming inside. There, in that dank curve of blackness, littered with ancient rubbish and smelling like a crypt, a bald and toothless old man stripping the clothes off the white body of a child . . . It did no good to think of it—she dropped the piece of pig-fat with which she had been larding the joints. Hammer, chisel, knife, whetting-stone—she counted them where they lay in the mud. Her father had brought them here; and, once she had rested a little and wiped her hands and face, she would put them into the sack and lug them back home.

Yet, sitting there with her legs dangling over the edge of the ditch and her warm face in her hot hands, she knew she had lost the knack of resting. Before she finished one task these days, her mind ran on to the next. While she washed the dishes, she thought how the floor called for a good scrubbing. While she sat mending shifts and sheets, she saw herself running out to skim the winter scum from the top of the well. There was enough to do—her mother was back on her feet and Jehanne had gone home to her hovel—but not nearly as much as she was making of it. These tasks distracted her from thinking of the time of the choice and the new building going up near the Nuns' Chapel. Cells—stalls for cows, pens for ewes—a week in one of them would put her out of her head.

Somebody was coming toward her down the muddy path—Eustace. I stand in need of him as a cat stands in need of a mouthful of nettles, she thought, and made a loud business of throwing the tools into the sack. "A good afternoon to you," she said over her shoulder, hating their sanctimonious "Peace" and hoping he would walk on. But he came straight to her and stopped so close behind her that the folds of his cassock brushed against the back of her head.

"It is a strange day," he said, "now cold, now hot."

She gave him no answer.

"In the shade I was cold, but here in the clearing I find myself breaking into a sweat."

And that, she thought, is the most startling piece of news we have had since the goodwife Gerda pricked her finger with a needle.

"It is the wrong weather for you to be doing such heavy work."

"There's no heavy work left to do. The mill wheel is finished, and I will be going home as soon as I catch my breath."

He stepped around and sat down beside her nevertheless. She could not bring herself to look him in the face; she stared instead at his hands. They lay in his lap in a loose purposeless way that was new—in the past he had always used them to ornament his easy eloquence. He had taken to biting his nails since she had seen him last—was that the result of an overdose of holiness?— they were raw at the quick and ragged at the tips.

"Well, I am glad to hear it," he said after so long a silence that she could not think what he was glad of. "How is your mother?"

"Up and about."

"And Jehanne?"

An idle question, asked simply to fill up time, since his mind was plainly on something else. But she could use it to her own advantage. "She is not with us—I have not seen her since she left—I was meaning to walk down and pay her a visit."

"Now?" There was something like dismay in his tone, and she glanced at him sidewise. His face, too, had changed: the eyes dulled and darkly circled, the tongue moving back and forth behind the upper lip. "I thought you said you were going home."

"Perhaps I did, but I must stop first at Jehanne's. I do not want her thinking I have put her out of mind now that there is nothing at home for her to do."

"It would be unseemly for me to go to Jehanne's with you—"

"I know that." And you can sit and squirm at the thought of all those evenings you spent in her company at the castle, when you shared mead and jests and talk with her and gave her all your split seams to mend.

263

"Must you go there now?"

"Yes, I must. So, if you will hand me the sack—"

"At least I can take the sack to your house and set it against the lean-to door."

She wished to God he had not made mention of the lean-to. Always, in the finished past, they had spoken of it when they took leave of each other for a little while: "I will see you at the lean-to" or "There is nothing to do tonight. We will sit and talk in the lean-to." The closed warmth of the place, its herb and animal smell, his voice reading aloud to her—she turned aside and wiped her sweating face on her shoulder. "Whatever you please, though there is no need for you to trouble yourself about it," she said.

"It is no great trouble to carry a sack of tools." He slung it over his shoulder, but plainly he had none of the peasant's strength or skill for bearing burdens. The weight dragged him to one side, and, as he stepped away, the tools clanked against his back. "A good afternoon to you, Liese. If your mother is there I will stop and have a word with her, though what I wanted was a word with you. Also, if you remember it, give my greetings to Jehanne."

All the way to the hovel she kept wondering what could be gnawing at him. It was not with him as it had been of late with the other members of the Brotherhood, who felt called upon to go about with long faces because Brother Rudibardt had fallen into sin. His trouble was less formal and communal. Worry over Alain? Some foolish lordly notion that a person's own pride went down along with his kinsman's pride? For the healing of such wounds she would not have wasted the commonest herb on the shelf in the lean-to. But she was sorry nevertheless, sorry for his back—hammer, knife, chisel, whetting-stone carried as a ten-year-old might carry them, bumping mercilessly against the small round bones of his spine. . . .

Jehanne's door stood open by two or three inches, which meant neither that she was there nor gone out, only that nobody was with her. For lack of a latch, when she did not want a visitor she barricaded the door with a three-legged stool. Through the narrow opening came a strong smoky smell: something strange, something not for eating was on the fire.

"Jehanne—"

No answer.

"Are you there, Jehanne?" She coughed because the smell had caught her in the throat.

"Is that you, Liese?" It was said in a flat and unwelcoming voice.

"Yes, but I can go away and come back some other time—"

"No, no matter, come in."

Once she was over the threshold she found it hard to believe that the chatelaine had ever been in such a room, or that its owner had ever sat companionably with the group in the great hall in the castle. Everything was in disorder: unwashed plates and bowls on the bench and the stool, garments strewn about, the bedclothes on the floor in a crumpled heap. Jehanne was as she had never seen her before—lying on her back on the stripped bed, staring at the ceiling, her arms, as thin as sticks, raised and crossed behind her head. She wore only enough to cover what it would have been unthinkable to expose, had nothing on her but her sheepskin vest and an old skirt cut off at the knee. Armpits, ribs, the concavity of her stomach were all bare, and she did not think to cover them or to sit up, thought only to grope with one emaciated foot for something on the floor. A crazy festoon, a kind of snake made of bits of colored cloth tied one to another—this she found with her sole and pushed with her toes into the darkness under the bed.

"If you were sleeping, I am sorry—"

"I was not sleeping. Sit down."

"But something is on fire."

"Yes, on the table. Don't trouble yourself, it's safe enough."

In the middle of the table under the single window was a tin trencher; and in the middle of the trencher was a clump of small flames, made the more ghostly and transparent in the afternoon light. Threads of wool and silk—all the precious hoarded stuff of her stitching—were curling and crimping in the fire.

"Why are you burning those?"

"Because I will not be needing them any more. Because I am finished with making gifts." She reached down and plucked a ragged blanket off the top of the heap and dragged it across her nakedness.

"But what has come over you?" She cleared the stool of a bowl and a tin plate, and sat down on the rings of wetness they had left on the wood.

"The lay brother has come over me—take that as you will. He came to urge me to repent, though once he was here he got his mind onto other things."

It was true that the lay brother was not such a one as a woman might yearn after. Still, others as gross as he had come and gone without leaving such grim chaos behind. "But he cannot have been the first to—to make ill use of you," she said.

"That would depend upon what a person means by ill use." She had not moved, she continued to lie on her back and stare at the beams. "Some do it out of love, but I do not ask for that. Some do it out of need, and they are welcome—I have that need myself. But he was the only one to do it because he wanted to do a filthy thing. Who could put a woman to worse use than that—to turn her into filth because he needed something filthy to wallow in?"

She had a brief vision of Brother Thaddeus laboring in hate and contempt over the poor body that all of them, from the chatelaine to Giraldus, had put out of mind because it and its doings were too pitiable to contemplate. "I am very sorry," she said. "If my father were alive, he would give him what he deserves." Feeble—so feeble that she herself almost had to laugh at it—the sort of boastful support one child will give another helpless child; and they two were women, which was scarcely a

266

matter for either of them to rejoice about. "Come, now, get up and wash yourself and go back home with me."

"Wash myself? Do you think I have not washed myself? Three times I have washed myself and I cannot get myself clean. I will never be clean again, not until I am dead. I want to be dead, I need to be dead."

She stared at the darkness under the bed and knew that the varicolored snippings had been knotted together to make a noose—a futile, riduculous noose: it would never have served, not to hold even her negligible weight. "It is harder than you think to do away with yourself," she said. "My father was an old man, and even so—God rest him—it took him days and days."

"You are right. It would never have held, and I suppose I knew as much." She propped herself up on her elbows and swung her legs over the edge of the bed.

"Will you come home with me?"

"No, and I will not hold you here any longer, either—I know that Berthe will be waiting. I will put this rat's nest in order, and then I will sleep awhile." Still wrapped in the blanket she went and opened the door. "I do not know what to say to get you out of here. I cannot say 'A good evening to you' as I did before they came over from the other side—we are different now, we have changed too much. And I cannot say their 'Peace' to you, either. I do not know why they say it, I am sure they have no thought of what it means, it goes into their ears and out of their mouths without passing through their heads. Would you believe it?—he stood here, just here, pulling down the skirt of his cassock with one hand and wiping the smell of my rut off his face with the other, and what he said to me was 'Peace.' "

She walked back home past bales of rotted hay, past the goodwife Angela's shut shamed house, along a fence of peeled and braided willow wands behind which the peasant families hereabouts kept their sheep. The rawness of the evening chill had begun to settle in, and the quiet was broken by constant and desolate bleating. She stopped and looked over the fence at

the sheep where they huddled together, all but one. Mortally
sick, blear-eyed and patchy, he stood in the angle of the fence
alone. The others—it was always so with animals, it was said to
make the difference between beasts and men—the others had
abandoned him in utter callousness; his suffering was no concern
of theirs; for them he was already dead. He stretched out his
neck in her direction, and a sound like the grating of a rusty
saw came up through his throat. A draught of brewed herbs, she
thought, the fire in the lean-to—but she did not open the gate
though the catch was almost under her hand. What was the
lean-to to her, or an ailing beast, either? She looked over the
fence straight into his vacant, scum-clouded eyes. "Stand in your
corner and die. Die and be done with it," she said.

✠ ✠ ✠

If Giraldus had turned up at the castle soon after the knifing,
the chatelaine could not have brought herself to take him in.
She received nobody but Eustace, and him only because he was
her source of news. She saw by his face, and by the faces of the
two old servants, that she was not managing very well in her effort
to hide her bereavement and fright. She was weak past walking
without feeling her way along the walls, weak past raising her
voice, weak past getting up without supporting herself on the
arms of her chair. It was her thought—and twice the thought
had been transformed into a vivid dream—that Mechthilde's
blade had passed through *his* body into hers, that she too was
bleeding from within. Her monthly cycle did not come round,
but it never occurred to her that she might be with child:
pregnant she was not, only driven by violence beyond the time
of fruitfulness: an aging woman now, haggard, stiff in her joints,
numb and fumbling in her fingers, all grace and luster gone.
    One night when she was walking the upper hallway in her
sleeplessness, she found herself face to face with her husband.
He had stepped out of his room, with a candle in his hand,

268

straight into the way of her walking: and she saw with other eyes than her own their two faces, as if detached from their bodies, isolated in a circle of light. Every line of hers dragged downward, as if by the pull of the grave. Every line of his as it had been since the morning after their wedding, frozen in icy irony. Their eyes stared at each other, and she would have blazed hate and defiance at him if he had not blinked and released a single unmentionable tear.

"It is hard to sleep on an empty stomach," he had said. "Go down and have some bread and a cup of milk."

She had gone down then to show her gratefulness, had crumbled some bread on the board, had poured milk out of the pitcher into a cup and back into the pitcher again to make it seem that she had taken his advice. Since that night, he had been coming into the great hall where she usually sat, to stir up the fire or fill the kettle or lay a piece of rug across a draughty windowsill. These kindnesses were dear wounds to her—they hurt her unbearably, yet she could not wish them away. And when Giraldus appeared at the door in need of tending, she received him with relief. The exigencies of his sickness, his loud voice, even his jibes about another luckier invalid were welcome because they clouded the exquisite, killing air she had been breathing with Alain.

When Giraldus was well enough to take his meals downstairs, her husband also appeared at table. Because after weeks of solitude he could not forgo an old fellowship? Because he would not have another see her eating in exile and disgrace? She did not know, but she was thankful nevertheless. And she had more reason for gratitude every evening: first he served her without addressing her; then, out of long habit, he fell into voicing the minimal courtesies—"If you have finished, let us get up," "Allow me to cut you another piece of meat"; then, whenever she found courage to ask him a question, he gave her more than a stripped yes or no. She was wary of Giraldus, and meted out his wine for fear of what he might say with a loosened tongue. But even when Eustace stopped by and reported the monastery news, Giraldus allowed himself no more than a knowing smile.

On the fifth of the evenings when the three had supped together, Eustace came somewhat later than usual, when Alain was on the point of going back upstairs. She and Giraldus were putting chestnuts into the fire, and her husband stood on the hearth, of half a mind, she hoped, to wait for the first pop in the embers. Supper had been scanty and tasteless, and she knew that he had eaten sparely so that she and the guest might have their fill. She hoped he would use his nephew's visit as a pretext for staying—she wanted no chestnuts until he had had his share.

"It is almost warm out there," said Eustace, with the overdone cheerfulness of his false position. He had learned to give the chatelaine the news she craved, along with other trivial items, when he found her alone with Giraldus; but he was less at ease now that her husband was in the room. "The dried beans have run out, so we will have no more thick soup. The holy Father got out of bed and walked up to the scriptorium. I have finished Ambrose and begun this day on Jerome."

To the scriptorium—Blessed Jesus, all the way to the scriptorium! She let her quaking knees give way and knelt and threw another handful into the flames. If he had walked to the scriptorium today, a day would come when he would walk elsewhere—to the crypt under the Nuns' Chapel, to the confessional booth near the Burning-Trees, to Jehanne's hovel; and then . . . She could not sustain it, could not imagine more than a gesture of awe: her hand testing the actuality of his presence, moving in wonder over his wasted face.

"I think we have more than half a bin of dried beans here— ask Adele and take what you need," said her husband, settling into a chair on the hearth. And she could not understand how two such disparate joys should mingle in her: joy that her lover might come to her again and joy that her husband should stay and eat.

"And that great tub of sanctified lard—is he still directing his betters?" said Giraldus, making for the most comfortable chair.

"No—not for the moment. Brother Thaddeus has been relieved of his duties—at least of those he took over from the holy Father."

"Really? And what brought that about?"

"Well, he has had a kind of falling-off."

"He has—has he?" He stopped short of the chair and turned to look at Eustace, gloating. His lips, still cracked and yellow from the fiery sickness, spread in an evil smile. "And may we ask what is the nature of this falling-off? Surely you are close enough to their high councils over there to furnish us with more particulars."

"I do not see why it should concern you."

"Oh, but it does concern me."

"Well, I suppose you will hear of it sooner or later. He has confessed to carnal doings with Jehanne."

"With Jehanne? There's a miracle out of Hell, if I ever heard of one! There's proof positive that the Devil can laugh, in spite of what is said in the books—Jehanne and Brother Thaddeus in bed!" And, seized with an uncontrollable laughing fit, he went down on the floor, sat hunched over with his head on his knees and his big hands flailing the rushes.

"Stop now," said the chatelaine, coming and standing over him.

"How can I stop?" His back and sides were jerking in spasms that might as well have been sobs or hiccups. "Oh, I would give my life to hear the rest of it! Be a good fellow, Eustace: tell a person how it came to pass."

"He went to exhort her—"

"To be sure! He went to exhort her to abstinence and the saintly life, and she exhorted him right back again—to the blessings of carnality—"

Oh, he was out of hand, past all circumspection. She prodded him with her foot to remind him where he was, and saw at once that she could have done nothing worse: he had turned mean, she had affronted his pride. "Oh, come, let yourself go

271

a little—you are not a nun, not as yet," he said, and caught her by the ankle, and squeezed so violently that the hurt went in to the bone.

"Myself, I do not find it uproariously amusing," said her husband.

She did not dare to look at him. She let herself down onto a leather cushion and nursed her throbbing foot in her hand.

"But it *is* uproariously amusing, whether you see it or not. Nobody but a blind man could live on this island and keep a straight face. Everything on Saint Cyprian's is ridiculous—cheap and ridiculous. This fat oaf—yes, and his master with him—before they came over the isthmus with their good tidings, we did well enough. Maybe our lives were aimless, hopeless—but at least we were not cheap. What made us cheap and ridiculous was this business of squeezing us all into a monkish mold. And now that they have led us around to sanctity, they set us a fine example: sneaking around in crypts and confessional booths and whores' hovels, grabbing whatever they can lay their filthy fingers on—"

"Ah . . ." she said, rocking from side to side, feeling it all as a pain spreading inexorably up from her ankle toward her heart.

"Remember, my friend," said Alain, getting up, "neither you nor I has allowed himself to be squeezed into any monkish mold, so I see no reason why we should concern ourselves. As for the doings of the lay brother—they have no fascination for me. So if you will excuse me I will take myself back upstairs."

"That's right!" He got to his feet and stood facing his host. "Turn your back on it, go upstairs and shut the door on everything! You were never one to let yourself be disturbed—you need your quiet, you need your peace. Even when Ottric was down at the mill making an end of himself, you never lifted a hand—"

"And you—what did you do to help him? Went over to the other side, as I recall. Ate devil's rye, made a sodden fool of yourself. Unless, of course, I do less than justice to the ecstatic visions you were having over there—"

272

"Oh, if we are talking about ecstatic visions, mine are nothing compared to yours. Which incident followed which in the life of the virgin Genevieve, whether the nave of the Cathedral was vaulted in blue or green, through such sublime revelations the whole island would naturally be saved—"

"Every man has the right to dispose of his life as he sees fit."

"And you saw fit to waste yours on a plaything. Look how it is with you: your friends dead or estranged, your holdings handed over to the Holy Father in Rome, your woman gone. Now that you have lived your life as you saw fit, what have you got? Nothing. A mouldy book and a pile of crazy stones."

She saw her husband's hand hanging down against the skirt of his cassock. It made a strange gesture, and in so doing became for her a leaf thrown onto a fire. It opened weakly and slowly, and turned palm outward. Then it closed and seemed to crumple. "What do I have left?" he said. "Nothing at all."

"Truly, I must go," said Eustace. "They will be locking the gates—"

"Go then, Nephew." He walked toward the stairway, looking straight in front of him. "What happened here was none of your doing."

"I am very sorry, Uncle, nevertheless."

She covered her face with her hands and did not take them away until both Alain and Eustace were gone and the chestnuts had begun to make their intolerable popping on the hearth. Giraldus stood above her, looking down. His face was drained of blood and malice, yellow as cheese except where the fiery sickness had left the marks of its blue fingers on his skin. "I, too—though you may not believe it, I am very sorry," he said.

"Ah . . . That you should have said such a thing, and to his face . . ."

"What can I do? I have told you I am very sorry."

"I never said it, though I was the one that had the worst of it to bear. So help me God, I never spoke a word of it, not to him and not to anybody else."

"What do you want of me?"

"Spare him the sight of you—get out of this house—"

"And you?"

"I? Whatever you have done to him, you have done to me. No, don't touch me, don't come near me. Go and never come back, never speak to me again, never, as long as I live."

✠　　✠　　✠

On his cautious little journeys from his bed to the refectory and the scriptorium, Father Albrecht became aware that there was trouble with his eyes. Not that his sight was in any way diminished. In fact, it was eerily heightened: he seemed to be seeing out of his ears and the back of his head; he saw too intensely; he saw too much. He would stop halfway down a corridor, transfixed by the image of a paving stone that lay behind him, a paving stone so singularly purple that he almost lost his balance in his eagerness to turn and go back and look—a piece of slate was all it was, and yet it had the color of an amethyst. Or he would halt and stammer in a conversation with a Brother because a moth—nothing, really, said the Brother, one of those little moths one finds in ancient garments—had fluttered past his face. Only, to him, it had seemed as big as his hand and marvelously iridescent, with innumerable rainbows weaving over the network of its wing.

Once when he was yearning after some word from the chatelaine, he realized that, even if he were to get such a letter, he might not be able to read it, and panic froze his heart. Though it was late afternoon and time to be going to the second meal, he hurried in the opposite direction, toward the chapel, pretending for the benefit of such Brothers as he met to be deep in prayer. The chapel was deserted. Brother Thaddeus and Brother Rudibardt had suspended their penance in front of the Cross, had gone to eat the crusts and water of their repentance in their cells. The rosy effulgence of the westward sun lay on a sheet of parchment on the altar—text for the next service—and he took it up and stared at it in fright. Read it? *Te Deum* leaped at his eyes as the blast of a trumpet assails the ears: ebony letters raised on a mottled ivory surface that seeped up light. He rested his elbow on the altar and covered his eyes with his hand and felt his dry cheeks inundated with a wash of plentiful tears. Why? In part because the lettering had dazzled his sight, but even more because he had remembered a time out of the past: Alain coming merciful and courteous into the great hall of the castle, holding out a book for the testing of his eyes. He stood a long time effortlessly weeping; and it was then that he understood the source of his affliction and exaltation. Some fragment of the fiery sickness—shred of a fog dispersed, echo of a sound already dead—had floated back upon him. When he took his hand away, the stark smoke-stained chapel shone with the luminescent greys and blues of mother-of-pearl. He blinked and stared the chapel and the service sheet back into reality. If he was to go on living in the world, he would have to master this visionary state, to make it come when he summoned it and go when he bade it be gone.

"Is it well with you, holy Father?" said Eustace, looking at him with concern over a plate of pork-fat and dried beans. He was in the refectory, had gotten to it brooding all the way on other images: a roof transformed into a stretch of meadow, a piece of masonry whose jointures dripped honey, a breathing tree, an emerald forest encircling a violet town.

"Perfectly well. I am completely restored."

"Are you sure? If there is anything amiss with you—any sensation of floating, any disturbance in your vision—"

"Yes?"

"Eat for the time being only meat and fish and vegetables. Refrain from bread—they say on Saint Cyprian's that in such cases it is well to refrain from bread."

He had not intended to eat of the brown rusk that lay to the left of his plate. Something in the Friday smell of it repelled him. "What day of the week is it?" he said.

275

"Tuesday, holy Father. If you would like me to take you back to your cell—"

"Not at all, not at all." And he launched—and carried on brilliantly until the reader for the day took his place at the lectern—a subtle but lucid discourse on time and memory: how memory, properly conceived of, would seem to disprove the existence of time, since a man knows nothing with more certainty, not even a page of written words held before his eyes, than the memory which is unfolding within himself.

"Lift up your heads, O ye gates," said the reader, "that the King of Glory may come in—"

And before he mastered things visionary and told them to be gone, he thought how every man could be a king if only he made himself welcome: one gate, and then another, and beyond that the holy of holies, rich with ointment and unguent, smooth as mother-of-pearl, restitution for all mortal affliction, even for death. . . .

He went to the service—indeed, he was sure enough of himself to officiate. Everything proceeded in a seemly and decorous fashion—no word left out or uttered with too much emphasis. Only once during the *Alleluia* was he tempted to give way; the rich bass and the high boy treble willed themselves to go on and on after the mouths that had uttered them were closed, but he put an end to that by raising his left hand and flicking his ear with thumb and fingertip. Long conversation in the corridor after service: "God has been good to you and to us, holy Father." "You cannot know what a blessed thing it is to hear your voice from the altar again." Eustace beside him all the way, thoroughly kind now, having become utterly remote. "Let me light your candle before I leave you, holy Father"—though the day's light was far from gone—lest I trip over a fold in the bearskin rug, lest I stumble against a chair. Then solitude in the cell, with the door pulled shut, and candle flame and natural light merging into one another and making a strangeness, and no reason to hold off the strangeness, no reason at all . . .

276

It came to him then—first as a floating shred of vision, then as a possibility in the world of actuality—that she and he might flee together to the new town. Smell of beams with the sap still in them. Paths laid out and strewn with shadows of leaves and coins of light. Brother Matthias, he of the red hair and the long chin, stood in the square, with his hands held out. There was sawdust in the folds of his cassock, and his eyes and the heaped building stones behind him burned like gentians, unbelievably blue. "A house for the two of you," he said. "The dust from the beams is still on the floor. But our oven is filled, and there will be bread, and such small game as we can lay our hands on, and well-water in a tin cup. Down the path, the second house to your right hand. Go in and rest and wait. Unlike the two whose sweet doings begot our sorrow in their Garden, you and she know that the setting sun will rise and the risen sun will set, and you can wait for the night."

Knock on the door. Flat knock, no echoes.

"Who is there?"

"Mechthilde, holy Father. I know you have forbidden me this place. But my need is very great."

"Go back to the courtyard. I will come to you there tomorrow."

"You will not see me alive tomorrow, Father. Out of Christ's pity, let me in."

He looked at the strengthening tongue of light above the candle and brought his wandering mind to bear upon Christ's pity. Sometime since—yes, on the evening when Ottric had sat on the hearth at the castle, staring sullenly down at his own ridiculous shoes—*she* had shown deep concern with Christ's pity: Had there truly been One who had given up His body out of pity for the rest? And had He asked, while the yield of the earth was passing for the last time between His lips, that they pity Him also, pouring out wine in remembrance of Him, breaking for Him a loaf of commemorative bread? Very well, then, it was enough—let the children of Saint Cyprian's celebrate the Eucharist. . . .

277

"Holy Father, I beg you—"

"Very well, then, daughter, since your need is great. Come in."

She came and stood before him, some ten paces off from his chair. He had not seen her, had only heard her voice since the raging mass of her had come pounding after him in the graveyard; and his mouth fell open at the appalling change that had come over her in the interim. She was a big gaunt woman, loosely swathed in rags, the flesh wrinkled and fallen in. Weight had dripped away from her—there was no fat left, only a mushroom puffiness in the large powerless hands and feet. A shudder passed over her, as if the cell were colder than the mouldy courtyard from which she had come.

"I was about to send you word that the time of your penance is over," he said.

"Ah . . ." It was not a sigh of relief. It was a widening ripple on the surface of a bottomless well. "And if my penance is over, then am I to say no more paternosters?"

"Only the same number as the rest of us. One on rising in the morning and one on lying down at night."

"And in the time between, what, Father—what in the name of Jesus am I to do with myself?"

He had a brief sense of some sort of kinship with her. Long ago, after the sodden box had been opened to reveal the alabaster hand, after the page had been cut from the chronicle and the jest about Saint Radigunde had grown stale, he had wakened every morning with the weight of the empty day crushing his chest. Morning and the noonday meal and the endless afternoon, the hollow vastness of evening, and the night a cavern of broken sleep. And what in the name of Jesus am I to do with myself? . . . But then she took one step forward and reached out to touch his resurrected flesh with her dead hand, and any thought that he and she were of a kind became a blasphemy against himself. Blood coagulates in the womb of time, and essence enters in. But sometimes—with her and with Brother Thaddeus and Brother

278

Rudibardt—the chance solidities conjured out of nothing are too opaque to harbor essence. Essence, entering by chance into a flawed solidity, becomes gross and monstrous—he was driven out of his chair by the horror of the revelation. "Live like any other, according to the capacity of your understanding," he said. "Live as best you can, within the limits of the law. Nothing more is required."

"And if I cannot bear to live?"

Then die, he thought, since you exude poison and taint the common air. But he did not say it, said only, staring past the candle, "Life is God's gift, and to throw away what is of His giving is the sin of sins, beyond absolution."

"I am standing on the edge of Hell, then, Father. Only one thing could deliver me."

He did not ask her what it was; he stood in the old, learned attitude of confessional attentiveness.

"If you could forgive me. Not in God's name. Out of your own mercy, out of yourself."

"It is not for me to forgive you, as I have told you before. God alone can forgive you, His boundless mercy passing to all sinners through me."

"Put that by, Father. I, even more than all the rest on Saint Cyprian's—seeing what I have seen and knowing what I know —I cannot set much store by the doings of God. It is you, not God, that I love—but we will say no more of that. It was you, not God, that I struck in the back with a knife. It is your forgiveness I want—yours and not God's."

"Well, then," he said in his weariness, "I forgive you against my better knowledge, since you insist upon it." But the joy that flared up in her withered face burned out in an instant because he could not sustain his words with his eyes. His eyes—he felt them as cold creatures sliding in their sockets—slipped away from her, rejected her utterly. Senses mingled crazily in the rejection: there was a Friday smell in the withdrawal of his glance, a wash of cold sea water into the vacuum left by the breaking off of their look.

She walked very slowly toward the threshold. "Thank you, Father. You have done your best, and nothing more could be asked of you," she said without turning her head. "Indeed, all on this island have done as well as they could by me. I have had bread from the chatelaine, clothing from Berthe and Liese, devil's rye from Giraldus, fish from Jehanne. If you remember it tomorrow, tell them so." She bowed, and closed the door.

Not long after her going, two of the Brothers stopped by to walk with him to Vespers. He told them that he was unusually tired, having said his first office after sickness, and they dissuaded him from stirring forth: the Brotherhood and the saints themselves, they said, would be happier to think of him resting in his cell. The little pronouncements of the monkish life, alien to their rude mouths at first, were slipping easily out of them these days. Give them another year, he thought, and they would master the fluent, edgeless discourse, would be able to pour over everything—death, madness, starvation, cruelty—the purling waters of priestly eloquence.

Secure now in his solitude, certain of his solitude for the remainder of the night, he took a fresh quill, a sheet of parchment, and the Abbot Benno's inkwell from the reading-stand, and placed them on the visitor's stool beside his bed. Not that he meant to write to her at once—he took and savored singly in its turn every small preparatory delight: the softness of his shift after the harshness of his cassock, the firmness of the propped pillows behind his back, the warmth of the coverlet over his feet. As he saw it now, it would be well to dream the letter through before risking his only sheet of parchment, and he could not have asked a better occasion for dreaming: the candle flame growing always more intense, ringed round by orange and violet aureoles, the chanting voices coming in from the chapel, never completely dissolving into silence, *"Credo"* continuing to sound above *"Sanctus"* and *"In Nomine Domini,"* and all three of them still trembling

there when *"Alleluia"* began, unearthly intertwining arcs of
sound, complexities innocent of incongruities. . . .

Beloved:
If Eustace brings you ill news of my state along with this letter,
discount it. I am well. The stain in my urine is less, I walk without
pain or effort, and this day I have officiated at the altar; so you have
no reason for distress.

It is true that I was somewhat addled in converse with him in the
refectory, but that was not because of the inward bleeding. Some small
shred of my earlier sickness has detached itself from that blessed time
when you tended me, and has floated back upon me. And how can I
bid it be utterly gone, seeing that it comes from the days and nights
when my flesh first knew your hands?

Nothing departs so long as it is remembered. I think of your forehead and the shape of your head under your hair. Your skull also is
a sanctuary holding a jewel, and the jewel has innumerable facets, and
carved into many—not to be razed out so long as there is essence in
your solidity—are images of me.

That is a wonder and a glory surpassing even the coexistence of
Sanctus and *Alleluia* and other such secret miracles, among them the
rainbows that are on the wings of moths and purple that is to be seen
in paving stones.

But what I have thought through to set down and send to you
would overflow all the parchment I have by me. Let me state it
briefly: come with me to the new town. They are building it up in a
cleared place somewhere in the forest between the island and the
world. And what have you—since you have opened your gates to me—
to do with the island? And what have I—since I have come in unto
you—to do with the world?

For lo, the winter is over and gone, and their streets are strewn
with the innocence of sawdust, and the sap is still in their hewn
beams, and every stone quarried from their mountains has its soul and
its color, the most ardent and precious among them breathing gentian
blue. Which is also the color of the veins that cross the milk of your
skin, especially the one that branches up out of your left breast. The
line of it I remember and could draw even in my sleep, for I have
loved you past all measure, beyond God and beyond myself.

281

Come, then, when I send to you and go with me to the new town.
I will send soon, before the time of the choosing—let another man
officiate at the choosing.

> Yours only, lying beside you in the womb of time, desiring
> this and nothing else, so long as my essence is compounded
> with my solidity,
>
> Albrecht

✠ ✠ ✠

Ever since the evening when the witch Mechthilde had leaped
from the stone of the virgin Genevieve and drowned herself in
the inland lake, a murmuring and a ferment had spread like a
plague among the folk of Saint Cyprian's. The ignorant among
them—and most of them were ignorant—showed an unseemly
concern over what had happened to the body. The body had not
come up to the surface; and peasant and goodwife, shepherd and
townsman carried on an endless argument as to its fate: The
great doors of the drowned Cathedral had swung open to
receive it, which meant that all things, even the foulest, were
now acceptable to God. The Devil had tied it to a spire by the
petticoat and would untie it in his own good time to rise again,
like the foetid wafer come out of the depths to sicken the Abbot
Benno; and when that day came the stench and the poison would
contaminate everything.

They gathered in tens and twenties at the edge of the leaden
water. There were more of them than they had thought, and their
numbers oppressed them. It was as if the fact that so many of
them still lived belittled what they had suffered; fewer should
have sown their seed after the tidal wave, fewer should have been
begotten during the Time of Blood. Being come together, they
saw too that many had been taken with the fiery sickness. This
year it had come upon them with unexpected virulence, so that
few who had conceived could bide the time of bearing, and many
were afflicted with dreams and visions. Nor was it always possible
to know a fever dream from a revelation. One spoke of a bell

282

tolling under the waters, and was mocked by others who said it was only his own heart thumping in his head; but then he died of the sickness and a peculiar smile appeared on his face, and because of that they carried him to the monastery and demanded that he be buried in a holy grave.

Some, afraid of imminent death and goaded past endurance by the questioning and the quarrels and the common restlessness, made the choice before they were called upon to make it, and went early to look for peace in God. The women began it. Four of the new-built cells at the edge of the moving waters were filled up: one by a very old woman who was said to have burned her life away in a foolish passion for the Abbot Ottric's predecessor, one by a deaf-mute in her fifteenth year, and the two others by a pair of ugly sisters to whom the world had given no light except the mild joy each of them saw in the other's eyes. Thereafter, the rolls of the brotherhood increased, and very rapidly, to the number of twenty-seven. But, though these came no longer to the edge of the lake to stare and point downward and speak of one thing or another that they saw or might have seen, they were not missed. There were still too many left to take up the best vantage points, to make the thick air heavier with the smell of their bodies, to afflict their neighbors' ears with questionable visions, dull conjectures, and petty tribulations.

Somebody said that in the spring of the year—and it was spring by the monastery calendar, though the fog had not dispersed—the best time to see the waters was just at dawn. Then, or so it was rumored, the first light of the sun turned the lead-grey surface into a transparency. Then, if ever, the mysteries would reveal themselves: gap in the roof-tiles, nave and transept strewn with the skeletons of fish and men, the holy book lying open on an altar hoary with barnacles, its pages constantly ruffled by the waters. So it was said, and they believed it since it helped them shorten the wearisome night. They took to rising in pitch dark and putting on their clothes in haste. They took to leaving the morning meal half eaten on their tables and coming with torches

283

from every part of the island to take a place as close as possible to the virgin Genevieve's stone. Some who were sick or drunken or otherwise addled would rise still earlier, would kindle their torches and start the desultory procession in the middle of the night. And, once the first of them had come past the castle with their loud contentions and streaming lights, there was no more sleep for the chatelaine.

None from the castle had gone down to the lake. It was beneath their dignity—even the dignity of the two old servants—to lend themselves to what was primeval and noisome in the folk: they had seen it at its worst in the murder that had come flying out of the bat-ridden cave; their kin had been its victims on the Burning-Trees. But the chatelaine could not despise the general obsession with the corpse. She herself was obsessed, especially in the loneliness of her nights. Where was the poor madwoman now? Caught by the arm or the neck by what slimy trail of seaweed? Wedged in what grotesque position into what crevice of ruined masonry? Yes, and sent there by jealousy of her own kindling: the ravages of jealousy still on the face, there until the ravenous fish had eaten down to the bone.

There were times of confusion between sleeping and waking when Mechthilde was not to be clearly distinguished from the two mastiffs she had poisoned, and then the chatelaine mourned all three. She walked back and forth in her room—since the quarrel with Giraldus she had not dared to open her door at night—holding a pillow against the aching emptiness of her body, talking to the pillow as she might have talked to the corpse or the beasts, saying to it over and over *"Kyrie eleison, Christe eleison."* They were the only words she knew of the service that had been brought over from the other side. Strange words, in Greek, an even more ancient language than their pure Latin. She had read them once in a book left in a crypt where she had waited for him to come to her, and had asked him about them afterward, and he had explained: "Lord, have mercy, Christ, have mercy." Upon what? Upon us all. *"Kyrie eleison, Christe eleison.*" Let the Son have pity on all the poor creatures of the Father's unfathomable making: fish and fowl, beast and man— all, all—the sinful living and the unforgiven dead. . . .

One night when she was walking with the pillow pressed against her—the night was far spent, it was getting on toward sunrise—she heard the sound of something coming down with a crash. A tower of the submerged Cathedral going down under the water? The Monastery of Saint Cyprian—and *he* in it—collapsed by the first shudder of another tidal wave? No, not as vast or calamitous as these, but calamitous enough. . . . She dropped the pillow, ran to the door, pulled it open, and heard not another sound.

But she could not put it out of mind or stay longer in the chamber that had become her prison. Barefoot, in nothing but her shift, she stepped out into the hallway and went downstairs. Everything there was undisturbed and quiet—so quiet that she felt an urgent need to rouse somebody, anybody. She went to the hearth and poked at the embers. She went to the table and clattered the dishes. She went to a chair and sat down in it, but could not sit still, had to thrust out her foot and draw a hollow discord from the body of the lute. It was Adele who came, slow but sure of herself, knowing the place blind, as a rat knows the labyrinths of his cellar. "Is that you, my lady?" she said in her quaking voice.

"Yes."

"How can I serve you?"

"Light me a candle." She was sorry it was Adele—she had hoped it would be Daniel. She had not been alone and face to face with the old woman since the knifing in the graveyard and Mechthilde's ranting had made common talk of her infidelity. And, once the candle was lighted and the worn, pouch-eyed face came toward her in the circle of yellowness, she felt for the first time an undoing wave of shame. Faithful—for fifty years or more the old woman had been faithful. Yes, and ate the last stale crusts of her bargain now without complaint, said "No matter, no matter

285

at all" when her husband's palsied hands lost hold on a stack of tin plates, took her napkin and wiped away a dribble of porridge oozing between his toothless lips.

"Is there anything else, my lady?" She put the candle into her mistress's hand and stepped back into darkness already diluted by the wan greyness of dawn.

"No, nothing. Only—did you hear a crash?"

"A crash? No, but then I am so deaf. Something might have fallen in the kitchen-house. I will go and see."

While the day came on—white, sullen, without sun—she sat holding the lighted candle and awaiting what might come of the looking about. But she knew that nothing would come of it. The crash—she perceived it more accurately now than when she had heard it—the crash had sounded in one of the upper rooms. "Oh, God, no," she said aloud, and broke into a sweat so weakening that the walk up the long staircase was a labor. In his room— yes, and there was the proof of it. His door, closed and latched against her since he had made a monastery of his chamber—his door stood partly open; and she saw as she might have seen some hideous and ominous presence the absence of him on the bed.

Not there. Nothing but tossed sheets. The bench cleared— sandals and cassock gone. And behind her—she knew it before she turned and saw it, knew it by a cold creeping down her spine —his Cathedral of Saint Cyprian, the toy on which he had squandered his life, the only palpable embodiment of his long seeking after God, in ruins. The floor by the window littered with the rubbish of his years—hundreds of scattered stones.

She had dropped the candle in her terror. It burned on a little rug and she stamped it out without feeling any pain. Go to him, wherever he is, go to him. Halfway down the stairs she met Adele on the way up. "Nothing—all's well, my lady. Go back and try to sleep."

"I must go out."

"In your shift, my lady?"

She was right: how could she walk in her shift among the folk gathered by the stone of the virgin Genevieve? "I will take a cloak—"

"And go barefoot?"

"Very well, then, I will dress myself," she said in anger.

"Shall I rouse up Daniel to carry a torch?"

"Who stands in need of a torch?" It came out of her in a shriek. "It is daylight. Let me alone."

Clothes, a brown dress, too heavy for the oppressive weather, but there was no time to find another. Shoes, a kerchief to cover the low-cut front. Her hair—she unbraided it with agitated fingers as she ran down the steps and out into the steaming air.

In the murk—for it was neither night nor day—she followed the torches of others at a distance. Past the monastery: and *Kyrie eleison* for you also, my Albrecht. Over the bridge and across a long stretch of beach, past the black trunk laid prone in everlasting memory of Brother Galbart: *Kyrie eleison* for you, Brother—those who give the greatest measure of pity stand most in need of it themselves. And for me also—*Kyrie eleison* for me. Close now to the inland lake. She could breathe the stagnant smell of it but could not bring herself as yet to look. Some of the folk were standing in small groups at the brink. They did not see her coming in among them—what might have been a lank trail of hair had just floated past them and shown itself for what it was: a weedy thin-stemmed vine clotted with mud.

She sighted her husband a little apart from and above the others. He sat where he would never have sat unless the taut strands that held his subtle brain in balance had sagged—on the fenced and sacred slope of the virgin Genevieve's stone. All the others were looking down into the water. Only he stared out and across it, and her eyes stared with his: a grey unmoving stretch, mirror of the blank sky, vacant of God and of everything. And his own emptiness drawn inexorably to that somber, deathly emptiness. Not now, not while the folk were standing by, but sometime later he would go the way of Mechthilde and the virgin Genevieve. Tasting the bitter leavings of his life like vomit in

287

her mouth, she walked toward the place where he sat. "That is my lady," said a child, and the mother said "Hush." I walk in my shame as the dead lie in their shrouds—forever—but that is no matter, she thought, and stepped over the fence, and went up onto the stone to him and said his name.

He turned his head slowly and looked at her, plainly neither knowing nor caring who she was. The flat grey water drew him back like a lodestone. She summoned up what small courage her life had left to her and did what she had not done since the morning after their wedding—put out her hand to him, was the first of the two to offer touch. "Come home with me," she said. He looked at her again, and this time his eyes did not reject her. He sighed and took her extended hand and went down the slope with her, onto the path that led back home.

✠ ✠ ✠

"If he sits too long with me—" so Berthe had said to her daughter—"and you want to be alone with him out in the lean-to, only give me a sign and I will yawn and say I have to go to bed."

And now they had been sitting for the better part of an hour in the room where the Abbot Ottric used to receive the members of the Brotherhood, and Berthe had yawned twice, gently and self-deprecatingly under Eustace's eyes, though Liese had given her no sign.

She had no wish to be alone with him, she knew it would yield nothing. Though her mother's offices were well meant, she rejected them; they grew out of a lie she had long ago stopped telling herself. Never, not in the most felicitous of the gone evenings, had he come to her as a lover. He had only so borne himself as never to indicate that he was *not* a lover, and the hope he had allowed to live had lain over all their doings as the red of the after-supper sun lay over the patched and yellowed tablecloth. In that faint glow they had shared nothing but childish things: he had read her tales from one of the castle books, she had made him an almost inedible cake flavored with herbs and mead, they two had worried together through the sicknesses of conies and sheep.

"Are you tired, Mother?" she said to save herself the embarrassment of another yawn.

"Yes—and I am very sorry, it has been so long since we had any company. But, when you are as old as I am—"

Age, loneliness—it pained her that they should be mentioned before him. "Well, I will see you comfortably into bed."

He got up, confused at first, but then took hold of himself and said with a certain deliberateness, "Yes, do so, Liese, by all means. I will wait for you in the lean-to."

She did not want him waiting in the lean-to, and why he should wish to see her there was beyond her comprehension. It had been pleasant sitting with him here. There was a mild, melancholy note of finality in this visit—his last, doubtless, before he made the choice and had the soft brown hair shaved in a tonsure from the top of his head. She would have liked to remember him as he had been until now: thin under his white cassock, talking courteously of inconsequential things. "If you wish," she said, "but there is no fire out there."

"No need of a fire. I will take my cloak. And do not hurry, I have plenty of time."

Talk between her and her mother could only be false, seeing that he had left the door to the lean-to standing open. In silence that seemed equally false but somehow less compromising, she turned back the coverlet, helped the old, sagging body out of its harsh clothes and into its softer shift, lighted a candle and filled a goblet and set them both on the stool beside the bed.

"You take the candle," her mother said in a whisper, in the foolish hope that he would outstay the sun. But she frowned and shook her head and went out to him, without so much as smoothing her hair.

He had settled down, with an insensitivity that surprised her, in the old way, in the old place. He had spread his cloak on the fireless hearth and was sitting on half of it, leaving the other half for her, as if she could overlook his absence and finish now some forgotten piece of conversation left dangling months ago. She walked past him and pulled up a stool. If I must sit, I will be the one to choose what I sit on and where, she thought, and took a mournful satisfaction in the fact that she could put herself apart from and a little above him and could hold her tongue—uneasy though the silence was—waiting for him to say the first word.

"Your mother seems almost wholly restored."

"She is as good as she will ever be and better than I dared to hope. God forbid that she should come down with another ague—it will be damp for her in one of those—those cells."

"Are you thinking of that?"

"I think of it as little as I can. But I suppose I must start to think of it seriously soon. The time of sowing is almost here, and the time of the choosing was set for soon thereafter—"

"Well, no need to think seriously of it as yet. The whole matter depends upon the holy Father, and he is abed again with a touch of the fiery sickness, and Brother Thaddeus—as you probably know from Jehanne—cannot serve in his place. The fact is, we seldom speak of the choosing. If you were to ask me what day of the month this is, I would not know. With us at the monastery, it is much the way it was before they crossed the isthmus: we float in time, we live from one day to another."

"And time is heavy on your hands." Which was an explanation of his visit, and she voiced it as such.

"No, Liese. That was not why I came. There is enough to do there, only the blood has somehow gone out of it. I mean, it is hard to have the same trust in it since—"

"Since your kinsman was affronted in his honor?"

"No, it is not that, either. And it seems hard, seeing that I came here to talk to you freely—you are, you know, the only one to whom I *can* talk freely—it seems hard that you should bridle at my every word. Since it came about as it did between the holy

Father and the chatelaine, we have had nothing but one misfortune after another: Brother Rudibardt and Peppi, the lay brother and Jehanne, Mechthilde dying the way she did, and my kinsman—since you choose to call him so, though he is your friend as well as my uncle—my kinsman utterly undone."

"I am very sorry for all of that."

"I see it as a wheel—if the hub is unsound, no spoke can hold. I am only a spoke, and sometimes it seems to me that I will not hold, either. I am in doubt, Liese, I am very much in doubt."

She did not ask him whether he was in doubt of God's existence or of the holy Father's power—weakened as it was—to hold together the shaken Brotherhood of Saint Cyprian. She was distracted by a sudden movement of his hand. It went out gracelessly and came down on her bare instep, and the palm was like no other she had ever felt: at once slippery with sweat and icy cold.

He went on talking, but his chill and purposeful hold on her so distracted her that she could catch only parts: A month ago he would have made his choice without giving two thoughts to it, but now it was different. . . . To choose the monastery over the world seemed rash, especially considering how little he knew of the world. . . . If Jehanne chose the nunnery, as some were saying she would, she would be choosing out of a surfeit of knowledge. He himself, on the other hand, if he chose the monastery, would be making his choice out of total ignorance. . . .

Her foot, as conscious as the hand that held it, had gone rigid in a hold that had become a desperate grasp. Jehanne had told her that a woman should expect next to nothing from a boy's first love-making: they knew so little, they were so anxious over their own powers that all a person could hope for was the satisfaction of bestowing a charity. Jehanne had said . . . And why had she refused to bring the candle? And would his advancing palm be affronted by the hair on her shins and thighs? And, if she had ever dreamed of such a thing, she would never have sat on a stool in front of him so that he had to reach and strain and clutch. She would have been on the cloak with him, and the cloak so

291

folded in as to cover them both, and their bodies moving easily from the old ignorant closeness to the new knowing closeness. . . . Oh, God, that she should have set barriers in her anger against him and against herself!

He went on talking as if silence were a chasm that would swallow him up: Nobody so far except Giraldus had chosen the world, and to go from the island with Giraldus was for him the same thing as walking into a wilderness alone. Though his parents had died early and he had neither brother nor sister, others had spoiled him out of pity—there had always been Alain and the chatelaine, yes, and Ottric, God rest his soul, Ottric and Berthe and herself—she above all the rest. . . .

Cautiously, allowing every part of her person to signal him that she meant to come closer, not to flee, she stood up and broke his grasp. "Wait a little, I cannot hear you clearly," she said, and came down to the hearth beside him, not daring to look at him, looking instead at the plank wall of the lean-to, made more beautiful than anything she had ever seen by the surge of hope and the red light of the sun.

Smell of his body—ink and candle wax and the faint sourness of the sweat that drenched his hands. He turned and kissed her on the mouth, and the kiss was too hard and too conscious; but then he too was going blind toward he did not quite know what —something more fearful to him than it was to her—he tensed his muscles, he closed his eyes. Carefully, always remembering that it should be a charity, she held him round as if she were cradling an infant, and stroked the nape of his neck under his fine hair.

Still talking. . . . Of a journey now, of the world on the other side. Of certain jewels come to him from his mother and father—garnets, an opal, a carbuncle said to have been sent to his forebears by the Emperor Charlemagne. They would not set out in poverty, they would have enough—

Enough? But what could she ever want beyond her present unbelievable riches? Her very body was a possession beyond price.

292

Palms, mouth, the warm folds between her thighs had begun together to make a sweet tingling. She lay back, wanting ridiculously to yawn at the luxuriousness of it, and he came down with her in her embrace.

"We could go," he said, "from one town to another until we found one to our liking—"

Ah, she thought, like a child telling himself a tale . . .

"We could find a house, or we could build one—"

Like a child too in his inability to give himself over to the tingling and the thrumming. That part which should by now have sprung to life—according to what knowledge she had of such things—remained under his cassock still in the bud. She would not be behindhand, she would offer him every possible encouragement.

She offered her bare breasts and he kissed them as if he had been told he should—but that kind of short, hard kissing only jangled the inward pulsing. The sigh he let out over them when he had done his duty by them chilled the nipples and turned delight into a strange pain.

"Wait," she said, "this is no way to go about it." And she got up and went into the corner where the herbs were stored on shelves, dark now with a webby darkness because the sun was gone. There—for what more could she offer him than the total nakedness of woman?—she stripped away smock and skirt and petticoat, all that could muffle the pulsing that their flesh would make together; she hoped, no, she was certain, that he too would be making ready, that when she came to him again he would meet and clasp her in his nakedness.

Not so. The ghastliness, the sense of light in eclipse began when she saw him sitting fully clothed on the hearth, staring at her with fixed and vacant eyes.

"I see that you have taken off your clothes for me, Liese. It was kindly intended, and I am grateful," he said.

She did not answer, only looked around for something with which to cover herself against the cold and the shame.

293

"But I am not yet ready for that—you must forgive me—as I told you, I have been deeply troubled of late. I scarcely know—" He got up and stared at the familiar room as if he had just begun to waken out of a terrifying dream. "Here—do you want the cloak?" He held it out to her at arm's length. "Keep it—I do not need it—it is not really very cold outside—no, keep it." And with that he walked past her, his eyes turned away from her, and out through the lean-to door.

For a long time she could do nothing but sit on the stool and shiver under the cloak. Wave after wave of the ghastliness—it was like a nausea of the spirit—broke over her, making her hands as clammy as his, leaving the taste of standing salt water on her tongue. Perhaps it is like this to be dying, she thought; and for the first time she knew that she was mortal and that she would never again be without the knowledge of her mortality. Her eyes, accustomed now to darkness, did not notice how much the dark had thickened. Old things, things whose ugliness was new because all their meaning had just been bled out of them, had an eerie half-life in the intensifying shadow: rude bench, foolish collection of boxes and jars, old bed of rags for sickly beasts, stiff with their spittle, littered with their hair. Die and be done with it, she thought, and felt a hard smile growing on her mouth. With such a smile she would walk the corridors of the nunnery, pretending to meditate. With such a smile she would sit on the edge of a narrow bed in a narrow cell and take off her habit for the empty night.

And then it came upon her suddenly—like the edge of the moon emerging out of the blackness of its eclipse—it came upon her suddenly that she would do nothing of the kind. Her body was hers, her body and all its tingling and pulsing. Why should she deliver it over to the God who had forgotten her and all the children of Saint Cyrian's? The curve of the land mass beyond the isthmus came into being, crescent-shaped, in her mind's eye. City after city, tower upon tower—foulness, yes, sewers and stews such as must always be in human habitations—but gardens also, and orchards heavy with fruit, and streets where multitudes came and went, multitudes of bodies, and many, many capable of answering all that she had asked of him while she lay on the hearth in his unripe and deliberate embrace.

There were ashes in her hair, left over from that moment. She brushed them away and stood up and went to find her clothes, shedding his cloak behind her on the floor. She would dress and put on a cheerful face in case her mother still lay waking, but there were limits to what she would do for her mother's sake. Berthe had had her life and her Ottric; with Jehanne to look after her, Berthe would do well enough in one of those little cells. As for herself—she was not afraid to set out in loneliness: it was no worse than the common lot to come solitary out of the womb and die alone. Without his moist hand upon her, without his jewels—with nothing but the pulsing body she had gotten from him against his will and the hard smile that his weakness had taught her lips—she would cross the isthmus and walk into the world.

⌗   ⌗   ⌗

The chatelaine had read the letter three times, though she had known from the beginning how she must answer it. A short letter —scarcely enough words in it to cover half a sheet of parchment, and all of them strictly to the point and apparently written in sickness and haste. But if it had been ten times its length, her answer would have been the same. It had been folded in two when it came to her. Now she folded it in four, and put it between threadbare silk and the spareness of her left breast, and went back downstairs.

Alain was where he had been for almost all his waking hours since the day when she had brought him back from the stone of the virgin Genevieve. He sat in a tall chair near the window, with a book on his knees, and the morning sunlight lay across the book and his unmoving hands. Not that he read—she had noticed the day before yesterday that the book was always opened to the

295

same place. The stitches that bound it had been stretched by the shattering of his spirit; the history of his despair had been set down without a word in the volume; henceforth, whenever it was opened, it would fall open at that page.

"What time is it?" he asked as she came in.

For now they spoke to each other—he in a flat and listless voice and she in a carefully measured one, too consciously worka- day, as if to assure him with every utterance that all was well, today was no different from yesterday, life and time would flow together at the same ordinary pace. "Past midmorning, getting on toward noon," she said.

It was really somewhat earlier. But the weight of time was so heavy upon him that for his sake she was forever outrunning the sun. Like a sick child who has nothing to do with himself, like an old man whose life has shrunken to the size of a porridge bowl and a wooden spoon, he waited for his meals, though he found whatever he ate savorless, and began to wait for supper before the taste of what he had eaten at noontime was gone from his tongue.

And, in spite of his preoccupation with food, he had begun to grow thin. His long cheeks had fallen in and his eyes, deep sunken, had ceased to dart about and gazed fixedly at whatever happened to lie within their sight.

"I thought I might go out and walk in the sun a little," he said.

That always struck terror into her. By day and by night, whatever he was doing to deal with his empty hours, she kept listening for the creak of a door. Going out meant walking toward the inland lake, and there were fewer and fewer watching there as the days went by. Someday there would be nobody, and he would go and sit on the stone and give himself over to the lode- stone pull of the blank water. "Then I will go out with you, Alain."

"No . . . I will stay where I am, at least until after we have eaten."

But if he was thinking of going out, she could not go up to her chamber to answer the letter. She sat down far off from him so that he need not see her, and took up a bit of grey cloth, a needle, and a length of purple thread. Years ago Jehanne had tried to teach her stitchery, and she had proved completely inept at it. Back in those days it had seemed unbearable to her to sit motionless, making one small stitch after another. But now she was thankful for what little of the skill had remained: the restlessness was gone along with the hope, and she could sit out half a morning, moving nothing but her arms and hands, covering a two-inch square of grey fustian with scrolls and flowers.

An A—she would have liked to send him an A or even his whole name stitched out on a marker for a book Then, reading in his cell in Cologne, he would think of her and run his fingers over the texture she had raised, and that would be a kind of touch. Not that she could finish even an initial—he would be gone too soon.

"I would be better off at the monastery. Eustace says the day goes by more quickly there, broken up as it is into little segments."

"You know, Alain, that I would want you to go anywhere, if only you could find your peace—"

"But I cannot go there—not while *he* is there."

It had not been uttered with bitterness, only with enough emphasis to tell her whom he meant without startling or shaming her with a name. She thought of the letter and wished she could show him a certain part of it: "Soon now, beloved, Alain will think of the monastery, and that will be well. Strange as it may seem to you, he is the one to succeed the Abbot Ottric. His mind is subtle and suited to dealing with complexities. His rank and blood will stand him and the island in good stead when he deals with the Holy Father in Rome. And, since he never raised a hand against either of us two, he has the singular virtue of Christian charity. . . .

"I cannot serve under him."

"You are the lord of the island—why should you serve under anyone? He will be leaving soon—I have had dependable word of it—he will be setting out now in two or three days."

297

"If that is so, I may very well betake myself to the monastery. Who knows?—I have read of some that were given a new life in the cloister."

"I am sure there have been many such." And she thought how men, in spite of their vaunted hard-headedness, believe in a resurrection in this life, and fix their dreams of it upon a certain place. One dreams of a cell in the monastery of Saint Cyprian, and another of a place briefly visited or conjured up out of nothing in a fever dream, a place nameless or as yet unnamed, known only as "the new town."

"But if I were to enter the Brotherhood—what of you?"

"Never think of me—it will be well enough with me." I am a woman, too grounded in the past to renounce it for another life. I am forever stopped at daybreak in Jehanne's hovel, coming out of sleep—oh, wonderful, oh, glorious—into laughter and gratified desire. . . .

"What time is it now?"

"Getting on toward noon."

"Strange as it is at this hour of the day, I am heavy-headed."

"And no great wonder—you hardly closed your eyes last night."

"Well, I will go upstairs and lie down for a little."

"Yes, do, and I will turn down the coverlet." And write my letter while you sleep . . .

To Father Albrecht at the Monastery of Saint Cyprian
Beloved:

Though I am yours and no other's, now and so long as I live, I cannot go with you to the new town.

I write it at once, lest by reluctance to set it down I would seem to beguile you; and as you know I have used no guile with you, save only that which I used on the night when you could not sleep and came and found me eating chestnuts by the fire. From the day you took me unto yourself I have been yours in truth, with no cause ever to turn my eyes aside or to lay a veil over my inmost spirit. And it is out of such truth that I must tell you I will stay on Saint Cyprian's, and you will find within you grace and truth enough not to beguile me when I have set down herein what binds me to remain.

The first reason is the hardest of the three to make plain to you: Were I to go now from my husband in his despondency, I would utterly change and reshape myself. If I could abandon him, then I would be otherwise than I was when I tended you, and wept on your going out of our house, and hastened to let you in when you returned, and lay with you wherever we found a place. I would then be another woman, and I wish to be one woman only: the one whom you loved beyond human hope, most gloriously, the one who slept and woke with you in Jehanne's bed. Such compassion as I have for him was in me then, the richest element in my compounding. And desire at the expense of compassion would work a more ruinous change in me than that which I must choose: compassion at the expense of desire.

Do not imagine for a moment, my Albrecht, that I will be his as I was yours. No touch will be upon me to raze out your touch. None shall touch me save those who wash me to make me ready for my grave. He will go to the monastery, and I will go to the nunnery. And though I go as God's bride—for so they speak of it—I am no man's bride but yours, no, not even God's.

The second reason is less obscure. Inasmuch as I am a woman, even though I am childless, I cannot tear from my mind concern for those who are yet to come. We cannot store up that which is wine for us and poison for others, especially for the children. Through us Mechthilde is dead and Alain is undone, and that is already a great price even for such joys as ours; and I would make you also other than you are if we were to bring evil upon those as yet unborn. Let them say of of me at a time far off: In that cell lived one called Julianne, the chatelaine, and she broke the holy law most flagrantly with one named Albrecht of Cologne. But he went from her afterward into his own country and did whatever he could to cleanse himself before the Lord, and she remained in the nunnery and in the end was absolved, after many years of penitence. And it will be a foolish tale, no more to be taken wholly into a wise heart than the virgin Genevieve's vision of the drowned Cathedral or the Abbot Benno's thornbush; yet it will be nourishing to the children, since it teaches, together with the immutability of the law, the sweetness of absolution.

The third reason you know already, if not in your mind, then in the secret places of your heart. What we have had of each other was a ripeness. There is a night at harvest time when the fruit on the

299

bough is perfect—sound of skin and sweet in to the stone, and with the coming of another night it is not more, but less. We have been fortunate in that we harvested in the ultimate hour. What could we desire that we have not been given? What could be revealed to us that we do not know?

Therefore, beloved, I remain with you in that ripeness, and you in your ripeness remain with me. I am everlastingly as I was in Jehanne's hovel, when the dawn awakened you and you awakened me, yours for all time,

Julianne

I send you herewith a jewel, a black pearl on a silver chain. Not as a token of my love, for of that you need no token. Only to keep you provided for on your journey, for I cannot bear to think you should suffer any need.

J.

✠   ✠   ✠

Monday of the second week of the month of May, in the year A.D. 1101. I, the Abbot Alain, elected by the acclamations of the Brotherhood of Saint Cyprian without dissenting voice, and duly ordained in my office by the holy Father from Cologne, write these things in the Book:

Three have been gone from us now for a week: the said holy Father, and Giraldus, and Liese the daughter of the Abbot Ottric, whose soul God rest.

The day of the choosing has been here and is gone, and seventy-two have elected to come into the monastery, and others have cast off their cassocks and have gone to labor on the land. The Sisterhood flourishes, numbering eighty-one, with not enough cells as yet to house them. But there is much building, and I have taken Brother Thaddeus from his penance before the Cross and have set him, after the old dispensation, to hewing down trees. Also, I have received this day a deputation from the nunnery, sent here to ask that the chatelaine— she who was my wife in the world and is now my sister in the Lord— be appointed as their abbess, and I have granted it, and they have gone back content.

Until another comes to us from the world, with the world's wisdom, to instruct us, let it be as I set down herein:

I: Let the services stand as the holy Father fixed them, for it is good that the day be broken into segments, so that those who are joyful may savor each part and those in despair do not find it a burden on their hearts.

II: Let these festivals be unchanged:

The Festival of the Nativity, since winter is long and there should be a time of rejoicing in it, especially for the children and the aged. The Festival of the Resurrection, since the earth is reborn, though man passes from the face of it.

III: Let the Eucharist be celebrated at intervals of the Brotherhood's choosing, even though it may not be demonstrable that God became a man among men and gave his body and blood in willing sacrifice. For man in his long seeking after God in some wise transforms Him. And man wrought greatly, with much tenderness and strong compassion, when he transformed Him into such a One as could be moved by pity to take on flesh and suffer our grief and go down to our death.

I will write in the Book diligently henceforth, every Monday after Vespers, so that there may be no further lapses and confusions. I will also do whatever I can for the children of Saint Cyprian's, partly out of pity for them—since it was their portion to live beyond Doomsday —and partly for my own sake. For my peace is in their necessities; with their necessities they fill my empty hands. Still, it will be with them and with me not as I fashion it, but as time fashions it.

The Abbot Alain

✠ ✠ ✠

For a week now the three of them had been journeying eastward by another and far more felicitous route than he had taken with Brother Thaddeus, along the outskirts of the great forest and over a range of mildly rolling hills. The weather was airy and light; the stars came nightly into their appointed places; there were rills and cresses and kindling sticks, and fish for the catching in some of the streams. And he wondered whether it was his particular lot or only the common one to hack a hard path toward fulfillment and go forward with ease toward utter emptiness.

That somber question kept asserting itself over all the sweets of May, like a Doomsday text written in a missal over a background of marigolds. It kept him lagging a little behind the other two: Liese on Cicero with the baggage piled behind her, and Giraldus traveling like a peasant, in a fustian smock, on his own big callused feet. He himself sat Asmodeus, more demon donkey than ever, nettled by long confinement in the monastery courtyard and wary of the inland air—did beasts also suffer from change and hoard up memories? Now, as always when his companions had gone on ahead, he thrust his hand inside his cassock and felt the black pearl against his chest.

To be alone with it was the last luxury left to him, and even that he bought at the expense of his conscience. The other two needed him—they stood on the brink of an alien world. All day yesterday they had come upon signs of human habitation: stumps bearing the marks of the ax, smoke rising from distant bonfires, charred bones left over from meals eaten a season ago. And their need and their curiosity yielded him one gain at least: it kept him occupied, it helped him to fend off all thought of what was to come.

They were waiting for him not far off, on the crest of a hill, with the glow of the afternoon light falling upon them through the leaves of an ancient sycamore. She had dismounted to give the beast a respite, and he was looking out over a wide expanse—dark pines for the most part, but some of the early leafage too, frail and almost yellow among the mounds of blackish green. "Look, another bonfire, Father. No, down there, more to the left of you," he said.

Smoke, no doubt of it, but not the small dispersing wisps of it they had seen before. A fine grey column, going straight up, such smoke as comes only out of a chimney. His eyes, older and more farsighted than theirs, made out the slant of a slate roof, and, still farther to the left, a relative openness, a sudden purposeful falling away of trees. It might have been a lake—but no, he knew it was a town. "Well, then," he said, "we have gotten to it far faster than I thought we would. There is some sort of house down there."

"Some sort of house?" They said it together, she apprehensively and he avid for the world.

"Yes, and a town, too, I think—over there where the trees thin out." But his voice was flat, there was nothing in him to respond to their eagerness. He was seeing in his mind's eye for the first time how it would be to live again among men. These two he had grown used to on the way: they knew him well enough not to rub against the rawness of his spirit, their questions were bearable interruptions of the silence and the solitude. But crowded streets and contending voices and footfalls coming and going all day long . . .

"If it is a house, let us go down to it," Giraldus said.

"Now? The road down there may be longer than it looks. It would be better to eat and sleep up here and go down in the morning. We might startle them, whoever they are, coming upon them in the dark."

"Ah, now, Father, we will have the sun for another hour at least."

She also was eager; she got up and mounted Cicero, saying, "I will be the one to knock. They could scarcely be startled by a woman."

"Very well, then, since you wish it." He let them go down the shale-strewn slope ahead of him, in and out among the boulders and trees. Inexorably now, no longer to be put off by expectations that he had harbored but never knowingly entertained—we may still lose our way, I may yet lie down like Patches in the wilderness—they advanced upon him: all the disheartening events that were laid up for him. "Move, then, get to it," he said to Asmodeus and started after them, hunching to avoid the boughs. One thing after another, and he ready for none of it. Hospitality in whatever house it was down there—and how can I expose my

303

flayed being to unfamiliar touch and jangling voices? Town after town, street after street, Chapter House after Chapter House, and how can I simplify and degrade what I have known to make it fit for uninitiated ears? Cologne, and the insatiable curiosity of the landlocked Brothers, and the long report to the abbot. And, after the questioners have grown weary of thrusting their prying fingers into what is too elusive and delicate for them to touch— what then? A book, a stolen candle butt . . . Shale underfoot and Asmodeus balking. A stolen candle butt and a little circle of light and the stagnant silence of a cell—

"No!"

Perhaps he had said it aloud, perhaps he had only stiffened with the fierce need to say it. Either way, Asmodeus felt the impulse and stopped and reared and flung him into the underbrush.

Not a bad fall—he got up at once, eager to prove his wholeness and gainsay the sense of sudden and shameful undoing: a cleric in a cassock, thrown from a donkey into the dirt—he was glad they had gone on ahead, glad they were not there to see him. After the one wild protest, Asmodeus stood still, as if he were ashamed of himself, head down and silken ears still stiff with a surge of affronted blood. Well, better not to mount him then, better to lead him down the rest of the slope onto what was plainly less forest than half-cleared lawn—few trees, more stumps, buttercups and dandelions startlingly yellow against mowed green.

He stopped and looked up and saw the sky, much more of it than he had seen for many days. It was a May sky, clear except for a single small cloud moving at so slow a pace he could not be sure it was really moving at all. And when he looked back at the ground, he wished that Liese and Giraldus had not gone on. Something—the sudden upward look, the intense blue of the sky, the queer slow movement of the cloud—something had begotten a disturbing light-headedness, a feeling of distance, of withdrawal. He went on walking, but he walked warily and overconsciously, as if by will. I am walking, he thought, one step after another, and these are buttercups and stumps, and that dark oblong is the wall of a sizable house, and that is the door, and Liese and Giraldus are coming out of the door.

"But there is nobody inside—nobody!" said Liese.

"And it is all very strange," said Giraldus. "Whoever was here has left a fire going at full blast, and a meal, too, only half eaten."

But he was too taken up with his own strangeness to pay due attention. As he walked between them the few steps to the threshold, he was overwhelmed by a wave of weakness and weariness. He had not even troubled to tether Asmodeus. He could think only of the benches inside, of how he would be sitting down to rest. . . .

"How fresh and new it is, Father," she was saying. "Come in and see—everything in it is new."

A thought had occurred to him, and he could not enter without testing it out. Holding himself steady on the doorframe with one hand, he felt the small of his back with the other. Wet, yes, oozing somewhat, and the tips of his fingers showing the red of it—he wiped them clean on the wood. "Let me take the place on the other side of the table—I am cold—I want my back to the fire," he said, and went the length of the board, steadying himself against the edge by brushing it with his thigh. Weak, markedly weak, too weak certainly to be setting out for Cologne tomorrow, or the day after tomorrow, or the day after that . . . And he could not master his face—he felt it shaping itself in a knowing, secretive smile.

None of the questions the other two kept asking each other concerned him in the slightest. To whom did this fine house belong? Where were its owners and when would they return? Was there really a town nearby, in that other clearing? He did not care. As the heat of the fire penetrated his back and the slow seepage continued—for all he knew, increased—he brooded on his own hidden excitement: Some process, awesome but welcome, had been set in motion in his body when Asmodeus threw him into the underbrush; his solidity was relieving his essence of further responsibility; he had been dismissed from his charge; and, even though it was shameful to step down and away, it was also sweet. The smell of pine had been carried into the house out of the forest. Beams, walls, table, benches all gave off its resinous somnolence.

"Are you tired, Father?" she asked with a bit of filched roast fowl in her hand.

"Very."

"There are mattresses in that room over there—I saw them. Go and lie down—we will keep watch—you stand in need of rest."

He waited until both of them were engaged in cutting a slice of white meat from the breast. Then he heaved himself up and made his way over an earthen floor that seemed infinitely far away, through slants of light that dazzled his mind as well as his eyes. This room was smaller than the other and had no furnishings except his sole necessity: straw sewn between rough sheets and laid flat on the floor. Ah . . . There was some pain when he stretched out and turned onto his back, but with pain also he refused to involve himself—he had known far sharper pain before. And here was a bare wall, such a one as he had lain against in Jehanne's bed, and here was shadow healing to his assaulted eyes, and here was his black pearl. . . .

It seemed to him that he had been sleeping for days, but he knew by the quality of the light that no more than an hour could have passed. Voices, unfamiliar ones, talked now on the other side; and he should have been relieved to find them so companionable: it was all to the good that the children of Saint Cyprian's should be going on like that with the children of the world. Once, long ago, in the days when he consorted with the dark whore Elspeth, he had gone drunken to a disputation between two learned bishops; and now he followed the conversation as he had followed the forgotten argument, merely to see what his dazed mind could make of it. The business of piecing it all together kept him from thinking of the sodden spot on the mattress under his back—of that and of the pain.

306

Clerks out there—three young clerks—and the house, of course, did not belong to them. They had simply taken it over for the time being on their way to Aachen. It was the bishop's property—and he managed to ride the crest of a wave of something close to agony while he waited to hear what bishop. The bishop who had ordered it for his hunting lodge, the bishop who would be coming early in June from Regensburg to serve in the town. And they, since they were vagabonds and renegades—they boasted of it—would be taking to their heels at the end of May, would clear out as fast as they had disappeared this evening in pursuit of the doe that had streaked past the window while they supped. . . .

"And you," said a boy's voice, not yet sure whether it was alto or baritone, "what are you? If you will forgive me for so saying, there is something of the stench of the cloister about you too."

"Well, then, take me for a renegade. Say I am on the run from it like yourselves."

"And that other one in there?"

"A monk of Cologne, on the way back to his Chapter House after a long journey."

"Rouse him up," said another voice. "We will all go together for a night of drinking in the town."

"No," said Liese, "he is old and tired."

"How old, sweetheart?"

"Very old—maybe fifty."

"Fifty? Fifty is nothing! I have known a man of fifty to drink a gallon and top a whore three times running. Rouse him up."

"No," said Giraldus, "he is not fit for it. He has a new wound."

"How did he get it—at dice?"

And her voice, charged with anger for his sake, said haughtily over the next surge of pain and weakness: Nothing of the kind; the holy Father was not the sort of man to risk himself in a a brawl over a dirty purse; he had come honorably by his wound, had gotten it in love, great love. . . .

So she would say of him afterward—not that it was of any consequence. His story, like all the stories that pass from tongue

307

to tongue, would become a foolish tale on the way, no more to be taken into a wise heart than the virgin Genevieve's vision of the drowned Cathedral or the Abbot Benno's thornbush, but nourishing to the children nevertheless. . . .

"But what is the name of the place?" Giraldus's voice came to him over a strange blending of her speaking voice and her written words as he had seen them on the page.

"Nothing—no name as yet—it will be named by the bishop when he comes in June, probably after some saint or other. For the moment it is called the new town."

But if that was so—if the paltry clearing he had sighted from the hilltop and the shimmer of turquoise and amethyst revealed to him when he floated in crystal air between Saint Pelagia and Brother Matthias were one and the same—if the Maker had wrought so meagerly that the world of His making shrank beside the visions of His creatures— No, he could make no sense of it, he wanted only to sleep. . . .

✠   ✠   ✠

Liese went on sitting in the bishop's hunting lodge, with her elbows on the bishop's table. Giraldus and the three new ones were staying late at the tavern, talking no doubt of the wonders to be met with in places whose names she had heard for the first time tonight. Aachen, Saint Gall, Munster, Regensburg— she saw their clustered windows lighted from within by innumerable candles: city after city, floating islands of light between the empty sky and the dark murmuring earth. And within the walls of those cities thousands upon thousands of mortals: babes coming red out of the womb, children seeing devils and angels in their dreams, lovers groping for each other in the blackness, old men and women pondering and remembering, corpses laid out on their biers. . . . I am one of a multitude, she thought. And if there was fear in the realization of her own insignificance, there was also a blessed lightening of the weight of her existence.

The bishop's lodge, unfinished as it was, let in the speech of night: twigs falling under the pressure of the restless wind, owl cries and the cries of small beasts caught in the claws or talons of big ones; and only the mind within the human skull—hers and all the others—to catch the sounds and record the little secret deaths.

At home she had always made the nightly rounds of the house, and here she could not lie down without doing the same. She closed the door, steadied a heap of plates that might come clattering down and disturb the holy Father's sleep, and stopped on her way to the other room to ponder a mystery: The hospitable vagabonds had asked her who and what she was, and she had said with pride, "An abbot's daughter," and they had laughed and told her it was no great distinction considering the way things went with Holy Church these days—nothing, certainly, for her to boast about. . . .

She stepped over the threshold and held the candle high so that its light went into the corner where she had seen the mattress, and—blessed Christ!—why had she not thought to go in to him before? He lay straight out in front of her, like a toppled image carved out of wood, and his cassock and the mattress and the floor around him were drenched with blood.

"Holy Father—"

"If you have come up out of the inland water, let me say that I forgive you. I was at fault when I refused to forgive you and put it all on God."

"In the name of Jesus—"

"No, in my own name I forgive you. And Jehanne also—that goes without saying."

"I am Liese, Father, Liese—"

He raised his head from the neck, and the candle showed it more like wax than wood. His eyes did not move in their webby hollows, and she knew he recognized her only by her voice: he could no longer see. "Ah, Liese, yes, to be sure," he said, and let his head fall back again. "I am sorry—I should have told you —I never imagined there would be so much blood."

309

"Are you in pain, Father?"

"No, it is very peculiar—almost no pain at all."

"Can I bring you something—wine, water?"

"Wine—that is a very good thought, my child. My mouth is dry, and I must do some talking."

She ran as if her tending could save him, though plainly he was beyond saving. She came back and knelt beside him and lifted his head by putting her hand under the cold nape while he swallowed—he took no more than a mouthful. But that was enough to bring him back to her and to the open, alien room. "Come here—no, closer," he said, and, after some fumbling, wrenched from his neck a silver chain with a black pearl on it and thrust it into her hand. "Now you must listen, and tell me afterward everything I tell you, for there is not much breath left in me," he said.

"Do you want to make a confession, Father?"

"No—I have neither the breath nor the heart. Only listen. When Giraldus comes back with the others, I will be dead. Let them delay their journey long enough to take my body to the new town. Tell them that they must ask there for a Brother Matthias—he is in charge of the building— Do you hear me?"

"Yes, Father, every word. A Brother Matthias, in charge of the building."

"Good. And ask him out of his courtesy to find me a grave and bury me in the new town. Ask also—for he is gracious and will not deny you—ask that he send you with a proper escort to Cologne, as my emissary— A little more wine. Good, and tell the abbot there all you know of what passed on the island since my coming, only do not tell him of the falling-off of Brother Thaddeus—that is none of his concern."

"I will do exactly as you say, Father. I have heard it all."

"And after you have spoken to the abbot in my name, ask that he have you taken to the house of a lady Ermintrude—say the name."

"A lady Ermintrude, Father."

"Good, my child. And take with you, as a gift to her, a pot of basil from the garden in the monastery, and say you bring it from me. And tell her that I have sent you—alone as you are—into her keeping, and offer in exchange for your board and bed that jewel you hold in your hand."

"I will do so, Father."

"Not that she will take the jewel. She will only lay it by against the day when she sends you forth from her house with a husband, and she will never send you forth with one you cannot love. Now, say it over from the start, beginning with Brother Matthias."

"I am to go to the new town together with Giraldus and the others, and give into his keeping your—your body—"

"This is my body, given for you in remission of sins. . . . Go on with it, my child."

"And ask him to find you a grave. . . ." She went on to the end with the rest of it, even though she could tell by the slackening of his jaw that he was dead.

✠   ✠   ✠

The twenty-third day of the month of May, in the year of our Lord 1101

I, Alain, Abbot of the Brotherhood of Saint Cyprian, have received this day on the island two masons, sent to me by one Brother Matthias, who oversees the building in a place as yet nameless, known as the new town. And, since all things are set down in his letter clearly, I enter it here in the Book:

> To his Reverence, the Abbot Alain, on the island of Saint Cyprian's greetings as from one Brother to another, and may you be given freely of His grace.
>
> There came to me seven days ago a company of three young wandering clerics, and with them two from your diocese, a young woman named Liese, niece of your predecessor, and one named Giraldus, whose station I do not know. They brought me, to my sorrow—for I knew him to be a worthy man in the brief time he visited me—the body of Father Albrecht, the

Pope's emissary, sent to the flock of Saint Cyprian's by the Bishop of Cologne.

I have had a grave made for him in a place that will lie under the nave of the new cathedral here, and I have said Mass for him, and we will remember him daily at Vespers in our prayers.

Giraldus went his way, together with the clerics, toward Aachen, immediately after the burial. But though I provided her at once with an escort, the young woman remained with us for three more days, in search of a certain kind of thornbush. Most of the thorns in these parts are touched with red at the tips of the petals, and she would not set out until she had found an entirely white one and planted it at the foot of the grave.

Be of good cheer, your Reverence, for you will soon be rejoined with the flock and provided with all that your bitter needs require. In the interim, may God be mindful of you, and cause His face to shine upon you, and grant you His peace.

Brother Matthias
In charge of the building
at the new town.